HAYDEN'S REALM

by Joe Gillespie

Hayden's Realm

By Joe Gillespie

ISBN: 978-0-9935265-3-4

Arkbound is a social enterprise that aims to promote social inclusion, community development and artistic talent. It sponsors publications by disadvantaged authors and covers issues that engage wider social concerns. Arkbound fully embraces sustainability and environmental protection. It endeavours to use material that is renewable, recyclable or sourced from sustainable forest.

Arkbound
Backfields House
Upper York Street
Bristol BS2 8QJ
England

www.arkbound.com

For Maevis, Oscar and Edgar

TABLE OF CONTENTS

PART 1

There were things in the air that shouldn't be there.

CHAPTER ONE

Max Hayden was a smug, self-centred bastard.

As he left the tall office building, he had smugness written all over his face. He was good, and he knew it.

He strolled out to his car, opened the door, tossed his briefcase into the back seat and climbed in.

Taking a smartphone from his inside pocket, he swiped across and brought-up his contact list. Near to the top, his finger stopped at 'Katie Cowell'. He was about to press 'Call' but stopped. He smirked and put the phone away.

Pulling out into the main road, he leaned across slightly and pushed the 'Play' button on the in-car entertainment system. He wound Bruce Springsteen's 'Back in the USA' up as loud as he could bear and bowled along the motorway.

Max turned his key in the lock of the solid wooden front door.

His shirt was unbuttoned at the top and his tie half undone. He set down his briefcase just inside and put his suit jacket on top.

A young woman was absorbed in grating carrot into a bowl of salad. He crept up behind her and put both arms around her waist, swung her round and pecked the nape of her neck.

Katie acted a little surprised, although she had heard him come in. She turned and smiled.

"Well, how did it go?" she asked excitedly, nodding her head in encouragement.

Max put on a poker face and looked her straight in the eye.

"You are only…"

He breathed on his right finger tips and stroked his

collar lightly.

"…Looking at the new Technical Director of McGregor Aerospace!"

She smiled and nodded deliberately.

"Oh…" she said.

He picked her off the ground again in a tight hug. They jumped up and down in a joyful dance.

"I just knew you would get it," she whooped.

He stuck out his tongue at her.

"So did I!"

He took the salad bowl from the kitchen worktop, opened the refrigerator door and stowed it inside.

"Tonight, we are celebrating," he said.

Katie gave him another big hug and kissed him again.

"Where would you like to go?"

"Giovanni's?" she asked, pausing slightly with a question on her voice. "Can…we afford it?"

"Whatever," he said. He lifted his briefcase from the hallway, unlocked the catches and removed his laptop. He took out a manilla folder, reconsidered and promptly put the folder and computer back in again. The briefcase was locked and pushed back under the hall table out of sight.

"They put me through three interviews but I had this sneaking suspicion that they'd given me the job already. It was just a matter of getting the head honcho on board," he continued.

"If we are going to Giovanni's, you might want to ditch the jeans and sweater."

Katie liked to dress casually - jeans, white trainers, sloppy jumpers. Her short blonde hair bobbed around her ears. She also liked to wear lipstick. Max hated it.

She knuckled him on the shoulder.

"I'll go scrub-up," she mocked, heading out into the hallway and up the stairs.

Max fetched the briefcase, unlocked it and took out the

manilla folder. His eyes glazed over as he flicked through the turgid contracts.

His mind wandered.

Max was neither tall nor thin. His scalp was shaved short, a perfect complement to the designer stubble on his face.

He had joined the Royal Navy as a graduate with a good degree from Cambridge at the age of twenty-five. That was eleven years ago. He had stayed in the Navy for five years and was licensed to fly both fixed-wing aircraft and helicopters. Most of his work was in avionics and control systems. When he left the Navy, he went to work for Advanced Aviation and had become a star player in his field. Now he had been headhunted by a major competitor and was about to move on.

Katie was ten years his junior. They had met in a pub where he often had lunch or drinks after work and hit it off right away. Within six months, they were living together.

In her teens, she had planned on becoming a fashion model. She certainly had the looks: tall, long legs, beautiful face. An unfortunate set of circumstances involving bulimia, anorexia and hospital put paid to that.

It was totally by accident that she fell into the antiques business. Her friend Judy asked her to help out at a fair one day. She really enjoyed it and was soon dabbling on her own, making a few quid here and there. It was more of a hobby than an occupation but she bought an old Mini Countryman so that she could lug stuff around.

Katie liked Max because…well, she never really worked that one out.

He loved her just because she was Katie.

Max put a measure of Arabica beans into his hand-cranked coffee grinder. He was a coffee snob, although he preferred the word 'connoisseur'. He tipped the aromatic grounds into a filter cone lined with unbleached filter paper. The boiled water was allowed to cool for a minute before he poured it over the coffee grounds. Fresh black filter coffee. He couldn't think of anything better.

Nearly half an hour later, Katie came back downstairs. Max was finishing his coffee in the kitchen.

"Will I do?" she asked.

Max gave a low wolf-whistle.

"Where did that come from?" he asked, nodding at the slinky red satin dress.

"Oh, just a little something I put away for a special occasion," she teased. "Isn't this a special occasion?"

"It certainly is," replied Max.

He put his suit jacket back on and straightened his shirt cuffs.

As they left, he double-locked the front door and opened the door of the black Audi A5 in the driveway.

"Are you sure that you'll be able to drive home?"

"I don't intend overdoing it," Max said, looking down at his watch. "I need to get into work tomorrow early and type-up my resignation letter."

"Don't you have to work out three months?" asked Katie.

"Theoretically," replied Max, "but when they hear that I'm joining McGregor's, I'll get the bum's rush. I'll be asked to clear my desk right away."

"So, what are you going to do for three months?"

"I have a few loose ends to tidy up and quite a lot of research to do, but McGregor's have asked me to go in a couple of weeks to meet the management so that when I do start in October, I can hit the ground running."

Katie pulled down the vanity mirror and checked her make-up.

They turned into the restaurant car park and found a vacant space between a yellow Porsche and a red Ferrari.

The other cars around them were just as grand.

"Mmm," said, Max tapping his Audi steering wheel, "I feel a tad underdressed in this!"

Katie chuckled.

Max removed his jacket and slung it over his shoulder casually. In a place like this, he didn't want to look like he worked for a living.

Giovanni's was right on the shore with a stunning view over the bay. The decor typified Italian chic – an odd mixture of traditional and ultra-modern that just somehow worked.

"Do you have a reservation?" asked the smart waiter as they stood in the foyer.

"Er, no," stuttered Max, "is that a problem?"

The waiter looked at them for a moment.

"Two?" he asked.

Max glanced around to see if anybody else had followed them in.

"Yes, two." He added "idiot" silently.

The waiter took menus from a rack and beckoned them to follow.

The restaurant was barely a third full. They were ushered to a table for two by a large panoramic window. The waiter pulled the seat out for Katie and pushed it back in under her. He handed them each a menu folder and tidied-up the cutlery and glasses on the table fussily.

"Would you like to see the wine list?" he asked.

Max took the thick bound drinks menu and pointed to the most expensive bottle of bubbly.

The waiter bowed and walked away.

He returned a few minutes later holding up a bottle of champagne to Max. He nodded. The waiter removed the cork with a twist and poured some into Max's flute and waited. Max waved has hand in dismissal and pointed to Katie's glass.

"So, what does the new job involve," asked Katie. "Is it much different from what you were doing before?"

Max lifted his glass and stared at it thoughtfully.

"They didn't say very much other than that it will be a 'little different' from what I'm used to. I don't know exactly what they have in mind for me but the 'remuneration package', as they call it, is double what I'm on at the minute. Then there's the Beemer that goes with the job."

Katie pulled a tight smile.

"I'll know more about it in a couple of weeks – but I won't be able to tell you anything," he smirked dryly. "Not only do I have to sign a watertight non-disclosure contract, there is the Official Secrets Acts too!"

"Ah," said Katie nodding knowingly, "military stuff?"

"That's par for the course in this business," explained Max. "In aerospace, it's just like that."

They passed on starters and ordered their main meals. Katie went for the pan-fried mackerel, Max the grilled fillet of beef. Max didn't want to embarrass himself attempting to pronounce the long Italian names.

Throughout the meal, Katie plied Max with question after question, most of which he couldn't or wouldn't answer. She gave up.

"How was yours?" asked Max, as she put her knife and fork on the virtually empty plate.

"Absolutely wonderful." The waiter was already hovering with a dessert menu.

"I'll just have the amaretto syllabub," Max indicated and looked across at Katie.

She patted her tummy and shook her head.

"No, full up!"

"Would you care for some coffee?" asked the waiter.

"Could we have two espressos on the veranda?" Max replied.

The waiter nodded graciously and left.

The veranda bathed in the warm glow of a July evening. Seagulls wheeled in the sky as waves lapped softly on the sandy beach, where a few oystercatchers pecked purposefully amongst the seaweed.

"This is so lovely," sighed Katie. "A perfect end to a perfect day."

Max put his arm around her and kissed her cheek. He presented her with a white rectangular box, opening it to display the contents. Her eyes widened.

"Maxie, it's lovely!" she exclaimed, taking the Victorian pendant necklace and holding it up to the light.

"Amethyst, my birthstone!"

Max smiled.

"For the luckiest girl in the world."

She fumbled with the clasp and put it round her neck.

"Thank you, oh thank you," she said.

Katie looked around to see that no-one was watching and went to sit on Max's lap. She put her arms around his neck and they kissed deeply.

On the horizon, out over the bay, sails bellowed lazily in the sea breeze.

"Oh, I'd love to have a boat," sighed Max, "maybe I'll be able to buy one now. Just imagine, lying back under the stars and drifting off to Nineveh."

Katie closed her eyes and took Max's hand.

She gazed out over the bay at the pale orange band of sky that spanned the horizon. Cotton wool clouds caught the last sun rays and were edged in the same soft, fiery glow. She would remember this night.

Max and Katie cuddled on the veranda but straightened-up abruptly when the waiter arrived with the two coffees, each with an amaretto biscuit on the saucer.

"Can I have the bill?" asked Max. The waiter nodded

and walked off.

Max started drinking his coffee. Katie leaned back in her chair and drunk in the atmosphere. She could have coffee anytime.

"Oh look, Max. Can you see that cloud shaped like a polar bear?" asked Katie.

Max looked.

"I can't see any polar bear."

"There's its head and there are its front paws."

Katie pointed.

"Pareidolia," said Max.

"You what?" asked Katie.

"Pareidolia. It's the psychological phenomenon whereby the human brain tries to make sense out of random shapes."

"Oh, you and your big words," scowled Katie.

"Some people can use them and some can't," said Max, giving Katie a gentle shove.

"Anyway, that's definitely not a polar bear, looks more like a squirrel to me," said Max.

Katie tightened her lips and continued to draw the outline in the sky with her finger.

"Aw, it's changed shape," she moaned.

She looked for more shapes in the clouds.

"Max, what's that?" she asked, pointing to a cloud in the distance.

"What now?"

"Look, there. There are three dots sitting just above that cloud." She moved her fingers in a circular motion.

"I can't see anything," said Max, shaking his head.

Then he sprang to his feet, putting his hand across his forehead to cut out the glare.

"Odd," he said, "I have no idea. Can't be birds, too far up and they're not moving. Not planes either, planes can't stop in mid-air. Too high for helicopters as well. I don't know," he shrugged.

"Are they UFOs, perhaps?" smiled Katie.

"Well," he laughed, "they are flying objects and I can't identify them so, therefore they are, by definition, UFOs. That doesn't mean that they are alien flying saucers or anything like that. There will be some perfectly ordinary reason for them being there. Weather balloons, atmospheric distortion…"

He shook his head. "There were reports from China recently of cities apparently floating in the clouds. Just a freak weather condition it turned out. Hell, I don't know, could be anything. In my business, you see a lot of things in the sky that you don't understand. You have to learn to live with it or it will drive you mad."

The three objects began to move off, first in formation and then shifting into line one behind another. For a moment, they were obscured by a fleecy cloud and should have re-emerged from the other side. Only one came out. It accelerated at an impossible rate straight upwards. The other two had just vanished.

Max and Katie stared at one another for an instant, mouths agape.

Max shook his head as if he had awakened from a bad dream.

"Odd!"

He took Katie by the hand and led her back into the restaurant. He paid the bill and left a tip on the plate

Back in the car, Max started the engine and turned the radio on. He pushed the pre-set for the news station. After a few minutes of banal jingles, the newsreader spoke.

"Reports have been coming from all along the coast about strange objects in the sky this evening. Let's go over to our reporter Milly Barnes…"

"Yes, I have here with me, some people who have just

witnessed bizarre and unexplained happenings in the sky. Tom, tell me what you saw."

A man with a thick country accent spoke into the microphone.

"I was just coming down the lane on my tractor when I saw these three…don't know what you call 'em…just sitting up there. They didn't have no lights or anything, they were just grey. Then, all of a sudden, they shoot-off like bullets from a gun. Odd thing is, two of the three just disappeared into thin air. Strangest thing I have ever seen in my whole life, it was."

"And Tracy, can you tell me what you saw?"

"I was coming home from work and there was a lovely sunset. Three flying saucers came out from behind a cloud – but I don't believe in those things," she giggled. "I don't know what they were. One was a sort of triangular shape and the other two were – oh, maybe they all were. They were a bit hazy, not distinct, like."

"And what happened to them?"

"Dunno. One minute they were there and the next minute they're gone," said Tracy.

"Thank you both. And with that, I'll hand you back to Carole in the studio,"

"So we weren't seeing things," coughed Katie, groping for a handkerchief in her pocket.

"T'would seem not," said Max, as they sped off home.

The four-armed alien monster reared up and gave a ferocious snarl. Sticky goo drooled from its extended mandibles and its bony arms flailed wildly towards the figure on the ground beneath it. The scantily-clad female screamed and put her arm across her face. The leviathan's red eyes were aflame with rage as it lifted the girl off the ground and glared. It raised its head to the sky and gave a triumphant roar.

"Oh Maxie, what's that rubbish you're watching?" asked Katie, sitting down beside him on the sofa.

Max didn't answer but pressed the volume up button on the remote.

"Do you want a drink?" she asked.

"On the rocks," he answered. His eyes didn't leave the screen.

Katie returned from the kitchen with two glasses. One held Soave, one had just ice cubes. She set the glass of ice beside him on the coffee table.

"Ta."

To the swooshing of plasma cannon fire, Max lifted the glass to his lips and recoiled. Just ice? He took two cubes from the glass and pulled back the neck of Katie's soft woollen jumper. She squirmed and shouted.

"Max! Don't you dare. Maxie!"

She clamped her two hands against the back of her neck to block the ice cubes from sliding down inside the back of her jumper. Max moved them round to the front and dropped them in.

"Ahhh!" she screamed as the cold ice slid down into her cleavage. She lifted the front of her jumper and shook the ice cubes out onto the floor. Before Max could get them, Katie picked them up and tried to get them inside Max's shirt. He was too strong for her and just held her wrists while the ice melted in her hands. He wrestled her down onto the floor rug. They fought some more. Max swept Katie up in his arms and lifted her off the ground. He raised his head to the sky and gave a triumphant roar. She put her arms around his neck and kissed him wildly.

"Take that, space cadet," she smiled.

Max managed to pick up the remote control and flicked the television off.

"Now look what you've done," he said accusingly.

"What?" she asked.

"Made me miss a classic," smirked Max as he carried her towards the stairs.

* * *

"Who the hell is this guy, Landers?" asked CIA Director Michael Thornton.

Schakowsky, sitting opposite replied, "He's a maverick. A pain in the ass that heads-up a group out at Groom Lake and has ambitions far beyond his station."

"What does he want from us?" asked Thornton.

"He's been requesting intel on encrypted radio signals localised to a small airfield in the East Coast England."

Thornton rocked back and forth on his chair.

"He contacted GCHQ in England," said Schakowsky, "and they told him to piss-off."

Thornton grimaced. "I imagine they did. Under what authority is he making these requests?"

"He told the Brits he was CIA. He's not. He has only the most tenuous connections with us but he is a master of bluff. He doesn't come right out and say it, he suggests it and lets the other party reach the wrong conclusion."

"And, what do we know about these signals?" asked Thornton.

"We know that they are military-grade encrypted. If we had to decrypt them, given enough time and resources, we probably could. We just don't have any good reason to do that."

"What do we know about the airfield?"

"Private. Belongs to McGregor Aerospace. They run a couple of Lear Jets from there with avionics test rigs. Mostly Brit MOD stuff. All above board. So, there's a perfectly good reason for military grade encrypted signals coming from there. It's not really any of our concern."

"So, why am I even being bothered with this?" asked

Thornton.

"I'm just worried about Landers, Michael. He has history. When somebody like that becomes a liability, they are usually promoted out of harm's way. He was, but it didn't work. He's ended-up in a no-man's land between CIA and military but it's one where he gets to call the shots."

"I don't understand," said Thornton. "He must answer to someone?"

"That's it," replied Schakowsky, "he is a law unto himself and seems to get off with it."

"But, he must have some areas of interest," argued Thornton, "somebody's paying him."

"There are budgets allocated to research work that even we don't know about. People in government with pet projects. They find the money and no questions are asked."

"Pet projects," repeated Thornton, "such as?"

"Groom Lake, Area 51. Do I have to draw pictures?" asked Schakowsky.

"Somebody is spending good money on that nonsense? Flying fucking saucers? Are they believing their own mythology?" asked Thornton.

"One man's mythology is another man's culture, is another man's way of life. Who am I to say?" shrugged Schakowsky.

"Look, let me make this clear," said Thornton. "I'm not wasting CIA resources on this bunch of clowns and their pet projects. If Landers asks for any more intel from us, just tell him to go shove it. He gets zilch. Okay?"

"And if his backers start making waves?"

"Refer them to me," barked Thornton, tapping his chest.

CHAPTER TWO

McGregor Aerospace headquarters was an impressive building: a glass and concrete structure some twelve floors high with a highly manicured garden out front. Quite a difference from the low, utilitarian buildings he was used to. The foyer was plush, if a little sterile. There were two people at the reception desk. The man was typing at his desk terminal. The young woman looked up and smiled.

"Can I help you?" she asked Max.

"Yes, name's Max Hayden, I have an appointment with Tony Davidson."

The receptionist lifted a telephone, pushed a few buttons and muttered something.

"Someone will be right down for you Mr Hayden, please have a seat."

Max sat down at a glass coffee table and put his briefcase on the floor. He stared all around him and admired the elegant light fittings on the walls and ceiling. A few minutes later, a lift chimed and a very business-like brunette walked over to him.

"Mr Hayden?"

Max stood up and lifted his briefcase. He smiled at the girl and followed her into the lift. They got out on the top floor and Max was showed into the Managing Director's office.

"Hello Max, nice to see you. Did you have a good trip?" asked the man standing at the end of the table.

"Yes, fine," replied Max, "I'm only fifty-five minutes away."

"Good," said Tony Davidson, the Chairman and MD of McGregor Aerospace. "You've met Doug Sinclair, our Head of Research?"

Max nodded and shook the man's hand.

"And Margaret Lynton from HR?"

Max shook her hand, remembering her too from earlier interviews. He thought she was a bit school-marmy with her black suit, thick glasses and hair tied-up in a bun.

"There may be others joining us later, but I think that we had better get started. Will you have some coffee?" said the MD, pushing across a tray holding a coffee jug, cups and saucers. Max declined.

"Right," he continued. "We know a lot about you from your CV and interviews, but more critically, from our private enquiries."

Max had a hunch about that. His interviews were just too easy.

"I suppose that you will want to know more about us and what we do?" prompted the MD, "but first, let's get the boring formalities out of the way. You have signed the contracts and OSA papers?"

Max took the manila folder from his briefcase and put it on the table. Margaret Lynton leaned over and took it, flicking through the pages inside. She sat back.

"Ok, where do I start?" began Tony. "We know about your impressive work with jets, helicopters and head-up displays. I think that it has been hinted that your work here might be a little more…diverse?"

Max nodded.

"Well, I won't go into any great detail today," said Tony, "that will have to wait until you start in October. This, of course, is our head office used primarily for administration purposes. We have other places spread around the country and overseas. Our main research centre is based at Heathfield Airfield nearby but you will be based at our special R&D facility about an hour and a half north from here."

Oh great, thought Max. *That's a potential two and a half hour commute. We'll have to move.*

"And," continued the MD, "you will be spending some time away!"

Now, that hadn't occurred to him. What did 'away' mean anyway?

Tony went on. "What you won't know is that McGregor Aerospace is just a subsidiary of a much larger global enterprise. I would like to think it's a very important and vital part, but all that will be explained in due course."

"Well, it doesn't look like the others have been able to make it today so here is some of our marketing and corporate literature to get you up to speed on our public image. Don't be surprised if the actuality is a little… different."

Tony looked round the table at the barely concealed smiles.

"If you have any questions, Margaret here will fill you in. She will show you round the offices. You will be coming here for meetings from time to time and there are other people you need to meet. She will also sort out your bank details for your salary and a car."

Well, thought Max, *that was short and sweet. Obviously a very busy man… or he had a round of golf lined up.*

They all rose and shook hands again. They were on their way out of the room when Tony's PA pushed past with a sheet of paper and showed it to him. He appeared to be taken aback. The door closed.

Walking around the offices with Margaret, Max was surprised about how little the building gave away about the company's business. The people he was introduced to were equally tight-lipped and non-committal. Sure, there were a few framed photos of aircraft of various types in the corridors and a big stainless steel sculpture suggesting 'flight' in the reception area.

He didn't know what he had expected, photos of radar

screens and computers? That's what they had in his old company. McGregor's was very different. This was a veneer. A facade, like the fronts of buildings in Western movie towns. What you saw was NOT what you got, he was sure of that.

Margaret Lynton was pleasant enough superficially but, at the same time, reserved, even stand-offish. The questions Max asked of her were glossed over or pushed aside. She wheeled him into a corridor and down a short flight of stairs. She held her palm against a glass panel on the wall beside a door and ushered him inside.

A man was sitting at a desk inside. "Alan, this is Max Hayden who will be joining us shortly as Technical Director at Mewton. Can you run him through the inception procedures and give me a call when you've finished?" She promptly turned and left.

"Hello. Alan Gibson, security. Pleased to meet you," said the thin man shaking Max's hand.

"Procedures?" quizzed Max.

Alan took him by the arm and led him off into another room.

"Yes, we run a tight ship here. I need to get some biometrics."

Max shrugged.

"Can you just put your hand flat on this pad and look up at that spot on the ceiling?" asked the security man. "You might feel a scratch."

Max winced.

"What was that?" he yelped, looking down at the spot of blood on the back of his hand.

"An ID chip, RFID. That will give you security clearance Level 2c throughout the company. Just put your hand against the security panel whenever you need access. It's more secure than palm or retina scans – unless someone cuts your hand off – and you really don't want them to cut your head off, do you?"

"Hmmp!"

"Oh," continued the thin man, "if the chip doesn't give you access, you're not supposed to be there."

Alan took Max over to a plain white wall and switched on some spotlights in the ceiling.

"Have to get a mug shot."

The security man took a photo with a small digital camera and said, "Right, that's it. I'll just call Margaret back."

Four minutes later, Margaret came thought the door and beckoned Max out.

Max nodded at the security man and followed Margaret.

"School dinners," said Margaret pointing at the door of the canteen. It was as close as she came to humour.

"It's okay, really," she remarked, "but I doubt if you will be using it much. Let's go to my office and see what we can do about a car."

They took the lift down to her office on the first floor and she asked him to take a seat. She sat at her terminal and brought up a new window.

"So, it's a BMW 640 is it?" asked Margaret. "If you would rather have something else, I'll see what I can do. Might take a bit longer to source."

Max pondered for a moment. They had mentioned a BMW at one of the interviews. He hadn't expected to get a Six Series.

"No, a 640 would be just fine."

Margaret scrolled down the screen.

"Manual or automatic? Oh, they only do automatic."

"That's fine," he replied.

"Black, white, silver?" she looked up at him. "I don't think they do any other colours in that model. Oh yes, there is a red."

"White."

"You are starting in October, so I should be able to get it for then. Excuse me if I sound pedantic but I am going to have to see your driving license."

Max looked puzzled.

"I know, I know," she apologised, "but it has to be done by the book. And you are going to have to fill-in an insurance form." She pushed over a sheet of paper.

"Can I ask a question?" Max said, grimacing and prepared to be knocked back.

"Try me."

"Tony said that I'll be based at the R&D facility. Where exactly is that? I might have to move."

She tapped a few keys on her computer and brought up a map. Twisting the monitor towards him she pointed at a small clearing in the middle of a large forest.

"Here," she said, writing down a postcode on a sheet of paper.

"It is difficult to find, a sat nav won't help either. Someone will take you up there first time to show you the way. The security guards will want to look you over and check that your bios are in order. Should be a bit easier after that."

Max left the building half an hour later. He hadn't been unduly stressed but he felt completely shattered. He got into his car and headed off home to the tune of Bob Dylan and the lure of a stiff drink.

* * *

"Ham. Two eggs, easy over. Hash Browns."

The large, middle-aged man sprawled out over the melamine diner table. He was dressed in combat jacket and trousers that were devoid of any identifying patches or insignia. His black sedan and a single Kenworth truck was parked outside in the diner parking lot, its driver nowhere to be seen.

"Coffee?" asked the perky waitress.

"Black," came the reply.

"Quiet?" asked the man.

"Graveyard," shrugged the waitress.

He looked out across the dust. A tumbleweed rolled past.

Godforsaken hellhole, he thought.

A sand-coloured Humvee pulled into the parking lot and ground to a halt. Two males sidled out, looked around and pushed the diner door open.

"Sir," nodded one of the men as they sat down opposite John Landers.

The waitress arrived with a tray and set it down on the table. She looked at the two newcomers. The big man raised his eyebrows.

"Coffee," said the black man, Walker.

"Two," said the other.

The waitress wandered off.

"Look," said the man in combat gear, pouring some sugar into his coffee, "I'm going out on a limb here. I've asked Langley for help but they just don't want to know."

"What do you want us to do, Sir?" asked Thompson, the white man.

The truck driver came into the diner and sat down in one of the spongy red bench seats. He waved at the waitress. He was obviously a regular as she shouted an order through the hatch into the kitchen behind without asking.

The military-looking man beckoned the other two to lean closer.

"There's something going on in England, I don't know what but I've been hearing rumours." He tapped the table with his finger.

"I want you to get in touch with our people over there. Get them to trawl the aerospace trade press for any interesting movements of personnel. Scan the job vacancies. Get a picture of who is doing what."

The black man nodded and sat back as the waitress arrived with two cups of coffee on a tray.

"Anything else?" she asked.

They shook their heads and waited till she was back behind the counter.

"And," continued the big man, "see if there are any reports of strange things in the air. I don't care how wacky they sound, I want to know about them."

"You mean UFOs?" smirked the white man.

"Yeah, they'll probably call them that, flying saucers, whatever. Look Thompson, this ain't funny. Wipe that smile off your face."

Thompson straightened up.

"And get this straight, nobody needs to know who is requesting this intel. As far as the agents in England are concerned, it's coming down from the top. Get it?"

The two men nodded.

"If you do hear anything, it comes straight to me, nobody else. Clear?"

They nodded again.

"Needless to say, you cover your tracks. None of this comes back to haunt me!"

He slapped his palm on the table. The truck driver looked across to see what the noise was. He sent a text from his mobile phone.

They went on eating and drinking.

* * *

When Max arrived back home, Katie was polishing a

table on the floor.

"Oh, what a helluva stink," said Max in annoyance, "why can't you do that outside instead of in the living room? Pooh!"

Katie went on painting.

"Flies," she said, "they stick to the wet varnish outside."

She put the lid back on the tin and wrapped her brush in some cling film.

"Needs another coat tomorrow. Want a drink?"

Max drew has hand across his forehead.

"Scotch. A large one," he replied.

Katie went off into the kitchen.

Max pulled off his shoes and put his feet up. Katie returned with a Scotch on the rocks and handed it to him.

"What have you got to report then?" she asked.

"Do you want the good news or the bad?" he teased.

"Okay, come on," she gesticulated.

"The bad news is; we might have to move."

"What?" she gasped.

"The place where I'll be working is two and a half hours from here in the middle of nowhere," he explained. "I certainly can't commute that far."

Katie went quiet.

"And the good news?"

Max produced two airline tickets and a travel brochure from his inside pocket and waved them at her.

"We are going away."

She snatched the tickets from his hand and opened them. Her jaw dropped.

"Bahamas?"

Max grinned.

"Just ten days but we could do with the break."

Katie flung her arms around his neck.

"Oh Maxwell Hayden, I do love you," she whispered.

Max splashed whisky on the floor.

They sat down on the sofa. Katie put her head on Max's shoulder and enjoyed the moment.

"Did you find out any more about what you'll be doing?" Katie asked.

"They haven't told me very much yet. I did get the impression that I was headhunted specifically for my work with helmet-mounted display systems. That's what they grilled me about most at the interviews."

"What's that then?" said Katie, only half interested and prepared to switch off immediately if anything vaguely technical was mentioned.

"Do you know what a virtual reality headset is?" he asked.

"I think so. Something to do with computer games?" she suggested.

"Yes, something like that except that military pilots wear them. It's a bit like having a computer display inside your helmet. It gives you all the readings that you would normally get on the dash. It projects maps for navigation and can be used for targeting weapons."

Katie made an "Oh" shape with her mouth and changed the subject.

"When are we going to start house-hunting then?"

Max winced.

"Not so fast. I've been thinking about this. I want to ease myself into the new job first. See if it fits," he mused.

"I'll get a room for a week or so until I get my bearings. Then I think we should get a place to rent until I can sell this place."

"Sounds like a good plan," smiled Katie. "I suppose I'll have to go around and meet some new dealers."

She opened the holiday brochure and transported herself mentally to a tropical beach.

The temperature was a comfortable thirty degrees

when Max and Katie stepped out of the plane at Lynden Pindling International Airport, Bahamas. It was a fast five mile ride in a yellow taxi to their smart hotel at Cable Beach on the outskirts of Nassau. The hotel was large, pristine white, mostly marble, and had an incongruous row of Doric columns running down to the two luxury swimming pools.

The driver lifted their suitcases out of the boot. Max paid him. A boy came running over and carried them into the lobby. Max didn't have any change so the boy got a larger tip than usual. He looked at it, beamed and ran off.

"I'll get someone to show you to your room," said the cheerful receptionist and rang a little bell.

Max tipped the bell boy with another note and went over to the window to gaze out across the pools and white, sandy beach. The sea was so turquoise blue it was surreal.

Katie explored the apartment. The main room was bright and airy and furnished in a colonial style that, being an English antiques buff, was not entirely to her taste. The four-poster bed in the bedroom was comfortable but what was the point of four posts with no canopy? Ah well, this was The Bahamas and they didn't plan on staying in the hotel room much anyway.

It was late afternoon when they stumbled upon a quirky beach bar constructed from bamboo and woven palm leaves. On top, it had a neon sign spelling-out 'Paradise Beach Club'. Caribbean music played softly from a CD-player behind the bar. They heaved themselves onto two tall stools in front of the bar.

There weren't many people about. The bar boy was young, couldn't have been more than twenty. He had a big bright smile and certainly knew his cocktails – which was just as well because none of the fanciful names meant anything to Max nor Katie. 'Beni', was only too happy to reel-off the ingredients, history and mythology for each cocktail in a well-rehearsed patter. The recital was almost incomprehensible due to the liberal interjection of patois. Max tried a 'Sky Juice' and Katie a 'Yellow Bird' to start off. They tasted even better than Beni's colourful descriptions.

An hour and a half later, they had each sampled four different cocktails – not such a good idea! You just don't get rum like that in England. Katie was beginning to slur her speech and giggle.

"First time?" asked a middle-aged woman dressed in a bikini, flip-flops and loose blouse. She had just sat down on another barstool, along with a man in a straw hat and plain blue shirt.

"Yes," said Katie, "isn't it lovely here?"

"Wonderful," said the woman.

"Where you from?" asked the man with a distinctly American twang.

"England," replied Katie, taking another sip of her Pineapple Upside-Down Martini.

"Oh. I've always wanted to visit England," said the woman. "I hear it rains a lot!"

Katie grinned.

"It does, but not all the time."

Max's phone rang. He took it out of his shirt pocket and looked at the name on the screen. 'Leo Whyte'.

"Excuse me, I need to take this," he said walking off down the beach to the water's edge. He dipped his toes into the warm water and wriggled them into the soft sand. Leo was his ex-boss at Advanced Aviation and Max was half-expecting this call.

"Hello Max. I expect you can guess why I'm ringing?"

"No," Max lied.

"I was just wondering if you might be persuaded to stay with us. What would it take to get you to stay at Advanced Aviation? If it's the money, maybe we can do something."

Max was a little tipsy after four cocktails and had to push his brain hard to get out a reply.

"Leo, I'm standing here on a beautiful beach in the Bahamas. The sand is white, the sea is blue and I've had a few drinks. I can't really talk about this now."

Leo persisted with his coaxing while Katie was getting merrier by the minute.

"Max has just got a plumb new job," she bragged to the American couple.

"Oh really, what line is he in?" asked the man.

"Oh, he's an avionics expert, specialises in helmet displays, you know, like the ones for computer games except for aeroplanes."

The Americans looked at one another.

"Sounds fascinating," said the woman, who revealed that her name was Martha and her husband was Bob.

At that point, Max returned and just caught the tail-end of the conversation. He didn't want Katie talking to anyone about his job. Normally, she would know better but the alcohol had loosened her tongue.

"Katie, I think that we had better go and change for dinner," he said, taking her firmly by the arm. She stumbled to her feet.

"See you later, honey," said Martha. Bob just raised his hand.

An hour later and Katie was out cold on the bed. Max let her sleep. He glanced at his watch and realised that dinner was already being served in the hotel dining room. She looked so peaceful that he didn't want to wake her.

It was ten o'clock when Katie stirred with a desperate need for a pee. When they eventually got down to the dining room, it was empty. A couple of cleaners had the chairs stacked on top of the tables and were sweeping the floor.

"Looks like we'll have to find a late-opening restaurant," said Max. Katie agreed, she was hungry – and still a bit groggy.

He asked for recommendations at reception and ordered a taxi. It was their first night – and it was still young!

After four days, The Americans became conspicuously absent. They no longer beckoned Max and Katie to come and sit with them at every opportunity. They hadn't even said goodbye. Max was glad. He had the impression that they were pushing just a little too much for information about his new job. Katie had told them a little on the first evening, but then, she didn't know very much other than the simplified version Max had told her. He changed the subject every time the topic came up.

Rain greeted them when they returned to England. A few days later, Max found himself in the middle of a muddy field.

"Oh no!" he cried, trying to wipe the mud off his shoes on a clump of grass. "If you'd told me we were going into a field, I would have worn my wellies."

"Car boot sales are usually in fields," said Katie.

"Why did you have to drag me along to this…this tatfest?"

Katie put her arm on her hip.

"I might need a lift with something."

The bargain hunters sifted through the folding tables piled with discarded household junk and haggled with the stallholders.

"What do you think of this?" asked Katie, holding up a wooden box stuffed with beads and imitation pearl necklaces.

Max grunted. He didn't have an opinion.

"Forget the beads, the inlaid marquetry box is the find," said Katie handing over five pounds to the seller without even bargaining.

They wandered through the untidy rows of tables and

cars. Katie picked things up, asked the price and put them down again. Then something caught her eye, a tall wooden coat stand.

"How much?" she asked the woman behind the table.

"Ten pounds," was the reply.

"I was thinking more like five," said Katie, expectantly.

"Eight."

"Seven"

The woman succumbed and Katie handed over the cash.

"What do you want with that?" asked Max.

Katie looked at him as if he was an idiot.

"If I strip the old varnish off and redo it, I'll get forty pounds for it!"

Max grimaced.

"Here, can you take it for me," she said handing the hat stand to him and heading off to another table.

"What a load of crap!" said Max loudly.

The woman behind a table gave him a scowl.

Katie was examining some African carved figures with great interest and doing calculations in her head.

Max spotted a table that had, amongst other stuff, some old cameras. He went over for a look. He had always had an interest in vintage cameras and had a few on a shelf in his living room.

"How much for the Voigtländer," he asked, pointing at a 1940s folding bellows camera.

"Fifty pounds," came the reply, "still in full working order."

"And where will I get 135 film for it?" asked Max.

"You can't," said the seller, "but the shutter has a delightful purr to it. Forty-five?"

Max wasn't one for haggling. He shook his head.

Katie came over with a used plastic carrier bag and held it up to him.

"I've got you a present," she smiled. "Something for your new car, when you get it."

Max didn't have high expectations. What could she possibly get for a Six Series BMW?

She pulled-out a cardboard box with a cellophane window. Above that were the words, "Car Back Window Nodding Alien."

The classic 'grey' alien had a large head that wobbled when shaken.

Max pulled a face. Katie gazed at him for a hint of gratitude.

He leaned over and gave her a perfunctory peck on the cheek and a hollow "Thank you dear."

They headed off through the mud trying to step on the dry patches of grass. The long hat stand wouldn't fit completely into the back of Katie's Mini Countryman. It was left hanging out through the back doors, tied to the handles with string.

Max was glad to get that experience behind him. He was starting his new job the next day.

CHAPTER THREE

Max took a deep breath as he savoured the new car smell. He tried the soft steering wheel and stroked the tan stitched leather upholstery. The controls looked simple enough. Beautiful. He was about to turn the key in the ignition when a hand slapped on the bonnet.

"Nice!" someone said with a soft Scottish accent.

"Doug."

Max climbed out of the car and shook hands with the older man with greying ginger hair.

"Welcome aboard," said the Scot that Max had met at the interviews.

Douglas Sinclair was a mainstay of the McGregor Clan. He had married old man Gordon McGregor's daughter, Marie some time ago, but was more than just family. For twenty years he had helped develop many of the concepts that had made McGregor Aerospace what it was. He had assembled a team of World class virtuosos in the field and Max Hayden was the final piece of the jigsaw. He was the visionary that that could bring everything together.

"Look, I know that you can't wait to try out your new toy but we'll be going in mine," said Doug, pointing to a mucky Land Rover on the other side of car park. "You'll see why."

"Uh, okay," sighed Max closing the door of the BMW with a soft click. Fiddling with the buttons on his key fob remote, he locked the door.

As they walked across to the tatty 4x4, Doug spoke.

"The BMW is for your own personal use. You won't be using it for work. You can drive from home to head office and use it as a shopping trolley but you can't take it anywhere near Mewton Base. You'll be given a pool car, something like this."

Doug tapped the roof of the Land Rover.

"Less conspicuous," he smirked.

"And, don't be surprised if it is a different one every day!"

"All a bit cloak and dagger?" beamed Max.

Doug tapped his nose.

"Smoke and mirrors. Smoke and mirrors."

Max and Doug chatted for the entire hour and a half journey, mostly personal stuff - where they'd been educated, lived, worked, family. Work was hardly mentioned.

Max lost track of the turn-offs that Doug had made. They were on a narrow road through a dense forest that had passing lay-bys every few hundred metres. The forest was dense and the undergrowth on either side of the track formed an effective barrier both visually and physically.

"How am I ever going to find this again?" asked Max.

Doug looked over at him.

"Don't worry, you'll get the hang of it. We are going in the back way today. There is a more direct route from the main road but you'll need to get the hang of the place first."

Doug pulled into a recessed gateway in the hedgerow. The gate was old and rusted and looked like it hadn't been used for years. The lock and chain were completely corroded by weather. The hinges looked like they were fused together with rust.

A sign on the gate had peeling letters: 'Forestry Commission. Authorised Personnel Only!'

"Here?" asked Max, with more than a hint of surprise.

"Watch this," smiled Doug pulling out his smart phone. He swiped it on and typed a password with his thumb. The gate, together with the gateposts on either side, rose vertically upwards from the ground. The left hand gatepost and its concrete foundation sat on top of a well-greased stainless steel pillar. The entire assembly rotated on the pillar and the gate swung open.

Max grinned. "Impressive!"

A movement in a tree ahead caught Max's eye. He spotted a security camera fixed to the trunk turning towards them. Doug pulled through the gate. It swung shut and lowered itself back level with the ground.

Half a mile further up an overgrown track they came to a high metal fence with razor wire along the top. A gate in the fence had a small metal box by the side. Doug slid his window across and held his hand up to the box. The gate glided open.

The track sloped down some way and then round a tight bend. A wide camouflaged shuttered doorway in the side of a small hillock wound downwards, taking them into an underground car park.

Max looked a more than a little bemused.

"I had a look at this place on my aerial mapping program," said Max, "it looked like a disused lumber camp."

"Yes, that's exactly what it is, on the surface," said the other man.

"Apart from a few tin huts, an old digger and lumber truck, you won't see much here. They load up some tree trunks sometimes, drive round the block with them and bring them back again. Smoke and mirrors, Smoke and mirrors," he said with a twinkle in his eye.

"So, the research facility is entirely underground," surmised Max, "how big is it?"

Doug pulled a face.

"Pretty big," he said, "about the size of a small town."

Max gasped.

"Apart from the research labs, we have a small manufacturing unit and there are some living quarters," said Doug, "but I wouldn't want to live here."

"There's no airfield," said Max, more as a question.

"Don't need one," replied Doug. "No aeroplanes!"

Max was puzzled, an avionics company with no aeroplanes. How could that be?

They got into a lift at the back of the car park and went down. Max counted six levels on the control panel. They stopped at the third. He had expected to be overcome with claustrophobia but no, it was remarkably bright and airy.

"Why does it not feel like an underground bunker?" asked Max.

"Ah," replied Doug, "advanced air conditioning. The air temperature and humidity is carefully controlled and just the right amount of ionisation and perfume applied."

"Perfume?" asked Max.

"Yes, people aren't normally aware of it but the smell of your surroundings can affect you mood considerably. Why do you feel elated when you walk by the sea or high in the mountains? The sea smell comes from the tiny organisms that live beneath the waves. Then there is a proportion of ozone mixed-in."

These things had never occurred to Max. There was a lot to learn.

"I'll show you to your office and then you can meet the team," said Doug, leading Max through a door. They seemed to walk for ages through the labyrinth of corridors. There were numbers on doors but no indication what was behind them. Some had pads to read RFID implants, a few had plain keyholes. There were a lot of them.

Max's office was a decent size. It had a large black desk trimmed with stainless steel. On top was a computer screen. Another workstation sat by the side. There were three white leather cantilever chairs and a matching couch. There was also a recess for books, a few decorative glass bottles and three nondescript modern prints in black frames hanging on the wall, together with a large television. All the office lacked was a window.

"Nice view," said Max sarcastically.

"The one big disadvantage of an underground workplace," commented the Scot as he went over to the television and touched a switch on its side. A slideshow of pastoral scenes and breathtaking vistas flowed across the screen.

"That's the best we can do down here," he said. "If you are desperate for a breath of fresh air, there's a lift up into the woods."

Max looked round and took it all in.

"Now," Doug continued, patting the monitor on the desktop, "this is an ordinary PC connected to the internet. You can use it for surfing the web, personal email and stuff like that. You *don't* use it for anything work related. It has a firewall and it would take a pretty clever hacker to get access to it but it's not totally secure – deliberately. If anyone does manage to get into it, it's packed with files filled with utter nonsense."

"Smoke and mirrors," grinned Max.

Doug pointed a finger at him suggesting that he had hit the nail on the head.

"The other one," Doug went on, "is not connected to anything outside this facility. This is where you communicate internally and do your real work. You can handle UNIX command line?"

Max nodded.

"There is a small kitchen along the hallway with a shower and toilet," Doug pointed to the right through the doorway.

Max went and tried-out the big white swivel chair behind his new desk. He looked round and nodded.

"This'll do nicely."

"Now, lets go and meet the others," said Doug tipping

his head sideways towards the door. "They are dying to meet you."

The main laboratory was big. Row after row of workbenches disappeared into the middle distance. Racks above each bench held oscilloscopes and other test equipment. It was all very neat and tidy.

A small group of people stood around talking. Some sat at workstations. Others were looking at machine drawings on a table.

"This is Doctor Sergei Bazarov, Head of Engineering," said Doug holding his hand out towards a tall dark man with tousled, wavy hair. Max shook his hand.

A fair-haired female sitting at a workstation turned round, smiled and gave a little wave.

"This is Jennifer Ryan," continued Doug, "she is our chief software wizard."

"Call me Jen." Max could just detect an Australian accent coming through.

From the other side of the table, a dark-haired Japanese man stepped forward with his hand outstretched.

"Ken Miyazaki," he said, "cybernetics and AI."

As the others introduced themselves, Max was taken aback at just how international the team was. Russian, Australian, Japanese, Chinese, Indian – but there were no Americans! Max wondered why and made a mental note to ask Doug about it later.

Max was intrigued by the Russian engineer but he wasn't totally comfortable with Russians. Doug called him over.

"Max, Sergei is our tame flight engineer. Actually, he's a bit more than that, he has a doctorate in theoretical physics – but he likes to take the hands-on approach."

Sergei smiled. "Actually, I'm a quantum mechanic. Trouble is, I can never find my spanners, they're so small!"

Max's doubts about him subsided.

"I think we'll get along just fine," said Max. "How come you speak with an American accent, you are Russian?"

"If you want to learn English in Russia, the teachers are all American," he answered. "I can't do English English. Sorry."

Max patted his shoulder.

Sergei Bazarov looked to be in his late thirties. His hair was on the long side and not very tidy. You could call it a mess. He wore small, gold-rimmed glasses and dressed strangely: blue shirt, green jacket, mustard yellow trousers. Nothing matched.

"Would you like to come up with us and meet the other member of our team?" asked Sergei. "Auntie Gertie."

Max did a double-take. He got his jacket and pulled it on.

"Sure," replied Max.

The three of them took the lift to the top level and stepped into a small hallway. A heavy metal door stood before them. The Russian man placed his hand on the pad on the wall, letting the door open into an airlock. He put his hand against another pad and the inner door slid open too.

Max was surprised to be in, what appeared to be, the hangar deck of an aircraft carrier. The two in front of him beckoned him through.

He looked about. The ceiling was a mass electrical and ventilation ducting. The walls were white and sported various gantries and platforms. On the hangar floor...

"Wow!" he exclaimed not quite believing what he was seeing. "What am I looking at here?"

Three unusual aircraft sat under the wide curved roof. Each was sitting on a motorised cradle and covered with a tarpaulin. Sergei motioned to one of the technicians to pull a cover off.

Doug held out his hand to the nearest craft.

"Its official name is AG-127-3, which is quite a mouthful. So during operations, it's simply Delta 3."

He pointed at the other craft in turn and counted them off.

"Delta 1, Delta 2, Delta 3."

It was smooth and dull black all over except for the corners of its fuselage, which housed glossy black spheres. There were no obvious wings or fins or anything aerodynamic that suggested it could fly. Printed in grey on each side was "D3", the 'D' being a stylised triangle.

Bewildered, Max shook his head. "What is it?"

Doug looked over at him and smiled.

"I told you that there were no aeroplanes here. This, I suppose, is what you might call a 'flying saucer', except that it isn't. It's an experimental test-bed that uses three vectoring gravity drives - 'G-Drives".

Max looked stunned.

"Sergei, would you like to explain?"

The Russian clasped his hands together as if beginning a lecture.

"During the Second World War, Nazi scientists experimented with gravity drives. Rumour has it that they captured an alien vessel intact – unlike the smashed-up ones they got at Roswell. Typical Americans, shoot first, talk later. Anyway, towards the end of the war, some of these scientists, and their experiments, were spirited off to Russia. The Americans were happy enough to get Wernher von Braun and his rockets. We got the gravity drives."

Gravity!

Max didn't know much about gravity. Yes, he was aware of its effects, but not its nature. He recalled a 'howler' read out by a former school science teacher. Some wag had written in his exam paper that before Isaac Newton had invented gravity, things had just floated in the air. Another had explained that gravity was what stopped the penguins falling off the bottom of The World. He was right, but for the wrong reason.

"How does it all work?" asked Max quizzically.

"It's quite simple really," explained Sergei, "the G-drives are based on a series of stacked superconducting coils encased in liquid helium that generate artificial gravity."

"But the war ended nearly eighty years ago," commented Max. "Why has it taken so long?"

"Power," said Sergei. "The German experiments used massive amounts of energy. Although they managed to achieve liftoff, their drives had to be hard-wired to the electricity generators, so their machines remained strictly tethered to the ground. It has taken all this time to come up with a power supply light and compact enough to actually leave the ground unrestricted."

"And that is?" quizzed Max.

"Fusion."

"You have fusion power?" Max gasped.

"Yes, of course," replied Sergei. "After Chernobyl, our government put all our research efforts into fusion energy. A reactor not much bigger than a suitcase can power a city and the only by-product is a small amount of Helium. There is such a micro reactor in here. It's perfectly safe."

"So, has this, thing, actually flown?" asked Max.

"Yes, all the time," bragged Sergei.

"You might have heard about the strange objects in the sky recently on the news," interrupted Doug.

A penny dropped.

Max's mouth gaped.

"That was you?" he asked.

Doug continued to speak. "Most of our activity is at night time but the public have, unfortunately, seen things they weren't supposed to see." He looked at Sergei accusingly.

"We fly far out over sea for the most part," explained Sergei, "but we have to get from here to the sea and lighting conditions can change without warning. We do have a couple of Lear Jets that we send up as escorts at the same time. They make sure that there aren't any other aircraft in the vicinity and relay encrypted comms to the Deltas."

"What's with the disappearing behind clouds?" Max asked.

"Haha," said Sergei, "disappear into them, you mean. We can sit inside a cloud almost indefinitely and drop a peri-cam down through. Like a submarine periscope but the other way up."

Max could seen the huge possibilities for covert surveillance – but in whose hands?

"This is an international project then?" pressed Max.

"Very much so, it's much too big for any one country to handle, even Russia," said Sergei.

"And, the Americans?" asked Max.

"No," sighed Doug, shaking his head. "The Americans have their own parallel projects based upon Roswell technology. They might have gravity drives but they don't have any practical way to power them. We know that we are way ahead of them and we don't share anything."

"Would you like to have a look inside?" asked Doug. "Delta 3 here, 'Aunt Gertie' to the family, takes a crew of three. The other two are semi-autonomous drones. The human body can't handle the G-forces that these things throw so Auntie Gertie is throttle-inhibited to 5G to be safe."

Max and Doug climbed a metal step ladder into the hatchway of Gertie's cramped cockpit. There were three reclining couches, two facing forwards and one backwards – or was it the other way around? There was no obvious front and back, nor any windows save for two tiny portholes. Max couldn't help thinking that the styling was more akin to that of a luxury yacht than that of a purely functional aircraft. The design was light grey minimalist instead of military stick-everything-where-it-should-be-and-to-hell-with-aesthetics.

Max squeezed into what the thought was the pilot's seat. There were a few controls but not many. He picked up a helmet and looked at it. He gasped in shock.

"Where did you get this?" he shouted. "I was still working on this when I left Advanced Aviation. It was top secret! Nobody outside the company knew about it."

He turned the helmet round to inspect it from every angle. It was identical to his JA-200 but obviously not manufactured at Advanced Aviation, the wiring was too neat. As he usually chopped and changed it during testing, it quickly became a rat's nest. This one was a work of art.

"A fine piece of work," smiled Doug.

"Where did you get it?" demanded Max.

"Oh, we got hold of it from some friends in China."

Max smacked his forehead in disbelief.

Doug smirked, "Now you know why you are working here."

"What is it that you want me to do?" asked Max in exasperation.

"Finish the helmet, basically" said Doug calmly, "and add a few modifications and enhancements that we have been working on."

"Aren't there patent problems?" asked Max.

"Stuff like this isn't patented," said Doug, "that would make the technology public knowledge and nobody wants to do that."

Max agreed, it made sense.

"Oh, and you have to work out how to interface it with Auntie Gertie. We don't have that expertise – yet!" said Sergei.

"Why do you call it Auntie Gertie?" asked Max.

Doug smiled. "Just a wee joke. A.G. – Anti Gravity – though some will tell you that it's not *anti* gravity at all. It works *with* gravity, not against it."

Max ran his hand over the smooth surface and crouched down to peer underneath. There was no sign of any moving parts and he couldn't fathom how such a craft could possibly fly through the air.

"It has no flying surfaces," he said.

"No, it is not particularly aerodynamic at all," said Sergei. "Doesn't have to be. It goes straight up like this." He demonstrated with his hand, keeping it parallel with the floor.

"When it gets out of the atmosphere, then it can move sideways. There, aerodynamics is not an issue."

Max shook his head.

"Do we have a timescale for interfacing the helmet?" was Max's next question.

"Oh, ASAP!" came the reply from Doug. "As quick as you possibly can."

Max frowned. He had no idea what he was supposed to do.

Max had a smug smile across his face as he drove back to his hotel. Gravity drives, this was the stuff of science fiction and he, Max Hayden, had been recruited to work on such a monumental project. That meant more to him than the doubling of his, already substantial, salary. He banged the steering wheel of his car with the palms of his hands. His brain was in overdrive; where he'd come from and where he could go.

Max's family were Navy through and through. His Grandfather had been an admiral and saw action in both the First and Second World Wars. His Father was a Falklands Veteran and his Mother was in the WRNs. He had been the first member of the family to leave the Navy early to follow a civilian career and now his prospects far eclipsed any that a potential senior naval position could have offered.

Oh, this was beyond belief. He pressed down on the accelerator and felt the power of his BMW surge forward. In his head, he could identify the parallel between the high performance car and Max Hayden. This was intoxicating. He looked down at his speedometer: it showed ninety miles per hour – way over the speed limit. It felt like he was doing only fifty. He glanced in his rear mirror and slowed down to a more reasonable seventy-five. He had been caught speeding before and it was such a blow to his self-esteem; not the fact that he had been speeding, the fact that he had been caught.

So, his task now was to marry-up his helmet electronics with the AG-127 craft cameras and sensors. Then, he had to devise a way to control the power of those micro fusion reactor powered gravity drives. At the moment, it was all done with levers. He could do better than that. Levers could be a liability at high acceleration because they are operated by frail human limbs and muscles. Max noticed that his speed had crept up again. All this thinking about speed and acceleration! He eased off.

How the hell did they get their hands on a JA-200 helmet from Advanced Aviation? He couldn't figure that one out. They said it had come from 'friends in China', how could that be possible? Security at his previous company was watertight, he just knew it was, but here was a fully functional helmet that he had been working on as a prototype six months earlier. He pictured his old colleagues one by one in his head. No, there wasn't one he didn't trust implicitly. He had known them all for years. There were no foreign nations, Chinese nor otherwise. It had to be a cyber attack, but he thought that their network was locked-down tight. He shook his head.

Previously, Max had toyed with the idea of micro-movement controls. He imagined that it should be possible to amplify small movements of fingers electronically but, the trouble was, that an unintentional jerk or muscle spasm would have devastating consequences with such huge amounts of power on tap. The trick would be to filter-out movements that exceeded expected parameters. He wasn't quite sure how to do that, there must be someone on his new team who could help. They were, supposedly, the crème de la crème of the aerospace industry. Then there were the facilities – a far cry from the R&D labs at his old job. Yes, he had worked wonders with what he had available but now, here was McGregor's with pockets virtually bottomless and the possibilities immeasurable.

Max's headlights beamed-out along the motorway. It wasn't far to his exit. He would ring Katie when he got back to his hotel. No, it was nearly 2:00am, she wouldn't appreciate that. He would leave her a text to meet up in the morning. They were going to look at some rental properties.

CHAPTER FOUR

"Hi Mum."

Katie held her phone to her ear as she walked round the cottage peering into cupboards and corners.

"We are just viewing the most wonderful cottage at the minute. Can I call you back later?"

"Okay. Love you." She hung up.

"I love it," she said to Max, taking his arm.

"It's only fifteen minutes into town," said the starchy estate agent.

"What's the minimum let?" asked Max.

"One year," came the reply.

"I can get to work in forty minutes from here," Max nodded at Katie.

"We'll take it," she said, clapping her hands.

The estate agent handed Max a pile of paper to sign and showed them out.

"I'll have the keys for you on Thursday."

Max and Katie gave the cottage a last admiring look as they climbed into the car.

"It's a pity there isn't a garage," Max said pulling out of the short lane into the main road.

"It's only for a few months until we find something more permanent," insisted Katie. "You still haven't told me about your job."

"Can't", shrugged Max. "You know the old spy joke about 'If I tell you, I'll have to shoot you?' Well, I won't shoot you, but somebody else might!"

Katie shivered and stared out of her window.

"I can't even take my new car to work. I have to play a charade where I park it in a car park below an office block in town and switch over to some old banger."

"That's ridiculous," she complained.

Max shrugged.

"Look, I'm going to have to drop you off at the station. Sorry love. I have a meeting in an hour at HQ. We'll talk more when I get back later."

"Hello, Max. Have a seat," said Tony Davidson. "I've been wanting to have a little chat with you but I've been very busy. You know how it is. How are you settling in?"

Max noted that Tony had an ice-cold stare.

"Oh, fine," said Max looking round at Tony's palatial penthouse office.

"Like your new car?"

"Oh, yes. Drives like a dream," smiled Max.

"Would you like some coffee?" asked Tony.

"No, I'm okay," said Max. He avoided office coffee like the plague. It was either instant or stewed.

"Max, I first want to make it clear that nothing we discuss here goes beyond this room. Okay?"

There was a pause. Max agreed. Tony continued.

"Now, you know what we are up to. You have been shown our G-drive project and asked to develop the JA-200 helmet concept to control it."

"Yes, I understand," said Max.

"Good. Good. There are some things that you won't have been told."

Tony scratched his forehead.

"Two things. First you have to understand that although the Americans are our allies to all intents and purposes, there are things that they don't share with us – and we with them. Truth is, we don't share a lot at all unless somebody stands to make money out of it. Usually them."

He drew circles on his desk with his fingertips.

"I don't underestimate them for a minute, that would

be very dangerous. I don't know how much, if anything, they know about our G-drives or your helmet research. We can't let them find out anything – for all kinds of reasons, which I won't go into. You can probably work them out for yourself?"

Max gave a slight nod.

"You have already seen the lengths that we go to hide our tracks. I'm afraid that you are going to have to live with that. We all do. Can I just make it clear that if there are any leaks, any slip-ups, any hint of indiscretion…!" Tony just stared at him long and hard and tapped the table. Max had a good idea of what he was trying to say. It frightened him a little. Hell, it was supposed to.

"You said that there were two things?" asked Max.

"Yes," said Tony. "There is something else important, very important. I'm not going to go into that now, you will find out soon enough. What I will say, is that it pales our little charade here into insignificance."

Max was feeling a bit punch drunk from all the intrigue.

Tony clasped his hands.

"Now, I'm afraid that you are going to have to excuse me, Max. I'm due at the MOD this afternoon. If you have any questions or concerns, you know where I am. If you don't, my PA does."

With that, he ushered Max out of the office.

A Chinese girl knocked on Max's door and walked in. People called her 'Li' but he wasn't sure if that was her first name or last. She was petite with short black hair and persisted in wearing a white lab coat. Nobody else did. She didn't exhibit the faintest hint of humour but carried out her work with faultless efficiency. She gave him a respectful nod.

"Can you give these specifications to Jen and Ken," he asked, handing her a USB stick. "I'd rather not put them on the server at this stage."

Li took the stick without comment and left his office.

"He waited a minute and lifted the phone punching in a number for Doug Sinclair.

"Doug, Max here. What have you got on Ms. Li, here?" he asked.

"Hmm, Li Yan. She prefers to use her family name. Doctorate in Computer Science from Beijing University. She is funded by the Chinese Government but they are aux fait with everything we are doing here. We are all partners these days, they have manufacturing skills that we could only dream of."

"Li seems a bit distant," said Max.

"Oh, when you get to know her well, she will still be the same," quipped Doug. "She has a friend, 'Ying Chen' who works in engineering. They are rarely seen apart."

"What, are they an item?" asked Max.

"Well, I wouldn't know about that," said Doug.

Max put the phone down.

He picked it up again and punched a button for another internal number.

"Jill, can you arrange a meeting for tomorrow morning with Doug, Ken and Jen in my office?"

The secretary made a note and asked. "Do you need Sergei there too?"

"No," replied Max. "I will have some stuff to discuss with him afterwards."

Max sat behind his desk with the others on chairs in an arc in front of him. He raised his hand in a submissive gesture.

"Before we start, I have a dreadful confession to make."

For Max, that was a hard thing to do.

There was a pregnant pause.

"I have just found out that Li Yan has a Doctorate and I

have been using her as an office gofer."

Jen coughed.

"I wouldn't worry too much about that, Max. Li is from a culture much different to ours. She is pretty much used to that."

Max scowled. It was not what he wanted to hear.

"Anyway," he continued, "I hope you had time to look at the specs I sent round with Li?"

They glanced round at each other and nodded.

Max started, "I have been working on ideas for a new helmet and I want to run them by you. This is just between the four of us for the minute."

"You are really considering retinal projection?" asked Ken, the cybernetics engineer.

"It's one of the possibilities, but it has many advantages if we can get it to work," said Max, as if it were a question.

"And the optical network?" probed Ken.

"Yes, provided you can conjure-up the bandwidth I need. I want a CineMax experience, not a magic lantern."

Ken nodded. "Sounds like the way to go."

"Sergei, if your people can work on the power relays... and Jen, can the programmers work with Sergei and whip up some drivers?" suggested Max.

"Sure," said the Australian girl.

"Now," continued Max, "there's only so much we can do on the ground. When we have all this stuff ready, the only way to test it properly is to take it up. Sergei will be piloting with the current equipment. I will wear the new Augmented Reality helmet - and Jen, I'd like you along with your laptop to tweak the parameters."

They all agreed, and set to work.

CHAPTER FIVE

Katie was threading new curtains onto a pole when Max came in. They were cream with dainty little red flowers.

"What do you think?" she asked.

"Yea," said Max with little interest.

He took off his jacket and slumped down.

"Hard day?" asked Katie.

Max pulled a face.

"Word has got out about what I'm working on."

Katie scrunched her eyes and peered at him sideways.

"Spies?"

Max tightened his lips and shook his head.

"Oh no, nothing like that. Just within the company. I was hoping to keep some stuff under wraps until it was further down the line but the top brass have got wind of it somehow and want to be put in the loop."

"Is that bad?" asked Katie, returning to her curtains.

Max squirmed on the sofa. "Could be. Seems that I've been a bit liberal with the budgets."

"I thought that this outfit had bottomless pockets," he added, "but that would not seem to be the case! I have to make a presentation to the board on Friday. I just hope that they understand."

"Oh, I have something to show you," said Katie, walking over to the corner of the room.

"What do you think of the seven pound hat stand now?" she smiled.

Max wanted to admit that she had done a good job, but that wasn't his style.

"S'okay."

Katie was used to him and let it pass.

"There's another car boot sale on Sunday, want to go?"

she asked.

"I've already got a car boot," he said without looking up.

She hit him.

"I don't think white cars and country roads were made for each other," said Max, looking out the window at his filthy BMW. "I have a board meeting tomorrow, can't turn up at head office like that."

"Want me to help you wash it?" asked Katie.

"No, too cold. I'll take it down to the car wash at the filling station in the village," he answered.

Max picked up his car keys from the kitchen worktop and headed out. When he got to the filling station, he paid for a wash and was given a pin number to enter into the keypad at the entrance to the mechanical car wash. It was only when the rotary brushes started flailing wildly that he began to have apprehensions about taking his new car into such a contraption. What if it scratched the paint or pulled a wing mirror off?

As the soapy wax bubbles slid down his windscreen, Max wondered about the board meeting lined-up for the next day. His experience of boards was that they were usually a load of stuffed shirts who overly valued their own self-important opinions. The committees that designed camels. He didn't want that to happen with his projects. His ideas were innovative and state-of-the-art. Would it all be too rich for them to stomach? Would they water everything down or start complaining about budgets? On the other hand, that's why they had hired him in the first place. He didn't know.

He flicked on his windscreen wipers to give him a clear view ahead – both literally and metaphorically.

Would the board even understand what he was talking about? It was all very advanced technically, but then, they had approved the development of the G-drives and micro fusion reactor. It could be argued that his work was relatively minor after those two earth-shattering developments. This was one of the few times in his life that Max Hayden was unsure of himself. Mister Infallible had doubts. He didn't like that.

When the car wash had finished, he drove out the other side and left the car. He walked all round it inspecting for damage. No problems: clean and shiny. The sign absolving the company from damage to cars caught his eye. He wished he had seen that on the way in. Maybe he would hand-wash in future. He had a hose – and Katie!

Going back to the cottage, he was careful to avoid driving too close to vehicles in front and steered around mucky deposits in the road. His car had to be in pristine, showroom condition the next day and his presentation just as flawless.

The head office car park was fuller than usual and the vehicles more lavish.

Max was still tweaking his slideshow when the others were led into the conference room. He pushed a key on his laptop and the screen on the wall went blank.

Tony Davidson introduced Max to the board members that he hadn't met before. Most were European but there were a few Asian faces in the gathering too.

Tony stood at the front, gave a brief opening statement, and handed the floor over to Max.

Max's first few slides gave a general overview of Helmet Mounted Display Systems. He had no idea how familiar the audience might be with the concepts and didn't want to appear to be talking down to them, or above their heads. Their straight-faced demeanour certainly didn't give him any clues.

When he got to retinal projection and modulated

laser diodes he felt he was losing them. He looked over at Tony who was making subtle movements with his hand suggesting that he ease-off on the technical details. Max produced an animation that described the process simply and succinctly. Tony relaxed.

"One of our main problems," said Max, "is that the G-drives put a lot of stress on the human body. Much as I'd like to use a mid-air gesture-based interface, the pilot is going to be pinned down hard to his couch from gravitational forces."

He looked round the hall and everybody seemed to understand.

"I want to use micro-gestures!"

Muttering came from the hall.

Max produced a cyber glove from under the table.

"This glove can register minute movements of hands and fingers. It can distinguish between a deliberate control gesture and a nervous twitch, so don't be concerned about that. If the movements are mapped to controls, a pilot can operate his machine easily, up to the point of black-out, then the AI kicks-in and takes over."

"Think of a trackpad on a laptop," he continued, "then put a trackpad on every fingertip of the glove. Add haptics, and visual feedback through the helmet, and you have a system that makes sense in a high-G environment."

A short film clip demonstrated the hand movements, their cause and effect. The audience seemed to be impressed.

"Now, if there are any questions, I will try to answer them."

Several hands went up.

"Is it safe to shine laser beams into people's eyes?" said one man, looking round the room for support.

"Perfectly safe," answered Max, "we are talking about very low power here. It's no brighter than an LED screen.

The brightness is continually monitored and governed."

"Next," he said, pointing to a woman at the back.

"How much of this technology is off the shelf and how much is proprietary?" she asked.

"Most all of it has been developed in-house," came the reply. "Only basic electronic components are not custom made."

A man at the side rose to his feet.

"Bob McGregor." Max recognised him from his portrait in the board room. "When are we going to see your ideas in action?"

Max held his hand up, palm outward.

"I can tell you now, that this is all ready to go, given a bit of fine tuning. We should be in the air by February."

Somebody started clapping. Max suspected that it was Tony Davidson from the expression on his face. Soon they were all applauding and stepping forward to shake him by the hand.

Tony Davidson gestured for silence.

"Well, that winds it up for today. I'm sure that you will all join me in thanking Max Hayden for a very informative and exciting presentation." He pointed upwards.

"And now, the sky!"

"Is he talking about budgets?" thought Max pessimistically. Then it occurred to him that he'd actually had quite an easy ride.

Max got home early. He only had to drive from Head Office.

"Want to go out tonight?" he asked, throwing down his things on the floor.

Katie jumped up. "Oh yes please," she said, giving him a big hug and kiss.

"I hear that the Dog and Duck in the village do a good steak," said Max. "It's a Friday night so they might be a bit busy. I'll ring and see if I can book a table."

"Super," smiled Katie.

The pub was as busy as Max had anticipated; people running around with trays full of glasses, lots of chatter and clatter.

They were shown to their table by a small waitress dressed head to toe in black. Katie took off her poncho and folded it neatly over the back of her chair.

"Table 5," it said on the menu holder.

Max ordered the meals at the bar and brought over two drinks.

"Do you want to talk about your presentation?" asked Katie.

"Oh, it went okay, I think," he said modestly but then changed his mind. "Rather well actually. Tony came over afterwards and congratulated me."

"Tony?"

"The managing director."

Katie mouthed "Oh."

"But," Max continued, tapping a finger on the table, "now the pressure is on to produce results. I'm going to be a little busy for the next month or so. You might not see much of me."

Katie took his hand to show that she understood.

"Might have to get a man in then," she teased.

"Oh Maxie," said Katie slowly, "I was in Bernie's Convenience Store in the village today and something very strange happened."

"Oh, what was that?" he asked.

"There was this big black car parked outside with two men in it. I think that they were watching me."

"Don't be ridiculous," said Max, "why would they be watching you?"

"I might be wrong, but I could swear that one of them

looked familiar."

Max smiled, "You're getting paranoid Katie."

"I'm not paranoid!" she snapped back. "I'm certain that I've seen him before. I just can't place him."

The waitress brought the steaks to the table along with a bowl of sauce sachets. Max looked up at her but said nothing.

Katie said, "Thank you," for him.

"Max…" She was about to chastise him for his bad manners when a thought came to her.

"I've got it!" she yelled. "It was Bob."

"Bob?" asked Max in puzzlement.

"You remember Martha and Bob in Nassau?"

"Yes"

"It was him."

Max threw his eyes up to the ceiling in desperation.

"Katie, my dear, why would an American tourist be here and watching you from a car in at the supermarket?"

"I don't know," she said sheepishly, "but it was definitely him. I know it was."

* * *

John Landers looked out across the desert landscape and watched an approaching Humvee kick-up clouds of dust in its wake. He closed his blinds.

He was about fifty with a flat-top crew cut and red face. With his impeccable black suit, he exuded authority.

"Ed," he said to the figure sprawled in an armchair, "I'm getting my ass kicked for results and you're not giving me any!"

Ed Mitchell shifted uncomfortably in his chair.

Landers sat down at his desk.

"We are doing our damnedest, John."

"It's not good enough!" Landers stressed each word

with a bang on the desk. "The Brits and Russians are pissing all over us."

Mitchell bit his lip and said nothing.

"They have some sort of drive that is light years beyond anything you have given us. They are flying it out of somewhere in Middle England and it's running rings round us. We haven't got a decent shot of it from our Condors or from our agents on the ground. All we get are these... amateur reports from news programs where they think they are seeing bloody flying saucers."

He ranted on.

"We are the ones that have the flying saucers. All tucked up in the Nevada desert for the last eighty years and still we don't know how they work."

Mitchell broke in. "John, if the Native Americans had come across a smartphone, they wouldn't know what it was or how to use it. Hell, they used smoke signals for communications. Even if the phone was charged up and they worked out how to turn it on, who would they call. You need two of them. You can't have a smartphone at one end and smoke at the other! We are the ones with the signal fires and blankets, the aliens have the smartphones. How am I supposed to square that?"

"You've reverse engineered some of the alien stuff," urged Landers. "You have all the money and resources you need. What's the problem?"

"It's slow going. What we need are more bright young graduates with open minds. People that can take a fresh look at the problems and try to make sense of how it all works."

"Or," said Landers, "we could shortcut the whole process and get a closer look at what the Brits are doing!"

"Can we do that?" asked Mitchell. "We are supposed to be allies."

"Pah!" exclaimed Landers, "we saved their hides from

the Germans in '42 and now they are in bed with Russians and Chinese. Ingrates!"

Ed Mitchell lifted his hat off Landers' desk, and stood up.

"Good luck with that," he said, leaving the room.

Minutes later, a knock came to Landers' door.

"Yeh," he barked.

Two men entered.

"Sir," one of them said.

"Thompson. Walker. Have a seat."

The two suited men sat down opposite him at his desk.

"Anything?" he asked.

Thompson and Walker looked at one another and shook their heads.

Landers pressed keys on his laptop and spun it round.

"This is Max Hayden. He is an avionics guru that has just moved from Advanced Aviation to McGregor Aerospace in the UK. Ex Royal Navy, and he's a damned clever son of a bitch."

Walker, a black man with a Fu-Manchu moustache pointed at the screen.

"What do we have on him?"

Landers turned the laptop back towards himself.

"We have his home address and his car license number. He switches cars at a park under McGregor's procurement offices and drives a 4x4, a different one every day, to a lumber camp which doesn't seem to do anything. Our Condors can't detect any heat signatures. Infrared photography shows no activity in the forest but there's gotta be something there."

He tapped an aerial photograph on his screen. "Our Condors detected gravitational anomalies in this area. I want you guys to go over there and find out what the hell it is!"

When they had left the room, Landers picked-up his

phone.

"Peterson, I want you to position Condor 4 over the co-ordinates in England I'm just about to send you. Okay?"

CHAPTER SIX

Max had shaved.

One thing that he had learned from his hours in a simulator was that stubble could get very uncomfortable in the confines of a flight helmet. At last, he was going to take his baby up into the air. Seventy miles straight up!

"How far upwards could we go?" he asked Sergei, who was going to be the main pilot on the test flight.

"Theoretically, all the way to the Moon," he replied in his quaint Russian/American accent, "but we are still some way off that."

Max and Sergei lay in the pilot and co-pilot couches which were level with one another.

Jen took the couch between them facing backwards. Their heads met level somewhere in the middle.

The craft was completely windowless but there were a series of high resolution monitors approximating the layout of a helicopter's viewports. Four faced forwards, two pointed down from the ceiling and two near the floor gave a view of the ground. Another monitor at the back showed a rear view and doubled as Jen's diagnostics display.

They wore compact pressure suits as they would be in the vacuum of space at the top of their travel. Sergei and Jen wore pilots' high altitude helmets and Max, his Augmented Reality helmet. White umbilical tubes carrying air and optical networking lines snaked from their helmets to a console in the middle.

The AG-127-3 was a good twenty-five feet on each sides of its round cornered triangular shape. A slight bulge in the top surface housed the cockpit. Apart from the spherical G-drive nacelles built into the three corners, the hull was fairly featureless.

Technicians removed the external power cabling and sealed the socket hatches. They were about ready to go.

Sergei requested clearance to lift off from the control room. There were no other aircraft in the vicinity. The craft inched forward on its three motorised dollies. The hanger doors slid open and Auntie Gertie was taken out into a small forest clearing decked with patches of frost. A quarter moon did its best to illuminate the patchy cloud cover.

Max was nervous. He had flown many times in all kinds of aircraft but this was different. He turned his head to see around the forest clearing with his night vision and saw the hanger doors close to mimic a small rocky outcrop in a hillside.

"Jen," he said, "I'm getting mis-registration between my left and right views, can you fix it?"

Jen typed something and tapped the arrow keys on her keyboard.

"Tell me when."

"Bit more," said Max. "Hold. That's it. Excellent."

"Wow!"

The full-colour, stereographic images projected into the back of his eyes were remarkable in their detail and clarity. It was as if he was standing alone naked in the night forest. The luminance amplifiers not only compensated for the darkness but also eliminated the blue cast of the moonlight.

His helmet was large with a mirrored visor taking up most of the front. A harness along the top had a protruding bump on either side housing the laser projectors. These fed into the visor via gold-coloured tubes and, at the bottom, a flexible umbilical tube carried oxygen and fibre-optic cables. The rear casing of a microphone sat in front of his mouth.

Through the helmet speakers an owl hooted in the distance. Max and Jen could hear Sergei's dialog with the control room through their audio. They were cleared for lift-off.

Like a trio of opera singers, the G-drives wound-up gradually to a high-pitched triad. They were very much quieter than any helicopter blades.

The floor moved and rocked a little.

Once on holiday, Max and Katie had stayed in a hotel room that had a water bed. This was the same slopping, unsettling motion.

There was clanking outside the hull as clamps detached and Auntie Gertie floated upwards to hover a few feet off the ground.

Sergei came on the audio.

"We'll be taking it quite slowly at first. We want to be at a good altitude to go through the sound barrier. It will lessen the boom effect on the ground."

Max's stomach dropped. It was like being in a high speed lift. He looked downwards with his helmet eyes and saw the dimly lit forest drop away. Beyond the forest, he could see the far-off glows of small towns and hamlets and the lights of vehicles moving along a motorway. His ears popped slightly. They passed through a cloud layer and the helmet display switched to a computer-generated image showing the ground recede. As they left the clouds, the sky above was filled with stars, millions of them. The moon looked as far away as ever.

Max felt his couch push into his back as Sergei accelerated off slightly sideways into a steep climb. There was a thump as Gertie broke the sound barrier. The rush of air going past the hull lessened off as the atmosphere got increasingly thinner. At seventy miles up, they levelled-off.

In his AR helmet, Max could see the curve of the Earth highlighted with a faint blue arc. It was beautiful. The stars no longer twinkled. He rubbed a finger on one of the two hemispheres built into the arms of his couch as his view swept through the entire gamut of the electro-magnetic spectrum from far infra- red to beyond ultra-violet. He was dumbstruck.

"Are you seeing this?" he called out over his audio link. Sergei and Jen could only see what was on their monitors, a very pale imitation of what he was experiencing.

Max called over to Jen to fine-tune a few helmet parameters.

"Wow! Wow! Wow!" he gasped as the view overwhelmed his senses.

Some fresh ideas came to his mind and he spoke them aloud into his voice recorder.

Through the clouds below, he caught glimpses of the British Isles and parts of the European Continent. In night vision, the image changed to monochrome but became much brighter. In infrared, heat sources on the ground showed-up in yellow false colour. He operated a control with his fingertips and suddenly his world was upside down with the planet spreading out above his head and the stars were at his feet. He felt sick. Only then did he realise that he was weightless and was being held in his couch by his safely harness.

He quickly switched back to right-way-up and closed his eyes to regain his orientation. He could see the laser light splay against his eyelids.

In his helmet speakers, chatter with control had eased-off but for the occasional report. "All functions nominal."

He breathed a deep sigh and wondered what Katie was doing far down below.

"You know, someday soon, there will be G-drive hotels up here. People will have dinners and wedding receptions and all that stuff," said Max. "And you will get up to them in G-drive elevators."

"Shouldn't be too far off," mused Jen.

"Just think of the money to be made," said Max. "The opportunities are enormous. Buy shares in McGregor Aerospace now!"

"Yes, I don't think that the possibilities have been overlooked down below," said Sergei. "One thing that we still have to solve though, is weightlessness. Can't have the wedding cakes floating off just as the groom and bride are about to cut into it, can we?"

"It shouldn't be too difficult to come up with some sort of local gravity situation to hold things to the floor," said Max.

"On interplanetary trips, you have the G force produced by the acceleration of the engines to hold you down. On space stations, they use the centrifugal force from spinning to achieve the same effect," said Sergei, in full lecture mode.

"Yes, but an orbiting hotel would have to be a big wheel," said Max. "I don't know the casual space tourist could handle that. They'd be puking all over the place. What we need is a floating island or castle in the air. The Earthside experience where up is up and down is down, but out here."

"Hmm. Watch this space," said Sergei with a chuckle. "My next project."

Max believed him. Then he sensed that Sergei was becoming agitated.

"Oh-ho," shouted Sergei suddenly. "We have visitors!"

Max overheard Sergei on the radio to ground control.

"Control, we have dolphins, repeat dolphins, at nine and three o'clock. Do you see them?"

"Negative," came the reply. "Nothing showing up here."

"Dolphins?" asked Max, "why dolphins?"

"You'll see," said Sergei.

Max started to shake as he used his helmet zoom to take a closer look at one of the craft paralleling their course. The hazy, pale blue shapes resolved into flat disks as he adjusted his view to the red end of the visible spectrum. One craft moved higher above his head and he could just make-out three shallow hemispherical protrusions on its base.

The two visitors travelled in a criss-cross path in front of them, backwards and forwards, up and down.

"Now you see why we call them dolphins," came a remark from Jen, who had been quiet until then.

"You've seen them before?" questioned Max.

"Yes, all the time," said Sergei.

"What are they?" demanded Max. "Is that the Americans?"

Sergei didn't answer for a minute while he took some readings.

"No, we don't think that they're American – too advanced."

"Who then?" said Max in aggravation.

Sergei pointed upwards. "ET!"

Max was shaken even more. This is what Tony had alluded to when they had their chat earlier.

"Are they hostile?" he asked quickly.

"No. No, they are only playing with us," answered Jen. "They are just giving us the once-over, they won't hang around for long."

As Max watched in his display, the two interlopers straightened out their courses and shot far ahead. In a second they were gone.

"Christ!" he said as the full implications hit him. UFOs were part of popular culture and had been for nearly a century, even longer if Ancient Egyptian and Mayan wall drawings were taken into account.

"Where did they go?" asked Max.

"No idea," replied Sergei. "They always disappear too quickly to tell. I think that they just vanish."

Max remembered that everything he saw in his helmet was recorded and put his display into playback mode. He wound back five minutes and watched carefully as the shapes streaked away. They did vanish. It wasn't just a matter of diminishing in size with distance.

He rewound the recording and set it for slow-mo playback. Sure enough, as some point in the mid distance, they had just ceased to be.

Max banged his fist on his thigh.

"Sergei, take us home?"

Max displayed his video of the dolphins on the big screen in his office.

Doug Sinclair looked at him and shrugged. "Yes, it's a mystery."

"And we are positive that it's not the Americans?" asked Max.

"Yes," replied Doug, "and no other nation on Earth has that kind of technology."

"Flying bloody saucers," said Max thumping his desk. "Have we ever tried to contact them?"

Doug shook his head slowly. "Max, we have not even been able to communicate with terrestrial dolphins so far. We have no idea if ET uses semaphore or pulse-code modulated tachyons. There are just no common terms of reference, even if we know the communications medium."

Jen had been sitting quietly in the corner.

"Can I just see the point where they vanish again? – and freeze frame."

Max jogged the video frame by frame backwards and forwards across the instant they disappeared.

"Look, just there," said Jen.

For just a hundredth of a second, the frame showed a very faint, fuzzy ring where the two craft vanished. It had rainbow tints, like oil on water.

"It's some kind of rift in space!" she exclaimed.

Max was trying very hard to take it all in. He had heard of things like this in sci-fi films but to witness it happening with his own two eyes was more than his brain could deal with.

"Can we call it a day," he suggested. "My head hurts."

It was Max's first time home for four days. Katie wasn't in.

He had a long soak in a hot bath and tried to get the jumble of images out of his head.

He put on his dressing gown and went into the kitchen to make some coffee. He could hear the sound of Katie's Mini coming into the small lane in front of the cottage.

The door opened and Katie put her shopping bags on the floor.

"Saw your car outside," she said throwing her arms around him.

"You might have given me a ring."

"Uh," said Max, "out of signal zone."

Katie slipped her hand inside Max's dressing gown.

"I missed you."

He didn't need any more persuasion.

It was Sunday.

"I hope that you're not going in today," scolded Katie.

Max threw back the duvet and sat on the edge of the bed.

"Er, no," he replied. "Why, have you got plans?"

"I was rather hoping that we could drive by where you work," she grinned. "I'd love to see it."

Max scoffed.

"Well, we could drive past it – but you wouldn't see it."

Katie looked puzzled.

"We could go and see your mother?" he suggested, happy that he'd been able to change the subject without too much exertion. He liked Katie's mother. She was just an older version of her daughter. Truth was, he thought that she fancied him.

Katie gave her a call to say they were coming. Alice would absolutely hate to have anyone drop in when there was a cushion out of place.

It was a pleasant drive to the seaside on a bright Spring morning. Every now and then on the journey, Katie would slip-in a question about Max's work hoping to catch him off guard. It didn't work.

Max even put up with Katie's complaints to Alice, about him being away from home so much and being so secretive. Alice took Max's side and told her to not be so 'bloody clingy'.

Perhaps it was because Max was there but Alice was all sweetness and light – not at all the nagging shrew she grew up with. Katie's father, Frank, had deserted them when she was a teenager. Alice always blamed herself for henpecking him too much. It wasn't entirely true. Katie was only too aware that he was getting itchy feet long before the divorce. She tried not to take sides. She loved them both dearly and they loved her.

Afternoon tea was served on the best Royal Albert china with paper lace doilies on the sandwich plates. Max wondered if all Alice's guests got this treatment. The truth was that she didn't have many visitors. Any that had come in the past were soon put off by her constant straightening of antimacassars and dusting of ornaments. Katie dreaded the prospect of becoming like her mother, but there was little chance of that, she was too easy going.

Alice didn't have her first G&T until five. Even though they had just dropped-in, she managed somehow, to whip-up a roast chicken supper with all the trimmings – and pudding too!

Max only took half a glass of wine knowing that Alice wouldn't allow him to drink just plain water. When he looked at his watch, Katie took the hint.

They both gave Alice a cuddle at the door as they left.

Max played loud rock on the car music system all the way home. Katie curled-up in the corner of her seat trying hard to block it out.

CHAPTER SEVEN

On Monday morning Max called Jen into his office.

"Look, I'd like you to write some filters for the helmet display," he said. "Narrow band, High-Q and I'd like to be able to sweep them. Can you do that?"

"Not a problem, Max," she replied.

"How long?" he asked.

"Oh, give me a couple of days. I have some code I can repurpose."

"Let me have a look when you have something."

Doug passed her in the doorway.

Max greeted him and said, "I'd love to have another look at the dolphins."

"I'll have Jill set up a meeting," smirked Doug. "Our place or theirs?"

Max smiled. "I don't think they will understand the concept of afternoon tea."

Max explained his ideas for modifications to the sensors and helmet software. Doug listened intently, asked questions and made helpful suggestions.

"We have a window coming up in March," said Doug. "Cloudy, dark Moon. Of course, I can't guarantee that anybody, stroke, thing will come to your party."

"We have the exact coordinates from our last encounter," said Max. "Hopefully, they will make a show. Sergei is optimistic."

"Doug," he continued, "I have an idea, what are the chances of taking Deltas 1 and 2 up with us. Can they fly formation with us under remote control?"

"You want to go in mob-handed?" asked Doug.

"Just a thought," said Max.

"Yes, talk to Sergei about it, shouldn't be too difficult."

"Can you tell me why you want to take all three Deltas up?" asked Doug,

Max winked.

"Smoke and mirrors, Doug. Smoke and mirrors."

"Village Antiques," it said on the door in gold foil lettering. Katie pushed it open and a little bell tinkled. There was nobody around.

She walked round the small shop looking at the items on the shelves and in glass cases. She picked some things up and looked for prices on the bases, but there were none. A silver and glass art deco brooch caught her eye. She lifted it and looked for the hallmark and maker's mark.

"Despres," came the voice from behind her.

She turned and looked at the grey-haired man in a waistcoat.

"It's lovely," she said, "how much?"

The man took it off her and examined the tiny paper tag hanging from a loop of white string.

"Two hundred and seventy-five," he said.

"Oh, nono, no," said Katie taking it off him and putting it back quickly on the glass shelf.

"Maybe I can come down a little on that," said the dealer.

"What's your trade price?" asked Katie, who really wanted it for herself. She produced a business card from her purse.

"Ah," said the old man, scratching his head, "what do you think?"

"A hundred?" asked Katie.

"No, can't do that," said the man, "I paid more than that for it."

"What's the best you can do?" asked Katie.

"Two hundred," came the reply.

Katie picked it up again and turned it round in her

fingers. It looked very masculine but worse than that, she wasn't sure that it was genuine. She had a feel for these things.

"No, I think I'll leave it," she said.

The man shrugged.

"I have something out in the car that might be of interest to you," said Katie indicating her Mini Countryman parked just outside. "Come and see."

The old man followed her outside. She opened the back doors of her car and showed him the antique oak coat stand that she had cleaned-up.

"I'm looking for fifty pounds for it," she said, taking it out and standing it on the footpath for the man to inspect. He looked it up and down.

"Mmm, how about forty?" he asked.

Katie deliberated for a minute and shook his hand.

"Forty it is," she smiled.

They took the stand back inside and the old man produced two twenty pound notes from a box under his counter.

"Pleasure to do business with you," he said. "Are you sure you don't want the Despres brooch?"

Katie twisted her lips.

"I'll think about it."

She left the shop and opened the door of her car. A large black sedan drove past. She didn't notice the passenger looking at her with more than a passing glance.

Sergei's team had Auntie Gertie suspended from a gantry in the hanger. External panels along the base had been removed and the G-drive nacelles were spread around the floor. Max saw Sergei checking drawings on a workstation screen.

"What's going on?" asked Max.

Sergei looked up. "You're a genius," he said.

Max was taken aback.

"What did I do?"

"You videoed the dolphin craft with your helmet system," said Sergei, grabbing him by both shoulders.

"Yes, I did, but so what?" asked Max.

"Can't you see?" said the Russian excitedly, "their engine nacelles are parabolical, whilst ours are spheres. They are able to direct more gravity energy than we can. That's why they are so efficient."

"So, you are changing the nacelle profile?" asked Max.

Sergei nodded vigourously. "I've modelled it on the computer. We can get more than double the thrust from the same energy. It's not just the shapes of the casings, it the quantum field coils inside too."

Max patted him on the shoulder.

"And you say that I'm the genius?"

Max went over and examined the disassembled drives. There were no visual clues to their operation at all.

"How do they work," he asked.

"Graviton field generators," said Sergei, "it's all about harnessing the spin-2 boson, which is massless as opposed to electromagnetism's spin-1 boson."

"So you are firing particles of gravity like particles of gas in a rocket motor?" asked Max.

"Oh, no, no, no," said Sergei, "not particles, strings, and they aren't fired anywhere!"

Max was lost. It was all beyond him and he needed to save face.

"Hey Sergei. Can I get one of these for my car?"

Sergei took him seriously.

"No," he said, "they wouldn't be much use on corners. Cars need to grip the road surface. A G-drive in a car would be like skating on ice."

Max flapped his hand to say, "Forget it!"

Sergei grinned.

"I need to go back to my lab and do some more calculations."

Sergei had access to what was probably the most sophisticated number-crunching power on the planet but when he wanted to work something out, he used a blackboard. That's the way he had done it at university in Moscow and he didn't see any great reason to change. It worked. He was trying to improve the power transfer efficiency between his micro fusion reactor and the G-drives' field generators. There wasn't anyone in the world he could ask for help. He was the expert.

"Doing hard sums?" asked Doug facetiously, as he entered the lab.

Sergei stepped back from the blackboard and surveyed his latest work.

"Bah!" he exclaimed, stepping forward with the blackboard duster and wiping-off huge swathes of his equation. "It's just not working."

"Maybe you should sleep on it?" suggested Doug.

Sergei turned round to him. "That's the trouble, I won't sleep!"

Doug nodded in understanding. "I have the same problem myself."

Sergei stood stroking his chin for a minute and then stepped up to the board again. He pointed at one part of his equation and then another. He stroked his chin again. In the blank space he had just cleared, he started filling-in some numbers and brackets.

"Hmm," he pondered some more.

"I'll leave you to it," said Doug. "Makes my head itchy…in the inside where I can't scratch!"

Doug was just about to leave the lab but turned round in the doorway.

"Sergei, I think it is time that Max had some flying

lessons."

"Max, this is Jeff King," said Doug. "He has been our chief test pilot on the development of the Deltas."

"Hello Max, I've heard that you have flown before," said Jeff, shaking his hand.

"Yes, Royal Navy. Hawks and Tutors," answered Max.

"And helicopters?" asked Jeff.

"Yes, mostly Lynx and Merlin."

"Excellent," said Jeff, "then flying Auntie Gertie should be child's play. Come to think of it, a child could fly her."

"It's that easy?" asked Max.

"If you have flown helicopters, you already know the flight controls."

Jeff beckoned Max inside Gertie's cockpit. He took the co-pilot's seat and patted the pilot's couch for Max to climb into.

"You have the equivalent of the cyclic stick here, works just like a helicopter but instead of changing the rotor's pitch, it controls the relative power to the G-drives. Push it forward and the power to the forward drive reduces slightly and you go forward. Now, where a helicopter maintains a constant rotational speed and the angle of the rotors vary the lift, the throttle here, varies the power to the G-drives in unison giving speed of ascent or forward and lateral motion."

Max nodded that he understood.

Jeff continued. "The pedals change your direction by altering the vector of the forward G-Drive. Of course, there's no anti-torque rotor but the effect is the same. The big difference between Gertie and a helicopter is that where a helicopter is basically unstable in the air and you have to work hard to control it, Gertie is rock solid and won't go anywhere unless you tell her to. That's why I said a child could fly it."

Max played with the controls. It was different from what he was used to as the couches were tilted back much more than helicopter seats.

"When can I take her up?" asked Max, enthusiastically.

"Tonight. I'll just have to file a plan with flight control and arrange for an escort," said Jeff.

Max was strapped into Auntie Gertie's pilot's couch and Jeff into the co-pilot seat. They were sitting in the forest clearing just outside the hangar at 1:00am. It was raining hard. The forest was pitch black, but to Max it looked like daylight through his helmet's enhanced view.

"Okay, we have been okayed for lift-off," said Jeff. "The escorts tell me that the sky is clear of traffic for thirty miles around. Start-up the drives."

Max flicked a control switch and immediately the three G-drives started their distinctive high-pitched hum.

"Now, just a little throttle," said Jeff.

Gertie lurched upwards.

"Easy does it," said Jeff. "The throttle is quite sensitive, there's a lot of power in there!"

Max eased off on the throttle and Gertie hovered thirty feet in the air with rain cascading off her hull. He could see over the tops of the forest trees and lightning arced in the distance.

"Okay, when you are ready, give it a little more juice," said Jeff.

Max felt the acceleration hit his back as Gertie cleared the first thick cloud layer.

"Ohhh," cried Max. You can't do that in a helicopter.

"Now, head east out over the sea," said Jeff.

Max pressed the right foot pedal and pushed the cyclic stick forward. Gertie headed east at a slight downward tilt.

"You need to compensate for the loss of power to the forward drive, a little more throttle," instructed Jeff. "We are working on a mod to do that automatically – this is a test bed to iron-out all these foibles."

Max familiarised himself with the controls and noted where improvements could be made to Gertie and his helmet.

"Don't be trying anything too fancy," said Jeff. "Don't try any loops or anything like that. Gertie is not aerodynamic at all and G-drives don't like being upside down."

"It would be good if you could combine Gertie's G-drives with a conventional plane to get the best of both worlds. Vertical take-off and fast forward flight."

"Yes, absolutely," said Jeff. "I believe that the Chinese are working on something along those lines."

"Think we'd better head back now," said Jeff. "Gertie has another trick up her sleeve. Just head back in the general direction of Mewton, same altitude."

Max headed West.

"Now you know how airlines have autoland?" asked Jeff, touching a button on the flight control screen.

"Just sit back and relax, Gertie knows her way home – to the millimetre."

She did.

"How long?" Katie tried her best to constrain the shriek.

"About a week," said Max stirring his coffee.

"Where will you be staying," she asked pointedly.

"They have some accommodation at work for people who need to stay over. The tests have to be done at night time so I'll be on nightshift."

Max buttered half a cinnamon and raisin bagel.

Katie put out her hand and grabbed his wrist.

"Maxie," she looked him in the eye. "Who is Jen?"

Max thought nothing of the comment at first and then he twigged.

"Jennifer Ryan, she's my lead software engineer."

At last, Katie had wrangled some information out of him about his workplace. She gave herself a tick.

"She rang when you were in the shower. Didn't say who she was but I saw it on your phone screen."

Max continued with his breakfast.

"Is she pretty?" she asked.

Max made a rocking motion with his right hand. His left was busy cramming bagel into his mouth. When he had swallowed the bagel he smiled at her.

"Katie, I know what you're thinking. You haven't got anything to worry about. Jen is okay but I get the impression that she's wedded to her computer."

"Probably more reliable!" she groaned.

Katie's posture eased.

"I hate it when you go off for days on your own," she scowled.

Max took the kitchen TV remote and turned up the volume.

"A group of UFO enthusiasts have published a video they captured off the International Space Station webcam downlink…"

The picture showed a low definition view of the Earth from space.

"…If you watch carefully, you will see two objects travel from the bottom left to the top right of the screen…"

Two bright objects disappeared behind one of the station's solar panel arrays.

"…If we zoom-in on the objects, we can clearly see that they are not aircraft, and meteorites don't travel upward."

The magnified image showed two very blurred ovals.

An unhealthy-looking man in a hooded jacket spoke into an interviewer's microphone.

"It just goes to prove, we *are* being watched by UFOs. The governments know all about this but they keep it all hidden from the public."

Max chuckled inwardly and turned the volume back down as the news bulletin went into cricket reports.

"How can I get in touch with you…in an emergency?" asked Katie.

Max sensed that she was fishing.

"No use calling my mobile," he said, "phone reception is virtually non-existent where I'll be."

He wasn't lying.

"If you need to get in touch desperately, ring head office and they'll get the message to me. I'll get back to you when I can."

Max picked-up his mobile and went out through the front door.

"Hi Jen, you called?"

"Yes, Max, are you about today? I have something to run by you."

"Yes, I'll be there in about an hour," he said and went back inside.

Katie was putting the breakfast things in the dishwasher.

"Will you be late tonight?" she asked.

"Oh, not particularly," he replied.

Max grabbed his jacket and briefcase, and was about to give Katie a kiss on the cheek. She turned her head and their lips met.

"See you later," he said emphasising the word "you".

"Ding dong."

Katie was expecting a delivery of brass polish she had bought online and opened the door with an expectant smile. The delivery man was taking a small package out of the back of his dark brown van, which had backed into the driveway.

"Max Hayden," he said holding out the package and a

clipboard.

"Oh, it's not my polish," she thought to herself.

She stepped out of the cottage towards the van, hand outstretched to take the package from the courier. Suddenly, someone grabbed her from behind. She shrieked, but a solvent-soaked cloth was forced over her mouth. She tried not to breathe the vile fumes but they soon took effect. Her body went limp and collapsed. Two figures dragged her into the back of the van. One climbed in with her. The other ran round to the cab, started the engine and drove off.

When Katie regained consciousness a few minutes later, she was gagged and had a jute shopping bag over her head. Her hands were tied together with some sort of twine or plastic tie. She could feel the motion and hear the sound of the van speeding along as she lay on the hard floor.

She made a muffled scream.

Katie couldn't tell in which direction they were going. Every now and then the van would stop, presumably at a road junction, and would tear off again. She could hear other traffic and car horns tooting. Maybe they were in a town, she wasn't sure.

Half an hour later, when the van had pulled to a stop, she could hear the back door creaking open and she was pulled out. She was frog-marched down a flight of stairs and into what must have been a building basement. It smelled musty. Inside, she was shoved into a room and she could hear a door being slammed. Behind the locked door, she could hear voices but couldn't make out what they were saying.

Max leaned over and looked at the image on Jen's workstation monitor. He recognised the home page from his helmet display.

"Now, this is just a simulation," said Jen, running down a menu to highlight a new item called 'Gravity Map'.

A perspective view with a green grid appeared on-screen. An image of the Earth dropped down from the top and visibly distorted the grid. It was joined by an image of the Moon, which caused a smaller dent in the grid.

"This is a new overlay for your helmet," explained Jen. "It's a lot more understandable than a stream of numbers flying past in a floating window."

"This is great," said Max tapping her on the shoulder. "Can you upload it to Auntie Gertie's computer?"

"I've done that already," smiled Jen. "Hope you find it useful."

Jen continued playing with the gravity map software, opening a code window and changing some variables.

"Who was it that I spoke to on the phone?" she asked, without looking up from her screen.

"Oh, Katie," replied Max, waiting for the next question.

Jen and Katie were very similar. Both were attractive. Jen's hair was a bit longer and darker but they were the same height and build. Their personalities were quite different though. Katie was warm and affectionate, Jen was distant and immersed in her coding. She had no rings on her fingers, nor any other jewellery for that matter. Max wondered if she had a life outside her work but didn't want to pry. Maybe when they knew each other better.

"Your other half?" asked Jen.

"Yes," said Max, "we've been together for some time now."

"No sign of you tying the knot then?" smiled Jen.

"No, I think we're okay the way we are."

"Family?" asked Jen.

"She's keen, I'm not," he replied.

Jen turned back to her screen and went on working.

"See you later," said Max, walking off.

Heading back to his office, Max passed Li Yan in the corridor. He smiled and nodded. She gave a curt "Hi!"

without stopping. He wondered if he had offended her when they first met. She certainly didn't give anything away.

He went into his office and sat down at his desk. He turned round, poked the head of his nodding alien on the bookshelf to make it wiggle, and got lost deep in thought.

CHAPTER EIGHT

Tony Davidson walked with Doug Sinclair along one of the many underground corridors at Mewton Base.

"I don't know quite how Max will react to this," said Doug.

"Doug, changing the subject for a minute, what is your own impression of Max. Please be frank, it's important."

"Well," began Doug, "first impressions were that he was a bit of a prima donna but…"

"Go on."

"There is no doubt in my mind that he is brilliant. If I have to put up with a little vanity and egotism, I can live with that."

"Do you think that he has the integrity for this job?" asked Tony.

"Yes, I think he has. He is totally engrossed in his work on the helmet design and the results speak for themselves."

"Mmm. Interesting," said Tony putting his hand on Doug's back and pushed him gently towards Max's office door.

"Ah, Tony," said Max, "don't see you round here much."

Tony closed the door as they came in.

Max pointed at his chairs.

"Max," started Tony, "I've had someone from The Ministry on the blower. Seems that someone from The States has been making waves."

"How so?" asked Max.

"They're not giving anything away but we know that they have stuff in orbit and nobody knows what it's for."

"Spy satellites?" prompted Max.

"More than that," said Tony. "I have intelligence that

they have been monitoring our tests."

"What are you going to tell them?" asked Max.

"Mind your own bloody business!" said Tony.

It took a moment for Max to realise that the message was for the Americans, not for him.

"We're not telling them anything," continued Tony, "but we have to get out from under their noses."

Max looked puzzled.

"Max," whispered Tony, "I want you to go up there and clobber a satellite."

"Huh!" exclaimed Max.

Doug produced a USB stick and plugged it into Max's big TV set. He went through a few menus and brought up a diagram showing satellite orbits over a map of the Earth. He tapped one particular wavy line on the screen.

"This one. They call them Condors, they have them all around the world but this one is locked in orbit right above us."

Max bit his lip as he pondered.

"Won't they see us coming?"

Doug waved his hand.

"The satellite is looking downwards. You are going to come in from above."

"Isn't that illegal?" asked Max.

Tony patted him on the back.

"The way we are going to do it will look like ET did it!"

Max smiled.

"Sergei is going to love this!"

"Tomorrow night!" said Doug.

The large articulated lumber truck drove through the front gate of the facility. A security man came forward and checked the driver.

"Hello, Jack. What have you got today?" asked the uniformed man.

Jack laughed.

"Can't see the wood for the trees," he quipped.

The load of tree trunks looked like they belonged on the lumber truck. What wasn't so obvious was that they hid a compartment for bringing in supplies.

The security man waved him through.

As the gate swung shut, a dark brown van drove past, slowed down momentarily, then continued off down the road.

The latest revision of Max's helmet was clamped to the test frame and hooked-up to a grey interface unit. Jen and Li examined diagnostics on a workstation monitor. Max walked in.

"Oh, Max," said Jen, "I was looking for you. I want you to try the latest tweaks we've made to the power coupling drivers."

"Oh, okay," said Max, "do I need to suit-up?"

"'Fraid so," said Jen. "Need your micro-motion controls. We'll do it in the simulator. I'll just call Sergei down."

The AG-127 flight simulator was an exact replica of the craft's cockpit – if not quite so claustrophobic. It was supported by three hydraulic jacks to mimic the movements of the G-drives and a multitude of meters and oscilloscopes were scattered around the periphery.

Max heard Jen's voice over his helmet audio.

"Max, what I want to test is the capability for the G-drives to handle a sudden surge of power and deliver a short pulse of gravitational energy."

"I hope it doesn't blow a fuse," joked Max.

"That's what we are attempting to find out," said Jen. "Are you ready?"

"Ready."

"Right, set the power level to fifty percent and give it a stab," said Jen.

Max stroked the hemispheres on his couch armrests with his cyber-gloves.

The hydraulic pistons spasmed, giving Max an almighty jolt.

"Ouch! I think my eyeballs just popped out and back in again."

"Take it up to sixty percent," said Jen.

Max knew what was coming this time and prepared himself for the whack. It didn't help. His whole body was subjected to an enormous kick as if by some giant's boot.

"Just once more…"

Jen's words were cut off by Sergei breaking-in.

"Only go to sixty-five percent. Any more will wreck the hydraulics."

Max sighed loudly.

"Damn the hydraulics, what about me?"

Again he was slammed back in his reclining couch.

"Okay, that's enough! Have mercy," he cried.

Sergei helped him out of the recliner and undid his helmet. Max steadied himself on an equipment rack and nearly keeled over. Sergei stopped the rack from toppling.

"Are you all right?" asked Jen, gently massaging the back of his neck.

"I'll survive," said Max, "that's nice but I think I think I've had enough for one day. I'm going home."

As he stepped out of the lift into the underground car park, Max was still in a daze from his simulator punishment. It was early evening and Katie was sure to be surprised to see him home. He climbed into the old Land Rover and keyed-in the numbers on his mobile phone that opened the roller doors. The vehicle took the bumpy lane in its stride and soon he was out on the open road.

Max hadn't gone very far when a brown van overtook him on a bend.

'Bloody fool,' he thought.

As he rounded the bend, Max could see the brown van half embedded in a hedge on the opposite side of the road, steam spewing from its radiator.

'I knew it!'

He pulled-in behind the van and set his hazard lights flashing.

Jumping out of the Land Rover, Max headed for the van's passenger door. He opened it and peered inside. The compartment was empty.

'Huh?'

Max had an uneasy feeling. The hairs on the back of his neck prickled. He sensed that someone was watching him but when he looked about could see no-one. This wasn't right, where was the driver?

Suddenly, he felt something cold and hard press against the back of his head.

"Don't turn round," said the voice.

Max froze.

"We have your girlfriend. If you want to see her again, pay attention."

Max identified a Texan accent. He had spent some time in Austin with Advanced Aviation.

"What do you w…"

"Shut-up and listen!"

The gun pressed harder against his skull.

"How do I know you have Katie?" he asked angrily.

Katie's amethyst pendant swung in front of his face.

He put his hands across his forehead and closed his eyes.

"What I want you to do…" said the voice from behind. He felt something being slipped into his right hand pocket, "…is to put this USB drive into your network computer. Do you understand?"

"What is it?" asked Max.

"You don't need to know that, just do it!"

"How do I know that you will give Katie back?"

"You don't. But if you fail to carry out my instruction, you will never see her again."

Max gulped.

"I'll do it. I'll do it. But if you harm a hair on her head…"

He couldn't get any more of the sentence out. He was lying unconscious on the road.

Max didn't know how long he was out. He pulled himself to his feet. First the bodily assault from the simulator hydraulics, now this. His head hurt and there was blood. He rubbed. It didn't help. The crashed van was nowhere to be seen, only a tyre track at the edge of the road betrayed its existence. He stumbled to his 4x4 and hauled himself in. He couldn't let Katie see him in this state. He decided to go back to Mewton Base.

Doug's door was open. Max tapped it as he walked in.

"Max, what happened to you?" asked Doug anxiously.

Max crumpled into a chair.

"Do you want a drink?" asked Doug.

Max expected a cup of tea or coffee. Doug produced a bottle of Glenmorangie from his desk drawer and plonked it down on the desk. He found a small whisky glass and poured Max a large one.

"We have a little problem," began Max, placing the USB drive in front of him. "They've kidnapped Katie."

"Who has?" snapped Doug.

"Don't know," answered Max, "but I think he had a Texan accent."

"Americans?" shouted Doug. "What did they want?"

"They want me to put this USB drive into my network computer. Presumably, it has a virus to open a back door into the system. They said that I wouldn't see Katie again if I didn't do it."

Doug, pondered for a second and then relaxed.

"Go ahead," he said. "It's not a problem."

He leaned over and pushed a button on his internal phone.

"Jen, can you come over here? I have a job for you."

Max put the USB drive into the slot on the front of his computer. There was no indication on the screen that anything was happening but he could hear the internal hard drive thrashing for half a minute and the activity light on his network hub blinked green. Then it went quiescent again. The virus had done its job.

Doug and Jen were standing behind him. Doug smiled.

"Well, I hope that they are happy," he said. "That should keep them busy for a while."

CHAPTER NINE

Max took Auntie Gertie higher than she had ever been before. The G-drive modifications had worked a charm. Sergei was in the co-pilot's seat and they were two hundred miles above the planet. Space officially began at sixty – unless you're American, where it starts at fifty miles.

"This is the height of the International Space Station," said Max. "We have a long way to go yet. Let's see what this thing can do."

He accelerated Gertie up to five G. Max had been up to eight G in a human centrifuge while training as a pilot in The Navy – but only briefly. A sustained five G was very uncomfortable indeed but his cyber glove controls did what they were supposed to. He didn't black out.

"This should do," said Max and the G-force diminished. "Now, all we have to do is find our target."

Max brought the orbit diagram up in his helmet view.

"No sign of it yet," he said.

"Should be along in twenty minutes," said Sergei.

They waited.

A bright dot in Max's display showed the oncoming satellite coming up to pass below them.

"Have to match velocities now," said Max as he accelerated in the same direction.

"Now, lose some altitude."

He took Auntie Gertie down gently until it was practically sitting on top of the car-sized spy satellite. It bristled with sensors – all pointing the other way.

"Now, we're going to whack it with some gravity."

They felt an almighty whump as the craft unleashed a massive pulse of gravity energy into the satellite. The recoil shot Gertie violently upwards.

The satellite tumbled and fell away. Max watched it fall in his helmet display. Switching to maximum zoom, he could see that some sensor arrays had been flatted against the sides as if they had been hit by a hurricane. Others were just stumps. It started to glow a dull red as it hit the upper atmosphere and went through orange and yellow to white hot. It disintegrated into a stream of glowing trails.

"Bit like playing tennis," joked Sergei.

"I think it's going out of court," added Max.

Auntie Gertie shuddered violently.

"Damn!" shouted Sergei.

"What happened?" called Max.

"Starboard G-drive's gone," yelled Sergei. "The surge must have burned something out."

"How serious?" asked Max.

Sergei wrestled with the diagnostics.

"Could be a rough ride down."

Max limped the tilted craft back directly over the lights of England and tapped an icon on his navigation screen.

"Going down! Hang on."

Gertie's autoland was totally out of calibration due to the loss of one drive. Max had to land manually. Back on the ground, he had missed the landing cradle and only just missed a group of tall trees. Auntie Gertie sat askew on the dark forest floor barely visible against the backdrop. Max and Sergei looked about as technicians scampered from the dimly lit hanger doorway with hand lamps. Doug came over.

"You two alright?" he asked.

"Just a bit shaken," said Max.

"Mmm," said Doug, scratching his head. "Got to get Gertie out of sight before daybreak. Plenty more eyes in the sky."

He shouted over to a group of men who were

examining the wrecked G-drive nacelle. "Can you get some tarps and camouflage netting over that!"

"How are we going to move it?" asked Max.

"With great difficulty," replied Doug. He pondered.

"Sergei, any chance we could swap-out the damaged drive for a spare out here?"

"Could do," replied Sergei in a slow drawl. "I'll need a tent over it?"

Doug explained to the workmen what was required and, within half an hour, Gertie was just another bump in the landscape.

Later, Max went out into the forest clearing and saw that, under the tent, Auntie Gertie had been raised on large hydraulic jacks and the damaged nacelle was being lowered onto a low trailer.

Sergei walked over to him.

"Half the coils are melted and fused together," he groaned. "Don't think we can salvage anything at all. It's scrap."

"Want me to take it down to the breaker's yard and see if I can get a few quid for it?" joked Max.

Sergei glared at him contemptuously.

"Hopefully, they won't ask us to pull a stunt like that again," he said.

Max agreed.

"How long until we can fly again?" he asked.

"About a week, if all goes well."

Ken Miyazaki and Li Wang walked into Max's office and put two helmets down on his desk.

"Now, everyone can have one," said Ken.

"They're the same as mine?" asked Max.

"Exactly. Even though they serve different purposes, the hardware is identical. The software determines their overlay capabilities."

Li spoke up.

"But you won't be able to swap yours with someone else. At the moment, each one has to be specifically tailored to the user to fit their skull shape and eye-spacing. We are working on ways to make them universal with the settings stored in memory."

"Like car seats?" suggested Max.

"Yes. Like memory car seat," said Li.

Max patted a helmet.

"Then we can take these to the tea party,"

Ken and Li looked at each other in puzzlement.

Max smiled but said nothing.

* * *

"Very interesting," said John Landers, looking at the 3D model of Max's helmet rotating on the screen. A window with numbers and formulae scrolled past on the side. Landers zoomed-in on an electronics schematic and grinned.

"Excellent!"

Thompson and Walker had smug looks on their faces.

"Let's get this stuff over to the backroom boys. We have the full specs here, they should be able to reproduce this."

The two agents got up to leave.

"What did you do with the girl?" asked Landers.

Thompson rubbed his nose.

"She's okay," he said. "Her ties will disintegrate in a few days and the window isn't locked. The building is unoccupied and nothing can be traced back to us."

The phone on Landers' desk buzzed. He picked it up and froze.

"What!" he screamed, "are you sure?"

He put the phone back on its base and put both hands

flat on the desk.

"What is it?" asked Thompson.

Landers looked up.

"We've lost Condor 4!"

"Lost?" asked Walker. "What do you mean 'lost'?"

"Don't know," said Landers. "One minute it's there, next minute it's gone. Somebody's taking potshots at our satellites."

"Maybe just a malfunction," suggested Walker.

"No way," said Landers, "it's just not there any more."

* * *

"Katie! Are you alright?" Max howled into his phone.

"I'm okay," she wept. "I got out the window and knocked on someone's door. They let me use their phone. Should I call the police?"

"No, Katie, you need to get away from there as fast as you can. Call a cab. Go to a hotel. I'll get there as soon as I can."

"I don't have any money," she sobbed.

"Katie, can you put me onto the person whose house you are in? I'll sort something out with them."

Max negotiated a temporary loan for Katie and said goodbye. They agreed upon the hotel that Katie should head for. He put the phone down and pondered what to do next.

Katie took a taxi to The Swan Inn, where they had once stayed for a wedding reception. It was a good fifteen miles from the cottage, which Max considered to be a safe distance for the minute. She locked herself in her room and was determined not to open the door to anyone but Max. He was nowhere to be seen. She tried to phone him but was repeatedly put through to his voicemail. She rang her mother, Alice.

"Mum," she couldn't hold back her tears.

"Katie, what's wrong?"

"Mum, I was kidnapped!"

"Don't be silly, Katie, what are you talking about?"

Katie recounted the events starting with the bogus courier to escaping from the basement and ringing Max from a stranger's house.

"Did they hurt you?" asked Alice.

"I'm okay."

"What did they want?"

"That's it, I don't know. I just don't know. They didn't say a thing. They just dumped me in a basement room and left me there. It took me hours to get free. I was terrified. I thought that I was going to die."

"You poor darling," said Alice, "have you reported this to the police?"

"Max told me not to. I don't know what to do. Oh Mum!"

"Do you think that this is something to do with him?" asked Alice.

"I just don't know. He's so secretive. He works on hush-hush defence stuff so I sort of understand. It just drives me mad."

"Katie," said Alice, "do you think that Max is right for you?"

"Oh, he can be a conceited bastard at times," she snivelled, "but I do love him, warts and all."

"Do you want to come and stay with me for a while?" asked Alice.

"No, I don't think that is a good idea. They might know about you."

"Know about me," gasped Alice. "How could they know about me?"

Katie jumped up and down in frustration.

"I don't know."

There was gentle tap at the door.

"Katie, it's me."

"Oh Mum, Max is here. Got to go. Bye. Speak to you later"

She opened the door for Max and threw her arms around his neck.

"Max, I was so frightened."

"I'm sure you were, love. We have to get to the bottom of this." He said.

"Why did you tell me not to contact the police?" asked Katie, drying her eyes.

Max thought about how best to explain it to her.

"Believe me, it will be investigated, but by people a bit higher up the ladder than the local bobbies."

"You mean military intelligence?"

"Something like that."

Katie sat down on the bed.

"What are we going to do? We can't go back to the cottage. They know that we live there," sobbed Katie.

Max cuddled her and considered the implications. He had kept his side of the bargain with the interloper at Mewton Base. On the other hand, he knew that they had been fed a load of crap. Would they pull the same stunt again? Unlikely, they had shown their hand and lost.

"Don't worry, Katie. You are safe now. The problem has been taken care of. I don't think you will be bothered again."

"Mum said I could stay with her for a while."

"If you want to, go ahead," said Max. "A break will help you clear your mind."

After three days, Katie remembered why she had left home ten years ago. Admittedly, there wasn't much demand for catwalk models in a sleepy little town bordering the

North Sea, but that wasn't half of it. She had suffered the wrath meted-out to all those who dared to desecrate this little shrine to Alice, the goddess of all that is clean and tidy. She really felt for her dad who had suffered Alice's ire for some thirty-five years. She phoned Max. The call went to voicemail and Max called back half an hour later.

"Katie, what's up?"

"Max, come and get me out of this place. I left some toast crumbs on the kitchen worktop and was verbally assaulted for the next half hour. Alice doesn't understand how she could possibly have reared such a slovenly child. TAKE ME HOME!"

Max agreed to pick her up at seven. At least she wouldn't have to share another evening meal with her Mum and the prospect of picking-up a fork with the wrong hand.

At five past seven, she heard a car horn outside and saw that Max was waiting in the car. He didn't want to be asked in to be lectured on the iniquities of his wayward girlfriend. They headed off home but stopped off at the Dog and Duck for a meal and to fill-up at the petrol station.

Katie was a little apprehensive about going back into the cottage. Max eased her concerns by telling her that he had his security people watching the house and that she was not to worry if she felt eyes on the back of her head. He was happy to let her believe that it was twenty-four hour surveillance when, in fact, one of the guys on the gate at Mewton had offered to pass the cottage on has way to and from work. On the kitchen worktop, there was the small carton containing brass polish that she had ordered over a week ago. The she noticed a pile of estate agent leaflets.

"Max, what's all this?" she asked, holding up the sheaf of paper.

"Oh, I've heard that there is interest in my old house at last. Someone has made an offer that is a bit below my asking price but I'm going to accept it. We can look for a new house now."

Katie's eyes lit up. She sat down at the kitchen table and leafed through the houses for sale.

"What will you do about this cottage?" she asked, "remember, we have a one year minimum let."

"Don't worry about that. We can sub-let it if need be. Nobody has to know."

"Max, do you like this one?" she asked, holding up a leaflet for a barn conversion. "Look, it has four bedrooms, a garage and outhouses that I could use for my furniture restoration. It looks lovely."

"Why do we need four bedrooms?" asked Max.

"I was thinking, one for us, one for visitors, one to use as a study and…"

"And what?"

"Maybe a nursery?"

Max smirked contemptuously.

"Okay," he agreed, "I'll see if we can view it tomorrow. I have the day off because I'm working tomorrow night."

Katie liked the idea of viewing the house but this was news she had been dreading. She had more than a little trepidation about spending a night alone in the cottage.

"Why do you have to work at night?" she asked.

"Simply because there are some things that can't be done in the daytime?" he replied.

"Oh, Max. I don't like the idea of staying here without you."

"You'll be fine," he said reassuringly.

"What if those men come back?"

"Katie, I guarantee that they won't come back!"

"How can you be so certain?"

"Well, if you are really worried, you could always go back to your Mum's."

Katie shut up.

CHAPTER TEN

Sergei turned his head from side to side.

"Oh, this is cool," he said.

Jen was in her centre couch adjusting the eye-spacing on her helmet lasers.

Meanwhile, Max was flicking through the overlays on his helmet display to get the best view of Auntie Gertie's two remote controlled sisters that followed them in close formation. They had no running lights and were black against a black background. All he could see was their outline shapes as they eclipsed stars on their upward paths. They had been careful to plot a path well away from any satellites and the ISS where they would have been visible silhouetted against the bright blue planet beneath.

"Sergei," called Max, "can you give us a bit more separation from Deltas 1 and 2?"

The drones moved further away.

"Now let's see if the dolphins take the bait."

The three Deltas were identical. Even though the drones had no occupied cockpits, the provision was there to add seating at a future stage. They were flying in 'V' formation with Auntie Gertie at the front.

"Sergei, Jen, just a thought. I want to swap our position with Delta 2. Our lead placement is a dead giveaway." The two craft swapped over.

"Now, I'll put us all in a slow clockwise spin. It will be easier to see all around us."

The dolphins were invisible to radar and the wide spectrum helmets were the best bet to spot them if they came.

Before long, two hazy discs overtook them and began

weaving backwards and forwards playfully in their path as they had done before. They flew ahead and fell behind, they hovered above and below.

"Sergei, take the drones further away from us and see what happens."

Deltas 1 and 2 moved away.

"That's interesting," said Max. "They didn't follow the drones, they are sticking with us. Somehow they know that this Delta is manned."

Max manoeuvred the drones into different relative positions much like playing 'find the lady' card trick but still the discs stuck with them. They flew in spirals around Auntie Gertie. The views in their helmet displays showed close-ups of the two discs. Through the haze, they seemed to be pearlescent white in colour and had no visible features apart from the three bulges on their bases. Jen switched her helmet display to gravity mesh mode.

"Look, they are using G-drives just like ours!" she exclaimed. The helmet display overlay showed deep gravity distortions surrounding each craft.

"Might as well send the drones home, Sergei," said Max.

Sergei switched them over to autoland so that they banked away and downwards. The discs didn't care.

Max nudged Sergei.

"Let's see if we can outrun them."

Max changed the vector of the G-drives and cranked-up the power. The discs fell behind for a few seconds but then flew past them rolling as they went.

"Damned cheek," laughed Max. "Faster, Gertie, faster."

The dolphin craft had no trouble keeping up and matched Max's every attempt to lose them. Max was enjoying it. Jen, not so much.

"Max, they seem to be getting closer," said Jen.

"I'm watching."

One of the discs came in over the top of Auntie Gertie until it nearly touched.

"I hope they don't plan to do what we did to the spy satellite," cried Sergei.

The second craft manoeuvred up tight below them.

"What's happening?" shrieked Jen.

Max tried to steer sideways out of their way but he couldn't. He took the power down to minimum and tried reverse thrust but they continued on at the same hectic speed.

"They have us trapped in a gravity hamburger," yelled Max. "Looks like we're being taken for a ride."

Auntie Gertie was locked solid between the two white discs. They were twice her size and considerably more powerful. They hurtled on a steep incline upwards and away from their previous paths parallel with the Earth's surface.

Max switched his helmet display to gravity mesh. He could see the grid of lines distort and intermingle between the three craft. He didn't understand what he was looking at. It was as if a giant spider had spun a huge web between the three craft. Never before had he seen such a complex entanglement.

Their speed increased. Max could feel the acceleration pushing him hard against his recliner.

"Shit, what's that?" he cried.

"My God," yelled Jen.

The grid of the gravity mesh was smooth and level in mid distance, but after that it went haywire. Whatever it was, they were headed straight for it.

Dimming the gravity mesh overlay in his helmet display, Max swept the visible light spectrum and out beyond. There was nothing to be seen but the backdrop of stars.

"Where are we going?" cried Sergei.

"I have no idea," replied Max.

Faster and faster they went. Max could feel his face begin to distort from the acceleration. Then he saw something. It was faint but looked like an animated Spirograph drawing. It rotated, changing shape and colour, expanded and contracted. Suddenly, the middle of the apparition burst into blinding white emptiness. The three helmet displays dimmed instantly to compensate or their retinas would have been fried. They headed straight into the whiteness and Auntie Gertie's three human occupants lost consciousness simultaneously.

Max came to. He could hear Sergei coughing in his helmet speakers and a pained groan from Jen. He was aware that they were no longer moving.

"Everyone okay?" he called.

Stressed acknowledgements came from his companions.

"Where are we," screamed Jen, in a state of shock.

Their helmet displays showed nothing but absolute whiteness with cascading error messages in red running top to bottom.

Max had the impression he was standing upright but with no visual point of reference, he couldn't be sure.

"Can you see anything?" he called out to the others.

"My display is blank," answered Jen, "total whiteness."

Sergei broke in, "It's like being in a snowstorm in Siberia." He had actually experienced that in his teens.

Max put his arms out and felt all around. There was nothing within reach. He tried moving his legs to walk but there was no ground under him to give traction.

"Can you feel anything?" he asked.

Sergei and Jen said, "No," in unison.

They were not inside their Delta 3, they were not connected up to anything. How could they possibly breathe and communicate? Max didn't know.

"I have a bad feeling about this," said Sergei. "Perhaps we are dead?"

"And talking to one another?" asked Max grimly, although it had crossed his mind briefly that Sergei might have a point. He had heard of people seeing a bright light ahead of them before they died. How they were able to report that, he couldn't imagine.

Jen breathed quickly and heavily. Max could sense her anguish.

"Take it easy, Jen. I'm sure that we'll be all right." He wasn't.

Suddenly, she screamed a terrible scream.

"Max! Max! Something's pulling at me!"

Max could feel something grip his ankles too. It was firm but not painful.

A muffled yell came from Sergei.

It was then that Max noticed that the blinding white nothingness had started to swirl. There was movement in it. The error messages on his helmet display faded away. Something else took their place. He didn't know what was going on. It looked like hieroglyphs or some kind of lettering. The symbols moved and twisted like a line wriggling worms and then morphed into words – in capitals letters.

<GREETINGS>

Max was dumfounded. Someone or something was communicating with them.

"Sergei. Jen. Are you seeing this?"

"Hello," he said tentatively.

<H E L L O> imprinted on his helmet display as he spoke the word. The letters morphed into symbols and faded.

There was no response.

A great fear took over his body. He felt so helpless.

"Who are you?" asked Max. "Do you have a name?"

Again, Max's words appeared in front of him, changed into hieroglyphs and faded away.

<NO NAME> <ONE IS MANY> came the reply.

Max didn't understand. How could someone not have a name? What did 'one is many' mean? There was total silence for several minutes.

"Perhaps it is describing a collective consciousness like a colony of ants," suggested Sergei. "Names are irrelevant."

Turning his attention back to the nothingness before him, Max asked, "Where are we?"

His view filled with symbols again. They twisted and changed shape for some time as if struggling to find translation.

Finally a word appeared before him. He didn't understand.

<REALM>

"Realm, what the hell is realm?" he cried in exasperation.

The symbols again had difficulty translating into English.

<YOU HAVE NO WORD> came the message.

Sergei chimed-in, "Are you from another planet?"

Their displays flickered and symbols changed shape.

<NEGATIVE> <REALM>

"What is realm," asked Max again.

His display went into a rapidly changing series of patterns. They eventually coalesced into an identifiable image. It was a slowly spinning cube made up of countless spheres arranged in a three dimensional grid. The view magnified into a fly-through of endless rows and columns of spheres. Eventually, the viewpoint left the cube to show the spheres disappearing off into infinity in every direction.

The view then zoomed into two adjacent spheres. Each sphere was made-up of masses of dots. *Stars,* thought Max… and then he noticed that some of them were spiral in nature. *No, galaxies.*

"They are groups of galaxies," Max said over his helmet microphone. Then it struck him. "Universes!"

"They are parallel universes."

He was aware of the 'Multiverse' theories thrown about by academics but thought it was all speculative nonsense. The two coloured spheres in his display moved together and merged into one another. The spheres alternated between red and blue, highlighting their differences. The red image faded leaving only the blue. The word <REALM> appeared. The red sphere and lettering faded and were replaced by the blue sphere and again the word <REALM>.

A green sphere moved-in over the blue one and the word <REALM> appeared in green. The same thing happened with a yellow sphere, then a purple one, then an ever accelerating number of other spheres crowded in and faded away.

The conclusion hit Max like a brick. He gasped, "We're in another universe. They have taken us to another universe!"

Through the swirling whiteness in his helmet display, Max could just distinguish moving shapes. They were hazy and indistinct yet there was definitely something moving out there, but what? Whatever they were, they were moving very quickly. It was like watching a video in fast-forward. His brain fought to make sense of what he was looking at. Jen sobbed.

The mist thickened again to an opaque white.

"How do you know our language?" asked Jen shakily. They all watched the words assemble.

<WE WATCH>

"How long have you watched?"

<TEN THOUSAND YOUR CYCLES>

"Ten thousand years," gasped Sergei.

"Why have you brought us here?" asked Max.

<TALK>

"You want to talk to us. Well, you should treat your guests a little better. Why have you kidnapped us and brought us to this place?"

<TALK>

Max tied to encourage them to be more forthcoming. "Talk then!"

The shapes in the display wriggled and danced but made no sense.

<WE HAVE NO WORDS>

"What do you want to talk about - football, the economy?" said Max impudently.

<WE WATCH TEN THOUSAND CYCLES> <YOU CHANGE>

"You have been watching our race develop for ten thousand years. Why do you wait until now to speak with us?"

<YOU MANIPULATE GRAVITY>

"Yes," said Sergei, "we have G-drives just like you."

<SOON>

Sergei felt insulted. This was his work they were putting down.

"Why is this so important?" he asked.

<MANIPULATE GRAVITY> <MANIPULATE SPACETIME> <MANIPULATE REALMS>

"I see," interrupted Max, "you think that we are on the dawn of a new age?"

<NEW AGE>

"When will all this happen?" asked Max.

<MATURITY>

"So, you think that we are not ready yet?"

<SOON>

"Why aren't we ready now?"

<YOU FIGHT> <YOU STARVE> <YOU SPOIL YOUR WORLD>

Max felt that he was being lectured by a schoolmaster. "Are you able to help us fix these things?" he asked.

<NEGATIVE> <YOU MUST DO> <ALL>

"Not even any hints?" asked Jen.

<YOU MUST DO> <YOU>

"Don't you have wars, poverty, strife?" asked Max.

<LONG TIME AGO>

"And you got over all that?"

<MATURED>

"Can we see what you look like?" begged Max.

There was no answer for a while.

An image appeared on all their helmet displays at once. It was just a head unconnected to a body of any kind. It didn't look at all photographic but like some identikit face or a low resolution character from a computer game. The mouth did not move.

<WE ARE WHAT YOU SEE>

Max knew they were hiding something. This was a surely a joke.

"This is not real," he insisted.

<WE ARE WHAT YOU WANT TO SEE>

"Ah," said Max, "you don't want us to see what you really look like?"

<WE ARE...>

Again the symbols twisted and turned for some time.

<YOU HAVE NO WORD>

"If we can't talk face to face, how can we trust you?" asked Jen.

<WE TRUST> <YOU TRUST>

There was a pause.

"Give us something," asked Max. "Are there other beings in our galaxy, like us?"

He pointed to himself but nobody else could see that.

<MANY>

"Do they have gravity drives?"

<SOME>

"Are they close to us or far away?"

<FAR>

"Have they visited Earth?"

<THEY VISIT YOU>

"How did they get there? Do they have faster than light drives? Do they travel through wormholes?"

<NEGATIVE>

"How do they do it then?"

<MANIPULATE GRAVITY>

"How many realms are there?" asked Max.

Their displays spun in whorls.

<NO NUMBER> <INFINITE>

"Do you visit other realms?"

<MANY>

"Are they all very different?"

<YOUR REALM> <THIS REALM> <DIFFERENT> <SOME REALMS ALMOST SAME>

"And you can just go between one and the other easily?" asked Jen.

<NOT EASILY>

Max heard Sergei say something in his helmet audio. He couldn't make it out but when his helmet display began to show Cyrillic characters, he realised that Sergei was speaking in Russian. The answers came back in Russian too.

"What is that all about, Sergei?"

"I was asking questions about quantum entanglement theories," replied Sergei.

"Did you get an answer?"

"Yes, <NO WORDS>."

Jen broke in with a question.

"Is it possible to travel in time? Go to the future or past?"

<MANIPULATE GRAVITY> <MANIPULATE SPACETIME>

"Can you go backwards and forwards in time?" asked Max.

The squiggles in his helmet display squirmed for a while, then…

<THIS REALM BACK> <OTHER REALMS FORWARD>

Max tried hard to understand what he was being told.

"Can you show us how to travel between realms?" asked Max.

<YOUR DRIVE> <NEGATIVE>

"Can you help us to improve our G-drives?" asked Sergei.

<NEGATIVE> <YOU DO>

The exchange went on for an indeterminate amount of time with little real information coming out of the captors. It was obvious that their concepts were so remote from anything the humans understood that they were impossible to explain meaningfully. The intelligence tried using more animated diagrams but none of them made any sense.

"Aren't you prepared to give us any help at all?" asked Max.

There was a long pause. The icons on the displays contorted and shifted.

<SOMETHING>

The swirling mist cleared a little and Max could again see the shadowy shapes. He tried to do a spectrum sweep but without his couch armrest, he couldn't properly operate the display menus with his cyber glove.

Max could feel a tremble all about him and a stuttering, humming noise broke the silence.

Symbols morphed.

<FINISHED> spelled-out the words on his display. He felt a sudden onrush of motion sickness and nausea and then blacked-out. They all did.

CHAPTER ELEVEN

Max fought the grogginess inside his head. It was like waking from a nightmare. His eyes were closed but his eyelids were bathed in a soft laser light. He opened them slowly. There, all above him, the familiar canopy of stars and below, the bright blue arc of planet Earth. Through his helmet cam, he could see the interior of Auntie Gertie's cockpit. Jen and Sergei were beside him, but not moving.

"Wakey, wakey," he called into his helmet mic.

"We are awake," said Sergei. "We're headed home on autopilot."

"I'm starving," moaned Jen.

Max realised that he was hungry too. Very!

"Max, have you looked at your clock", shouted Jen.

"Yes, it's four thirty-five," replied Max.

"No Max, the date, not the time!"

"What!" yelled Max. "That can't be right."

"It looks like we have lost four days somewhere," said Sergei. "It's Friday. We have been out of it for four days."

"But we only left Mewton Base yesterday," said Max.

"No," said Jen, "the clock is correct. We have been unconscious longer than we realise."

"They will have given us up for lost," said Max. "Better get in touch and tell them we are on our way home."

Down they went on the vertical approach vector for Mewton Base.

"Altitude, twenty miles," said Max over the helmet audio, "looking good."

"I'll be glad to get my feet back on the ground," said Jen. They all agreed.

"Hey, wait a minute," cried Max. "We have two blips on

tactical below us."

"I see them," said Sergei. "Reception committee?"

"Look like F-15s to me," said Max, "American jets from Lakenheath. They seem to flying in a wide circle."

"Could just be a routine exercise," called Jen.

"Don't want to take any chances," said Max. "They could be on the lookout for us."

"Would they attack us? Surely not," asked Jen.

"I don't want to find out!" said Max. "As far as they are concerned, we would be unidentifiable bogeys. They could take us out without any comeback whatsoever and we don't have any counter measures. Gertie isn't designed for combat. If they send missiles after us, we're toast. I'm going to manual and stopping our descent. We'll sit up here for a while and watch them."

"Couldn't we outrun them?" asked Jen.

"No," said Sergei, "not in the atmosphere. We could outrun them higher up, but they are up about as high as they can go. I think that we need to consider giving Auntie Gertie some firepower."

"And what would our dolphin friends have made of that?" asked Max. "If they had detected weapons, I very much doubt we would be here now."

"The fighters are still circling," said Jen.

"We're just going to have to wait them out," said Max. "They are going to run out of fuel, we're not."

"Do you think that they know we're here?" asked Jen.

"I don't think that they will be looking up here," replied Max, "and anyway, our stealth coating should keep us invisible to their radar at this range. Luckily, they can't detect gravitational anomalies. If they had our helmets, it would be a different story."

"Look, I think that they're pulling off," said Sergei. "They are heading North West."

"Let them get well out of sight," said Max. "Then I'll

take us back down."

"Hey," said Max to Sergei and Jen, "there's something weird going on. I'm not quite sure what it is."

"What is it?" asked Sergei.

"I've got a very strange feeling," replied Max.

"Auntie Gertie, she feels different. Let me just try something."

Max tilted the Delta's nose down a fraction and opened up the power to the G-drives. The craft shot forward in level flight. He kicked down on the rudder pedal and completed a tight U-turn.

"There," he said, "did you feel that?"

"Feel what?" asked Jen. "I didn't feel anything."

"That's it," said Max, "I've just accelerated and pulled a very tight turn and it was as if we were sitting still."

"That's impossible," said Sergei, "I didn't feel any sense of movement at all."

"Okay," said Max, "hang on, I'm going straight up, full power."

The three occupants waited for the G-force of the acceleration to push them down hard into their couches as it had always done before.

"Go on then," said Jen.

"I've done it," said Max, "we are going full whack upwards and there is no sense of G-force whatsoever."

Max reversed the thrust plummeting them Earthwards. He expected the sick feeling of going down in a very fast lift but no, there was no sensation of movement.

"I don't feel anything," said Sergei. "Is this some strange by-product of what happened up there?"

Max threw Auntie Gertie all around the sky and they all felt they were sitting in an armchair at home. A bleep in Max's helmet speaker heralded a message from the control room below.

"Control to Delta 3, you seem to be all over the place, where have you been?"

"Er, yes," replied Max, "we are…just fine. We'll be back shortly."

The message end signal sounded.

"Have you any idea what's going on here, Sergei?" asked Max. "It would seem that all G-forces have been neutralised inside this cockpit."

"These diagnostics are looking all wrong," said Jen. "I think that someone…something has been messing with Gertie."

"Mods?" asked Max.

"We'll, these readings are off the scale," said Jen. "It couldn't have happened by accident."

"It looks like our friends up there have given us a little goodbye present," said Max. "Now, all we have to do is figure-out how they did it."

"Inertial dampening," said Sergei, "they have given us an internal gravity field that cancels-out the external effects of gravity. That is quite some going away present. Let's get back down home so that I can have a look at what's going on."

When they reached ground level, Auntie Gertie stopped and rocked for a moment then dropped softly onto the waiting landing cradle. The clamps locked on with a solid 'clunk'. As soon as the G-drives whined down, the dollies glided them slowly into the hanger and the doors slid shut.

Max was first out of Gertie's hatchway as his couch was closest. He had trouble standing. He wasn't sure if it was the lack of weightlessness or just his head still swimming from the ordeal. He and Sergei caught Jen when she collapsed. They took off their helmets and breathed the fresh air.

Max put his fingers up to his itchy chin.

"Huh!"

He had more than designer stubble, it was practically a beard.

He was shocked. He usually kept his facial hair on the bristly side, except when he was wearing a helmet. He *never* let it grow any longer than that.

A buggy was waiting to take them for the short ride to the suit room.

It had taken a full thirty minutes to suit-up before their departure. De-suiting should be quicker except that, after four days, their suits stank. Auntie Gertie was too small to have a toilet and their maximum absorbency underwear was only designed for short trips.

They each went to a wet-room shower and washed down with high pressure jets of hot water. Max was drying himself off when he caught sight of himself in a steamy mirror. He wiped off the condensation with his towel. How could his facial hair have grown so fast?

Max dried-off in the hot air drier and put a jumpsuit on. He headed off to the suit room water cooler.

"Where have you been for four days?" asked Doug.

"Not in space," said Max. Then he corrected himself. "Well, not all of the time."

"So where then?" asked Doug impatiently.

"Mmm, that's a long story," said Max, nodding in the direction of his office.

* * *

Landers snatched the incessant phone from its cradle. "Yeh!"

"Sir, those files you sent through, is somebody jerking us around?"

"What do you mean?" said Landers angrily.

"You sent us some working drawings and schematics

for a helmet mounted display system, an airplane and a load of software."

"Yeh, is it good?"

"The animated 3D model and schematics are good, but…"

"Come on man, out with it!"

"I don't quite know how to tell you this, Sir, but the helmet is one of ours. Not only that, it is the very latest revision of the F-35 unit."

"What?" spat Landers. "They had the specs of our latest helmet system?"

"Yessir!"

Landers moaned.

"What about the airplane working drawings?"

"Detailed instructions on how to fold a paper airplane using A4 paper!"

Landers fumed.

"And the software, is that ours too?"

"No sir. It's not."

"What is it then?"

"Well, it was written in assembly language for a chipset that we don't use."

"Did you get anything out of it?"

"After a lot of work, yes."

"And what was it?"

"Sir, it was a Space Invaders game!"

Landers threw the phone across his office, smashing it to pieces against the wall and leaving a dent in the wood panelling. Opening his top drawer, he took out a bottle of pills and swallowed a handful. He sat down at his desk and put his head in his hands and shook it backwards and forwards.

Landers reached out for his phone. It wasn't there. It was lying in bits at the other side of the room.

He took out his mobile and tapped a number in his

contact list.

"Dwayne, I need you to do something for me…"

Max and Doug sat opposite each other in Max's office.

"Not sure where to start," said Max. "We went up looking for dolphins and got more than we bargained for. Two of them snagged us in a gravity field and took us back to their place."

"To another star system," asked Doug.

Max took his nodding alien off the shelf behind him and put it on his desk. Had Doug dyed his hair? There used to be wisps of grey in there. He said nothing.

"No, not another star system. It wasn't anywhere. It wasn't even in our universe."

Doug stared blankly.

"We were able to communicate with them through our helmet displays," continued Max, "I can't begin to imagine how they worked out how to do that, but they did. They said that they have been watching us for over ten thousand years."

Doug sat with his mouth open. Max played with the nodding alien unconsciously.

"Sergei thinks that they are some sort of collective, like ants or bees. I don't know if there's any hierarchy involved or not, the translation was fairly basic – like pidgin English. They told us that manipulating gravity was the key to unlocking interstellar travel, time travel, all of the spacetime continuum, but wouldn't give us any hints how to do that whatsoever. They said we had to work that out for ourselves. Oh, and I asked them if there were other beings in our universe. There are lots. Some of them have gravity drives and have visited Earth."

"You asked them to help us?" asked Doug with a frown.

"Yes, at first they gave a blunt no and then hinted that they would do 'something'. I'm not entirely sure what that meant but they seem to have modified Auntie Gertie. We found out on the way back down that we have something that counteracts natural G forces. Sergei is going to try to see what they've done, if anything."

Doug sat back in his chair with a puzzled look on his face.

"What else did they tell you?" he asked.

Max shook his head, "We were rather rudely cut off at that point."

"Cut off?"

"Yes, knocked unconscious."

"Damn. Does Sergei or Jen have any ideas?" asked Doug.

"Jen was scared shitless, poor girl. Sergei was probing them on quantum physics in Russian but I don't think he got anywhere. Maybe we should ask him."

Max and Doug headed for Sergei's lab. They passed Li in the corridor.

"Nice glasses Li," said Max as she walked past.

Li turned round and gave him a look of puzzlement.

"What did you just call her?" asked Doug.

"Li, it's her family name. She prefers that."

Doug paused for a minute, shook his head slightly and continued down the corridor to Max's office.

"She has always worn those glasses," he said, "and everybody calls her Yan."

Max was quite taken aback, he had always been proud of his attention to detail.

Sergei was standing in front of his blackboard when Max and Doug walked in.

"All of a sudden, my calculations have come into focus," smiled Sergei. "I've racked my brains on this formula for months and now I've come back from…up there…it is all much clearer now."

"So, what is this the 'something' they spoke of?" asked

Max.

"Don't know," said Sergei, "I've been over Gertie from top to bottom and I can't see any sign of modifications."

"Damnedest thing," he said pointing at his blackboard. "I have always used yellow chalk – better contrast against black. How could it have turned white in the four days we were away?"

Max didn't know - maybe Sergei's retinas were damaged by his helmet display lasers too.

"Sergei, meeting tomorrow morning at Head Office, nine sharp," said Doug. "And you might want to smarten up, there will be VIPs there!"

Sergei waved a gesture of dismissal. He hated meetings at the best of times, but VIPs?

Max headed back to his office and met Li in the corridor again. She gave him a big smile.

Jen was waiting for him in his office. She gave the nodding alien's head a little push and smiled.

"Max, there's a heap of data from our sensor logs and helmet videos in Gertie's computer. We need to get that all off and analysed. There is so much we need to learn about those…things. I don't know how much we've got, maybe they wiped it all."

"Yes, I agree, I want to see that," said Max, "Can you ask Li, I mean Yan, to handle it?"

"Good idea," said Jen.

"And Max…"

She went over and gave him a little cuddle.

"Thanks for getting us back."

Li Yan turned into her small lab. Jen had asked her to download Auntie Gertie's logs and video recording onto the local network storage drives. There were petabytes of data. Somebody, probably her, would have to sift through it all and analyse it. It took a good three hours for all the files to copy across but while she was waiting, she opened a few for a quick check.

Li just couldn't comprehend what she was seeing. She shook her head in disbelief. Max's helmet recording showed the dolphin craft playing in front of Gertie and then close in and entrap her. It showed the strange pyrotechnic display as the portal opened into another realm. After that, the video was just blank white for hour after hour. Had the video been wiped, it would have been black but no, it was saturated. She fast forwarded at maximum speed to try to find what happened next. Nothing. But there was still four days worth of data to sift through.

She opened a log file. There were environmental reports for several hours and then nothing but meaningless error messages.

She opened the video file again and skipped forward to the appearance of the dolphins. Looking around to see that no-one was watching, she produced a USB drive from the pocket of her white lab coat and inserted it into one of the workstation's USB ports. She made an edited copy of the video sequence up to the point where the white nothingness began. Looking around again she ejected the drive and put it back into her pocket.

The people who funded her research deserved to get something in return for their money. They were unlikely to get it any other way.

Ying Chen opened the door for Li and smiled. She slipped into the small apartment and closed the door behind her. Li took the USB drive from her pocket and pressed it into her friend's hand.

"What's this, Yan," asked Chen.

"I know that I shouldn't be doing this but it is something so devastatingly important that I can't let it be buried away. The World has to know about this."

"Know about what?"

"Get your laptop," said Li.

Ying Chen retrieved her laptop and charger from her bedroom and plugged it in.

Li put the USB drive into one of the laptop's ports and launched the video she had made from Max's helmet recordings. Chen watched it without a trace of emotion.

"I see what you mean," she said when the video had finished. "Impressive technology."

Li was taken aback at her friend's fascination for the dolphin gravity drives and apparent inability to see the bigger picture.

"But don't you see, it's another race of beings totally outside our terms of reference," said Li.

"Yes, I understand that," came the reply, "but I would just love to get my hands on one of those gravity drives to see what makes it tick."

Li sighed in exasperation.

"Can you make sure that Xu gets this. He will know how to get it to the right people."

Chen blinked, "Of course."

CHAPTER TWELVE

Max sat in the Head Office reception with Doug. Jen came through the swing doors and saw where they were sitting.

"Seen anything of Sergei?" asked Doug.

"I think I saw him drive into the car park, should be here in a mo," replied Jen.

Doug glanced at his watch.

Max looked round the foyer and his eyes fell on the bronze 'Flight' sculpture. He looked at the floor and then back up at it again. There was something wrong that he couldn't quite place.

Sergei walked through the foyer door looking flustered. If he had tidied-up, it didn't show.

Tony Davidson's blonde PA exited the lift and asked the four of them to come with her. They went up to the top floor conference room. There were several familiar faces there but two men in pinstripe suits took Max's particular attention. Tony welcomed them and pointed to four vacant chairs at the end of the large table.

"We are privileged today to be joined by two distinguished guests," started Tony. "I'm sure that you will all recognise The Secretary of State, Michael Reece and his Minister, Ethan Shaw."

The two men nodded.

"I'm sure you are wondering what brings them along today but what you are about to hear is of monumental significance. Three of our research people have made a voyage to the edge of space in one of our experimental aircraft."

The room was hushed.

"Gentlemen. I won't beat about the bush, we have made first contact!"

At first there was stunned silence. Then a cacophony of questions assaulted the quartet from Mewton Base.

Tony held up his hand for calm.

"Gentlemen, please allow the pilot and our leading avionics expert, Max Hayden, to tell you about their experiences."

Max got to his feet and related the story about the dolphins, Gertie's capture, the portal into another realm and their conversation with the intelligence on the other side. When he had finished, there was shocked silence.

Ethan Shaw held his hand in the air to gain attention.

"This is probably…no…definitely, the most important event in the history of humankind. I can't begin to comprehend the implications and ramifications. Needless to say, not a word of it goes beyond this room. I will study the written report at length over the next few days and then decide where we go next."

He stared at each face round the room to emphasise his words.

"First, I have a question for the team. Can I ask if this rendezvous is repeatable?"

Max squirmed uneasily in his seat.

"What you have to remember," he said, "is that they found us, not the other way round. They took us to… wherever it was. We don't have the knowledge nor the technology to go there ourselves."

"Don't you have the co-ordinates of this…this…portal as you call it?" asked Shaw.

"Yes, we have, but it is not likely to be in the same place again. We can't see it, detect it – or find it ourselves," said Max. "This is some kind of rift in spacetime that they control. Don't ask me how they do it. All I know is that they say we have progressed but we are not yet ready to join their elite club of spacetime travellers. It could take centuries for that to happen."

A man in a pinstripe suit rose to his feet, clearly familiar with the techniques of gaining attention.

"Can you explain this term 'realm'?" asked Michael Reece. "I understand it to mean 'kingdom' in the historic sense."

Max stuttered for a second. This was a hard one.

"Mr Secretary, they couldn't provide an exact translation for this. A lot of the stuff we discussed was hampered by the fact that we don't have the words nor even the concepts to put the words to."

Max looked round the waiting faces at the table.

"Realms. Here's my take on it, I could be wrong but it's my best guess. It's nothing to do with kingdoms. Think of a radio. It has dozens, if not hundreds, of stations available when you turn the dial."

He demonstrated with a twist of his hand.

"You can only tune-in to one station at a time. When you are at that station, you know nothing of what is happening on all the other stations and the actors on Radio 4 know nothing about what is happening on Radio One. They are each in different realms and have their own separate timelines. Our present existence is only one realm of an infinite number of others."

Max paused for a moment and looked round to make sure they were keeping up with him.

"From what the…intelligence told me, it is possible to *see* into the past within your own realm – it didn't suggest that you could visit it. You can't, however, see or visit the future of your realm. Makes sense, it hasn't happened yet and there are countless possibilities that branch off from any point in time. You can see forward in time, but you will be observing an arbitrary alternative universe that probably has no bearing on your current timeline. Sorry, that's the best I can do."

Max's explanation left the delegates confounded. This

was all too hard to digest.

"There are just so many things that we can't comprehend and maybe never will."

The meeting wound down with other people coming over and asking more questions. Max patted his written report.

"It's all in there! Anything else is pure speculation."

After the meeting, they made their separate ways back to Mewton Base via the interchange car park. Max and Doug went in the Land Rover, Sergei and Jen in the Toyota.

"I wonder how much of all this they are going to share with our international partners?" asked Max.

"That will be interesting to see," replied Doug. "My guess is that they will keep shtum about it until they can make some political capital out of it."

"You can't hide something like that forever," said Max.

"They have done before!" smirked Doug with an upturned eyebrow.

On their drive back to Mewton Base, Doug pressed Max for more information. Had he forgotten something?

"Max, tell me more about this G-force nulling experience."

Max stared down at his feet.

"If it had just been me, I could pass it off as my imagination but Sergei and Jen were with me. They confirmed the lack of G-forces as we came back down. I tried hard to pull some Gs but there just weren't any."

"And Sergei can't find any modifications?" asked Doug.

"No, he insists that there are no modifications."

"Perhaps you were all hypnotised," suggested Doug. "Post hypnotic suggestion is where you are given an instruction that is triggered by a pre-determined event some time in the future."

Max felt very frustrated and uneasy. Something was

gnawing at him but he just couldn't put his finger on it.

"As far as you are concerned," said Max, "we were away for four days. To us, it seemed like a couple of hours. What happened the rest of the time, I don't know. It's just blank. Look, the only way to find out if this is a figment of our collective imagination is for someone else to take Gertie up and throw her around a bit."

"Yes, I'll get Jeff to do that tonight," said Doug, "and it might be an idea if you, Sergei and Jen had a talk with Mary Dubranski."

"Mary Dubranski?" asked Max.

"She's the company psychiatrist."

Max shuddered. Never mind Auntie Gertie, had their brains been tampered with up there?

"Okay," he said begrudgingly. "There's definitely something wrong and I need to get to the bottom of it. I still feel like I have a hangover but I haven't had the satisfaction of getting it."

Doug took the Land Rover through the security system and into the underground car park.

"You need a good night's sleep," Doug said as they waited for the lift. "Things will be a bit clearer in the morning."

Max went into his office and locked his papers in the filing cabinet.

"I'll see you tomorrow, Doug," he said patting the man on the back and heading for the lift back to the top level car park.

He took a pool 4x4 and drove over to the car park gates. His palm against the security pad opened the door. A few hundred yards down the lane, he pulled into a lay-by and took out his phone. He dialled the number for the cottage landline. A strange voice answered.

"Katie?" he asked.

"You've got the wrong number," came the reply.

"Sorry," said Max. The phone went dead.

He rang again. The same voice answered.

"I'm so sorry," said Max, "must have the wrong number."

He rang Katie's mobile number. There was an unobtainable signal.

"What the hell's going on?" he said to himself.

Sitting in the lay-by, Max felt a heavy tiredness wash over him. He sank back into his seat and almost immediately dropped into a slumber.

Max dreamt that he was in a long corridor. On the walls hung framed photos of aircraft and radar dishes. It seemed familiar. Further along the corridor, he could see two figures. He immediately recognised the taller man: Leo Whyte, his old boss from Advance Aviation. The smaller man appeared to be Chinese. They were examining a helmet, *his* helmet. They were muttering in a language that Max couldn't understand. Leo lifted the helmet above the smaller man's head and lowered it, as if crowning a king. Max was puzzled. Could Leo be the one who gave the helmet to the Chinese? Why would he do that?

Max saw another figure further down the corridor. It was a woman dressed in a nightdress. She had her back to him but it looked like Katie. He moved towards her and as he got near, she turned around and looked up at him. It wasn't Katie, but her mother, Alice. She smiled and took his hand. She led him down the corridor, glancing round every few steps to give him a sexy smile. Where was she taking him? Bed? Mmm. Max followed, but it became obvious that they weren't walking - he was floating along behind her. They came to a door at the end of the corridor. Alice opened the door and invited him to go through. Max hovered through into a cloud. There was no sign of Alice.

The mist swirled. Again, Max felt he had been to this

place before. It was a blinding white nothingness. He was floating inside a cloud but it didn't feel damp. Something stirred in the mist in front of him. He floated closer. There was a voice.

"Maxwell Hayden, you didn't show your calculations for this answer."

It sounded like his old physics teacher from school, Mr. Burrage.

"How did you come to this conclusion?" asked the voice.

"It's so obvious," said Max, "I didn't think it needed any workings."

Max moved yet closer to the figure in the mist and what he saw shocked him to the core. There was a face – of sorts – there were things that could have been eyes but all over the visage were flaps that flickered and holes that opened and closed. It was like looking at an open-heart operation. Below the conical head was a body that resembled a skinned animal – all bones and exposed muscles. Part of Max's mind was revulsed, yet he was a strangely calm. He blinked. All of a sudden, the thing looked more human and less like – meat. He blinked again.

"Hayden, you have to tell me how you worked this out."

It *was* Mr. Burrage. Even though he was considered to be a tyrant among his classmate, Max alway respected Mr. Burrage. He was tough, but fair.

"Sir, can't you see, this is only one of an infinite number of universes. They all exist together, one on top of the other. Every event, every action in any universe that has a choice of outcomes, spawns a new universe and each one of those universes branches off into others, ad infinitum."

Mr. Burrage spoke, "Yes, I know. You have come to the correct conclusion, it's your calculations I want to see. Do you understand the theory? Have you considered the scope of the dimensions involved."

"There are four dimensions, the coordinates describing three dimension space plus the dimension of time," answered Max.

"Hayden, have you not learned anything? Each realm has its own versions of your four dimensions and there are countless realms so a realm must be a fifth dimension. There are further dimensions concerning scales and wavelengths but the basic five are enough for your workings."

Max gulped. He had no idea how to provide the train of thought he had used. Five dimensions? He was an avionic engineer, not a theoretical physicist. How could *he* prove the multiverse theory, you would need a report from Einstein's impartial observer to do that. Max became aware of a click-clicking sound in the background.

"Sir, it would take too long to explain, the exam only lasts for two hours."

"How long would it take?"

Max shrugged, "Forever?"

The clicking grew louder.

Mr Burrage launched into one of his famous rants about what *his* physics teacher would have said if he hadn't shown his working but mercifully, Max woke up. He looked at where the clicking was coming from and there was a police woman tapping his window with a key.

"Are you all right, sir?" she asked.

Max straightened up and wound down the window.

"Er, yes. I was feeling a bit tired and decided to pull over."

"You haven't been drinking, have you?" she asked.

"Oh, no, nothing like that. I've been working night shifts and my body clock is all over the place."

The police woman smiled and gave two slaps on the roof of his 4x4. She moved back into the passenger seat of the police car behind. She was typing something into a computer as the car pulled out and sped down the road.

Max composed himself, checked his seatbelt and turned the key in the starter.

Max pulled into McGregor's Procurement Office car park where he kept his BMW. He parked the 4x4 and looked around for his car. He couldn't see it anywhere. He took out his remote and pushed the 'Unlock' button. Lights flashed and a bleep sounded. His BMW was more or less where he expected it to be except it wasn't white. It was a creamy-beige colour. Max shook his head and blamed it on the fluorescent car park lighting – was he still dreaming?

He got in, buckled-up and headed off home.

* * *

They called him 'Mad John'. Once when a subordinate suggested a better way to do something, he pulled out a Beretta .92, held it to the poor man's head and cocked the hammer. Even those above him didn't dare chastise him for it.

John Landers paced up and down the dimly lit operations room bathed in the glow of workstation monitors. The view on the large wall monitors showed a satellite image of a part of Central England passing below. Superimposed along the bottom of the image, a set of GPS co-ordinates, accurate to less than a foot, changed too rapidly to be read.

Landers peered closely at a monitor on the wall. He signalled to an operator with his upheld hand – left, left, left.

A long, bullet-shaped satellite in low Earth orbit fired wisps of gas to minutely change its orientation.

"Take me in closer," called Landers.

The view zoomed-in to a forest clearing with a lumber

truck and some shacks.

"There," he said, tapping the screen with his forefinger. "There!"

A cross-wire was centred exactly on a corrugated-metal shack.

"Lock!"

A door swung open on the satellite missile bay and a precision-guided weapon's holding clasps released.

"There, we have it, Sir. All locked in," said the uniformed operator. "Shall I go for it?"

Landers paused for a moment with a mad look of joy in his eyes and then nodded.

"Go!"

The operator lifted a cover over a red button, looked up at the screen and pressed down hard with his thumb. The missile received a short push from a small rocket motor and fell silently into the atmosphere. Heat shields turned orange hot and were jettisoned on the trajectory. Down it fell, going faster and faster. With a joystick, the operator kept the corrugated tin hut centred on his cross-hairs.

The missile sped through the wispy cloud cover, slammed through the flimsy hut and tore downwards into the ground. It exploded in a thunderous fireball. A huge mound of earth heaved-up and from below, a cloud of smoke and dust mushroomed out wide over the forest.

Landers smiled a rare smile and tapped the desk with his forefingers.

"Bastards," he growled, trailing his hand along the wall as he walked out.

* * *

As Max drove home in his BMW, he had a very strange feeling. It was something to do with the colour of the sky, it wasn't quite right. He had never seen a sky like that. It had a green tinge to it. It was just then that he realised that the laser projection into his retinas must be having some effect on his eyesight. That's why the car didn't look white anymore, it wasn't the fluorescent lighting in the car park at all.

It must be affecting the blue receptors in my retinas. God, I hope it's just a temporary effect, he thought to himself. *I could go colour blind.*

He drove through the village. There was the filling station and car wash. There, Barney's Convenience Store. There was the familiar hanging pub sign with the fox holding a mallard duck in its mouth. Something nagged at his mind. Was this sleep deprivation?

The car on the gravel path beside the cottage wasn't Katie's. Whose car could that be? Max pulled-in behind it. The gravel crunched.

There was a flash of lightning in the distance and a crash of thunder.

"More bloody rain," he thought.

He looked at the cottage window and something was amiss.

The curtains were now plain beige. Surely Katie hadn't changed the curtains? It was only a few week ago that he saw her putting up cream curtains with dainty little red roses. Was this his eyes playing tricks again? He needed to get this seen to by the meds at Mewton Base.

Max put his key into the front door keyhole and tried to turn. It didn't turn. He checked to see if it was the correct key. It was. He tried again and it still wouldn't work. Katie wouldn't have changed the lock, no she wouldn't do that – would she?

Max rang the doorbell hard and impatiently. He saw the shape of someone coming to the door through the glass. It wasn't Katie's shape. The door opened.

"Yes?" said an elderly man.

Max gulped.

"Who are you?" he asked.

"What do you want?" asked the man. "We don't buy anything at the door."

A woman arrived behind the man.

"What is it, John?" she said, peering out from behind him.

"Look, I don't know what's going on here, is this some kind of joke?" asked Max. "What are you doing in my house?"

"I can assure you that it's *not* your house," said the man. "We have lived here for over thirty years."

Max was speechless.

The man tried to close the door but Max pushed back and squeezed through into the hallway.

"I'm calling the police," said the woman, storming off into the kitchen.

"Where's Katie?" asked Max.

"There's no Katie here," shouted the man angrily.

Max glanced around the hallway. It had flowery wallpaper and a bow-legged, mahogany hall table with a fancy flower arrangement. On the wall hung a slightly faded print of 'The Hay Wain'. This wasn't his hallway.

"The police are on their way," announced the woman with a scowl.

Max held his hand up in submission.

"Sorry, I don't know what's happening here, I lived here last week and I went away for a few days. When I come back…" He gestured around the hallway.

"Did you get a knock on the head?" asked the man. "Could you be suffering from amnesia? You should see a doctor."

Max shook his head in a state of utter bewilderment. He opened the door and sidled out. The door shut loudly behind him.

He looked up at the cottage and all around the view in front of it. It looked the same as ever – except for the car and curtains – and the occupants.

He got into his car and held his head in his hands. He was in a complete daze.

Max drove along the road slower than he usually did. He had no idea where he was going, he just needed time to think. He had no home to go to, Katie couldn't be reached by phone. Did she even exist? Had he imagined his relationship with Katie? This definitely wasn't right. Was he still dreaming? He banged his hands on the steering wheel in frustration. Up ahead, he could see a lay-by at the side of the road. He pulled-in and turned the engine off.

He needed to talk to someone. Who? One of the doctors at Mewton perhaps? He thumbed the number for Mewton switchboard. No answer! The line was dead. Couldn't be, he had been there just over an hour ago.

He sank back into his seat and closed his eyes. No, he didn't want to go to sleep and dream again. He thought for a minute, then opened his eyes again. He leaned forward and looked at the bonnet of his car. It *was* cream, it should be white. So, it wasn't the fluorescent lighting in the car park. Everything else was the correct colour, so it wasn't his eyesight. Then, he remembered Sergei's blackboard and the chalk that had turned from yellow to white. Sergei had seen that, it wasn't just him. He thought hard about other things that had changed since he came back from – up there. Yes, it seemed odd at the time but he remembered the sculpture at head office reception being stainless steel. How could it have changed to bronze? And, another thing, why did the 'Dog and Duck' pub have a sign showing a fox and duck? Why had he not noticed Li Yan's glasses?

Max's mind rushed. It was becoming clear that things were not the same now as they had been before his encounter with the intelligences in space. What was it they said?

<YOUR REALM> <THIS REALM> <DIFFERENT> <SOME REALMS ALMOST SAME>

'Almost the same.' ALMOST!

Then he remembered Jen's question about the ease of travelling from one realm to another and their answer, <NOT EASILY>.

With an infinite possible number of universes, it suddenly hit Max that they had simply got their sums wrong. Maybe their computations couldn't handle so many decimal places, how could they? They were *almost* right but this definitely wasn't his world.

This wasn't his realm.

* * *

Somewhere in a bubble in the vastness of time and space, countless synapses fired. Waves of thoughts flowed and intermingled. Arguments and counterarguments were postulated, considered, accepted, rejected. Radical ideas were introduced, coalesced, nourished, tempered.

Deep inside the entity, an observation was introduced.

"The organic beings were not returned to their original space-time co-ordinates. This cannot have been an error?"

Thoughts seethed, twisted and swirled.

"Not an error. In a few of their years, they will have the technology to manipulate gravity and not long after that, the ability to traverse space-time. They are at the threshold of maturity technologically but they are not mature in other respects. They still have strife, hunger and planet-wide pollution. It would be irresponsible to allow them the freedom of space-time in their current stage of development."

Fractions of a nanosecond passed. Billions of opinions streamed-in, were considered, consolidated, solidified, channelled and filed.

"It has been calculated that a subtle deviation from their normal space-time would be beneficial to their evolution."

"Have these calculations been verified?"

Further nanoseconds passed.

"Modelling shows a high probability of success – but there are some uncertainties. Even with the telepathic implant embedded in the one called Max Hayden, we can only make suggestions. It is not total mind control."

Using the information available and an immeasurable numbers of projected possibilities, nodes wrestled, distorted, squirmed, coagulated, resolved.

"Suggest reversal."

Amidst the cacophony of calls for endorsement and disagreement, one line of thinking flourished and prevailed.

"Agreed! They must be returned to their original realm."

PART 2

There were things in the air and nobody knew what they were.

CHAPTER THIRTEEN

"I'm very sorry, Miss Cowell. I can't tell you where Max is."

Katie Cowell sobbed into the phone.

"I appreciate that your work is all very hush-hush and everything, but surely you can tell me something. Max and I have been together for ten years. He went to work about a week ago and I haven't heard from him since."

"Miss Cowell, I think that I'd better put you though to Tony Davidson, he's our Managing Director and CEO. Just a second and I'll see if he can speak to you."

The phone gave a hold signal and Katie waited for one minute, then two. Max had never spoken about his work at McGregor Aerospace. She knew that he was a specialist in avionics and designed augmented reality helmets for pilots. He mentioned a couple of his colleagues' names in passing but he was bound to secrecy by his contract – not to mention the Official Secrets Act.

"Miss Cowell," came the voice from the phone. "I am Tony Davidson. My secretary tells me you have been asking about Max Hayden."

"Yes, I haven't heard from him for five days. Can you tell me … is he all right?"

"It's Katie, isn't it?" began Tony. "The honest truth Katie, is that we just don't know where Max is. He went on a high altitude test flight with two other people and we lost contact with them. It could have been a radio malfunction but there is no record of them having landed – anywhere."

"Has there been an accident?" begged Katie, "I have to know what happened. Is there something you are not telling me?"

"Katie, there is only so much I can tell you. You know that our work is highly classified. It was a test flight in a small experimental aircraft and they have not returned. Rest assured that we are doing everything we can to find out what happened. As soon as I know something, I will let you know immediately."

"Thank you," said Katie stiffly.

"Now, I'll just pass you back to my secretary. Give her your contact details and I hope to have news for you very soon. Goodbye."

Katie gave her mobile and landline numbers to Tony's secretary, and her postal and email address for good measure. She thought of giving her mother's details too but realised that she was probably overdoing it.

After she hung-up the phone, Katie scanned the news sites on the internet, again, and did every possible search she could think of regarding aircraft crashes within a couple of hundred miles from where they lived. Nothing. Against her better judgement, she rang her mother, Alice. They didn't get on well together but she had to talk to someone.

"Mum, Max has disappeared."

"What have you been doing to him?" asked Alice suspiciously.

"No, not run off. He has been test-flying some experimental aircraft and hasn't returned. Even his company don't know where he is. I've been looking-up air accidents and there haven't been any in England in the last two weeks. Where could he be?"

Alice softened a little. Even though there was a history of animosity between them, she did like Max.

"I'm sure that everything will be all right, Katie. He's probably sitting in a bar somewhere. He'll be back very soon. Why don't you come over and see me some day?"

"Maybe," said Katie unconvincingly and hung up without saying goodbye. Max's narcissistic bluntness was definitely rubbing off on her.

Max Hayden sat in his BMW with his head in his hands. His designer stubble had not been trimmed in the last week because he was wearing a helmet most of that time. It felt rough on his palms. He was in a state of utter confusion. He had just been to the cottage where he and Katie lived only to find that someone else lived there, and had done for over thirty years! Apparently, Katie didn't exist in this world.

This world!

Max banged his head on the steering wheel in desperation and frustration. He had tried to ring Katie and her mother but the phone numbers were either not available or belonged to someone else. Even stranger, the phone number for Mewton Base, which he had left less than two hours ago, was unobtainable too. He decided to phone head office to speak to the company's managing director, Tony Davidson.

"Max, thank God you are safe. There has been an incident at Mewton Base. We are just investigating now but it looks like there has been an explosion."

"An explosion?" gasped Max. "How did that happen. How bad is it?"

"It has all the hallmarks of a precision guided bunker-buster bomb, as far as we can tell."

"Christ!" coughed Max.

Tony continued, "The bomb went down one of the lift shafts to the bottom level and did a lot of damage to our storerooms, kitchens and some recreational facilities. Luckily, the upper floors, the hangar and workshops escaped most of the damage thanks to the blast-doors. We haven't been able to access some areas as yet as there have been cave-ins."

"Are there any casualties?" asked Max.

"Unfortunately, yes. Eight dead and a couple of

dozen injuries, some life threatening."

Max was stunned.

"I'd better go round there," he said.

"Sorry, you can't," said Tony. "The entire complex is in lockdown. There are journalist and TV news crews trying to get access to the area but the MOD have put a five mile exclusion zone round the base. Nobody, but nobody, goes in until it is completely safe to do so. It could take a year to make it operational again."

"What about my team, Sergei, Jen, Doug, Li?" asked Max.

"Sergei and Jennifer were off-base at the time, so they are okay. Doug and Li are in hospital but not seriously injured. I don't know about the others, reports are still coming in."

Max tried hard to take it all in. First, the realisation that this was not the world he had left behind when he set off on his last flight, now he finds out that his workplace has been damaged and some of his colleagues injured.

"Who would do this?" asked Max. "What bastards did this?"

"We haven't had time to analyse the bomb fragments but, assuming that it wasn't ET, there is only one nation on Earth that has the technology. It didn't come from an aircraft and the fact that it came straight down makes a surface-launched missile unlikely. It could only have come from a satellite – an American satellite."

Max sighed. "We should have seen that coming. The Americans have been doing their damnedest to find out what we are doing. I think we must have pissed them off."

"But," said Tony, "that would constitute an act of war. A war with the USA. That hasn't happened since 1812. Excuse me but I have to speak to Whitehall."

Max tried to ring Sergei on his mobile but went straight

through to voicemail. He asked him to ring back. Then he rang Jen's number.

"Jen, it's Max. Have you heard what happened?"

"Yes," replied Jen, "I've just heard from Sergei. It's terrible. He has gone to the hospital to see Doug and Yan."

"Can we meet up somewhere?" suggested Max.

"Where do you suggest?"

"Do you know the White Swan?" asked Max.

"Yes, of course," said Jen. "I can be there in half an hour."

Max put his phone away and headed off towards the pub. Somehow, he had the impression that she didn't like him all that much. It didn't matter, they were colleagues, not friends.

He waved to her as she walked through the door. She came over and sat down.

"I'd just come home when Sergei rang me," said Jen.

Jen's Australian accent was tempered by her years in England and only the odd word gave it away.

"Jen, I have something to tell you. Have you noticed anything strange since we came back?"

"Strange, what do you mean strange?"

"Little things," said Max, "colours, shapes, little details that are not as you remember them."

"To tell you the truth, Max, I have been totally zonked-out. I'm pretty much in a daze at the minute."

"Let me get you a drink," said Max, "what would you like?"

"Oh, just a white wine spritzer," she replied. "I'm driving."

Max got a couple of drinks and came back to the table.

"The only thing that struck me as different is that someone has decorated the stairwell of the flats where I live. The walls used to be blue but now they are white. It's strange though, they look very scuffed for something that must have been painted in the last week."

"Mmm," said Max. "I have noticed a lot of things different. So different, in fact, that I now realise that this is not our world."

"What do you mean, not our world?"

"Jen, I just went home, to the cottage where Katie and I live. Katie was not there. Another old couple live there and say they have done for over thirty years."

Jen's jaw dropped.

"You didn't make a mistake and go to the wrong house?"

"No," said Max, "I know my own house for Christ's sake – except it's not my house."

"Have you tried to ring Katie?" asked Jen.

Max nodded. "I have tried to ring Katie's mobile. The number is unobtainable. I tried to ring her mother, Alice, but there was a stranger there as well, never heard of her."

Jen stared.

"I also rang an antique dealer in the village that Katie sells thing to. She was in and out of that place every week. He couldn't remember her at all. Nobody would forget Katie. She does not exist in this world! When we came back down from … up there … we returned to a different realm. One that is very similar to the one we left, but it's not the same. Apart from Katie not being here, I have noticed all kinds of little differences – the colour of my car, the pub sign in the village, the name on the convenience store. Remember Sergei complaining that his blackboard chalk had turned from yellow to white?"

Jen gasped.

"To make matters worse," said Max, "I am now homeless!"

Jen took a sip of her drink and thought hard.

"Want to bunk up at my place," asked Jen, "for a few days," she added quickly. "I have a sofa bed in the living room."

Max patted the back of her hand.

"Thank you Jen, I need time to …" He raised his voice in anger. "Get my fucking head round this!"

He looked away.

"Sorry, I'm a mess," he said quietly.

Max's phone buzzed.

"Hi Sergei, I'm at the White Swan with Jen here. We need to talk."

"Do you want me to come to the pub?" asked Sergei in his peculiar Russian/American accent.

"No," said Max. "Can you come to Jen's place, I'm going to be staying there for a few days? We can't really discuss things in a pub. How are Doug and Yan?"

"I know roughly where Jen lives, what's the number?"

Max asked Jen what her address was and passed it onto Sergei.

"Doug is suffering from acoustic trauma. The pressure wave of the explosion. Don't know how it will affect his hearing. It will take time to discover if there is any permanent damage. He is not physically injured apart from that. Li Yan took-in a lot of smoke. She is on a ventilator but they say she should recover okay. Again, it will take time."

"Okay, thanks, Sergei. See you at Jen's in about an hour," said Max, ringing off.

"Did you get the gist of that?"asked Max. Jen nodded.

"Excuse me, Jen. I need to get something a little stronger at the off-license. See you at yours."

When Sergei arrived at Jen's flat, Max had already downed half a bottle of malt whisky. Max held the bottle up to him and Sergei lifted an empty glass waiting for him on the coffee table. Jen had opened a bottle of Jacob's Creek and was also half way down.

"Why are you here?" asked Sergei, his eyes flicking

between Max and Jen.

"Sergei, you never met my partner, Katie. It would seem that nobody else has either."

Sergei looked at Jen and then back at Max.

"What do you mean, Max?"

Max related the story about him going home to the cottage and trying to ring Katie and her mother.

Sergei sunk deep into his chair.

"So, it's not just me then?" he whispered.

He looked around half expecting other people to be listening-in.

"I thought I was going crazy," he said. "I was going through the CDs in my glove compartment and I hardly recognised any of them. How could someone change my CDs without me knowing?"

Max nodded in recognition.

"This is not our world, there is no doubt about it. We were sent back to the wrong realm. Maybe it's not possible to go back to the same realm, I don't know. You don't think that those … things … are taking the piss, do you?"

Sergei smiled a worried smile.

"How the hell do we fix this?"

They talked into the small hours, getting increasingly inebriated. Sergei was in no state to talk, let alone drive. He just passed out on the floor while Max sprawled out across the sofa and fell asleep immediately.

Max had a nagging dream. Even though he staggered out to the toilet in the middle of the night, when he went to sleep again, the same dream came back. His dream seemed familiar, like a sense of déjà vu. There in front of him was his old physics teacher, Mr Burrage, standing in the middle of a thick mist.

"Do you understand about realms now, Hayden?" said Mr. Burrage, although his lips did not move.

"Yes, I think so," stammered Max.

As Mr. Burrage became clearer in the mist, Max was somewhat taken aback to see a ventriloquist's dummy dressed in a cap and gown and holding a bamboo cane – not at all like the reality. His jaw was moving up and down but not with any concept of synchronisation with his speech.

"Are your realm and my realm the same, Hayden?" came the voice from the dummy.

"I don't think so," dreamt Max.

"How are they different?"

Max was puzzled. What realms were this bizarre apparition speaking of? Max knew of three realms. The one that he had lived in most of his life, the one he had come back to, and that strange misty place in the sky that seemed so like where he was now.

"You are not Mr. Burrage, are you?" asked Max.

"I am what you see," came the cryptic reply.

Max tossed and turned on the sofa.

"I am what you see," the voice repeated.

"You are not THE Mr. Burrage, are you?" insisted Max.

The dream continued in a loop until Max finally woke up with a very dry mouth and a headache.

"You guys want some coffee?" asked a much too lively Jen.

"Thanks," said Max. Sergei just beckoned, 'bring it on.'

It was lunchtime before any further sensible discussion was had.

"You know that I don't have any great love of Americans," said Sergei, "but I don't think they would do this. There has to be some other explanation but, off hand, I can't think of one."

"I think we had better go down to head office and see if Tony has any answers. Strange as it might seem after all this, we are still employees of McGregor Aerospace."

Max and Jen went in his BMW, Sergei in his.

During the drive, Max remembered his dream – particularly the bit about 'I am what you see'. That is more or less what the intelligence said to him when he asked what they looked like. He also recalled his dream earlier in the day when Mr.Burrage had the visage of an open-heart operation. Horrible.

Tony Davidson looked at the people seated round the boardroom table.

"I have been speaking to the Minister and he to his counterpart in the USA. They swear that they know nothing about this bomb. I don't know if I believe them or not."

"So, Max, from what you tell me, there is another me in another realm not having this conversation?"

Max gave a slight smile and looked around the wood panelled room. "There could be a you in another realm that is a fishmonger, or a ballet dancer – theoretically."

"In our realm," he pointed at Sergei and Jen, "we wouldn't be having this conversation. We don't belong here."

Tony looked uneasy.

"Look, this isn't getting us anywhere," he said. Until we get Mewton Base back in working order, I suggest that you take a holiday. Report back in a month's time and we will take it from there."

Max and Jen said goodbye to Sergei in the car park and Sergei headed off home. Max and Jen were going back to her flat.

"Jen, I've just been thinking about what Tony was saying. The Tony we have just been speaking to knows both of us, right?"

"Yes," said Jen, "why?"

"As far as you are concerned, your old realm and this

one are virtually identical. It makes little difference which one you are in. For me, the old realm and this one are radically different. If Tony knows me, then I must have a history in this realm but I can only remember the past in my old realm."

"Seems reasonable," said Jen.

"Don't you see, Jen. I must have a home in this realm that is not the cottage where I lived with Katie. Maybe we chose a different place to live in this realm."

"Maybe there is another me that didn't leave Australia and another Sergei teaching at a university in Moscow?"

Max pondered.

"No, I don't think it works like that. I don't think we are likely to run into our other selves. I hope not anyway. The way I see it, what were refer to as a 'realm' is a just a collection of individual timelines. Some of those timelines are identical, some nearly identical but, in my case, significantly different. I don't know why mine is so different. Perhaps I am a special case for some reason? Hell, I don't know."

"Max, have you got your driving license with you?"

Max took out his wallet and handed it to Jen.

"Have a look in there."

Jen found his driving licence and removed it from the clear plastic pocket in the wallet. She handed it to him. Max looked down at the license.

"Damn, he said. That's where I used to live when I worked for Advanced Aviation. I need to find what my recent address was."

"Margaret Lynton in HR would have your details on file," suggested Jen.

They hadn't driven far from headquarter so Max did an about turn.

"You're right," said Max. "The trouble is that I don't want to look stupid not knowing my own address.

'Margaret, can you tell me where I live, I've forgotten?'"

Jen smiled, "Then, don't ask her like that!"

"I'll think of some excuse," said Max as he pulled into the company car park. "You wait here, won't be long."

Max tapped on Margaret's office door.

"Oh, hello Max," she said looking up from her monitor. "What can I do for you?"

"This might sound strange," stared Max, "I'm applying for membership at my local golf club and they've given me all these forms to fill-in. Would you believe, they want a letter from my employer confirming my address and how long I've worked here."

Margaret peered over the top of her glasses.

"Mmm. Must be a very exclusive golf club?"

"Oh yes, they are very particular who they let in!"

"Could you just do a little note for them? Please."

She screwed-up her mouth and accessed the employee database. The address was copied and pasted into a new document, she added something to it and set it to her office printer.

"Do you want an envelope?" she asked dryly.

"No, that just fine. It's going in with some other forms."

Max thanked Margaret and headed out the door. In the corridor, he looked at the letter and gulped.

"Where the hell is that?"

Back in the car, he asked Jen if she knew where the address might be.

"Head out of town towards the motorway. I think it's down that way somewhere."

Max drove in the direction of the motorway while Jen did her best to read the street name signs as he sped past.

"Slow down a bit," she complained. "It's around here somewhere but you are going too fast for me to read the signs. Look, ask that man over there."

Max pulled over to the side of the road and lowered his

window.

"Do you know where Church Lane is?" he asked.

"That's the lane that goes past the church. That church," the old man said, pointing at a nearby steeple.

"Oh, thank you," said Max and turned off into – Church Lane.

"Number 18," said Jen. Must be on that side. Fourteen, sixteen, eighteen. There it is."

Max looked at the house. It was another cottage like the one he remembered but quite different in elevation. It had two dormer windows.

"You would think that I would recognise this place," he said, "but I don't."

He and Jen got out of the car and went up to the door.

"Of course, I don't have a key to this house," he said patting his pockets. He stopped.

"Jen, I am terrified what we might find here. What if Katie's here? What if some different girlfriend is here? Christ, what happens if I am here! I might meet another me from this realm!"

A middle aged-woman on a bicycle rode past in the roadway. She waved.

"Hello Max," she shouted.

"Who was that?" asked Jen.

"I don't know," snapped Max. "I never saw her before in my life but she seems to know me."

Max ran off down the road after the woman at full pelt.

"Hello, hello, can I have a word?"

The woman stopped and got off her bicycle.

"Hello," he said and muttered something intelligible. He was embarrassed to admit that he hadn't a clue who she was. How was he going to bluff this?

"Ah, you don't happen to know if…" he waved his hand in the direction of the house next door.

"Arthur?" she prompted.

"Yes Arthur, I have a terrible head for names," said Max. "Do you happen to know where he is likely to be?"

"He's probably in the house," she said. "He doesn't go out much these days since he had his accident."

"Yes, of course," said Max. "I'll just go and ring on his bell."

He waved to the woman as she pedalled off and went to his neighbour's door. When he rang the bell, he could see the curtains twitch. Then he heard a deadbolt slide across and the door opened.

"Hello Arthur, how are you keeping?"

"Mustn't grumble, Max," he said.

"Look Arthur, I seem to have lost my keys. Did I leave a set with you, I can't remember?"

"Yes, I have your back door key somewhere," said Arthur. "Just a minute."

Max looked round at Jen and gave a 'sorted' sign with his fists. Arthur returned with a key tied to a paper label with a piece of course twine and handed it to him.

"Thank you very much Arthur. It's a good job that somebody around here is organised!"

Arthur closed the door and Max and Jen headed down the side of the house to the back door. Max looked round the small back garden. The grass needed to be cut. He went up to the door, put the key in and turned it. He froze on the spot and looked at Jen, shaking his head.

"Here goes nothing!"

Jen followed Max through the back door into the small kitchen.

"Hello," he shouted, but there was no reply.

Max looked around the kitchen. It was tidy, but unfamiliar. He opened a few cupboards and examined the contents. He did recognise the ceramic mug with a big "M" on it that he had since his university days and the half empty bottle of 'Highland Park' single malt whisky. It was his favourite tipple. All kinds of little details struck a chord but the overall kitchen did not.

He wandered into the hallway. On the front doormat was a heap of mail. He picked-up the top letter and it was indeed addressed to him. It looked like a bank statement. He would examine all this stuff later.

Jen had already found the living room when Max walked in.

"Nice collection of vintage cameras," she said, pointing at a shelf.

"Yes, I love old cameras," said Max. "Look, here's a Leica IIf." He picked it off the shelf, turned the film advance knob and clicked the shutter. There was a soft click.

"Not like the clunkers they make nowadays," he smiled.

The cameras were all familiar and belonged to his prized collection. He picked-up a pair of wooden bongoes with animal hide skins.

"Got these in a souk in Tunisia," he remembered.

The possessions were definitely his. When he last saw them a week ago, there were in the cottage where he and Katie lived. Now there were in the house where Max Hayden lived. There was no Katie.

"Well, this looks to be my house," said Max, "so I won't be crashing out at your place anymore."

Jen just smiled.

"No worries."

Max shook his head.

"No, plenty of worries, Jen. I don't belong in this house. I don't even belong in this world."

"I'm afraid that it will have to do," shrugged Jen. "It's all we've got."

"Not if I can help it," snapped Max.

He went quiet in his thoughts for a few minutes.

"Can I get you a coffee or a cup of tea?" asked Max.

"No, I'm okay," said Jen. "I think that I should go home and let you sort yourself out."

"Yes, I'd better get a new lock for the front door and some extra keys. I'll drop you off and go to the hardware store. Might need some groceries too."

Max took Jen home. He stopped outside her flat. Maybe he had the wrong idea about Jen all along. They *were* more than colleagues, she had just proved that. They sat and looked at each other for a minute. The thought of giving her a peck on the cheek crossed his mind briefly, but no, that was dangerous ground; he didn't want to go there. He leaned over and gave her a friendly hug.

"Thanks for putting me up Jen," he said, looking into her eyes. She remained unmoved.

"I've always meant to ask, do you have someone special Jen?"

Jen sunk back into the BMW's plush leather seats and closed her eyes.

"Used to have. Mark and I backpacked from Oz five years ago. We were pretty close by the time we reached London. We decided to get jobs and stay for a bit, we liked it here. As I have a MA in software engineering, I didn't have any trouble getting a work permit but poor old Mark didn't have any special qualifications, unless you count surfing. He had to go back to Sydney. Maybe I'll jump on a plane and go visit him, unless he's teamed up with someone else!"

"It would be a good idea to find that out first," said Max. "You don't want to make a trip like that for nothing."

"It would be nice to see my mother, so it won't be a wasted journey. How about you?"

Max shrugged.

"I guess I'll try to track down Katie. I don't know if she even exists in this realm. Maybe she just went down a different track and we never actually met. It was just a chance encounter in a pub when I clumsily knocked a drink out of her hand and offered to replace it. If I had, by chance, just walked round the other side of a pillar, that would not have happened and I wouldn't have met Katie. It seems that, maybe, every little decision you make spawns a new realm."

Jen smiled and patted his knee.

"Catch ya later."

Max knew where Katie's parents lived: in his realm. They had split-up years ago but he had been to Alice's house several times. He did try to ring her but a stranger answered the phone. He decided to make the two hour drive to the little seaside town where they lived to see what he could find out.

He knew that Alice was fond of reading and gardening so the public library might be a good place to start. He could look up the local telephone directory.

He searched for both Frank Cowell and Alice Cowell but they weren't listed as such. He did find a F Cowell and two A Cowells. He rang all three but none where Frank or Alice.

He went over to the librarian's desk.

"Hello," he said to the woman behind the desk, "I wonder if you could help me. I'm trying to find Frank or Alice Cowell who, I believe, live around here.

"I'm not allowed to give any personal details," said the librarian.

"Yes, I know, but could you confirm if they have joined this library or not, that's all I want to know," begged Max.

The librarian did a search on her computer.

"No, neither of those names show on my computer," she said.

"Can you suggest anywhere else I could try?" he asked.

"You could try the electoral roll. If they have registered to vote, they should be in the White Pages. That's in the reference section over there."

She pointed at a rack of shelves in the corner.

"Okay, thanks,"

Max leafed through the book but there was no sign of Frank or Alice. The F and A Cowells he had already rung were there but nobody else.

What if Frank and Alice never met, just as he and Katie obviously hadn't in this realm? Then there would be no Katie! Max stopped off at a coffee shop and had a double espresso. Where to now? He was tired and fed-up and decided to give up for now and head home.

Max decided which of the two bedrooms in his house was his. One was obviously for guests as it was tidy and looked unlived-in. The other had a duvet that he recognised. He decided to have a nightcap of Highland Park and went to bed. He tossed and turned until about 2am before falling into a deep sleep. Eventually, he found himself in a familiar dream... but Mr. Burrage was no longer a ventriloquist's dummy, nor did he have a cap and gown. This was the Mr. Burrage he remembered from his teens at school – dishevelled grey suit, v-necked pullover, maroon tie.

Mr. Burrage smiled.

"You've done well for yourself, Hayden. Always thought you would," said the schoolmaster.

"Yes sir," said Max.

"You went to university?"

"Yes, Southampton. I did a PhD in electronics and joined the Navy," said Max.

"Mmm, very good," replied Burrage.

Then things started to get a bit weird. Even in his dream state, it didn't seem quite right. Mr Burrage's grey suit began to look metallic grey. So did his skin. He went on speaking.

"What do you know about dimensional realms, Hayden?" asked the … robot, still in Mr. Burrage's voice.

"Not a lot," said Max, "it's a new area for me."

"Do you understand the granularity of spacetime?"

"No. Not at all," confessed Max. "What does that mean?"

The robot continued.

"There are an infinite number of realms. We can't possibly resolve them all. We concentrate on a small subset but even then it's not an exact science," said the silver man. "You have already noticed that this is not the same realm as the one you came from?"

Max was confused. Was he dreaming or was this real? His recent visit to the intelligence in space has seemed like a dream at the time.

"I want to go back!" said Max.

"Yes, I'm sure you do," said the robot, "but it won't be easy."

Max found himself awake in a strange bed, in a strange room, and he was shaking. As his head cleared, he recognised the duvet and the room he had found in the unfamiliar house a few days ago. He swung out of bed and headed for the shower. As the warm water cascaded over his body, he closed his eyes and caught brief glimpses of the dream he had just had. Was the intelligence communicating with him through his sub-conscious? He had no idea what they might have done over the four days he and his team had lost while they were 'guests' up there.

CHAPTER FOURTEEN

The tall security fence rattled and shook as it was skimmed by three large Black Hawk helicopters. They left a cloud of desert dust in their wake as they glided across the compound towards a cluster of low buildings amidst a forest of huge satellite dishes. In unison, they settled to the ground. Immediately, from the wide doors on each one, a group of men in black uniforms jumped to the ground and took up kneeling positions with their assault rifles ready.

Two suited figures strode towards the nearest of the buildings accompanied by four hawk-eyed guards. Two other men ran forward with a large battering ram and three deft strokes, shattered the plate glass doors. People inside scurried for cover as the black-clad men pressed forward. At gunpoint, a security guard was beckoned to open an inner door that led to a stairwell and lift shaft. Two of the armed men took the stairs downwards. The four others opened the lift and pressed a button for the lower basement.

Two security guards in the basement pulled pistols but when they saw that they were outnumbered by six armed men, dropped them to the floor.

"Where's Landers?" barked Schakowsky, one of the suited men.

"He's not here," came the reply from a nervous security man.

The man pointed to the double swing doors and the two wielding Colt M4 assault rifles burst through into a corridor. Along the corridor, they came to a control room manned by some very surprised-looking technicians.

"Is Landers here?" asked Schakowsky.

"Er, no sir," said a man in spectacles wearing a camouflaged peaked cap. "He's not due in today."

Schakowsky beckoned the technicians out of the room.

"I want this place locked down," he ordered his subordinates. "Nobody touches a thing – but nobody! Bring me the guy with the glasses."

The man with the glasses was bundled into the control room.

"What's your name," demanded Schakowsky.

"Fredricks, sir."

"What do you do here?"

"We track satellites," said Fredricks.

"Who for?"

"NASA, sir."

"Don't bullshit me, Fredricks. NASA are damned well capable of tracking their own satellites."

Fredricks looked scared.

"Our work here is classified," he said.

Schakowsky stepped up and grabbed him by the throat.

"I'll ask you one last time, where's Landers?"

"He's probably at home," gasped Fredricks.

Schakowsky pushed him hard against the wall.

"Now we are getting somewhere," he sneered.

Schakowsky looked over at one of his armed guards and nodded towards Fredricks. A swift blow to the guts with an assault rifle brought Fredricks winded to his knees.

"You were saying…?"

John Landers was shaving in his bathroom when he heard the thrashing of a Black Hawk helicopter landing in front of his ranch house. He peered out of the window and grabbed a towel to wipe off the shaving foam.

"Shit!"

Landers knew very well that his unauthorised use of a military satellite to wreck an English Aerospace company would bring big trouble but he firmly believed that his action was the right thing to do. Apparently, others disagreed.

He leapt down the stairs and out through a back door in his t-shirt. He had only made it into the barn when he saw the Special Forces men surround his house. He heard a woman scream, "John!" but he had already left the barn and was taking cover behind a small ridge to the rear. He crept along with his head low and soon found cover in a wooded area. He knew the place well and, completely out of breath, crawled into some thicket and lay still. Not long afterwards, he could hear men scouring the wood but without dogs they didn't have much chance finding him here. Half an hour later, he heard the helicopter taking off and breathed a sigh of relief. He didn't dare go back to the house, they might be waiting for him to return. He made it down to the highway and waved down a passing truck.

"Give me a lift into town, Buddy?" he said to the driver.

"Sure thing, jump in," said the man with the stetson. "Did you leave in a hurry? Did her husband come home?" he grinned.

"Something like that," snapped Landers.

Landers made his way into a bar and found a public phone down the back.

"Thompson, we are in deep shit," he said. "Can you come and pick me up at the Crazy Horse – quick – and bring me a shirt and jacket?"

Twenty five minutes later, Thompson's head appeared in the bar doorway and Landers brushed past him and out into the waiting car. The car tyres screeched as Thompson swung about in the street and headed back out of town.

"What happened?" asked Thompson.

"CIA! That's what happened. I need to get as far away from this place as fast as possible."

Landers struggled to put on the shirt and jacket in the front seat of the car.

"Did you really think that you could get away with dropping a precision-guided bomb from a satellite onto England?" asked Thompson.

Landers glared at the man, with fire in his eyes.

"Shut it, Thompson, if I go down for this, I'm taking you with me."

Thompson drove off into the night.

* * *

Almost every night, Max dreamt of Mr. Burrage, his old physics master from school. Sometimes, he appeared perfectly human. At other times, he was some variation of a cyborg, robot or computer monitor. Even in his dream-state, Max would think, "Here we go again!"

Mr. Burrage would admonish him for his stupidity about spacetime theory and make him feel small. Then he would praise him for his academic achievements after leaving school. Max didn't know where he was.

One night, the 'Mr. Burrage thing' asked a stranger question than usual. "When are you going to come and visit again?"

Max remembered this clearly as he was having his morning shower. Did he mean visit his old school? Mr. Burrage would have retired by now, if he was even still alive. No, that doesn't make any sense but then, none of it did. It was when he was drying himself that Max made the connection. The intelligence, up there, was influencing his dreams somehow. It was inviting him to 'come visit' again. Of course, there was no way to get there without Auntie Gertie and she was locked-up tight in Mewton Base, maybe even smashed beyond repair. He decided to ring Sergei.

"Hi Sergei, do you know if Auntie Gertie is still operational?"

It took a few seconds for Sergei to reply.

"I haven't been able to get in to find out but Tony said that the upper levels were fairly intact. The hangar deck was well blast-proofed, but then we never expected a blast to be incoming."

Max pondered for a minute.

"Sergei, have you been having any strange dreams recently?"

"Me, huh, no. I never remember my dreams," said Sergei.

"I have been having dreams," said Max. "It is almost as if the intelligence that we encountered up there is communicating with me through my sub-conscious. It is inviting me, us, to come visit again. I did suggest that it was their turn to visit us but I was told that that wouldn't work, but I didn't understand why."

"There's no way we will be taking Auntie Gertie up again anytime soon," said Sergei.

"No, I guess not," shrugged Max. "Keep in touch."

Max put his phone away and wondered what to do next. His mind wandered back to thoughts of Katie but he had already explored all the possibilities to find her that he could think of. In the pile of mail that was waiting for him on the doormat was an appointment for a dental checkup that afternoon, so he headed off into town.

"Max Hayden," he said to the receptionist behind a tall counter. She pointed at a door at the side. The dentist's waiting room was small and airy. Max could hear the sound of a drill coming from the surgery and pitied the poor bastard that was getting it. He picked up a magazine from the table. 'Why do they only have these dreadful celebrity magazines?' he thought to himself. He had never heard of any of the people in them. Pop idols, footballers, soap stars – what did he care. He flicked quickly through the dross and suddenly something caught his attention. Katie!

He folded the page of the magazine back and read the caption, "Catwalk superstar Katie Henderson's second marriage on the rocks."

Max was stunned. He tore the page out and stuffed it in his inside pocket. Katie Henderson. Married twice. His Katie had started-out wanting to be a model but she almost starved herself to death and became very ill. In this realm, Katie had made it. She was called a 'catwalk superstar'. She was a celebrity.

After his eventless check-up, Max decided he had to find this Katie. First plan was to ring the magazine. He spoke to some hip sub-editor. Although they were both speaking in English, they had great trouble understanding each other.

"I'm trying to contact Katie C… Henderson," he said.

"Yeh, you and a lot of other perverts," came the reply.

"But," said Max, "we used to be friends."

"You could try her modelling agency, Hamptons, but I very much doubt if it will get you anywhere."

Max rang off and headed for his laptop. A quick search told him that Hamptons Modelling Agency was just off Knightsbridge in London. He decided to go there in person.

Max hadn't been to London for a while. He took the train and got the tube to Knightsbridge. He found the modelling agency in Beauchamp Place and went up to the first floor. He was expecting it to be a pinnacle of high fashion but instead, it was drab and dingy. He looked round the large room. On the walls were lightboxes with photos of beautiful women in haute couture clothes. A few of the lightboxes were flickering or not working at all. A massive brass chandelier hung from the ceiling gathering dust.

"Can I help you, ducks?" asked the man at a mock Louis XIV desk. Max pulled the magazine page from his inside pocket and spread it out on the desktop.

"Any chance you could tell me where to find Katie Henderson?"

"Oh, no. We don't give out personal information like that to any Tom, Dick or Harry," said the skinny man in purple velvet trousers.

"She's an old friend of mine," said Max. "I need to get in touch with her."

"Oh, Mickey Henderson would have something to say about that, sweetie," said the camp man, punching his palm.

"Yeh, okay," said Max. Who was Mickey Henderson? He had never heard of Mickey Henderson but the way the guy had spoken of him, he sounded hard. Max left the building and found a pub nearby that offered free wi-fi. He bought himself a beer and sat down. Taking his laptop from his briefcase, he did a search for Mickey Henderson. There was a whole page of hits. Mickey Henderson was, apparently, a very wealthy man. There was no mention of any business interests, just gossip stuff and photos of him aboard a yacht with several bikini-clad women. No sign of Katie. Eventually, he found an article about their wedding on a beach in The Seychelles. Digging deeper, he found that Mickey Henderson had a large house near Aylesbury. There was a photo of it. Max bookmarked it for later. He had done all he could in London and headed back to Liverpool Street station.

Max daydreamed on the train. He was very fond of Katie and, despite all his egotistic traits, she like him too. She must have, they had been together for ten years. He thought back to the holiday they had been on not so long ago. Ten days in the Bahamas. It was idyllic. He also remembered the scare that he had when Katie had been kidnapped briefly. She managed to escape after a few days but not before Max was coerced into stealing some files from McGregor's computer system. As it happened, he had only stolen files that were meant to be stolen. 'Smoke and mirrors,' his colleague Doug insisted. He wondered about what he would do if he couldn't find Katie. Life would be so empty without her cheeky smile.

Before setting of to drive to Aylesbury, Max did some more research online. Nothing told him exactly where Mickey Henderson's mansion was so he brought up an aerial map of Aylesbury and looked for anything that looked like a mansion. There were plenty of farmhouses but nothing that was obviously a mansion. He was expecting to find a large old house with a drive going up to it, and a swimming pool. When he eventually found the swimming pool, the street view photograph confirmed that it was indeed Mickey's house, except that it was relatively modern and not as big as he had imagined. He zoomed-in and found the road name to enter into his satnav.

The mansion had all the characteristics of a prison – security fence, CCTV, electric gate with entryphone and keypad. From what the guy at the modelling agency had hinted, Mickey Henderson was not someone to be messed with - a rich playboy tycoon, maybe even a villain? Max decided to ask around to see what information he could find out about the Hendersons. The local pub would be the best place to start. Max bought himself a half of bitter and a thick ham sandwich with English mustard, served on a plate with a salad garnish.

"I was wondering," said Max to the barman, "who lives in the big house up the road, the one that looks like Fort Knox?"

The barman laughed. "Mickey's place, yes it does look rather forbidding."

Max didn't want to push too hard so threw-in a few unrelated questions.

"Nice little place you have here, love the thatch. Mostly locals or do you get droves of tourists?"

"Mostly locals," said the barman. "It's a bit out of the way for casual tourists. We do get some but they are usually real ale fans out on a beano."

Max sipped his beer.

"I was reading somewhere that old Mickey was having some marriage problems," said Max.

The barman raised his eyes to the ceiling.

"Not surprised," he said, "That Katie is a lovely girl, I don't know how she tolerates all his philandering. She is obviously fed up to the back teeth with him."

"And she's on her second marriage," said Max. "These celebrities have a time of it."

"Yes, but her first husband died in a skiing accident."

"Oh," said Max. "Didn't know that. "Is that Mickey's Roller sticking out of the garage?"

"Yes," said the barman, "but he doesn't take it out on the road. It's a very valuable vintage Rolls Royce. He usually drives a Porsche 911, when he's around but he spends most of his time galavanting round the Mediterranean or Indian Ocean on one of his boats."

"Mmm," said Max, "okay for some. Does Katie go with him?"

"Hmph, no way. That would cramp his style too much. Katie stays at home. I saw her yesterday in that Mini Cooper of her's. Very distinctive, white with black go-fast stripes."

"And Mickey, what line of business is he in?"

The barman flustered. "I wouldn't know about that." He rushed off to serve another customer further along the bar.

Max took his sandwich and beer to a small table. When he had finished, he waved to the barman and left. He drove back past the house. The Rolls Royce was being washed by a young man in his shirtsleeves. There was no sign of a Porsche or a Mini. He headed off back into Aylesbury town centre and drove round the town a few times hoping to see a white Mini Cooper with black stripes. He saw one but a man was driving it. There was no sign of Katie.

The next white Mini Cooper Max spotted was parked outside a garden centre. It had the black go-fast stripes on the bonnet that the barman had mentioned. He pulled-in and found a parking space. The garden centre was quite big but he walked round looking at the potted plants before heading outside to the back where the shrubs were. As he rounded a tall Acer in a large pot, there she was, standing in front of him in all her radiant glory.

"Katie!" he yelled.

She looked up at him with a puzzled expression.

"It's me, Max," he said.

"Sorry, have we met?" she asked scornfully.

"Katie," he said again, as he relished the sound from his lips. "Don't you know me?"

He watched for a glimmer of recognition.

She shook her head, turned and walked off. Max was devastated. He had found Katie but she obviously didn't know him. How could she, she had never met him in this realm. It finally struck Max that he was on a fool's errand. This Katie was married to someone else and he, Max Hayden, meant nothing to her. He looked to see where she had gone, but she had dissapeared. So had her car. Max slipped back into his BMW and set the satnav for home.

CHAPTER FIFTEEN

Landers was shacked-up in a motel room. All he had with him was the clothes he was standing in. Thompson loaned him a hundred dollars but that wouldn't go far. He was certain that his ranch house would be under surveillance so he couldn't go there and if his partner, Ellie, went out, she would be followed. The only thing to do was to send Thompson round there. Thompson was smart, he could remain inconspicuous and throw-off a tail. Lander's didn't have a cell phone so he had to use the payphone in the motel office. He called Thompson.

Thomson drove up to the ranch house in a beat-up old Chevrolet pick-up truck. He was dressed in dungarees and had a peaked cap with a John Deere leaping deer logo on it. He dropped the tailgate of the pick-up and took a large heavy toolbox from the back and dragged it off into the house. Ellie was in the kitchen when he found her. She was fiftyish and plump, wearing a grey tracksuit and a sweatband on her head. She was taken aback to see this stranger in her house and was about to scream but Thompson put down the toolbox and put his forefinger of his lips.

"Shsss! I'm a friend of John's," he whispered. "This place might be bugged." He looked all around for any hints of wireless bugs but thought that the CIA were more likely to use a laser microphone to pick up vibrations from a window pane. He found a sheet of paper and wrote on it.

'Need John's cellphone, wallet, cash, credit cards, pistol and some clothes, and a toothbrush.'

"What seems to be the trouble with the waste disposal?" said Thompson loudly and deliberately.

168

Ellie wasn't too bright and it took her a minute to realise what Thompson was up to.

"Oh, err, it's not working," was the best she could come up with.

"I'll just have a look," said Thompson and waved her off to find Lander's stuff. He took out a wrench and started rattling it in the stainless steel sink.

Ten minutes later, Ellie returned with a large laundry bag.

Thompson thought to himself, 'too big.' He started-up the waste disposal.

"There, seems to be all right now. You shouldn't put those large bones in it you know."

"Oh," she replied. She would never have made it as an actress.

Thomson removed the bottom tray from his toolbox and put the important things from the laundry bag into it and winked. He tidied-up the tool box and said, "That'll be forty bucks, Mam."

"Okay," said Ellie and mimed the counting out the bills. Maybe there was hope for her yet.

"Thank you very much, if it gives you any more trouble, you know where to get me."

Thomson waved an arm as he left the house and threw the toolbox into the back of the truck. Ellie was standing at the door waving. He scanned the area looking for any signs of parked cars or semi-concealed CIA agents. He couldn't see anything. The road was straight as he drove away. He watched for cars following him in his mirrors. None.

Five miles further on, Thompson pulled into a weather-beaten gas station and drove round the back to where his black Ford SUV was waiting. He transferred the toolbox over to the Ford, drove back onto the road and headed back the way from which he had just come. He felt pleased with himself for evading the CIA.

                              * * *

The next three weeks went by slowly for Max. He felt so helpless and was suffering from borderline depression.

Sergei and Jen were already waiting in the boardroom and Tony Davidson held the door open for Max.

"Hello, Max. Had a good holiday?"

Max smiled weakly and nodded. He sat down at the table and Tony addressed them.

"Right. The good news is that Mewton Base has been stabilised and made safe. The bad news is that the two lower floors are pretty much a write off. We are going to have to find space in the middle floors for storage and one of the small labs is going to be turned into a kitchen. Work is progressing well."

It was Sergei that spoke-up first.

"What about the Deltas, when are they going to be operational again?"

"Well, theoretically," said Tony, "they could fly today but some of the backup services, maintenance and engineering, will take a few days more. Should be ready by the weekend if there are no more hiccups."

"Tony," said Max, "do we know what happened?"

Tony thought for a minute.

"We've been in touch with the Americans, at the highest level. As far as we gather, some group of rogue operators took it upon themselves to drop a precision-guided weapon from low-Earth orbit into Mewton Base. Lucky for us, they hit the wrong lift shaft. Had they hit the main shaft, things would have been a lot worse. The Whitehouse have assured us that they are dealing with the perpetrators."

"And, you believe all this?" asked Jen.

"I don't know," said Tony. "It seems very unlikely that they would do that deliberately. We'll just have to be extra careful."

"Can we go down there today?" asked Sergei.

"There is still a cordon round the place but I'll arrange special passes for you three. Go in the back way to avoid any press or sightseers."

Max, Sergei and Jen headed off to the procurement offices underground car park and swapped their BMWs for two dirty 4x4s. The lane up to the back gate was blocked off by soldiers but they produced their passes and were allowed through. The RF chip implanted in Max's right hand caused the rusted gate to lift into the air and swing round on a shiny, stainless steel pillar. The same technique opened the rolling door of the car park.

"Doesn't look any different," said Jen.

"It would look a lot different if they had hit the main lift shaft," said Max. Sergei pulled up beside them and they headed off to sub-level two where their offices were. Max noticed immediately that the light level was a lot dimmer than he remembered and the air was not as fresh. When he switched on his computer, there was no network connection. He headed off to Sergei's office.

"Do you have network access?" Max asked.

"No," said Sergei, "we need to get that sorted-out pretty quickly."

"There seems to be issues with the lighting and ventilation too," said Max.

"Yes, they are working on it," said Sergei.

"Let's go and check-up on Auntie Gertie," said Max.

He and Sergei headed for the lift but it was fenced off. They took the stairs to the top level and accessed the hangar with Sergei's embedded RF chip. The three Delta craft were sitting there with covers over them in the dim light.

"Can't wait to get these beauties back in the air," said Sergei patting Auntie Gertie's sleek black hull.

"Yes, we need to talk about that," said Max.

Doug Sinclair was sitting on an armchair beside his hospital bed playing with his tablet computer when Max came round the door.

"Hello Max," he said. His head was wrapped in gauze bandages and he was wearing a dressing gown.

"Hi Doug, how are you feeling?" asked Max.

The Scot spun his forefingers round his ears.

"I'm stone deaf. Can't hear a bloody thing," he said. "I may never hear the melancholy lilt of the pipes again."

"Well, I suppose there has to be an upside," grinned Max.

"What?" said Doug handing the tablet to Max who keyed in a message.

'That's a shame,' he wrote.

"What about Li Yan?" asked Max.

Doug pointed at the tablet.

"Oh, sorry," said Max and wrote, 'How is Li Yan?'

"Discharged yesterday," said Doug. "She's fine. Can't wait to get back to work. Pity about her mate."

"What?" said Max with a start.

"Unfortunately, Yan's friend Ying Chen didn't make it. They were so close those two."

"Aww," cried Max, "that's so sad. I didn't really know her but I saw the two of them running around together all the time."

Doug couldn't hear what Max was saying but could tell from his demeanour that he was devastated.

Max put another message on the screen.

'Are they looking after you here?'

"Yes, can't complain," Doug sighed. "Private hospitals like this cost an arm and a leg but McGregors are picking up the tab, so ..."

Max was finding it hard trying to communicate with

Doug. He kept forgetting that Doug couldn't hear a thing and was getting more frustrated. Max examined Doug's tablet, which was showing a strong wi-fi signal. He wrote another note.

'We can keep in touch by email.'

"Yes, Max, that would be good. Are you back at Mewton now?"

'It's a bit of a mess but they are getting it back together,' wrote Max.

A nurse walked into the room and signed to Doug that they wanted him somewhere.

"Oh, more tests," said Doug. "Have to go. Thanks for coming in, Max. Good to see you."

Max helped Doug out of the chair but he was perfectly mobile. He, Doug and the nurse headed out of the ward and down the corridor. When they came to the lift shaft, the nurse led Doug further down the corridor.

"Poor bugger," Max said to himself.

It was a week since Max and his team came back to work. Slowly, the others trickled back in too. The air conditioning was working again, as were the lights and, more importantly, the computer network.

"Max, you really need to see this," Sergei called down the corridor, beckoning him wildly. He and Jen were peering at numbers scrolling down the screen of Jen's workstation.

"I was just running some diagnostics on Gertie's main computer when I saw something very peculiar. The readings were all wrong. Input, output, no co-relation whatsoever. When I checked the code, there was a whole load of sub-routines in there that I didn't recognise at all. I didn't write them and I haven't a clue what they do. All I can tell is that they are something to do with the power relay drivers."

"So, ET did make some modification after all?" asked Max.

"I can't figure out what it does but it is a very clean bit of coding," said Jen. "They certainly knew what they were doing. Sergei!" Jen pointed to something he was holding in his hand.

Sergei put a computer daughter board on the table.

"I would never have spotted this in a million years if Jen's hadn't told me where to look. You know that I checked-out Gertie for modifications when we came down last time. I couldn't find anything unusual at all. I was looking for something major. The way the artificial gravity was counteracting acceleration in the cockpit suggested significant hardware changes but no, look at this."

Sergei pointed to a small hole in the printed circuit board. Six fine strands of what looked like fibre optical cable went from various places on the board and disappeared through the hole.

"You see the fibres going into the hole?" said Sergei. He turned the board over. There was no matching hole on the other side.

"First you see it, then you don't. Now, watch this," he said poking a thin drinking straw into the hole to almost its full length. He turned the board over again, there was no sign of the straw on the other side. He pulled the straw out of the hole again and ran it between his fingers to show that it hadn't been bent or broken.

Max gasped.

"What are we looking at here?"

Sergei shook his head.

"You're guess is as good as mine but I suspect that our friends up there," he pointed at the ceiling, "have technologies that we have never dreamt of."

"Oh, that's scary," frowned Max. "Let me see that."

Max took the circuit board from Sergei and examined it

closely. He took the drinking straw and pushed it into the hole and took it out again several times.

"It seems to be a miniature spacetime portal," he said. "God knows where those fibres are going or what they are connected to on the other side. He gave the fibres a slight tug. The hole rippled as if it was a black liquid.

"Don't mess with it," said Sergie, snatching it back from Max. "You don't know what you are doing. It could implode and suck half the country in!"

Jen smiled at the idea at first, but when the implications sunk in, she shuddered.

"We need to get this back into Auntie Gertie and see what it really does," said Max. The others agreed.

Lander's had let his beard grow. It did a good job of disguising his face and his fishing clothes, rods and bag gave him a believable facade. He and Thompson were in Blaine, in North Washington near to the Canadian border.

"Don't want to risk going through the border crossing," said Landers, "They will be on the lookout for me. That's why we are going on a fishing trip."

The car pulled into a side road that led down to a fishing jetty. They were obviously expected as a boat skipper called them over.

"Hi John," he said, "Good to meet you."

They shook hands.

"Where do you plan to drop us off?" asked Thompson.

"There are lots of little islands between Vancouver and Vancouver Island. Some of them are inhabited, a lot of guys doing animation work there, but there is a house that is up for let and I've got the keys. You can stay there for a few days and then a Canadian ferry will pick you up and take you to Victoria. Fishing's good on Victoria Island. You'll like it there."

"Wouldn't it be better to do this at night?" asked

Landers.

The skipper looked at him as if he was mad.

"No way. That would bring the border patrol boats down on us for sure. We do this in broad daylight. It is just a fishing trip after all."

"Border patrol?" asked Thompson nervously.

"Yeh, but they are after drug smugglers and terrorists, not folk on legitimate fishing trips. They know me and my boat well by now. They won't bother us."

The small white fishing boat's twin outboards churned-up a long wake as it headed out to sea. The heavily wooded islands in the Salish Sea off Vancouver were covered with mist as it sped through the narrow channels separating them.

"Beautiful part of the world," said the skipper.

Lander's nodded, trying not to get into any conversation.

At last, they pulled up at a small jetty, just glancing off some old car tyres hanging from the side as buffers. The skipper threw a rope over a post and tied a tight knot.

"There ya go," he said, helping Lander's and his heavy fishing gear off the boat. Thompson carried a travel bag.

"Here are the keys. You will find that the house is well stocked but it might be a bit damp until you get some heat going. There are logs out back."

He followed Lander's and Thompson into the small wooden house near the jetty. They hefted their things onto the floor.

He pointed to a pin-board on the wall where there were business cards, menus and brochures.

"If you need anything, ring some of these people. There are a couple of ferries pass by every day and they will it drop it off for you. Give it a week or so until they get used to you and then you can take the ferry to Victoria or Vancouver.

"Great," said Thompson and went off to explore the house.

Lander's handed the skipper a roll of notes, which he counted and nodded.

"Thanks," he said as he headed out back towards the jetty and his waiting boat.

CHAPTER SIXTEEN

Max, Sergei and Jen were waiting for clearance for takeoff. It was a moonless night and the forest was still.

"The Lear Jets are up and reporting no local traffic," came the voice from control over Max's helmet speaker. "You are clear for launch."

Max lifted Auntie Gertie off the dollies very gently. She rocked gently a few feet off the ground for a few seconds before shooting rapidly upwards.

"Just want to explore the capabilities of the mods," said Max into his helmet mic. Hang on tight."

There was no need to hang on, since there was no sense of motion whatsoever.

"Wow!" exclaimed Max, "we should be pulling four Gs at this rate but there is nothing."

"Can you push it a bit harder?" said Sergei. Max opened up the G-drives to 75%.

"We are already at escape velocity," gasped Max. The craft cleared the upper atmosphere and was technically in space.

"Better not go any further," said Max. The drives can do it but I'm not so sure that the hull can stand it. We are also a bit light on radiation shielding. What do you think Sergei?"

"You're right, Max. Auntie Gertie is only a flying test bed. She was never designed to go this high. This is twice the altitude of the ISS. We are well on the way to The Moon.

Max laughed. "Only two hundred thousand miles to go then."

Jen interrupted. "I didn't bring my Moon boots!"

"Any chance we could be spotted?" asked Max.

"I very much doubt it," replied Sergei. "Our stealth coating can hide us from anything I know of."

"Except dolphins," smiled Max.

"Except dolphins," confirmed Sergei.

"I think that's enough for tonight," said Max taking them back down Earthwards. "Note, no sinking feeling."

Auntie Gertie floated down like a parachute. When they were given the all clear to land, she settled onto the landing dollies and they winched her back into the hangar.

"It's a shame that Doug is missing all this," said Jen. "It was his project and now he's festering in a hospital bed."

"I wouldn't say he was festering, exactly," said Max. "There is nothing wrong with him physically, he has just lost his hearing. I'll drop-in tomorrow and keep him in the loop. He will probably try to follow me out!"

"Can they do anything about his hearing?" asked Sergei.

"They are giving him bionic ears," joked Max. "No, seriously, they do have aural implants these days that stimulate the cochlea directly but a ruptured eardrum will heal itself eventually, so they tell me, usually in a few months. I think that he would prefer to wait than have ear trumpets grafted on."

As they left the hangar, Max turned to Sergei.

"Now, what do we need to do to Gertie to make her properly space worthy?"

Sergei scratched his head.

"Let me think about it. Shouldn't be too difficult for short jaunts. You are not thinking of going to Mars or anything daft like that?"

Max pouted his lips.

"Mars? You never know, but I have another priority in mind. And it involves another visit with our friends up there."

* * *

Thompson was looking out the window of the wooden house.

"Hey, John. Don't want to worry you, but there's a red police patrol boat just offshore and two guys heading this way in a RIB."

The powerful inflatable boat skimmed across the water, and swung round as it reached the jetty. The policeman that wasn't steering carried an assault rifle.

"Hey, you in there," shouted the armed officer.

Thompson came out of the house, smiled and waved.

"Saw the smoke," called the officer. "What are you doing?"

"Hoping to bag some salmon," said Thompson.

"Salmon? Here?" said the officer. "You need to be further up north at this time of the year."

He got out of the RIB and walked up towards the house.

"Can I just have a look round inside?"

Thompson held out his hand towards the door.

"No problem."

The policeman went inside and saw Landers sitting at a table.

"Hi," he said. "Mind if I look around."

The officer kept his rifle pointed towards the floor as he walked from the main room into the bedroom and back. He opened a couple of cupboards and rummaged around inside.

"You got any identification?" he asked Landers.

"Driver's license," said Landers pulling the license out of his wallet and handing it to the officer.

"You are a long way from home, Mr. Landers."

"Yeh, Abe and me come up here for a week every year for some R and R and a bit of fishing."

"He tells me you are looking for salmon?" said the officer.

Landers dismissed the thought with a wave of his left

hand. His right hand slipped under the cushion on the couch and felt around for his Beretta M9.

"Abe doesn't know shit about fishing. He's more interested in watching the whales. We'll be here for a few days and then we are heading up to the north of Vancouver Island. Plenty of salmon and whales up there."

"Sure is," said the policeman, who took one last glance round the room, then walked out. He headed back to the RIB moored at the jetty. Back in the RIB, Landers could see that the man was on the radio and looking back in his direction. He hung up the microphone and climbed back onto the jetty.

Landers shouted, "Abe!" and pointed at the policeman coming back towards the house with his rifle at the ready. The two men were standing just outside the door of the cabin but started walking towards the officer.

"What is it now?" asked Landers.

"John Landers, I want you to come with me. Both of you."

Landers brought out the Beretta he was hiding behind his back and shot the officer right in the face. He sprawled back onto the ground with a bloody hole in his forehead. The officer still in the RIB pulled out his sidearm and started firing. Landers jumped to the ground and grabbed the fallen policeman's M16 rifle. He rolled over and fired three shot at the policeman in the boat in rapid succession. All three found their target and the man tumbled into the water.

"Quick," motioned Landers to Thompson. They ran down to the jetty and jumped into the RIB. Thompson pushed off as Landers got the outboards purring. He climbed into the driving seat and headed off, keeping parallel with the shoreline.

Gunfire from the patrol boat sent plumes of water into the air all around them. Thompson picked up the M16 and returned the fire. The patrol boat was no match for the twin-engined RIB and couldn't follow it in the shallow water near the shore. Landers soon had the island between them and the patrol boat and headed out into the The Haro Strait. The radio came to life.

"Landers, stop your engines. We have you on radar, you can't get away. There is a chopper on its way."

"Head for Vancouver Island," said Thompson. "There's no point in landing on one of these little islands, we'd be trapped."

Landers weaved in and out of the islets. The shoreline of Vancouver Island was only a mile or two away and was heavily wooded. He headed for a small rocky beach and drove the RIB right up onto it.

"Help me pull this up into the trees," he shouted to Thompson. The RIB was much heavier than it looked so they didn't drag it very far. The took the guns and smashed the radio.

"It will take them a while to find this," said Landers. "Now let's get inland and find ourselves some wheels."

They could hear the thrashing of helicopter rotor blades in the sky some way off. There is no way they could be spotted from the air amongst the tall conifers.

* * *

Sergei was drawing a diagram on his blackboard. Max was sitting watching when Jen came in.

"What's this?" she asked.

"Radiation shielding," said Sergei. "You are probably aware that the Earth is protected from solar radiation by a shield in the upper atmosphere some 6,800 miles up. Low frequency electromagnetic waves deflect the incoming radiation into neutral gas atoms and render it harmless. What I need to do is create the same effect on Gertie's hull."

He drew a round cornered triangle on the blackboard with a dotted outline around it.

"I can set up an array of antennae on the hull and feed it from a low frequency oscillator modulated with white noise. That should give us localised radiation shielding – in theory. Now all I have to do is put that theory into practice."

Max interrupted. "Is it not possible to use the G-drives to repel radiation?"

"No," said Sergei. "The electrons pass through virtually anything. They can wreck our electronics and our bodies. Magnetic or gravity fields are completely transparent to them."

"Well, we had better try out your low-frequency white noise then," said Max.

Sergei looked over at Jen. "Can you knock me up such an oscillator in software?"

"No problem," smiled Jen. "Just give me the specs and I'll get onto it."

"Won't it take a lot of power to drive such a thing?" asked Max.

"The oscillator won't use much power itself but it needs to be amplified and fed into the antennae. It's the amplifier that will suck up the watts. The fusion reactor should be able to handle that. I am going to need some help with the antennae design, it's not my area of expertise."

"Some of the guys in radar and communication should be able to help with that," said Jen.

"Exactly what I was thinking," said Sergei. "I'll head down there now."

Two hours later, Sergei found Max in his office.

"Well, did you get the information you need?" asked Max.

"Mmm, not as simple as I thought," said Sergei. "It's going to need a lot of antennae, very fragile antennae. In a normal space launch, everything is protected by an outer shell until the final stages leave the atmosphere. Then it is jettisoned and all the fragile stuff doesn't have to worry about fast moving air. Obviously, we can't encase Gertie in a shell so, I'm thinking retractable antennae. Will need a lot of work to the hull."

"Yes, I see what you mean," said Max. "But it is doable?"

"Given time, yes," said Sergei. "It's a pity that the dolphin people are so tight lipped. They must have solved all these problems thousands of years ago."

"Yes," said Max. "I intend to have a serious man-to-man talk to them when we meet-up next time. I hope that that is sooner rather than later."

Just then Doug walked in.

"Doug, good to see you back," said Sergei.

Doug did the whirly thing with his fingers round his ears.

"I'm not back to work," he said, "just dropped-in for a visit to see how things are getting on."

Jen went over and gave him a hug.

"Hey, steady on," said Doug, somewhat surprised.

"How's your hearing?" she mouthed very slowly and deliberately.

"Not very good yet," he said. "I can hear some frequencies but not others. It will take a month or two before I can have a sensible conversation. What are you up to?"

Sergei showed Doug the working drawings for the radiation deflector array and tried his best to explain what it was all about with a combination of mouthing and pointing at the different parts of the diagrams.

"Very clever," smiled Doug. "So, you can get on fine without me here. Might as well go home and grow vegetables."

"Vegetables?" grinned Jen. "From what I've heard, Scots don't do vegetables."

Doug was able to lip-read what she said.

"You don't want to believe everything you hear from Sassenachs," said Doug. "I love my tatties and neeps."

Max came into the room.

"I heard you were in," he said, going over and putting his arm around Doug's shoulder.

Jen spoke up. "His hearing has not totally returned, Max, but Sergei has brought him up to speed on the radiation deflector array."

"Excellent," said Max. "Anyone fancy a pint?"

He didn't have to ask that twice.

"But take it easy, we have been called-in to a meeting with Tony tomorrow."

"What's that all about," asked Sergei.

"He said that there's someone he would like us to meet."

The boardroom was busy. Max recognised the Secretary of State, Michael Reece and his Minister, Ethan Shaw. There were others that he hadn't seen before.

Tony Davidson raised his hand.

"I know most of you have met before but I'd like to introduce you to Edgar Openheim."

He held out a hand towards a man in a neat black suit.

"Robert has flown across from Washington DC with a personal message from The President. I think you will find what he has to say very interesting."

Openheim stood up and cleared his throat.

"Gentlemen, and ladies," he started. "I would like to thank you for the opportunity to come and speak with you today. I do know that you have had a recent catastrophe and we are all very saddened by it. Not only have you been attacked by a missile from one of our military satellites, you have suffered grave losses of personnel and kind. The President has asked me to express his most humble and sincere condolences and apologies for this most despicable and heinous transgression. He speaks not only for himself, but for all the people of The United States of American. We, of course, recognise the United Kingdom as one of our oldest and most cherished allies and that you should have these horrors inflicted upon you, is beyond reprehension."

There was a hushed silence.

"Can I first of all state that this act of aggression was, in no way, sanctioned by The President, nor by our government. It was carried out by a very small group of demented individuals who put their own personal aggrandisement and selfish interests before their national duty. I would just like to echo The President's extreme contrition and hope that it does not affect the exceptional historic relations between our two countries."

Sergei leaned over to Max and whispered into his ear.

"Pompous git!"

Michael Reece stood up and turned towards Openheim.

"Mr. Openheim, thank you very much for coming here today and explaining this most unfortunate matter. Please pass on the most sincere thanks of Her Majesty's Government to your President."

Openheim nodded slowly.

"Now, the question that I think everyone here would like to ask and I'm going to ask it for them is: have you caught the buggers who did this?"

There was a shuffling of feet in the audience.

Oppenheim tried his best to sound positive.

"Yes, we have raided the facility responsible for this and have the perpetrators in detention."

"All of them?" asked Reece.

Openheim looked embarrassed.

"We have most of them under lock and key."

"Most?" bellowed Reece.

"Unfortunately, the ringleader managed to get away," breathed Openheim. "But we are on his trail."

"Where is he now?" asked Reece.

"The last I heard, he had crossed over into Canada. The Canadian Police are in pursuit. He and one of his cronies are known to have crossed over from Vancouver Island into the mountains in British Columbia. It's pretty remote and inhospitable up there but you know what they say, 'The Mountie always gets his man.'"

"Quite," said Reece. "Does anyone else have any questions?"

Max put his hand up.

"Max Hayden, avionics engineer. Some of my closest friends and colleagues were killed or injured in that blast. Tell me, what are the realistic prospects of tracking two men down in that wilderness?"

"Mr. Hayden, I am very sorry for your losses. I can assure you that everything possible is being done to bring these men to justice. The Canadian Police are expert at operations like these, as you well know."

Max looked over at Sergei, who didn't seem at all convinced.

The meeting went on for another twenty minutes with more questions, and apologies. Finally, it broke up and everyone shook hands dutifully and shuffled out of the room. Tony saw the dignitaries off in their cars and headed back to his office. Max and Sergei were waiting outside his door.

"Can we have a quick word, Tony?" asked Max.

"Sure Max, come in."

Max and Sergei went in, closed the door and sat down.

"Tony," Max began. "I don't have any great hopes of The Mounties catching these guys. I don't know if you've ever been to British Columbia but it is vast." He gestured with his arms outstretched. "Even if they did scour the area with many helicopters, the trees are so dense that somebody could hide in there forever."

"Yes, I know Max. What are you suggesting?"

"Gertie," said Max. "We have technology way beyond what The Americans have. I would think that the Canadians are even less well equipped."

"No, Max. You can't go trespassing in other countries like that. What if you were spotted."

"We can do it at night, from inside the cloud base. Our thermal cameras could pick out their heat signatures from a thousand feet up. If they light a campfire, we could see them for miles."

"And what would you do if you found them?" asked Tony. "You can't very well radio it in or you will give away your location."

"We'll think of something," said Max.

"Narrow beam," said Sergei.

"We could hit one of their communication satellites with a narrow beam transmission. They wouldn't know where that came from. Remember, they have no idea about our technology. We might as well be ET for all they know."

"Mmm. Let me think about it," said Tony. "I think it is very risky."

Max took a large breath of fresh air as he climbed out of the Delta into the cold, open hangar. Sergei and Jen followed him out.

"Sergei, can we do something about the night vision camera. It's not sensitive enough, too much noise?" asked Max.

"I know what you mean," said Sergei. "Definitely needs an upgrade. I'll try to find some low noise amplifiers – tomorrow. I'm ready for bed now."

"Yes, me too," said Max. He quickly filed a report on the

computer in his office and set off in the Land Rover to pick up his BMW in town. At home, his head had barely hit the pillow when he fell asleep.

'Hayden,' came the voice from the mist. He recognised it as being Mr. Burrage, but he couldn't see anyone.

'I'm here sir,' dreamt Max.

'Have you done your homework?' asked Mr. Burrage.

'What homework?'

'The homework I set you on realms,' said Burrage impatiently.

'But sir, I don't know anything about realms. You haven't taught me that yet.'

'You can manipulate gravity, can you not?'

Even in his dream, Max had a small degree of understanding how the Delta's G-Drives worked. He didn't understand the quantum mechanics, that was Sergei's forte.

'Sir, I have some inkling of how to manipulate gravity, how does that allow me to work with realms?'

Mr. Burrage became agitated.

'You have a neural network, don't you? You have a quantum computer?'

'The only neural network I have is inside my head, in my brain. I don't know anything about quantum computers.'

'Oh, Hayden. You disappoint me. Can't I get anything into that thick skull of yours?'

'Yes sir, I mean no sir.'

'Be off with you boy. Next time I see you, you had better have some answers for me.'

Max woke up. The dream was so vivid. It was as if he had just had a conversation with his old physics master in the next room and just walked back into his bedroom. He rubbed his eyes.

Later, Max managed to corner Sergei in his lab.

"Sergei, can you tell me a bit about neural networks and quantum computers?"

"Oh Max," said Sergei, "how long have you got? I've spent years working with this stuff and I only know a fraction of it. Why do you have to know? Want to take over my job, is that it?"

Max smiled. "No, Sergei, nothing like that. I'll tell you if you promise not to mention it to anyone. They would lock me up and throw away the key."

"I won't tell anyone, Max. What is it?"

Max explained about his strange dreams, about Mr. Burrage and his quizzing about quantum computers and neural networks.

"It's almost as if they are communicating with me through my dreams," confessed Max.

"I think you might be right," said Sergei. "We lost all concept of the passage of time when we were up there with the dolphins. We know that they did tamper with Gertie. Maybe they tampered with us too."

"You mean, implanted something in our brains?" gasped Max.

"Maybe not something physical, like a chip, although who knows? I was thinking of something more like a memory. Something that is part of your brain but not normally in use. There are parts of the human brain that we know nothing about."

"So, let me get this straight. You think that they have flash-programmed my brain like an EPROM?"

"Exactly!" said Sergei. "Are these dream you are getting becoming more lucid?"

"Yes, I think they are."

"That is your brain adapting to the programming. It is building new neural pathways. As it does, the communication will become more efficient."

"Do you think I'll end up becoming a remote controlled zombie?" asked Max.

"No, nothing as dramatic as that," said Sergei. "It is obviously only affecting your subconscious. When you are dreaming, your brain is just doing its daily housekeeping. It's like when you defrag and optimise your computer. All this background activity manifests itself as dreams. Dreams rarely make any sense but can be influenced by events and past memories. Somehow, this programming is injecting data into your dreams. Your brain is trying to make sense of it, but can't – yet! When the new neural pathways are more robust, the dreams will become clearer. Maybe, you will actually learn something."

"But, what am I going to tell Mr. Burrage. I can't answer his questions?"

Sergei patted Max's head.

"Don't worry about that. The Mr. Burrage interpretation will gradually fade away and be replaced with … well, I don't know. You'll just have to wait and see."

"Telling me to not worry is like asking me to float in the air." said Max. "I am *more* than worried. It's my brain that's being messed with!"

Max took Auntie Gertie straight down from two hundred and fifty miles up. The trip from England to the west coast of Canada had taken barely an hour. They had done their homework back at Mewton base and much of the huge landmass they had to search was eliminated due to its inhospitality. More than seventy five percent of the area was above a thousand feet in altitude. There were very few roads or settlements in the area and Jen had programmed a filter for all known habitations into Gertie's computer. They knew that Landers and Thompson had crossed-over from Vancouver Island to the mainland but not at which point. Due to the nature of the rugged terrain, a patchwork of islands and creeks, some locations were more likely than others.

"I'm sure that this is lovely in daylight," said Jen. "What a lot of trees. Makes our little forest at Mewton Base look like a window box."

It being a pitch black moonless night, Max, Sergei and Jen had to rely on their helmet displays to make out features on the ground. Even the night vision cameras were struggling to render any detail and were being augmented with computer-generated graphics of the ground. Max levelled off about twenty five miles up and Gertie just floated there motionless.

"These guys aren't stupid," said Max. "They will most likely rough-it for a few weeks and gradually head down towards Vancouver once the heat has eased off. There are only two ferry crossings further up the island. One requires several hops between islands and the more southerly one goes directly from Courtenay to Powell River. They could have taken either but it cuts down the area we have to search significantly. Lets start at the Campbell River crossing."

The potential northerly route from Campbell River was relatively complicated but they searched the intervening islands. Most of them were inhabited and had rudimentary road systems but getting from one island to another would have been a problem for anyone without a boat and sound local knowledge. The only heat signatures they could pick-up were from small settlements. What they wanted to see was a reading that was well away from a populated area.

They followed valleys leading into the Strait of Georgia back into the mountains. Several times they came across camper vans and RVs parked in clearings. They came in low over each one and dropped the remote camera pod down for a closer look. They all looked like legitimate holidaymakers with canoes and mountain bikes. The fugitives wouldn't have stuff like that.

After several hours of fruitless searching, Max decided to move to the more southerly crossing from Courtenay to Powell River. It was considerably more populated than the other route yet still had plenty of scope for hiding in the wild.

"Do we even know what these guys look like?" asked Jen.

"Not exactly," replied Max. "All we have to go on is a pair of American military types with not much baggage. They could have bought some supplies on Vancouver Island. If it was me, I'd buy a tent for starters. If we can spot a campfire, it's either them or scouts. They are going to need a source of fresh water so, maybe by a river or lake."

Max turned up the sensitivity of the thermal imaging camera to maximum. The picture in the helmet display was very noisy due to the high amplification. The heat signatures of some larger wild animals glowed red against the black – a herd of small deer, the odd grizzly bear.

Another hour of searching left Max a bit perplexed.

"It really is 'needle in haystack' stuff," he groaned. What's more, the sky was starting to lighten. He didn't want to hang around in broad daylight.

It was Sergei that spotted the frame tent pitched on the edge of Lois Lake in the early morning light. Only the faintest hint of the previous evening's campfire showed a dull orange on Max's display.

"That looks interesting. I'm going down for a closer look," said Max. "Luckily, we have some cloud cover so we will have somewhere to hide."

From inside a small, slowly drifting cloud, Max lowered the remote camera pod. The wind buffeting made the camera swing back and forth violently on the long tether.

"This isn't much good," he said. "I'm going to have to go down even closer. I just hope that they are not early risers."

Gertie emerged from below the cloud and dropped slowly and silently to thirty feet off the ground. There, the camera was much more stable. Max was now able to see clearly in the visible light spectrum.

"Yes," he said, "definitely not scouts nor a family camping trip. There is virtually nothing outside the tent. It is well camouflaged, I'll give them that."

They sat hovering in the air directly above the mottled tent.

"Look, someone's coming out," said Sergei.

A man with a short beard and crew cut left the tent and stretched in the morning sunlight. He was standing there taking-in the breathtaking scenery around the lake and doing limbering-up exercises when he happened to glance upwards. He shouted into the tent and another man stuck his head out. Max put Gertie into a fast climb and made it into the cloud cover with only the camera pod still hanging through. He could see the man on the ground pointing into the air. The other was now out of the tent and looking upwards with a pair of binoculars.

"Looks like we've been rumbled," said Max. "Better get out of here." Upwards they shot at full pelt. Any other aircraft climbing at such speed would have pulled ten G or more. They felt nothing.

"Sergei, get the GPS co-ordinates of those two and poke them through to the local police network on the satellite link. We are heading for home."

"What the fuck was that?" yelled Landers.

"What, I didn't see anything," said Thompson. "Are you getting paranoid?"

"It was a black triangular thing," said Landers. "The way it shot up into the clouds was like nothing I've ever seen. It's certainly not one of ours. Nothing goes at that speed."

"Are you sure you're not dreaming. You put away a good dose of Jack Daniels last night," said Thompson.

"Christ, I'm not imagining it," barked Landers. "It was just floating there above the tent with something hanging out of it then whoosh, it was gone – except that it didn't whoosh, it didn't make any sound whatsoever."

"Are we talking UFOs here," grinned Thompson.

Landers put his hand to his head.

"Fucked if I know, let's get the hell outa here."

They removed their belongings from the frame tent and collapsed it. It fitted inside a long nylon bag. They put on their coats and slung the tent and haversacks over their shoulders and headed off into the forest. The ground was a carpet of dead pine needles that smothered anything but ferns from growing through.

"Better head south," said Landers, "the going should be easier."

The path through the dense forest was difficult to negotiate. There was a path but it didn't look like it had been used for some time. The landscape was all spruce trees as far as they could see in every direction save for the odd rocky outcrop. It seemed like they had walked for hours but the landscape didn't change.

"Let's take a breather," said Landers, putting down his rucksack and taking a swig from his water bottle. "There was a time when a twenty mile hike meant nothing to me. I must be getting soft in my old age."

In the silence of the forest, Thompson could hear the distant sound of a motor vehicle.

"Must be getting near a road," he said. "It would be good to get a lift."

"And have some idiot go blabbing to the police," snapped Landers.

"We could, at least, have a look?" said Thompson.

"Be careful!" said Landers, "and for Christ's sake, watch out for bears. You are not going to want to dance with a grizzly."

They eventually made it to a small dirt road but stayed well back so they could see who was passing. Nobody passed at all.

"It would be easier on the legs if we followed the road," suggested Landers. They trudged off southwards. The road wandered through the forest avoiding small hills. There was no sign of any life except for the scampering of red squirrels and the occasional bird call.

The road wound downwards around a sharp bend. Suddenly, there, blocking their way was a large, white Royal Canadian Police 4x4. Two officers had their rifles levelled at them over the bonnet. They turned to run in the opposite direction but two more policemen emerged from the trees with raised guns.

"Put your hands where I can see them," ordered one of the policemen, waving the nozzle of his rifle towards them.

Landers and Thompson looked at each other in dismay and raised their arms slowly into the air.

CHAPTER SEVENTEEN

It took a full six weeks working flat out for Sergei and his technicians to get the antenna array incorporated into Auntie Gertie.

"Now, we will have to go up and see if it works," said Sergei. "Jen, I want you along to adjust parameters on-the-fly."

"Of course," said Jen.

"How are we going to know that it works?" asked Max.

"I've had to install some new sensors," answered Sergei.

"What, geiger counters?"

"Something like that," smirked Sergei. "We are dealing with lots of different kinds of subatomic particles. Some just rip through DNA and damage it immediately. Other types are accumulative and prolonged exposure does the damage. They cause cancers and other nasty diseases – and you don't feel a thing, at the time. When we go beyond low Earth orbit, we have to pass through the Van Allen Radiation Belts. Further out, we are hit by solar radiation and cosmic rays. If we are exposed to those, we are in big trouble. I'm using a couple of radiation assessment detectors which will give Jen a readout of what we are dealing with both outside and inside my deflectors. If we were to use just metal, it would have to be a metre thick to have any effect."

"Jeez," said Max, "I had no idea."

"What I suggest that we do," said Sergei, "is just go up and stick our heads out of the trench for a few minutes. If that is okay, then we can venture a bit further."

With the new inertial dampers installed by the dolphin race, the team were less concerned about being detected, although they still had their Lear Jets go up first to check for middle-distance air traffic. Their radar was more effective than ground radar. Auntie Gertie could now get to a hundred miles up in the proverbial 'blink of an eye'; they just had to try to minimise the sonic boom effect. No manned space rocket could get anywhere near that kind of acceleration.

The Van Allen belts started about six hundred miles up. When Gertie had climbed nearly six hundred miles, Max slowed down and they deployed the deflector array. The whining of servos gave way to a solid 'thunk' as the antennae locked into place.

"Okay, I'm applying power now!" said Sergei and a dull throbbing could be heard throughout the hull.

"What's it looking like, Jen," asked Sergei.

"I'm reading 90MeV outside the shield and almost nothing inside."

"That's what I want to see," said Sergei. "Max, take her up a bit more."

The readings outside the deflector array varied wildly as they travelled through the Van Allen inner and outer belts. The internal readings hardly budged at all.

"That looks promising," said Sergei. Now, if I can just do something about that bloody humming noise, we'll be in business."

"Last time we met the dolphins, they found us," said Max. "Now, how are we going to find them?"

"Well, if I was going to snoop on Planet Earth from space," said Sergei, "I would park at one of the Sun-Earth Lagrangian points. Do you know what they are?"

Max spoke up. "Isn't that where the gravitational pulls of The Sun and Earth cancel each other out?"

"It's not quite as simple as that," said Sergei, shaking his head and drawing on his blackboard. He drew the orbits of the Earth and Moon and a series of contour lines showing the strength of gravitational pull of the objects in the system. He drew a couple of crosses on either side of The Earth.

"L1 and L2. This is where they park satellites and space telescopes. They just sit there in the equilibrium," said Sergei.

Max shook his head backwards and forwards.

"So, let me get this straight," said Max. "You are proposing that we go straight on past the Moon and half way to Venus?"

"It is past the Moon but nowhere near as far as Venus," said Sergei.

"And, you think that we can do that now?" asked Max.

"Don't see why not," shrugged Sergei. "We have Gertie and the radiation shielding. Your helmet can see way beyond the visible spectrum. I think we can do it."

"Even if what you tell me is correct, and I've no doubt that it is," said Max, "we still can't go up there and knock on their door like a couple of Mormons."

Sergei smiled. "Max, I think if we get anywhere near their portal, we will get an escort. I just hope they are as friendly as last time and don't take our visit as an intrusion on their privacy."

"No, wouldn't want to get their hackles up," said Max. "If it came to a shoot-out, we wouldn't have a hope in Hell's chance."

"I sure hope it doesn't come to that," frowned Sergei.

"Do you realise that we will be going further into space than any human has ever gone before?" said Sergei. "About four times further away than the Moon, around a million miles. It will take about one and a half days to get there."

Max groaned. "We won't even be able to go out to stretch our legs."

"Or go to the loo," said Jen.

"Don't worry," said Sergei. "We will be wearing proper space suits. They can take care of bodily functions. And, you won't have to wear your helmet all the time. There won't be much to see anyway."

"Have you been able to do anything about that dreadful droning noise when the deflector array is powered up?" asked Max. "I would go mad if I had to put-up with that for any length of time."

"Oh, simple," replied Sergei. "I just borrowed an idea from noise cancelling microphones. Half the antennae get the signal in phase and the other half get it out of phase. It cancels out the noise but has no effect on the deflection effect."

"Good," said Max. "I had no doubt that you would come up with something."

"Now, something you are not going to like so much," smiled Sergei. "Before we go up there, we need to tone-up in the gym. Our bodies need to be in tip-top condition for an extended time in space. A couple of weeks on an exercise bicycle would be good."

Max groaned again. He was never a great keep-fit fan. Jen seemed to enjoy the idea. Getting paid to go to the gym was, to her, a dream come true.

Mewton Base's small gymnasium was well equipped. Jen was having a workout on the running machine when Max came in. He came over and had a peep at the digital readout which was set to display calories used.

"You're doing well," he said.

"Just another five minutes and I'm calling it a day," she panted.

Max sat down in a rowing machine and adjusted the settings. He pulled on the handle and glided backwards and forward. The bleep on Jen's running machine told her that her time was up and she slowed down to walking pace. The machine came to a stop.

Max continued to row but his thoughts were far away. Katie was never far from the front of his mind. He could still see her smile. He could still smell her perfume. Max wanted to get back to her, back to his realm. He didn't have a way to do that – but the dolphins did. He wanted so bad to meet-up with them again and have this cruel situation disentangled. Max was so engrossed in his thoughts that he lost track of time. Suddenly he became aware of the pain in his arms and legs.

"Don't overdo it, Max," said Jen. "There's always tomorrow."

'A tomorrow without Katie,' he thought to himself and swung out of the rowing machine exhausted.

* * *

Three large black people carriers were waved through the gate at the Canadian Police detention facility just outside Vancouver. In the compound, two men in suits got out and pressed a button on the entry phone. They were admitted immediately.

"We are here to collect Landers and Thompson," said the man pushing some paperwork across the desk.

The uniformed male receptionist looked over the papers.

"Yes, we've been expecting you. Can you take a seat for a few minutes?" He picked up his desk phone and spoke into the receiver. "The American escorts are here for Landers and Thompson. Can you bring them up?"

Ten minutes later, two armed guards led a handcuffed Landers and Thompson through security doors into the foyer. They stared at the floor.

"We have orders to take you to Seattle," the suited man

said, waving a sheet of paper. "You will be travelling in the middle vehicle."

The armed guards prodded the prisoners in the direction of the main door, which opened automatically with a whirr. Landers and Thompson were bundled into the passenger seats of the middle vehicle and their handcuffs were latched onto rings beside their seats. The three people carriers headed out of the compound and southwards towards the border.

At the Peace Arch border crossing, the escort convoy took an express lane and went right through unimpeded. They drove down the freeway for an hour and a half and then took an exit for Highway 5.

When Landers noticed the detour, he called to the escort in the front passenger seat. "This isn't the way to Seattle."

The man turned round and stared at him but didn't say a word. An hour later, the convoy pulled off the highway into a side road leading through farming country.

"Where are you taking us?" yelled Landers.

There was no reply. Landers tugged at his handcuffs in desperation but to no effect.

A mile along the side road they turned into a lane that led to a large barn. The three vehicles stopped one behind the other and the two suited men jumped out of the one in front. They opened the side door of the passenger compartment where the prisoners were, undid the handcuffs and motioned for them to get out. Landers and Thompson leapt onto the dusty ground and were pushed towards the open barn doors. Landers could just make out two figures standing in the shadows inside. As he got closer, he could see that one of the men was black – and grinning.

"John," he said walking towards him with a hand outstretched. "I would hardly have recognised you with that beard. Hi Abe."

"Walker!" gasped Landers. "Son of a bitch."

They shook hands firmly and then Walker shook hands with his old partner, Thompson.

"Good to see you both," said Walker. "Come with me."

He led Landers and Thompson through a small door at the back of the barn. Sitting in a field behind the barn was a small Bell helicopter finished in army colours.

"Your ride to somewhere safe," said Walker. Landers gave him a pat on the shoulder.

"You have new identities," smiled Walker, "and there's some cash there too." He handed over two manilla envelopes. "Now, let's get outa here."

The three of them climbed into the Bell helicopter and strapped-in. They all put on headsets as it was impossible to talk normally because of the rotor noise.

"So, you've been sightseeing in Canada?" asked Walker sarcastically.

"Yet, had a lovely time huntin' and fishin' in British Columbia," sneered Landers. "It's a few years since I roughed it. Don't like it now."

"See anything interesting?" Walker continued.

"Now you come to mention it, I did," replied Landers.

"Oh, what was that?"

Landers pointed at the pilot with a question on his brow. Walker put his thumb and fingertip together and mouthed, 'He's okay.'

"Now that I've had time to think about it, I have an idea. We saw an unidentified flying object."

"*You* saw," corrected Thompson.

"*I* saw a triangular aircraft that moved like a UFO. Straight up faster than it could fall down. It could only have been from McGregor's in England. I thought we had taken that place out but apparently not – or they have another base that we don't know about."

"Damn," said Walker. "We won't be able to pull that stunt again. SatComs will be locked down tight."

"We'll have to put that on a back burner for now," said Landers. "I have other pressing matters on my mind at the minute."

The helicopter banked steeply and headed south.

* * *

Two and a half weeks of gym and Auntie Gertie's crew were fitter than they had been for years. It had taken nearly half an hour to get into and test their bulky space suits and they were doing pre-flight tests in the cockpit.

"All looking ship-shape," said Max.

A brief exchange with the control room and the hatch was sealed.

"We are all clear to go," said Max, floating the craft off its dollies to ten feet in the air. "Jen, if you need the loo, it's too late."

"I'm okay," laughed Jen. "Just as long as we can have a 'comfort break' on the way."

"There are no hedges," joked Max.

"In space, no one can hear you pee," said Sergei. The giggles trailed away as Max whacked up the power to the G-drives and they shot upwards.

Auntie Gertie's cockpit was small. There were three reclining couches, two facing forward and one facing to the rear. The floor space barely gave access to the three couches and standing upright was totally impossible.

To the front was a rather sparse console in a horseshoe arrangement. There were some storage lockers towards the rear. The overall impression was more that of a luxury yacht than an aircraft – but then, this was no military craft.

"Radiation levels are looking good," said Jen.

"Do you know what they've put in for us to eat?" asked Sergei.

"Is that all you can think of," asked Max. "Stuff in tubes, I imagine. Can't think of eating at the minute."

"Will we be doing a fly-by of The Moon?" asked Jen.

"No," replied Max, "not this time. The Moon is away over there." Nobody could see him point.

"Can we take the helmets off?" asked Jen.

Max checked the cabin pressure and oxygen level and made a small adjustment.

"There, switching displays to the main screens."

Removing the helmets was simply a matter of undoing a collar clamp and lifting them straight up. They were stowed on cradles beside their couches.

The large high definition screens mimicked helicopter windows, which lit up and gave them a view of the stars. Behind they could see the blue orb that was their home.

"What are we going to do for a day and a quarter?" asked Sergei. "No in-flight movies, I suppose?"

"I think that it would be a good idea to plan our strategy for when … if … we run into ouR friends out there," said Max. "I think we were a bit dumbstruck the last time. Didn't get much out of them."

"I have some questions," piped-in Sergei.

"About quantum mechanics?" asked Max.

"That, and other things," said Sergei.

"Sergei, my friend, the purpose of this mission is not a fact finding exercise. If you find out anything useful, that will be a bonus. As far as I'm concerned, I want them to send up back to our own realm. That's all I want!"

Jen agreed.

"There is so much we can find out," said Sergei. "Just give me a chance."

They took turns to sleep. The uneventfulness of the journey was sheer boredom. The hourly reports back to base were brief but had the useful side effect of interrupting

Sergei's constant renditions of Russian folk songs.

"We are just a few hours from target," said Max. "Better put the helmets back on. The screens are okay but they're not the same." It was true: direct laser projection into the retina gave much clearer images and the ability to see wavelengths beyond the visible spectrum.

Max swept the display from infra-red through to ultra-violet but the stars still looked much the same.

"Have a look at M42 in Orion's sword," said Max. Unlike the stars, the Orion Nebula changed colour dramatically at different wavelengths. At maximum magnification, it became a breathtaking cloud of marbled colours.

"It's beautiful," sighed Jen. "How far away is it?"

Sergei went into his familiar lecture mode.

"It's about thirteen hundred light years away and between thirty and forty light years across. What you can see now is what it looked like one thousand three hundred years ago. It will be quite different now."

"Maybe, someday, we will get a closer look," said Max.

"Only if I can get the principles of spacetime travel off the dolphins," said Sergei.

"Don't hold your breath," said Max.

As they neared their target, the team scanned the area, looking for any sign of hardware or unusual radiation. Max was the first to spot something.

"Look, at two o'clock, what's that?"

Sergei zoomed-in the view on his helmet display.

"Ah, space junk," he said. "There loads of stuff out here. It's too far out to be economically serviceable with regular repair missions. They usually send it into a harmless orbit or even into The Sun. What we are seeing here was probably too far gone to send it anywhere so it has just been left to rot."

"Rot?" asked Jen.

"Yes, it might take a few billion years," said Sergei. "But now that we have the technology, we could give it a nudge."

"What, now?" screamed Max.

"No, not now," laughed Sergei. "It's just another use for ships like this in the future. Space salvage. It will have to be larger than Gertie to pull that off."

"There's another," called Jen.

"I don't suppose that some of these are even officially logged," said Sergei. "God knows what they are."

Over the course of an hour, a total of nine inert probes of various shapes and sizes were located and photographed.

"I'm sure that somebody will find all this very interesting," said Max, "but it's not what we came for. I would hate to think that we have come all this way only to be stood up."

Another two hours passed and no more debris was logged.

"I think that we had better head back," said Max. "The dolphins are not coming out to play today."

"Just a minute," called Jen. "I'm picking something up."

"Where?" yelled Max, "I can't see anything."

"No, I can't see anything," said Jen. "It's an anomalous radiation reading, very faint. Max, take us to bearing left 30° down 72° from our present direction."

Max made the course correction.

"It's getting stronger," said Jen. "Still can't see anything on any wavelength."

"I'm getting it now," said Max. "That is peculiar. It's either very small or invisible."

"If it wasn't for the radiation detectors, we wouldn't be aware of it at all," said Jen. "By isolating some of the arrays, I can triangulate an approximate location. I'm putting it up on navigation now. Better slow down, Max, I think it is quite close now."

"I can't see it," said Max, "but I can see where it is. It is blocking-out part of the star field behind it. I'm going to put it between us and The Sun."

"Whatever it is, it is very black," said Sergei. "I'm switching on spotlights."

"Max, it's only a few hundred feet away from us," said Jen.

"Must be covered in black velvet," said Sergei, "the spotlights are having no effect whatsoever."

"I'm going in closer," said Max.

"Be careful," cried Jen.

The object blocked out The Sun as Gertie fell into its umbra.

"And I thought it was small," said Max. "It's huge. I can't make out any detail at all. Do you think I should try to land on it?"

"No, Max. Keep your distance. We have no idea what we are dealing with here," said Sergei.

"It's not natural," said Max. "If you look at its edge as it passes The Sun, you can see that it is an artefact. It has … bits. Sensors, antennae, I know not what. I am not able to detect the overall shape but the details are definitely 'made' – but not 'man-made'. I'm going to do a full circle."

Much as Max tried, he could not see anything more. In silhouette, it was black and where Gertie should have been casting a shadow on it, there was nothing.

"Maybe it is as defunct as all the other space junk around here," suggested Max.

"Maybe it's asleep," said Jen, "and I don't think we should waken it!"

"You might be right," said Sergei. "I think we should get out of here."

Max headed for home.

Max realised that he was very tired, unsurprising as the excitement of the events of the past two days had kept all three of the team at high alert. They agreed to take turns at having a nap. Nothing much was likely to happen for the next twenty-four hours when they would hit the Earth's upper atmosphere. Max went out like a light.

Mr. Burrage wasn't looking as stern as he usually did. He was standing there in limbo swishing a thin bamboo cane backwards and forwards.

"Ah, Hayden, there you are."

Max wasn't sure if Burrage was limbering-up with his cane and that he was going to feel its sting as he had done on several occasions as a youth.

"You wanted to see me, boy?"

"Yes," stuttered Max, "I have a few questions."

"Well, you know that I am always here to help, what do you want to know?"

"Sir, I tried to find you but you weren't there," dreamt Max.

"Where were you looking for me?" asked the master.

"At the Sun/Earth Lagrangian point L2, Sir."

Mr. Burrage laughed.

"And what did you find there?"

Max tensed. He knew this was a dream.

"Sir, I found some space junk orbiting the L2 point and …"

"And what, boy. Out with it!" snapped Mr. Burrage. "I don't have all day."

"Something large and very black," whispered Max, "sir."

Mr. Burrage laughed again.

"Ah, the night watchman. Yes, it would be about there."

"Night watchman?"

"I hope that you didn't go near it?" scowled Burrage.

"Not very near," said Max. "What is it?"

"A sentinel, dear boy. A sentinel that is there to protect your race should … 'The Old Ones' choose to come and visit."

"What!" exclaimed Max. He thought about what he had just been told. "It can't be very effective, we flew right up close to it."

"But your puny craft was of no threat," smiled Mr. Burrage. "What it is watching for is many millions of times the mass of your craft."

Max gulped.

"And hostile!" continued Burrage. "There are bullies in the playground."

Max began to shake. Then he realised that Sergei was shaking him.

"Wake up, Max. You've had your six hours. It's Jen's turn."

Max was in a cold sweat. The dream was so vivid. It could have happened in real life five minutes ago.

"Oh, I had a most disturbing dream," started Max.

"Lucky you," said Sergei. "I have to stay awake for another six hours."

Jen had already fallen asleep half an hour ago but Sergei didn't say.

"Sergei, I've found out what that black thing was."

"You found out? How?"

"It came to me in my dream. It is some kind of device to guard against invaders."

Sergei rolled with laughter.

"And who told you this gem of information?"

"Mr. Burrage."

"Who the hell is Mr. Burrage?"

Max paused as he knew that his answer sounded ridiculous.

"He was my physics teacher at school."

There was silence for a few seconds, then Sergei burst

into laughter again, even more vigorous than before.

"Oh, Max. It was a dream. Dreams are not real."

"It seemed real to me," replied Max. "I am convinced that it is their way of communicating with me." He was about to point upwards when he realised where he was – as 'up' as he could be.

"Mr. Burrage called it 'the night watchman' and said that although we were too insignificant to set it off, there was some threat from – way out there – that …"

"Nonsense," interrupted Sergei. "Your sleep pattern has been compromised."

"But, I don't have a sleep pattern in this job," cried Max. "It's not like I work nine to five. Never have."

"It was dream, that's all. Now, get over it," said Sergei sternly.

Two days later, Max and his crew were sitting at the board room table at McGregor's head office. Tony Davidson was listening attentively as they told them what had transpired on their mission.

"We have no idea who some of that space junk belongs to," said Sergei. "It is not in our database."

Tony wrote some notes on his laptop.

"Interesting, and you said there was something else?"

Max and Sergei looked at one another. They had agreed not to mention Max's dream.

"Yes," said Max, "something large and very black and not from planet Earth."

Tony peered over the top of his reading glasses.

"Is this something to do with our friends?"

"Yes, er, no. I don't know," said Max. "All we know is that it is artificial and has a very faint radiation signature."

Tony pushed his laptop to the side and removed his glasses.

"So you are telling me that you have found an alien

artefact?"

"Yes, exactly that," said Max.

"But what is its purpose?" asked Tony. "Why would it be there?"

Max swallowed hard.

"Um…"

Max felt Sergei kick his leg.

"I have a theory about that," said Max. He looked at Sergei sitting beside him and Jen at the other side. "I think it is a remote sensor that the dolphin people put there, a kind of early warning system."

"Warning about what, exactly?" asked Tony.

Max shrugged. "External threats."

Tony looked round the table.

"Any other 'theories'?" he asked. "Preferably ones that don't involve alien invasions."

Jen answered.

"You remember how they told us that they had been monitoring humans for thousands of years? Maybe this is what they use to do that."

"Why then, would it be dormant?" asked Max.

"I don't know," said Jen agitatedly "It's just an idea."

There was a silence in the room.

"Okay," said Tony. "Needless to say, this conversation doesn't leave this room." They all nodded. "I have some hard thinking to do about where we go from here."

CHAPTER EIGHTEEN

Michael Thornton, Director of the CIA in Langley, Virginia gasped.

"Looks like we've been taken for a ride," said Schakowsky, sitting at the other side of the desk. "The Canadian Police tell me that Landers and Thompson were picked-up from their detention facility in Vancouver to take them to Seattle. The paperwork was all in order. They passed through the border control at Peace Arch with a high priority authorisation. They were spotted by Washington State Police heading south on Highway 5 going over the speed limit but were instructed to take no action. That was the last we heard of them. They never reached Seattle. Gone!"

"I want them found!" yelled Thornton. "Get the footage from all the Washington State Highway cameras between the border and Seattle. In fact, get back onto the Canadian Police and get the footage of the convoy between Vancouver and the border too. They might have switched vehicles. And, while you are on to them, get copies of the authorisation papers. I want to know where they came from."

"Yes sir," said Schakowsky, and quickly left the room.

Some hours later, Thornton and Schakowsky were sitting in front of a large monitor in a control room. On the screen was footage of the convoy of three large black people carriers. On another screen, a map of camera locations along Highway 5.

"This footage was from the camera here," said Schakowsky. "The footage from the next camera, here, has no sign of them… so they must have left the highway here.

There are no cameras along that road."

"They would have known that," said Thornton. "They could be anywhere in Washington State, if they are even still in that State!"

Thornton became silent for a minute and scratched his head.

"Schakowsky, we've been fools. Here we are thinking that Landers is behind all this. He may be a slick son-of-a-bitch but there is no way he could have pulled-off this stunt by himself. I think that he is just a pawn. He is working for someone higher up the chain."

"Who?" asked Schakowsky.

"I don't know," said Thornton, "but I'm bloody well going to find out if it kills me."

John Landers now had a new identity and a full beard. His previous neat military crew cut hair was now longer and unkempt. Thompson had left for Florida and the Everglades, Landers was shacked-up only twenty miles from his ranch house in Arizona. He had driven past to look at the old place but he could see that it was still under observation from an inconspicuously parked car that anyone else would have ignored. He drove on until he came to a gas station and pulled in. He walked-up to a man sitting on a chair outside the office and said, "Hi, Hank."

The man, in grease-stained overalls and a baseball cap looked up and did a double take.

"Landers?" he said with a look of surprise.

"Not anymore," said Landers stroking his beard. "Name's Jeff Murray now. Look, I need a favour."

"Sure, John, I mean Jeff. You name it," said the mechanic.

"I need to get into my ranch house but it's bugged and under surveillance. I need to see Ellie and get her to move … somewhere else. You let Abe Thompson borrow your old pick-up truck and go round there with a box of tools not so long ago. I want to do that again."

"Why, sure. Anytime you like. The keys are above the sun visor. Just help yourself."

"Great!" said Landers patting the man on the back. "I'll be round tomorrow."

Next day, Landers pulled up at the door of his ranch house. Dressed in dungarees and wearing a peaked cap, he dropped the tailgate and took out a toolbox. He opened the ranch house door and walked in. Even with his disguise, Ellie instantly recognised him and gasped. He put a finger to his lips.

"Believe the waste disposal is acting up again?" he said.

Ellie recognised the ruse this time and said, "Yup, broke again."

He went over and put his arms around her and gave her a kiss.

"Let me have a look," he said pointing to a piece of paper and a pen on the worktop. He set a mobile phone down beside it and wrote, 'Ring me at this number from this phone when you are well away from the house.' She nodded.

Landers clanked around the waste disposal for a few minutes.

"Bones again?" asked Ellie.

Landers took the hint. "Yeh, you will need a more heavy duty disposal unit if you are going to put bones in it. There, it's fixed for now."

"How much?" asked Ellie.

"Same as last time," replied Landers. He gave her another hug and left with his toolbox.

That evening, Ellie rang Landers from the shopping mall.

"You sure you weren't followed?" asked Landers.

"Don't think so," replied Ellie. "Why would anyone follow me to a shopping mall?"

"Now, listen carefully Ellie, the house is still being watched and it's probably bugged too. You are going to go to the realtors and put the ranch on the market. I expect that will draw a lot of unwanted attention so I want you to move out immediately. Take just what you need for a vacation and have a short break in the Bahamas."

"The Bahamas?" asked Ellie with surprise.

"Yes," said Landers. "I'll meet you there and we'll go somewhere else - but make sure that you get a return ticket, a one way would be a dead giveaway."

"Where will we go?" asked Ellie.

"It's better that you don't know for now," said Landers. "Somewhere safe. I'll see you in a week. Don't worry, we are being well looked after."

* * *

"Max, I've had a word with The Minister," said Tony Davidson on the phone. "He wants to keep this hush-hush for now."

"Understood," said Max.

"And Max, you are not to go anywhere near L2 until this has all been sorted out."

"Of course," replied Max. "It's not as if it's on the way to anywhere."

"No, it's not. What about your Moon trip?"

"Yes, preparations are well advanced for that next week. Just a few orbits to do some mapping."

"Good luck then," said Tony and hung up.

"Was that Tony?" asked Jen, who was curled up on Max's office sofa with a mug of coffee.

"Yes," said Max, "just saying that we shouldn't go near

L2 but that's not a problem. I have no immediate plans to return there."

"I'm really looking forward to seeing The Moon up close," said Jen.

"Mmm, always a romantic," smiled Max.

"It's not that," she snapped back, in typical Jen fashion.

"I know, I know," said Max. "I'm quite looking forward to it myself."

"It's a pity we're not landing. I'd love to see the flag from the original Apollo 11 mission and put my boot marks beside Neil Armstrong's," grinned Jen.

"Vandal!" shouted Max. "They should put a glass dome over that site and keep people like you out!"

Jen was amused at the idea. "Tranquillity Base preserved for posterity. No walkabouts then."

"I should think not," said Max.

"Yeh, I suppose you're right," signed Jen.

"We are going to do a few equatorial orbits and a few polar orbits, can you plot some trajectories for best coverage?" asked Max.

"No problemo," said Jen, getting off the sofa and taking her coffee mug with her. "Later."

Max's phone rang.

"Max, Tony. Look, I'm afraid that your Moon jaunt will have to go on the back burner for now. Something has just come up. I've had The Minister on the phone, seems like the Canadian Police handed your runaways over to a ghost squad. The CIA have lost them again."

Max slapped the side of his head. "Christ! What a bunch of idiots. What do we do now?"

"It gets worse, Max. This thing is bigger than we thought. They tried to make out that it was some maverick operational manager that was behind the incident at Mewton but he was only taking orders from someone higher up. I think that even the great United States Central

Intelligence Agency are out of their depth here. Whoever is behind it wants our activities nipped in the bud."

"Do you think that they will attack again?" asked Max.

"I think that that is a distinct possibility," said Tony. "Much as it galls me, I think that we're going to have to co-operate with The Americans."

Doug Sinclair's first day back at work started out to be a celebration.

"Is your hearing back to normal?" asked Sergei.

"What?" said Doug, looking around and waving his hand. "Only kidding, Sergei. Yes, I can hear just fine. The doctors told me to stay away from noisy night clubs thought."

He patted Sergei on the back.

"I hear that your Moon trip is off?"

"Yes, Doug. For the time being anyway. I think that the powers that be have another mission up their sleeves. Do you have any idea what they have in mind?"

"No, they haven't told me anything," said Doug, "but from what I gather, things are happening in high places."

"What, higher than The Moon?" smiled Sergei.

Doug scowled. "Sergei, this is deadly serious."

Sergei realised that he had touched a raw nerve.

"We have a meeting at Head Office tomorrow," said Doug, "and I believe that there are going to be some big-wigs there."

"The MOD crowd?" asked Sergei.

"Americans!" said Doug. "CIA!"

Sergei looked aghast.

"I know," said Doug, "I am well acquainted with your attitude to Americans and I can't say I'm overjoyed at the prospect of working with them either but I don't think that we have any option. There's something very dangerous going on and we need to pool our resources."

"We're not going to show them The Deltas?" asked Sergei angrily.

"Over my dead body," spat Doug. "I don't object to giving them a wee hand but we are not going to divulge anything about our technologies or methodologies."

"The fugitives in Canada might have got a glimpse of Gertie. We didn't expect them to be up so early," said Sergei.

Doug stared down at the floor. "Well, it's too late to worry about that now. We'll just have to see how things go."

Max recognised Edgar Oppenheim from before but the other two Americans at the board room table were new to him. They introduced themselves.

"I am Michael Thornton, Director of the CIA, and this is Robert Schakowsky, Director of Operations."

Max leaned back in his seat. This meeting was going to be interesting.

Tony Davidson introduced himself and the rest of his team, without saying too much about their positions.

"Mr. Thornton," started Tony, "You have come all this way and I realise that you are very busy people. This must be very important?"

"That is an understatement," said Thornton. "I know that you people have suffered at the hands of some of our countrymen and I apologise for that most sincerely. Initially, we thought it was the work of a madman working on his own but subsequent inquiries have shown that this is not so. This is the work of a highly resourced subversive network. We don't yet know who they are or what their aims are. What we do know is that they are a threat to our national security and that of many other nations. So far, we have only identified a few of them. Some are under detention but we haven't been able to glean anything useful from them. The individuals you helped apprehend in Canada were spirited off as soon as they got back on

American soil. We know that one has gone to ground in Florida. The more dangerous one, Landers, thinks that he has slipped us but we are letting him run for now. We know his every move. He may be smart, but he's not that smart!"

"Mr. Thornton, not to beat around the bush, you didn't come all this way to tell us about your, em, misadventures. What exactly is it that you want from McGregor Aerospace?" asked Tony.

Thornton held up his hand. "Yes, you are right Mr. Davidson. We do need a favour. It has come to my attention that you might have certain … facilities … at your disposal. Now get me straight, I … we … are not trying to pry into your business. It's just that you might have some capabilities that we don't currently possess."

The room went quiet.

"And these 'capabilities'", said Tony, "what would they be required to do?"

Thornton gave a twisted smile. "I'm not here to point any fingers," he said, "and, I can assure you that there's no question of any incriminations. A few months ago, an American military surveillance satellite mysteriously disappeared from orbit. We don't know exactly what happened to it."

Max glanced over at Doug and Sergei.

"Other satellites were mysteriously repurposed and, I am embarrassed to say, one such satellite was compromised and used to commit this act of wanton destruction upon yourselves. As you are well aware, the so-called 'Star Wars' initiative was supposedly put to bed decades ago. Today, armed satellites are not meant to exist and as far as the US Government are concerned, they don't. Unfortunately, there are those of the belief that scrapping killer satellites was a mite premature. Gentlemen, there are still such weapons in orbit round this planet. These satellites are NOT under our control."

There was a nervous shuffle round the room.

"All I can say is that if theses rogue satellites were to mysteriously fall out of the sky, the world would be a safer and more secure place."

"Can you actually identify these satellites?" asked Max.

"Mr. Hayden, isn't it? Correct me if I'm wrong but I imagine that you know a thing or two about all the stuff that's spinning around up there in low Earth orbit, and further out?"

Max was flabbergasted, or was he just being paranoid?

"We don't know what half of that shit is, or who it belongs to. Some of it used to belong to us. I say 'used to' because somebody lost track of it. You might ask how somebody…" he pointed at himself, "could lose a satellite that cost billions of dollars to develop and send into orbit. Well, let me tell you, it happens! We're not proud of it, but it does."

Thornton peered around his audience like a comedian pacing a joke.

"You ask me if we can identify these things? Well yes, if you give me a drawing or photograph, point at one across the room and say, 'is this it?' I can identify it. Anybody could. What we are talking about here are things the size of a small car a couple of hundred miles away – or more. They have no lights. Their electronics have been put to sleep so they put out no tell-tale signals. We might just know there is 'something' there but no, to answer your question, we can't identify it. That, Mr. Hayden, is where you can help!"

Max's paranoia got even worse.

"What I'm suggesting, Mr. Hayden, is that we give you the drawings, you get up close and whack them. I know you can do it."

Tony broke in, "Mr. Thornton, I'm not sure where you got your information but, for the sake of argument, if 'somebody' was to get up close to these satellites, identify them and 'whack' them, as you so colourfully put it, it sort of suggests that we might have some offensive capabilities. I can assure you that we do not. Our operations here are purely scientific research."

"Oh, come on," said Thornton, "I know that you took a surveillance satellite out without using weapons. I don't know how you did it but the fact is, you did. I'm not going to ask how you do it, I'm just asking that you do."

Thornton put a USB drive on the table. "Here's what they look like, now please, do the world a favour."

The meeting broke up with no agreement or commitments whatsoever, but Max had a pretty good idea what was in store for him.

Max, Sergei and Jen were in Doug's meeting room at Mewton Base. They were viewing pictures of killer satellites on a large monitor.

"I'm sure that we saw one like that out at L2," said Jen.

"Yes, you're right," said Max. "But why it is way out there is anybody's guess. It's not as if they could do any damage at that distance."

"Oh, but they could," said Sergei. "Once missiles are launched, given an initial kick, they would just travel to Earth. It would take a week or more but eventually, they would get here and, given a few minor course adjustments from another satellite or two in low Earth orbit, they could hit anywhere on the planet with the precision of military GPS."

"And nobody would have a clue where they came from," said Doug. "Neat!"

"But, how will we find them?" asked Max.

Jen jumped up. "Max, remember how I used the radiation deflector array to locate 'the night watchman'. I'm pretty sure that these satellites must have atomic fission reactors, dirty ones. We'll be able to spot them from a hundred miles away, or more, even in their quiescent state."

"Okay," said Max, "suppose that we do locate them, how do we knock them out – remembering that the last time we used the G-drives to do it, we damaged one and nearly didn't make it back?"

"Yes, that's a problem," said Sergei. "I don't like abusing tools."

"And, I wouldn't want to get too close to a satellite that might have nuclear warheads on board," said Max.

"I have an idea," said Sergei. "We don't need any explosive weapons, I can rig-up a railgun."

Max smiled. "You're a genius Sergei. It wouldn't need to be particularly sophisticated. Poke a few heavy iron bars at the satellites using electromagnetic coils and the sheer kinetic energy should shatter them, even if they didn't have warheads aboard. We have all the power we need on tap with our little fission power plant. It could just be slung under Gertie's belly and I can do the targeting with the helmet display."

"The electromagnetic coil is no problem," said Sergei, "but we don't want it to be a one-shot affair like a musket. What we need is a magazine or a belt feed. Let me sleep on it!"

* * *

John Landers had his phone to his ear as he swung the small speedboat towards the sandy beach. He cut the engine and glided in until the nose touched the sand. Ellie got up from her wicker seat at the beach bar and waved furiously. Landers pulled the boat out of the water and headed up the beach towards Ellie. They didn't hear the 'click, click, click' of a camera shutter on an offshore cabin cruiser.

"Ellie, how've you been?" said Landers, giving the woman a hug. Ellie's body more than filled-out the jazzy swimsuit. In her straw sunhat and dark glasses, she could have been anybody, but Landers had known her since their teens. She waved the barman over.

"Jack Daniels on the rocks," she ordered, "and I'll have another of your 'Yellow Birds'." She looked Landers up and down. "I like you clean shaven," she smiled, "really suits you."

Landers stroked his smooth chin. He still hadn't had a haircut and it was starting to get long.

"Oh, it would be nice to live here," said Ellie, "but I suppose that you have other plans?" she added disdainfully.

"We'll be out of here tomorrow," said Landers.

"Where are we going?" she asked.

"Florida."

"Ooh," she said, sitting up.

"But not the nice part," Landers continued. Ellie sank back in her chair.

"I'm meeting someone here. Don't say anything about when and where we are going," he said.

Not long after, another blonde-haired man joined them at the beach bar table.

"John," he nodded.

"Hi Frank, this is Ellie," said Landers.

"Hi," she said. The man didn't respond.

"Want a drink?" asked Landers. The man waved his hand in dismissal.

Offshore, the camera shutter clicked again and again.

"John, I don't quite know how to tell you this but the word is that they're going to retire you," said the blonde man.

"Retire?" gulped Landers, sitting upright.

"You have become a liability. My advice is to watch your back." He gave a little wave as he walked away.

Ellie put on a grim face. "I don't think that I am going to

like this."

"Ellie, check out tomorrow morning and meet me at the airport at three - except pretend that you don't know me, and sit well away from me on the plane."

Ellie was liking this less and less.

Landers headed back to his speedboat at the water's edge. He heaved it backwards into the sea, waded out and got in. The outboard sprung to life and the boat left a long frothy white wake as it left the bay.

The camera shutter continued to click.

* * *

Sergei's solution to the railgun problem was simple and elegant. Instead of wrestling with the engineering problems of auto-feeding the iron projectiles onto the rails, he fitted Auntie Gertie with six single shot railguns.

"Nice," said Max, patting the device hanging from Gertie's underside.

"You realise that once you have fired one of these babies, that's it?" asked Sergei.

"Yes, I am more used to firing conventional guided missiles," said Max, "at least you can steer those to the target."

"Haha," said Sergei, "These slugs will be travelling at upwards of a thousand metres a second. If you miss, they will just keep going."

"More like firing a long range rifle then," said Max "except I won't be able to sight-in. I also won't be able to 'point' the railguns at anything, since they are rigidly attached to Gertie. All I can do is point Gertie."

"Yes, but Gertie is a much more stable firing platform than any conventional aircraft. All I have to do is to align the railguns so that their shots converge on a point, say, five kilometres away. If you track the first shot and it is slightly off target, you can compensate for subsequent shots with the computer. Railgun shots go perfectly straight for a very long distance, even in the atmosphere. In the void of space, they will just keep going forever, until they hit something – or not!"

"I'd still like to have something to calibrate my helmet display," said Max.

"How about a sighting laser?" asked Sergei.

"Yes, that might work," said Max. "Sergei, you have this knack of coming up with the most simple solutions. I doff my cap to you."

Sergei beamed broadly. A compliment from Max was rare indeed.

CHAPTER NINETEEN

Michael Thornton grinned. The photos his men had taken from the cabin cruiser off Nassau clearly showed Landers having a meeting with Frank Sanchez.

"Sanchez," he said pointing at a photo. "So he's mixed-up in all this."

Schakowsky smiled. "Well, we know whose pocket he is in. Benjamin Rafael!"

"Now, things are starting to make sense," said Thornton. Rafael was a failed politician whose right wing views were even too strong for the Republican Party to stomach. He had inherited billions from his father, a semi-respected industrialist, but the money was not invested nor put to any good use. Instead, it was used to promote his political ambitions and provide financing for anyone else who shared his warped ideals. He liked to think of himself as a puppeteer, the trouble was that some of his puppets were also in high places – including in the military. Instead of pulling strings, he pushed dollars.

"We have a file on Rafael that goes on and on, but he's Teflon coated. Can't get anything to stick," said Thornton.

"Give him time and he will make a mistake," said Schakowsky.

"I think that time is near at hand," smirked Thornton. "Now we have a link with a paper trail."

John Landers left the plane at Miami International Airport. Ellie stayed a respectable distance behind him on the long walk through to the arrivals lounge. When he stopped at the car-hire desk, she kept her distance. She had packed light for Nassau so she only had a grip to carry. When he moved off towards the hire car parking lot, she stuck behind him. When he had found his car, he opened the back passenger door and she got in.

"John, I'm a bit worried by all this cloak and dagger stuff. Won't you tell me what's going on?"

"The less you know, the better," he said as he started the car, "for both our sakes."

He headed off down Highway 41 in the direction of Naples on the Florida west coast. When they reached Big Cypress National Reserve, they turned off into The Everglades. The two hour drive took them to Chokoloskee Island and they pulled into a trailer park. Landers found the office trailer and went in.

"Hi, you have a trailer booked in the name of Murray?" he asked the disinterested woman behind a small desk.

"Sign in," she said, pointing at a form on the desk. She fumbled with her computer.

"Pre-paid for a month?" she asked.

"Guess so," said Landers. He didn't know exactly what Thomson had arranged. The woman turned to a rack of keys behind her and took a ring down.

"Number forty seven," said the woman abruptly, slapping down the keys on the desk. "Here's a list of dos and don'ts."

It was about eight in the evening when Landers heard a knock on the trailer door. He opened it cautiously. There was Abe Thompson.

"Abe," said Landers, holding out his hand. "Thanks for setting this up."

"No problem," said Thompson. "Hope everything is okay?"

"Yeh, fine," said Landers. "Look, I have something important to tell you." He took Thompson by the arm and led him away from the trailer. "Seems that we have lost favour in high places."

"Huh?" said Thompson.

"I've been told by one of Raphael's gooks that we are no longer needed."

Thompson looked stunned.

"What did he say?"

"He said that I was being 'retired'. That's means that *we* are being retired."

"John, nobody leaves that organisation alive," said Thompson.

"I know," said Landers, with a worried look. "We had better keep on the move for a while. And Abe, I don't think we should meet up like this. If one of us is being trailed, they will find both of us."

"Right," said Thompson.

They shook hands and parted.

* * *

"The Americans have given us the last known orbits of a couple of their rogue satellites," said Jen, tapping the keyboard of her on-board computer. Max's helmet display showed a diagram of the satellites' paths with dots representing their current projected positions.

"Have to start somewhere," said Max. "This one looks to be the closest, I'm heading over there."

Auntie Gertie was three hundred miles up so objects in low Earth orbit would be below her. Max closed the distance between him and the nearest satellite and dropped altitude. His helmet display showed their position and that of the satellite. As they approached the satellite's supposed position, Max switched to visual scan.

"Nope, there's nothing there," he moaned. "Nothing but us in a hundred mile sphere. Radar shows a couple of objects but they have matches in our database. What we are looking for won't be in the database."

"Okay," said Jen, "I will tell the computer that and get it to alert us to unknown objects."

Max changed course towards another suspect. Ten minutes later, an object position blinked in his display.

"That's an unknown," said Jen. "Let's have a closer look."

Max manoeuvred to within a hundred feet of the object and matched its orbit. The camera zoomed-in to show the details on the satellite.

"Yup, that's one," he said, "perfect match."

"You absolutely sure?" asked Sergei.

"Yes, look for yourself," said Max. He superimposed the live camera feed onto a stock shot that the Americans had provided. He altered Gertie's position slightly until the two images corresponded exactly.

"Yes," said Sergei, "we have our first target. Better move back a bit, Max. If that thing has nuclear warheads aboard, we could be in the blast zone."

"Won't our radiation shielding protect us from that?" asked Max.

"It will protect us from the radiation," said Sergei, "but not from the expanding sphere of debris travelling at thousands of miles per hour in every direction."

"Mmm, yes, I see what you mean," said Max.

Sergei continued, "It will just keep going until it succumbs to The Earth's gravity, then it will re-enter the upper atmosphere and burn up on re-entry."

Max backed Gertie up from the target a good ten miles.

"Should be safe here," he said and lit-up his targeting laser. Even at that distance, he could plainly see the bright green dot playing on the side of the satellite.

"Okay, here goes," he said pressing on the mushroom-shaped protrusion on his armrest. There was a noticeable lurch as the railgun sent its slug of iron towards the target. It only took a few seconds before the satellite erupted in a white hot sphere.

"Bingo," shouted Jen.

"Prepare for incoming," called Sergei, but there were only a few light bumps as pieces of metal that weren't vaporised in the atomic explosion bounced-off Gertie's hull.

"I had half expected a shock wave," said Max.

"Not in space, Max," said Sergei. "You need atmosphere to propagate shock waves."

In the following three hours, Max had identified and disposed of two more satellites. One of them flared like the first one, the second just disintegrated without any fireworks.

"Well, that should have taken care of the ones in low orbit but we've still got to deal with whatever is out at L2."

"Oh, not another long trip," said Jen.

"'Fraid so," said Max, "but we've done enough for today. The first duck-shoot was a big success."

Max, Sergei and Jen worked to fine-tune Auntie Gertie and her systems. Max's first priority was to be able to fire the railguns from further away. In outer space, the expanding mass of debris from exploding satellites would not be affected by gravity and would just go shooting off in every direction indefinitely. Feedback from Gertie's computer showed the offset from the laser targeting spot to the railgun projectile's point of impact. It was only six inches out but as the firing range increased, so would the offset. He made adjustments.

Jen tweaked some of Gertie's computer's sub-routines. Some she had coded on-the-fly when they were up in space. They needed to be cleaned-up and optimised. It was easier to do this with her system in the lab. When she was happy, she uploaded the new code to Gertie.

Sergei was happy with the way Gertie was performing. The new railguns worked surprisingly well too, even though they had been installed in a hurry. Instead of tinkering with what was working just fine, he decided to install a microwave oven and a small fridge. Gertie's cockpit was tiny, and cramped, but he managed to find space at the side of *his* couch for the two appliances. He hated the food in tubes. It looked like toothpaste and tasted vile, mostly because of its pasty texture. He wanted some real food onboard, if only for himself.

The second million mile journey to the Sun-Earth Lagrangian L2 point was more relaxed than the first. This time, they took turns to sleep. Max was more familiar with Gertie's handling now and took their acceleration up to ninety five percent. They could do the million miles in a day and a quarter. He sunk back into his couch and dozed-off.

Mr. Burrage was waiting for him in his dream.

"Boys like to make things go bang," he said. "Explosions are fun."

"I wasn't doing it for fun," explained Max, "it was a job that had to be done."

"Quite so, boy. Quite so."

"Can I ask you a question?" said Max.

"What about?" asked Burrage.

"Time travel," said Max.

"Mmm, tricky subject." said Burrage. "Do you have something specific in mind?"

"Yes," said Max. "I have been in this realm for months now. Katie will be wondering what has happened to me. She will probably have assumed the worst and moved on with her life. If I can go back to my own realm, is it possible to go back to the time when I should have returned?"

"Interesting question, Hayden." Mr. Burrage stroked his chin. "Theoretically, yes. It is possible, but finding the correct realm entry point is an extremely difficult task. The mathematics would require working with trillions upon trillions of places past the decimal point. The total number of realms is a number approaching infinity. You can only approach infinity, you understand, you can never reach it."

Max's nod passed from his dream state into real life. Sergei could see his head move up and down and wondered what was going on in there.

"So, it is possible if you have the technology to do the calculations involved?" asked Max.

"Yes," replied Mr. Burrage. "Do you have such technology?"

"No," said Max. "I don't, but I bet you do?"

"Me?" said Burrage in mock surprise. "I still use my slide rule."

Max didn't believe Mr. Burrage. Even in his dream state he could tell when he was being lied to.

"Okay, Mr. Burrage. Can you tell me what sort of computer would be required to do that kind of calculation?"

"Well, it would take massive processing power, even with quantum computers. Take the brain power of every being on your planet and multiply that by a centillion – that is 10 to the power of three hundred and three."

Max had no concept of such numbers.

"Does such processing power exist?" asked Max, hopefully.

Mr. Burrage looked flustered.

"I think that's enough for today." He vanished.

Max's dream changed theme, which was unusual. He dreamt of Katie and the good times they had together. He thought about her all the time in his waking state - now, she had joined him in his dreams. Was that the best he could hope for?

Max awoke.

"Must have been some dream?" smiled Sergei.

"What?" said Max.

"You were nodding in your sleep. Must have been

agreeing with someone. Who was it?"

"Oh, Mr. Burrage," said Max. "He tells me that to return to our exact realm position would require nearly infinite processing power."

"I suspect that he is right," said Sergei, somewhat puzzled. Max had spoken of his old physics master on several occasions before but never in such lucid detail.

Max sighed. "The dolphin people obviously have the processing power; they were able to send us back to a very similar realm than the one we came from. It should be possible to get us to a more accurate realm point if they really tried."

"If they were so minded," said Sergei. "I don't think that they care all that much."

Jen snored in her reclining couch. It was only possible for them to sleep on their backs. They were firmly strapped-in so there was no way to turn to the side.

"Better wake her up," said Max, "she's not going to want to miss the fireworks."

Two hours later, they had the target satellite within visual range.

"Seems to be a variant on the ones we hit before," said Max.

"Yes," said Jen. "There are some bulges that were missing on the others."

"Let's go in for a closer look," said Max, taking Gertie in to a few hundred feet of the object.

"I'm getting quite strong radiation readings," said Jen. "There must be a nuclear power plant and multiple warheads."

"I wouldn't want to be too close to that when it goes up," said Sergei. "Take Gertie back as far as you can."

Max lit-up the target with his targeting laser. He could see the green spot with his helmet display on full magnification but it was wobbling around considerably.

"Fire," shouted Max, as he released the railgun projectile. They waited for the inevitable explosion but it didn't happen.

"Bugger, missed," said Max.

"Take it easy," said Sergei. "No need to rush it."

Max's second shot missed the target too.

"Focus," shouted Sergei. "You are shaking too much when you press the trigger."

"Okay," said Max and relaxed back into his couch. He centred the laser spot right in the middle of the satellite and waited. Then he pressed the button. All hell broke loose. The satellite exploded like a supernova. An expanding sphere of hot plasma spread-out to fill most of the sky in front of them.

"Wow," said Jen. "That's a big bang. What did they have in there."

They waited for the expected rain of metal debris to hit Gertie, but nothing happened.

"Totally vaporised," said Serge. "Everything was blasted to atoms."

They watched as the explosion faded away to a point. Max scanned the epicentre of the explosion with a sweep of wavelengths.

"Well and truly gone," he grinned. "Mission complete. I've got some good footage to show the folks back home."

"Great," said Jen.

"Ah, wait a minute," said Max. "Look over there. The night watchman, I think we have just woken him up." The massive object that had previously been impossibly black was now quite visible. It was egg-shaped, metallic and seemed like it was coming to life. Lights came on, details on the surface resolved and rotated.

"Oh my," said Sergei. "Got to get some shots of this. Max, can you give us a tour?"

The crew were so engrossed in examining the object that they didn't notice the approach of two circular craft until they were above and below them.

"Oho," cried Jen. "Dolphins!"

As the two craft got closer, Max could feel himself losing control of Gertie.

"They have locked-on to us," he yelled. "Stand by to be taken for a ride."

The speed readings in Max's helmet went off the scale as they were pulled through space in a gravity lock. He had never before seen stars fly past, but he did now.

"We must be approaching light speed," said Sergei.

Suddenly a hazy bright ring opened before them and everything went black.

Just like the previous time, Max came-to floating in the middle of a white haze. He felt a little apprehensive, curious maybe, but certainly not fear.

"Everybody okay?" he called.

Sergei and Jen were present and correct.

"Hello," called Max. "Anybody here?"

He was expecting words to coalesce on his helmet display as they had before but no words came. He was puzzled.

"Hello," he called again.

The mist started to thin. It looked like it was being sucked into a nozzle in the ceiling. As the mist cleared, Max could see a figure standing in front of him – a human figure.

"Hayden?"

It was a familiar voice with an English accent.

"Can you see this?" Max called to his companions.

"Nothing but white smoke," answered Sergei.

"Same here," said Jen.

The figure stepped forward. It was Mr. Burrage.

"Can you see him now?" asked Max.

"No," replied Sergei and Jen in unison.

"Why did you attack the night watchman?" asked Burrage.

"We didn't attack it," protested Max. "We were blowing-up a rogue satellite."

"With nuclear weapons?" asked the figure.

"No," said Max. It had nuclear weapons on board, they exploded when we hit it with a kinetic projectile."

Mr. Burrage sighed. Max looked around but couldn't see his crew.

"Have we done any damage?" asked Max.

Burrage chuckled. "No, no damage but you have woken the night watchman up."

"Is that a problem?" asked Max.

"No, when the perceived threat is gone, the watchman will go back to sleep," said Mr. Burrage.

"Oh," said Max and then called out to his crew again. "Sergei, Jen, are you getting all this?"

"No, just white smoke here," said Sergei. "Can't see or hear a thing."

Mr. Burrage spoke again, "They are alright, only you can see me. Now, you asked me about time travel?"

"Did I?" asked Max.

"You might not remember it, but you did."

Max could remember parts of his Mr. Burrage dreams, but not this particular question.

"You asked me if it was possible to go back to a particular point in your original realm. I told you that it was very difficult but I think that I have found a way to get you close to that point."

"Really," gasped Max.

"Yes, it has taken the sum total of our processing power but I think we have the answer."

"You say 'our processing power', who exactly are you?" asked Max.

"You wouldn't understand," said Burrage. "It is something beyond the scope of human knowledge."

"Can't you just try to explain?" asked Max.

"I will try to put it into terms you can understand," said Burrage. "Many of your brains connected together."

"Inside heads?" asked Max.

"No heads, just brain," said Burrage.

"Are they organic brains?"

"A long time ago, they were organic – and separate. Now there is unity and the organics have been replaced with synthetic."

"So, you are one big massive artificial brain?" asked Max.

"In your terms, yes. You wouldn't understand the actuality."

"And what about individual personalities?" asked Max, " or have they all 'unified' as you put it?"

"I can't begin to explain this to you, Hayden. You will have to accept what I have told you and leave it at that."

"So, what is this Mr. Burrage thing? Why do you look like my old physics teacher?"

"I told you before, you see what you want to see."

"Okay, what about helping us with our technology?"

"I have told you that before too, I am not allowed to do that. I can only observe. I gave you a little help before, but I was reprimanded for that."

"You were reprimanded," cried Max. "Who reprimanded you, you said you were one big brain?"

"You wouldn't understand. There is one 'big brain' as you put it, but it has many nodes. I suppose that you would refer to them as personalities."

"Right," said Max. "I think I know where you are coming from. Now, you are going to send us back to a point in time, in *our* realm and everything will be as before?"

"No, that is impossible. What I said was that it would

be close to the point where you were before. It won't be identical, it will be close."

Max considered the possibilities. Was Burrage talking about the difference in hue of a coat of paint somewhere or about people going off into different timelines?

"I think that you will be happy," said Burrage.

"And what happens to the little gift that you gave us, the inertial damper?"

"Sorry, I have to take that back. Everything has to be returned to its previous state. You craft will be exactly the way it was when you first visited here."

Max didn't care about that. The prospect of being with Katie again pushed everything else out of his mind.

Max woke up in low Earth orbit. Sergei was on the couch beside him and Jen, somewhere between and further back. It took a few minutes to think what he was going to say.

"Sergei, Jen, what did you get from that meeting?

"Meeting?" asked Sergei. "I didn't meet anyone. I asked questions but didn't get any answers at all."

"Me neither?" said Jen. "What did you find out?"

"Quite a lot," said Max. "Mr. Burrage told me…"

"Mr. Burrage," snapped Sergei, "Max, have you slept all through this?"

"No," said Max. "I'll try to explain – but you might not understand me."

First thing they noticed on the way back down was that they were experiencing G-force again.

"Oh dear, that's going to slow us down," said Max. "No more million mile trips in twenty seven hours."

Familiar voices greeted them as they approached Mewton base.

"Clear to land, Max," said Ivan in the control centre.

Max looked down as they came into land. There was no sign of the rubble that had been excavated from the lower levels that were so badly damaged.

Doug met them in the hangar as they stepped down from Gertie's cockpit.

"You've been away for a long time," said Doug. "Where have you been?"

"How long were we away?" asked Max. "I've kinda lost my bearings."

"Six days," said Doug. "I thought that you would only be gone for a day at most."

Max shrugged. "Doesn't time fly when you are enjoying yourself?"

The team de-suited and Max went straight to his office. In the corridor, he met the two Chinese girls, Li Yan and Ying Chen. They greeted him as they walked past. Everything looked normal except Ying Chen - surely she had died in the explosion? Max shook his head.

"Haven't seen you for a few days, been away Max?" asked Li Yan.

"Oh, yes," said Max, "company business."

He sat down at his desk and lifted his phone. He wanted to call Katie but was totally afraid. Doug walked in and he put the phone down quickly.

"Max, I'd love to hear what you have to report."

Max paused, "How's your hearing, Doug?"

"What, my hearing is fine. What are you talking about?"

Max shook his head again. In this realm, the explosion at Mewton Base had never happened.

"Oh nothing, forget what I just said, Doug. I'm a bit punch-drunk from the trip."

"You'd better head off home and recuperate for a couple of days," said Doug. "When you feel fit, we'll have a debrief and then I have something interesting lined-up for you, but

I won't talk about it now. Off with you."

Doug shooed Max out of his office and Max didn't object. He wanted to get back home and see that Katie was where she should be more than anything.

CHAPTER TWENTY

John Landers paced up and down the dimly lit operations room bathed in the glow of workstation monitors. The view on the large wall monitors showed a satellite image of a part of Central England passing below. Superimposed along the bottom of the image, a set of GPS co-ordinates, accurate to less than a foot, changed too rapidly to be read.

"I know they are there somewhere," he said to himself. "I'm bloody sure of it."

"What was that, John?" said a man seated at one of the workstations.

"Oh, nothing, just talking to myself," said Landers.

A phone rang.

"Sir, there's a General Thompson on the phone."

Landers snatched the phone and turned to face a wall.

"Thompson, I told you not to ring me here."

"John, I have a message for you. Rafael's people want to talk to you – immediately. Usual place."

Rafael's people? he thought to himself, *is this a trick?*

"Huh? Okay, tell them I'll be there in an hour."

Landers handed the phone back.

"Gotta go out for a while," he barked.

Landers could see Thompson and two others sitting at a table inside the diner. They seemed to be having a heated argument. The two strangers glared at him as he walked over from the door.

"What's the problem?" he asked.

"Sit down and shut up," said one of the two and pointed at the empty seat. "You promised us some drawings for an avionics system and experimental aircraft. The boss is getting impatient."

Landers shuffled in his chair.

"Yes, there was a slight hitch with that."

"Hitch, what do you mean hitch? Have you got them or haven't you?" snarled one of the strangers.

"Not exactly," coughed Landers. "One of my men screwed up."

The stranger drummed the table with his fingers.

"The boss doesn't like hitches!"

The two men got up and walked over to the door of the diner. One turned round and brought his finger down to point at Landers. He mimed shooting and blowing away the smoke. They left.

Landers took a bottle of pills out of his pocket and swallowed some dry.

"What can I get ya?" asked the waitress.

"Nothing, we're just leaving," said Landers.

"Bloody nerve," said the waitress, "use this place as a meeting room and don't even buy a cup of coffee." She gave him an up-stretched finger.

Landers and Thompson walked over to where their cars were parked.

"Abe, I don't like this. I think that we'd better lie low for a while. I'll take Ellie on vacation, have you got somewhere you can go?"

"Oh yes," answered Thompson. "I have a little shack in the Florida Everglades. It would be nice to go down there for a while."

They drove off in opposite directions.

Max's first clue that things were going to be all right was that his Six Series BMW was white, as opposed to being cream the last time he came back. Next was the pub sign on the way into the village: it showed a dog and duck. That was right. He drove to the cottage and pulled into the lane. Katie's Mini was there where it usually sat. He looked at the curtains in the window. Yes, they were cream with a rose pattern. That was right. He put his key in the door and turned it. It worked.

He was only just inside the door when Katie burst into the hallway.

"Max! Where have you been? I've been so worried."

Max held her tightly. He tried to hide the tears in his eyes.

"Oh, had to go away for a bit, top secret stuff, you know."

Katie stood back and looked him up and down.

"Somewhere exotic, no doubt?" she asked.

"A bit," said Max. "Can't really talk about it." He pulled her towards him and kissed her.

"Oh, Maxie. I wish you weren't so secretive."

"I'm sorry, Katie. It goes with the job I'm afraid," he said, still holding on tight.

"Maxie, I have some news," she said standing back. She patted her tummy. "I'm eating for two."

Max didn't see that coming.

"What?" he yelled, "you're pregnant?"

Katie smiled and did a little curtsey.

Max's gasp of surprise turned to a huge grin.

"You are pleased about it, aren't you?" she asked.

"Yes, of course I am. Why wouldn't I be? Oh Katie."

They danced round the room in a tight embrace.

Max hadn't yet taken it all in. They had always been so careful. They hadn't even talked about kids. How could this have happened? Then he remembered Mr. Burrage's words: 'Close.' Well, if this was the worst that was going to happen, he could live with it.

"Oh, and I've found the most wonderful antique crib," she added.

Max went looking for his bottle of single malt. Katie curled up on the sofa with a book of knitting patterns.

Max slept well. Mr. Burrage no longer invaded his dreams and Katie was wrapped around him in bed. Much as they liked the cottage they were renting, it was time to start looking for a house of their own. Katie really relished house hunting, Max not so much. They spent the next day visiting estate agents and searching online. Katie knew exactly the kind of house she wanted, something big and Victorian. Max preferred something more modern. He fancied Art Deco but there was nothing remotely like that where they lived.

It was the mid afternoon when Max suggested that they go out for an evening meal. They had, after all, something to celebrate.

"Maxie, remember Giovanni's?" she asked. "It would be lovely to go there again."

"Yes, but it is a two and a half hour drive," said Max, shaking his head.

"Oh, I don't mean tonight," she said slapping his shoulder. "Just sometime."

"Yes, if we are ever in the area, we'll go to Giovani's."

"Remember we were sitting having coffee on the veranda and we saw those things up in the sky?"

"Yes, I remember, where would you like to go tonight?" Changing the subject didn't work.

"Did you ever find out what they were?" she asked.

"Oh, yes. I asked around and it seems that they were weather monitoring platforms," he lied.

"How odd," she replied. "I quite fancy something fishy tonight."

"The Crooked Bough is good for seafood", said Max, "or so I hear."

"We'll go there then," said Katie.

"Katie, there is something I've always been meaning to ask you," said Max, slowly. "Why did you not go on with your modelling career?"

"Oh that," she said. "An unfortunate set of circumstances."

"How so?"

"I was with this modelling agency in London, Hamptons in Knightsbridge. They got me a few jobs but nothing like enough to make a living. This guy that worked there, real bitch he was, told me that I was too fat, that I needed to lose weight to get work. Anyway, I started skipping meals then it gradually progressed to full blown bulimia. Didn't get me any more work. I just became very ill and ended-up in hospital."

"And that was the end of you modelling career?" asked Max.

"Not immediately," she said. "I had my portfolio with some good pictures and took it to another agency. They got me some work but it was for mail order catalogues. Horrible, horrible clothes. I just couldn't stick it any more."

"So, if you had stuck with your modelling, you might be hitched-up with some rich playboy and lying on the deck of a yacht in St. Tropez by now?"

"Instead, I am stuck with an ugly, bald-headed so-and-so who goes off for days without telling me where he is, all under the guise of 'secret missions'." She went over, sat on his knee and wrapped her arms around his neck.

"And, I suppose we are going to have an ugly, bald-headed baby," he smiled.

She tugged his cheek and kissed him.

She jumped up. "Oh, I need to see if my purple dress still fits for tonight!"

Max was in a state of confusion. He found it difficult to separate two sets of memories. In one set, he had come home to find Katie expecting a baby. In another set, Katie was a top model and had never heard of him. In one memory, Gertie had been armed with railguns and had destroyed four rogue satellites. In this realm, there was no inertial damper and all was well at Mewton base. Now, however, he had to face a debriefing session with Tony and the men from The Ministry. He had to tell them, again, about the encounter with the dolphins – the first one. The second one never happened in this realm. Sergei and Jen also had two sets of memories, he had checked. They agreed that they would try to forget what happened and never to speak of it. It was difficult. They each had months of memories of the future and, with time, it would become increasingly difficult to separate them.

When Max and his team had told the audience in the board room what had happened, the first time, they asked the same questions as they did before. Was the rendezvous repeatable? Did they share any of their technology? Max rolled out the same answers. No, he couldn't find the dolphins and their spacetime portal. No, they did not share any of their mind blowing secrets. Had Max not showed the close-up videos of the dolphin 'saucers' rolling playfully in their path, the others round the table would have come away very disappointed. Max handed out his report and, again, they all agreed to keep the whole affair under wraps.

As they left head office, Doug came over to Max.

"You handled that very well," said Doug, patting him on the back. Max wanted to say that he had a dress rehearsal a few months ago but he didn't. The fact that he had gone back in time to be where he was now was causing him great mental difficulties.

"Oh Max, can I see you and Sergei in my office in the morning. I told you that we have some ideas and I want to run them past you. I think you'll like them."

"Yes, sure Doug. Oh, by the way. I've just found out that I'm going to be a daddy. I just wanted you to be the first to know."

"Oh Max, I'm so happy for you," said Doug, giving him a man hug. Then a thought occurred to him.

"I hope that this isn't going to affect anything at work?"

"I haven't had time for it to sink-in, Doug," said Max. "I can't begin to think about the future just yet."

It was a strange thing to say; he was trying his damnedest to forget the future.

Max and Sergei were sitting round a desk with Doug.

"What do you think of old Max here," Doug asked of Sergei, making a cradle with his arms.

"Yes, I've heard," said Sergei grinning. "It doesn't seem like Max."

Max scowled. He still didn't believe it himself.

Jen came into the room and put her arms round Max from behind.

"Just heard the good news, Max. Congratulations."

Max turned and smiled at her.

"Do you want to join us, Jen?" asked Doug. "You might find this interesting."

Jen sat down and folded her arms on the table.

Doug started, "The powers that be are very impressed with your work. They have asked me to pass-on their sincere congratulations."

He smiled and paused.

"Needless to say, they have been thinking hard about how we progress with this technology."

He paused again, waiting for a reaction.

"This kind of work requires a *lot* of financial backing and although McGregor Aerospace and its partners overseas are prepared to invest in the future, their pockets are not bottomless. We do get some money from the government at the minute but they want to increase their contribution substantially."

Doug looked round the room.

"Of course, there is a catch, before you ask, they want something in return," he said.

"I know what you are going to say before you say it," said Max.

Doug smiled.

"Yes," said Doug. "How do you feel about arming Auntie Gertie?"

Max looked at Sergei for a reaction.

"It's got to happen sometime," shrugged Sergei.

"And when it does," said Doug, "we want to be the leaders in the field."

"What kind of weapons are they thinking of?" asked Max.

"Anything that they put on modern fighters, I guess," said Doug. "Missiles, precision-guided ordinance, cannons."

"What, no ray guns?" asked Max.

Doug grimaced. "The Americans have advanced laser weapon technology but they don't share it with us. Maybe somewhere down the line."

Sergei interrupted, "How about railguns?"

Doug nodded. "Yes, that is a possibility. Have you had any experience with railguns?"

Max put his head in his arms on the table to hide his amusement. Jen put her hand over her mouth and feigned a cough.

"Oh, I'm sure that I could fix-up something," said Sergei seriously. Max and Jen struggled to cover-up their mirth.

"Is there something I'm missing out on here?" asked Doug. "I get the impression that I'm being left out of something."

Max straightened-up and composed himself. "Sounds like an excellent idea, Sergei. Maybe rig-up a targeting laser too?"

Sergei pointed at him and gave a nod to the suggestion.

"Maybe something a little more powerful than a targeting laser. We have the power source. Anything The Americans can do, Sergei Bazarov can do better."

"Well, as far as the company is concerned, we would like you to proceed with this project ASAP. We are also thinking of converting the Delta 2 drone to carry a crew. The frame is identical, we had anticipated that we would want to do this at some time so most of the superstructure is already in place. Delta 2 is not quite up to Gertie's current specs but we can work on that."

"Oh, we have some other ideas," said Max. "We were thinking of adding some radiation shielding so that we can go further out from Earth."

"Yes, good suggestion," said Doug. "Look into it and give me some costings."

"Before you go," said Doug, "I'd just like you to know that we have appointed a new member to the team. She will be starting tomorrow and I hope that you give her your full support."

"What does she do?" asked Max.

"Er, she's a pilot," smiled Doug. "From the Navy, just like you, Max. She will be a little more up-to-date with modern weaponry. Her name is Abi Bristow."

Max was taken aback and a bit annoyed. It wasn't the fact that a girl was potentially taking over his job, it was the fact that somebody considered him to be getting a bit long in the tooth with naval weapon technology. When he thought about it longer, he wasn't really a pilot, he had fallen into that position by default when he came to McGregor's because he had flying experience. In reality, he was an avionics engineer first and foremost. Flying Gertie was a lot easier than flying a helicopter or carrier-borne fighter jet. Why did they need a fighter pilot? He put the thought to the back of his mind.

An hour later, Jen appeared in Max's office.

"You're a dark horse, then," she smirked. "I didn't figure you for the family man."

Max looked down at his feet. "Yes, it was a surprise to me too, if I'm honest," he said.

"I'm sure that it will be just fine," said Jen in a motherly way. "Anyway, that's not what I wanted to talk about." She went over and made sure the door was closed. "I've been running over Gertie's operating code. You know that code that the dolphins injected to give us inertial dampers?"

"Yes," said Max, "and they took it away again, bastards."

"Actually, they didn't," smiled Jen. "They didn't purge the backup drive, so I was able to restore it."

Max smacked his forehead. "You mean that we have the gravitational compensation back?"

"Don't know until we go up and try it," said Jen pointing at the sky.

CHAPTER TWENTY-ONE

"Welcome to McGregor's Aerospace, Abi," said Doug to the attractive young woman with short-cropped brown hair. "I think that you will find that this is a completely different kettle of fish from what you are used to. We don't have any aircraft carriers; in fact, we don't even have anything that you would recognise as a runway."

She looked puzzled.

"Och, where's my manners?" said Doug, "These are the people you will be working with."

Doug introduced Abi to the team one-by-one and gave her a brief summary of their jobs.

"I'm pleased to meet you all," she said, without any hint of shyness. Abi was dressed in skin-tight jeans, brown leather jacket and matching brown thigh-length boots.

Max remembered his first day and the total culture shock of encountering the McGregor's workplace. He had the advantage of working with another avionics firm after leaving the Navy – but it was still a shock.

Doug continued, "No doubt, you will have had all the usual induction routines at head office. I hope that you weren't too bored with it all?"

"No, it was fine," she said, "but they didn't tell me very much about the job. You said that you don't have a runway, will I be flying choppers?"

"Not exactly," said Doug.

Abi shook her head.

"What?"

"I think that we'd better take you up to the hangar deck, Abi. All will become clearer."

Abi waked into the hangar with the others. The

three Deltas had their covers off and Delta 2 was partly disassembled with engineers working on the innards.

She stared at them with a dry smile.

Abi went over to Auntie Gertie and peered underneath. She ran her hand over the nacelle of the forward G-drive. It was very cold.

"Nice piece of kit," she said. "Humour me, are these planes?"

She looked round for confirmation.

"Actually, closer to space shuttles," said Sergei.

She tightened her lips but didn't show any hint of surprise.

Max remembered his reaction when he first saw the Deltas. This girl was cool.

"I'll take you for a spin later," said Max. "You don't mind if she borrows your couch, Sergei?"

Sergei held his hands palms upright as if he didn't care.

"I'd better come along as chaperone," smirked Jen. "Max likes to pull the old, 'out of gas' stunt when he has a girl aboard."

Max gave her a hard push.

"Jen, do something useful and show Abi the labs."

It was late when Max, Abi and Jen sat on the launch dollies outside in the forrest. Abi had been told a little of what to expect.

"I'm loving the helmet," said Abi. "Is this your work Max?"

"Yes, I've been developing that for quite a few years now."

Max showed her the rudiments of operating the display parameters with the mushroom on the armrest.

"Hold on," said Max as he gave Gertie a surge of power. Gertie shot up though the lower cloud layer.

"Jen, I though you said that you'd sorted-out the inertial

dampers," yelled Max.

"Oh," said Jen as she tapped on her keyboard. "Just a tick." All of a sudden the G-force completely disappeared.

"Have we stopped?" asked Abi.

"No, we are accelerating upwards at about 8G at the minute."

"Neat!" said Abi, "can I have a go?"

"Oh, no," said Max. "You will need some simulator time before you can be let loose with Gertie. She's nothing like a jet. No wings, no aerodynamics. Much more like a helicopter in fact. To go forward, you drop the nose, like so, and change the vectoring of the two rear G-drives. It's a bit difficult to master when you are in lower atmosphere but, further up, it's a doddle."

Max pulled some high speed turns, spins and aerobatics. The view in Abi's helmet totally contradicted what she was feeling in her body. Nothing!

"What we can do is constrained by the fact that we don't want anyone to see the Deltas. We only operate at night time when we have been given clearance by our control room. They operate a couple or Lear Jets with long range radar and we just hold back if there's any other traffic in the vicinity."

Max checked with control and operated the 'home' button. Gertie dropped rapidly through the atmosphere, coming to a wobbling halt just feet above the launch dollies. The rest of the way was like floating down in a hot air balloon, until the clamps took hold with a sharp clunk.

"Mmm," said Abi, "I'm impressed."

As she walked off with Jen, she half tuned and gave Max a little smile.

"What do you think of the new recruit?" asked Doug, coming over to meet Max in the hangar.

"I thought that Jen was laid back but this is the veritable ice maiden," said Max. "What do you know about her?"

"I'm told she's good," answered Doug, "how good remains to be seen. There's just one thing that bothers me though."

"What's that?"

"Her father is an ex-admiral and now a big-wig at the MOD. I think that there has been a certain pulling of strings, if you get my meaning." He tapped his nose.

"I was surprised at her reaction to seeing the Deltas for the first time," said Max. "I know that I was blown off my feet when I first saw them. She acted like she was in a second-hand car showroom. No emotions at all."

"There can only be two explanations for that," said Doug. "Either she is, as you say, ice cool or … she knew exactly what to expect. Keep a close eye on that lassie, Max."

Doug turned to walk away but then turned round again.

"Oh Max, something I've been meaning to ask you. I was watching your last flight on the telemetry display. You must have been taking a lot of Gs up there?"

"Yes, a little trick the dolphins taught us," grinned Max.

"And you didn't see fit to tell me about it?" quizzed Doug.

"Didn't know it would work until now," said Max. "Jen did something in software, I don't understand half that stuff."

For the next month, Abi was put through every test in the book, both physical and psychological. She didn't even break sweat. Her time in the Delta simulator showed that she had absorbed everything Max had taught her, knew all the controls and the foibles of piloting this most unconventional of aircraft.

Sergei and his team were busy manufacturing the railguns and the radiation deflector array. He had done it all before, but his men didn't know that. Delta 2 had undergone a refit and was at the stage that Auntie Gertie had been a few months earlier. Now they had two manned Deltas and one autonomous drone.

Despite Sergei's earlier chest thumping, making the targeting laser into a viable weapon was proving difficult. He could produce a laser weapon, a good one - it was just too big to fit into the confines of the Deltas' small frames. A laser that could fit could be used for little more than targeting, so that plan was put on a back burner until either the laser could be miniaturised or they had a bigger craft. There was one on the drawing boards, but it was still a long way off.

Abi's first go at Gertie's controls brought no surprises. She handled them like a veteran. Max would never admit it, but she was a much better pilot than he was. Her reactions were quicker, her intuitions were better. She was, after all, a lot younger and fitter than him and she had been in action in the Navy only months before. But he didn't like her. Maybe it was because she showed him up at nearly everything she did. Maybe it was something else. He determined that it wasn't going to affect their professional relationship and he didn't have any other aspirations towards her. He had Katie, a Katie that was getting more bulbous by the day.

"Wouldn't it be good to have a dogfight?" asked Abi. "The three Deltas up together and we could beat-up on the drone."

"As long as we are only using targeting lasers," said Max. "Don't want to be firing railgun projectiles around willy-nilly."

"Yes, that's what I was thinking. If Sergei's people could rig-up some hit detectors, it would show how well we did," suggested Abi.

"Mmm," said Max thoughtfully.

All three Deltas hadn't been in the sky together since they encountered the dolphins some months before. Max and Jen took Delta 2 and Sergei teamed up with Abi in Auntie Gertie. For this exercise, they didn't need third crew members. Gertie had six railguns mounted under the hull but they hadn't been fitted to Delta 2 yet, just the targeting laser. In re-engineering the railgun mounts, Sergei had given them a small amount of lateral travel which could be controlled from inside. This gave them an adjustment of convergence so that they could hit the same point at varying distances. Some World War Two fighter planes could do this but as guns were moved inwards from the wings to the fuselage on later jets, it had become unnecessary.

"Okay," said Max. "Delta 1 has been programmed with random evasive manoeuvres. The game is to hit the target sensor on top as many times as possible."

"Here goes," cried Abi.

It was one hundred and fifty miles up so no Earth-based radar could detect the twisting and gyrating of the three small Deltas. With their G-drives, they could accelerate at ridiculous speeds and come to a dead stop almost immediately. Delta 2's software had been cloned from Gertie's hard drives but they had no way to reproduce the mysterious circuit board with the one-sided hole. Only Gertie had the inertial damper.

Abi was in her element. She threw Gertie round the sky like she had been doing it all of her life. She pulsed the targeting laser at Delta 1 in rapid bursts. Max could hear the 'ping, ping, ping' of the hits being registered in his helmet speakers. He tried himself. 'Ping, ping.'

Abi was a born fighter pilot and had the benefit of Gertie's inertial damper but Max was much more au fait with the workings of his helmet's capabilities and even had a few tricks built-in that his opponent didn't. He knew how to lock onto the target and let the laser fire automatically.

The random evasion that had been programmed into Delta 1 was proving to be very efficient. Even with his laser lock, the sudden changes of direction were making it extremely difficult to score a hit. He noticed that Abi was having trouble too.

"Jen, if I'm ever being chased by a bandit, I would like to have your random evasion program on board," called Max.

"I can add it to Gertie," she replied, "but you would black out if you tried those manoeuvres in Delta 2."

Max followed Delta 1 on a tight curve. He was getting some hits on the target. Suddenly, Gertie was right in front of him and he was headed towards her fast. They were on a collisions course. The options ran through his mind like wildfire. Go up? Go down? Go right? Go left? He had to make a decision quickly, but couldn't. Before he had time to react, Gertie shot straight upwards and he passed beneath with inches to spare. As he composed himself, he could hear the 'ping, ping, ping' as Abi hit Delta 1 time after time. She did a barrel roll.

Max thought to himself, 'bloody show-off,' but really, he was glad to have such an ace on his team.

From the altitude they were at, they could see the Sun starting to rise over the curved horizon and decided to call it a night. The Deltas dropped like stones towards Mewton Base. Max had to go slower because of the enormous G-force he and Jen were experiencing. Then he realised, Mewton Base wasn't just below him as he had expected. He found himself over an unfamiliar landscape and just above the tall tree tops.

* * *

Ollie Palmer and Matthew Beckley were a couple of nerds. They had a web site that ran very dubious reports of UFO sightings and weren't averse to a bit of Photoshopping to bolster their hits. To keep their consciences clear, they often ventured out into the night with a pair of binoculars and a camera. Tonight, they were going to strike it lucky.

Delta 2's navigation computer was throwing error messages on Max's helmet display.

"Jen, what's wrong with this bloody thing, I'm not getting a lock on Base?" called Max.

"Sorry, Max, the sensors seem to be acting up. I can't do anything about it from here, you'll have to take manual control."

Max steadied Delta 2 at treetop level. Nothing below him looked familiar and the mist over the forest didn't help. He did his best to get his bearings but there were no distinctive features in the terrain below, just trees.

Max radioed through to the control room to see if they had a fix on his position.

"No Delta 2, you just dropped off the radar, you must be very low," said the controller.

"I'm going to have to switch on the infra-red spotlights," said Max, "can't see a thing."

The three strong beams were almost invisible to the naked eye but gave Max a clear view of the ground though his helmet display.

Ollie and Matthew had managed to squeeze through some undergrowth into the dense forest and had a couple of small torches to light their way. The torches formed bright beams in the forest mist. They found a track through the trees and followed it. Every now and then, the sky would be light for a moment and then go dark again.

"What's that?" asked Mathew. "I keep seeing flashes."

"That's just the lighthouse on the coast," said Ollie. "It's amazing that it shines so far inland but I've seen it before and tracked its location."

"I'm a bit worried by this mist," said Matthew. "If it gets much thicker, we could be in trouble."

"Don't worry," replied Ollie, "I have our locations fixed on my mobile phone. We won't get lost."

The silhouettes of tree trunks punctuated the thick mist with every sweep of the lighthouse.

"Are you sure that this is the right place?" asked Matthew.

"Absolutely," replied Ollie. "Load of reports from around this area."

"It's a bit eerie in here," moaned Matthew. "I don't like this."

"Oh, give over," said Ollie, "or I won't take you with me again. Bloody wuss. Are you going to be a bedroom ufologist all your life? Are you afraid of being abducted and having your orifices probed?"

"Oh, shut up, Ollie. It's all right for you."

They meandered on though the mist, getting more frightened by the minute.

Max scanned the sky with his helmet display.

"There's a small private plane a few miles away," he said to Jen. "I'm going to keep low until it passes."

He lowered Delta 2 into a forest clearing as best he could, snapping-off some treetops as he did so.

"What's that?" whispered Ollie.

"Now, you are just trying to spook me," said Matthew. "Stop it!"

"No, look. There's a strange glow coming through the trees from over there."

"Ollie, stop it. I'm frightened enough without you going

on."

As they burst through into the forest clearing, the mist took on a dark red glow. Delta 2's infra-red spotlights were being diffused and refracted by the mist.

"Oh, my God," said Ollie stopping in his tracks. There in the clearing they could see three glowing red orbs and three fainter blue ones. Ollie whipped out his camera and pointed it in the general direction. He fired-off a sequence of shots in flash mode. The flash illuminated the mist but all he got was fog, and more fog.

"I'm out of here," shouted Matthew, running in the opposite direction.

"Wait for me," cried Ollie, "you'll get lost without my phone."

Max eased Delta 2 back above the trees and took her in the direction of Mewton Base. Despite the navigation being down, he was now back in familiar territory and soon found the back road into the base and followed it to the landing zone.

Ollie and Matthew reached the car they had left in a lay-by and got in, breathless. Ollie switched-on his camera and flicked through the images in the LCD screen on the back. All he could see was forest and mist.

"Have you got anything?" asked Matthew.

"Don't know," said Ollie. "Can't tell from this, I need to look at the photos on my computer."

"And maybe give them a little hand?" said Matthew smiling.

"If necessary," said Ollie. "There was definitely something there so my conscience is clear. It's not my fault if the camera couldn't pick it up."

"Wait!" he cried. "Look at that." He held up the camera for Matthew to see. Where the lighthouse was momentarily illuminating the mist behind Delta 2, he could see a distinct triangular shape hovering in the treetops with coloured lights shining downwards.

"Wow," said Matthew. "Can't wait to get that online."

Deltas 1 and 3 were already clamped to their dollies and wheeled into the hangar when Max landed. Landing on a dolly manually would have been difficult if it had not been for the camera on the bottom of the hull. Max touched down softly and heard the clunk of clamps.

There was a substantial audience in the hangar deck as they climbed out of their Delta. They were applauding. Max was a little embarrassed but waved to the crowd like a pop star. Doug came forward and shook their hands.

"What you didn't know," said Doug, "was that your little 'battle' up there was being closely monitored on telemetry and by cameras on the three Deltas."

"Huh?" said Max.

"Instructions from the top," smiled Doug. "They want to keep tabs on their investment."

"They should be pretty damned tickled pink in that case," said Max.

"Aye, I think they will be," said Doug.

"And did you keep tabs on the score," asked Max.

"Oh yes!" said Doug.

Max raised his eyebrows in anticipation.

"Tough luck Max, you were absolutely slaughtered!"

Max twisted his lips. Abi saw Max and Doug talking and came over.

"That was exhilarating," she said, giving a little shake. "How did we do?"

"Oh, we'll just call it a draw," said Max in his most composed voice.

Doug threw him a dirty look.

* * *

"Abe, I've found it," an excited John Landers shouted down the phone. The web page on his laptop showed a fuzzy triangular shape hovering among some treetops. "It's what we've been after all this time. McGregor's gravity technology. It says here that the photo was taken yesterday in the very forest in England we have been watching."

"Who is saying this?" asked Thompson.

"It's a web site called mattandolliesufos.co.uk."

"You can't be serious," cried Thompson, "some stupid kids!"

"No, listen. These two guys called Ollie and Matthew were in that forest last night and they report that they saw a triangular shaped UFO just floating in the treetops not making any sound. They got a very clear photo of it."

"You telling me that you are believing a couple of English UFO nuts?"

"I'm looking at the photo, Abe. It looks real to me," said Landers.

"So, what are you going to do about it, John?" asked Thompson. "If you go near Rafael's mob, you'll probably be shot on sight."

"Screw Rafael," snarled Landers. "This is an aircraft that floats silently in the sky using some sort of anti-gravity drives. We haven't been able to crack that technology since we got the stuff at Roswell. It's as much a mystery now as it was then and here are the Brits with a fully working model."

"Okay, John. What's in it for us? Tell me that."

"Money Abe, lots of money."

"And who is going to pay us?" asked Thompson.

Landers laughed. "Abe, If this technology comes on the market, nobody is going to buy helicopters any more. A lot of airplane firms are going to be in big trouble too. I know a certain American helicopter manufacturer who would pay handsomely if this little problem was taken care of. Are you with me?"

* * *

In the near infinite vastness of time and space, a boundless intelligence had a conversation with itself.

"Seems that we have a problem!"

"A problem? What problem?"

"The sentinel at Sun-Earth Lagrangian point L2 has been activated."

"Something to do with the human's nuclear explosion an Earth year ago?"

"No, it went back into its quiescent state when there was no further threat."

"What is it then?"

"It's a real alarm this time. There is a large mass heading for Sol's inner solar system in real space and on a path perpendicular to the ecliptic. I think it means trouble."

"The Old Ones! They have been there before but Earth was just a mass of volcanoes at the time. Now, there will be more of interest to them. How far out is it?"

"Still some way off. At its present rate and bearing, it will get to Earth in about four of their months. They will obliterate all lifeforms, sterilise the planet and strip it of its resources. They will probably alter the atmosphere, set-up a colony, and then move on."

"The humans won't stand a chance! We'll have to help them."

"No, intervention is forbidden, we can only observe. Our remit is to gently guide promising civilisations along a path to maturity and a state where they can be at one with the multiverse."

"You are prepared to watch this planet's annihilation for entertainment, surely not?"

"We can't be overly concerned with a single planet. They come and go all the time. Survival of the fittest, that's how everything works. Anyway, in other realms, it won't happen at all."

PART 3

There was something in the air that shouldn't be there.

CHAPTER TWENTY-TWO

A remote controlled multi-spectral camera dropped down below the cloud layer and swivelled round.

"Can you see any leaks, Max?" asked Abi.

Max adjusted the display in his helmet to sweep through the visible light spectrum and beyond. The view of the forest below changed to false colours as he reached the infra-red end of the range.

"It's subtle, but I can definitely see where the earth has been disturbed over the base," he replied.

"Yes, I see what you mean," said Abi, concentrating on the ground below while Auntie Gertie floated on her three G-drives inside the cloud.

"Max, we have two bogeys approaching fast from the East," Abi yelled.

Max switched his helmet display to radar.

"Christ, where did they come from!"

Two Royal Air Force Typhoon fighters flashed past and broke-off in opposite directions.

"I thought that Gertie was invisible to radar," cried Abi.

"Normally she is," said Max, "but we have water condensed on the outer hull from the cloud. It must be defeating the radar reflective coating.

The two jets circled in a wide arc around where Gertie was floating.

"They know we are here," said Max. "I'm pulling-in the camera. Take us straight up. Fast!"

Abi hesitated.

"Let's play with them for a bit. I'd love to see how Gertie can perform in a 'real' dogfight. They've seen us now so there's nothing to lose in that respect."

"Be careful," barked Max. "I don't want to see anyone hurt or any damage done."

"I know, I know," smiled Abi. "We can leave any time we want."

Abi played 'sitting duck' to see what the RAF pilots would do. They didn't seem sure. Maybe they were checking with their control for orders. The fact that Gertie was sitting absolutely still in mid-air just above the clouds meant that the Typhoons could only do fly-pasts to look at her. Abi kept still. As the two jets screamed past, she decided to follow them. Gertie wasn't designed for horizontal flight in the atmosphere but her fusion reactor gave her more than enough power to keep up with a Typhoon.

"Ha, that's spooked them," laughed Abi as the two jets split off from each other. She followed one, moving in right under it and matching speed.

"He can't see us down here," she said. "We're in his blind spot."

"Watch out for the other one," yelled Max, as the second jet sped towards them.

Abi stopped Gertie dead still in the air. Had she not been equipped with alien inertial dampers, the G-force would have squashed them flat. The two jets flew past and continued in a wide sweep. The next thing they saw was the tell-tale trail of two Meteor air-to-air missiles.

"Are you playing chicken?" asked Max. "Time to leave, perhaps?"

Abi put Gertie into a fast vertical climb. This is what she was good at. Far below, the missiles tried to track the rapidly climbing Gertie, but couldn't catch up. They exploded as they reached the limits of their range. Gertie continued straight up for two hundred miles.

"Oh, there will be hot gossip in the barracks tonight," laughed Abi.

"You really enjoyed that," said Max accusingly.

"Max couldn't see Abi's face because of their helmets, but he could certainly hear her giggles.

"Better give them an hour to lose interest," said Max, "and then home."

"What was all that about?" asked Doug.

"Three things we learned," said Max. "First, Gertie is not invisible to radar inside a cloud. The water droplets on the hull reflect radar instead of absorbing it. Two…" he giggled and looked over at Abi, "the RAF's finest are no match for our two girls."

"Two girls," asked Doug, with a puzzled expression.

"Yes," said Max. "Abi and Gertie."

"Look, I don't want any comeback from the MOD," scowled Doug. "There were two explosions in the sky not far from here but there's another thing." Doug turned his computer monitor towards Max. On it was a ufologist's blog with a hazy photo of Gertie hovering above trees in a thick mist.

"So what?" smirked Max. "This area is renowned for its UFOs. The RAF pilots will, or maybe not, report a UFO sighting. These clowns with the website are saying it's a UFO. It's a UFO."

"I hope you're right, Max," said Doug.

"It's the third thing that you should be more worried about," said Max, "Mewton Base *is* detectable from the air if you are viewing in the right wavelength."

"Really," asked Doug. "How is it visible?"

"In infra-red, you can see the difference between disturbed earth and undisturbed earth. The excavations made for building the base are visible."

"Oh," said Doug, typing on his keyboard. "We'll have to do something about that."

"Katie, I'm back," yelled Max as he entered the cottage after work.

"Hi Max," came a voice from the bedroom. "You're home early for a change."

Katie came out of the bedroom with a towel wrapped around her head, a few strands of blonde hair flowing down her forehead.

"Er, yes," said Max. "Slow day at the office. Have you found any houses?"

"There's a couple that we should look at," said Katie. "They're not far from here. I'll make arrangements for viewing, provided that you can get home early. Why do you need to work so many nights?"

"Well, if I know I'm going to be working late, we can see the houses early in the day."

Max was more tired than he realised. In bed, he fell asleep immediately. Somehow, he knew what was going to happen. Mr. Burrage appeared in his dream as he had done so many times before.

"Hayden, I have to tell you something,"

"What?" dreamed Max. "You don't usually tell me anything. You just give me cryptic clues with little hope of me understanding them."

"This is important," said Mr. Burrage. "I'm not supposed to tell you anything. I could be deactivated for telling you this. But I can't stand by and watch an entire race being wiped out."

At first, Max thought that it was a joke. Then he realised that Mr. Burrage didn't have a sense of humour. He was serious. Deadly serious.

"What are you talking about?" asked Max.

Mr. Burrage took time to compose what he was going to say.

"Billions of years ago, when Earth was still in its

formative state, it was visited by a race that we call 'The Old Ones'. We have no idea what they call themselves, but this race is hostile. They travel the galaxy searching for planets to modify for their own requirements. They wipe out any indigenous life-forms, sterilise the planet, and change the atmosphere to a mix that they can breathe. They set up colonies of their own and then move on to the next system. We have seen it happen so many times."

"Why don't you stop them?" asked Max.

"Because, Hayden, we are not allowed to interfere - we are merely observers and cataloguers. Some races develop to maturity. Some never make it. I'm afraid that your planet will go down as one that changed hands. I'm sorry. I shouldn't even be telling you this."

"When is this going to happen?" asked Max.

"Very soon. Their spacecraft will be with you in a month. You will not be able to stop it."

"What can we do?" begged Max.

"Nothing," said Mr. Burrage. "It is inevitable."

Max awoke in a cold sweat. The dream was still clear in his mind. Was it just a dream? It seemed so real, it always did. From what Mr. Burrage had told him, Earth was about to be invaded and everyone, everything, would be wiped-out.

"What's wrong, Max?" asked Katie from beneath the duvet.

"Oh, just had a bad dream, love. Don't worry about it," whispered. He ran his hand over Katie's baby-bump and cried. If the revelation from his dream was true and not some cruel trick of the mind, he would never see his baby. Dare he tell Katie? Dare he tell anyone? There seemed little point. If they were fortunate, the end would be quick.

The houses that Max and Katie viewed in the village were beautiful but Max couldn't summon any enthusiasm.

Knowing that he only had a month to live made the whole exercise quite pointless.

"Max, don't you like any of these houses?" Katie asked.

"Not really."

"Oh, Maxie, that last one was lovely. I can really see us living there. It ticks all the boxes."

"Yes," said Max, "but I think we should see some more. There must be one that's better out there."

"Maxie, we need to make up our minds. It takes ages to complete a house transaction." She rubbed her tummy.

Max patted Katie on the knee.

"Be patient, Katie. I'm sure the perfect house will turn up."

Later that day, on his way into Mewton Base, Max wrestled with the idea of telling his team about the dream.

They'll think I'm mad, he thought. *I wouldn't believe it if somebody told me.*

Sergei came into Max's office.

"Max, I've been looking at the problem of water condensation on the Delta's hulls. I think I have a solution."

"Oh, good," said Max without looking up.

"Don't you want to hear it?" asked Sergei.

"For all the time we spend inside clouds on the way up and down, I don't see it as a big problem," said Max.

Sergei's eyes went up to the ceiling.

"Max, what's wrong with you? You seem to be in a daze. Is it the prospect of fatherhood that's sinking in?" asked the Russian.

"No, nothing like that," said Max, waving Sergei off with his hand.

"What is it then, Max?"

"Please, leave me alone, Sergei," said Max, putting his head on the table.

"Okay," said Sergei, slamming the door on his way out. He headed straight for Doug's office and paused for a moment outside the door. Should he tell Doug about Max's strange behaviour? Yes, he should.

Half an hour later, Max was flicking through documents on his computer when Doug walked in.

"Hi Max. Can you tell me what's troubling you? It hasn't gone unnoticed that you seem to be a bit depressed."

Max shook his head. "There's nothing wrong, Doug. I'm just fine."

"Are you sure, Max? If you ever need a friendly ear, you know where I am."

Max looked up. "Thank's Doug. I appreciate it. I'm just not sleeping too well at the minute."

The test flight in Auntie Gertie that night was uneventful. Abi threw the craft around the sky with the same aplomb as she always did. She noticed that Max was quieter than usual. No snide quips. No sexist remarks. So far, Abi hadn't been told about the dolphins.

"Abi, there's something we haven't told you yet. It will be a shock to you, I'm sure, but I think you should know. You will find out eventually."

"What is it Max?" said Abi, with a note of concern.

"Well, you know that we have been working on the Deltas for some time? Sergei designed the G-drives and brought the fusion reactor technology from Russia."

"Yes, all that was explained to me on my first day," said Abi over her helmet mic.

"You haven't been up in Delta 2, Abi. She is quite different."

"How so?" asked Abi. "I thought they were identical."

"Delta 2 hasn't got the inertial dampers. She can't accelerate the way Gertie does. Well, that not strictly true:

Delta 2's performance is on a par with Gertie's, it's just that the crew couldn't withstand the enormous G-forces."

"I thought that was because Delta 2 has just been upgraded from being an unmanned drone and hasn't had all the work completed."

"No," said Max. "Delta 2 will never have the inertial dampers. We have no idea how they work."

"What?" said Abi. "How can you not know how something works?"

"Fact is, Abi, Gertie was modified by…"

"Modified by what?" she asked.

"Modified with technology that is not of this world."

Abi sat in stunned silence.

"Are you telling me that Gertie has alien technology?"

"Yes, er, no. Not alien exactly," said Max.

Max explained about the encounter with the intelligence somewhere up in the sky. He told how Gertie had been captured by two circular craft they nicknamed 'dolphins' and eventually dragged him, Sergei and Jen through a portal into a different universe. He explained that their 'hosts' - he couldn't call them captors - had been observing Earth society for thousands of years. They were hopeful that it would reach 'maturity' in the very near future, at which time all the wonders of the universe, and others, would be revealed. Much as Max and his crew tried to beg the intelligence to share its technology, it refused – but made a slight modification to Gertie in the form of the gravity-defying inertial dampers.

"So, now you know," said Max.

Abi was having trouble taking it all in.

"So, these…creatures…did share their technology in the end?"

"No, they aren't creatures," said Max. "It isn't even 'they'. Oh, this is very difficult to explain! As far as I can work out, this race left organic bodies behind a very long time ago and are now just a consciousness, except that the overall consciousness has many 'nodes', like a huge split personality. Abi, it is so much more advanced than us. Its brain power is gazillions of times more than ours. It is not constrained by space or time."

"God," said Abi.

"Yes, that is a good word for it," said Max facetiously, "but there is something else."

Abi waited.

"Not only did it modify Gertie, I think that it it modified me."

Abi choked. "What do you mean?"

"Well, I get these dreams. Very vivid, recurring dreams. It communicates with me when I am asleep. It tells me things through an image of an old schoolmaster, Mr. Burrage."

"Why an old schoolmaster?" asked Abi.

"It was someone I looked up to and respected. Oh, he was a right bastard at times and gave some of the other pupils a hard time, but I always found him fair and he taught me a lot."

"I see," said Abi. "So what has this Mr. Burrage told you that is of any significance?"

Max didn't want to go there.

"I could be imagining all this," said Max. "It could all be utter nonsense. It told me that we are going to be wiped-out by aliens in a month's time."

Abi giggled.

"No, seriously," said Max. "I believe that it is true and there is absolutely nothing that we can do about it."

"Have you told anyone else about this?" asked Abi.

"No," said Max. "I don't want to be laughed at."

"There's a very easy way to prove it one way or the other," said Abi. "Take a photograph of this oncoming menace."

"And how could we do that?" asked Max. "It is a month away and travelling at God knows what speed."

"Then, we'll have to use a telescope," said Abi. "But we'd have to know where to look."

"Yes, that might be harder than it sounds. It's not as if I can lift the phone and ask the intelligence for the spacial co-ordinates. I have to wait for…Mr. Burrage. I have no control over that."

Max and Abi continued to toss ideas back and forward all the way down to Mewton Base.

Abi didn't waste any time in telling Doug about her conversation with Max.

"Damn, so that's what's been troubling him," said Doug.

"He's just not certain," said Abi. "He doesn't want to make a fool of himself. You know what his ego is like."

"Yes," said Doug, thoughtfully. "He doesn't like to be wrong. Abi, just leave this to me. I know how to handle Max." Doug went to look for Max but he had already left.

Katie met Max at the door with the latest tranche of estate agent's blurb. He tried his best to feign interest but wasn't totally convincing.

"What's for supper?" he asked.

"I've made a leek and onion tart," said Katie.

"Yum," said Max as he poured himself a stiff malt whisky. He sank back in his chair and took a few sips. Katie had to take the glass from his hand when she noticed that he had nodded-off.

Mr. Burrage was standing with his back to him. Max got the impression that he didn't want to talk.

'Sir,' dreamed Max.

'What is it boy, can't you see that I'm busy?' moaned the master.

'Sir, I wanted to ask you about…The Old Ones.'

Mr. Burrage turned round with a scowl on his face.

Max continued excitedly. 'I need to know what we are up against.'

The master gave him a 'calm down' signal.

'They are an ancient race. Should have matured eons ago but never quite made it. They are spread out across this galaxy and are slowly taking it over.'

'Are they technologically advanced?' asked Max.

'In your terms, I suppose they are. They don't have gravity manipulation; they still use atomic propulsion.'

'And their weapons?' asked Max.

'Blunt instruments,' said Mr. Burrage. 'Crude but effective.'

'How can they wipe-out an entire planet? Some massive nuclear missiles?'

'No, they need their habitat radiation-free. They use biological weapons. Organisms that destroy all indigenous life-forms and then die-off when there is nothing left to consume. Then, The Old Ones move in. The whole process only takes a few of your days.'

'And you said that they were headed towards Earth on a course perpendicular to the ecliptic?'

'Yes, they will be with you in about twenty-five days.'

'Which direction will they be coming from?' asked Max.

'Look in the direction of Delta Cassiopeia. Their craft is large.'

'What's that shaking?' asked Max.

'I don't know,' said Mr. Burrage.

"Max, Maxie. Wake up. Supper's ready," said Katie, holding two hot plates in her hands.

Max sat up and composed himself. He made his way to the dining room in a daze.

"Max, you seem so distant these days," said Katie as she dished-out the tart. "Help yourself to some salad."

Max didn't dare tell Katie about his dreams.

"You were mumbling in your sleep," smiled Katie. "Something about nuclear missiles."

"Really," said Max, "I don't remember. We don't have much control over dreams or what we say in them."

Katie grimaced.

Max started into his leek and onion tart.

"Nice," he said, but his mind was elsewhere. *Where was Delta Cassiopeia?* He didn't know much about astronomy, even if he had been further out into space than anyone else. Cassiopeia is the big 'W', he remembered, and the stars in it are given Greek letters based upon their brightness. It must be the forth brightest star in Cassiopeia. He got up and went over to the window.

"What is it Max?" asked Katie.

"Just want to see what the weather is like," he replied and sat down again. "Fancy a little walk after supper? It's a lovely moonlit night."

It was a late summer's evening and the sky was deep blue. Max slung a pair of binoculars over his arm and he and Katie walked down the lane hand in hand. She thought she was going for a romantic stroll. Max was studying the heavens.

"Do you know much about the stars and constellations?" he asked.

"I know The Plough and Orion and maybe a couple of others?" she mused.

"Yes, that's about my limit too," he added.

Max pointed his binoculars at Cassiopeia. One star was dimmer than the others, but he couldn't say which one was the fourth brightest.

"It doesn't matter how strong the binoculars are, they still look like pinpoints," he said.

"Why the interest in stars all of a sudden?" asked Katie.

"It's a navigation project that I'm working on. Sailors used the stars for navigation for centuries. Now we have GPS, but I'm still intrigued by astra-navigation."

"What happened when it was cloudy?" asked Katie.

"They got lost or shipwrecked," said Max.

She gave him a shove.

Back at the cottage, Max took out his laptop and looked-up Cassiopeia. Delta Cassiopeia was the one that dipped down the lesser in the 'W' and was also called 'Ruchbah'. Now he knew where to look but he was going to need something more powerful than a pair of binoculars.

* * *

"Hack the Hubble Telescope? You gotta be kidding me," cried Jen.

"How do you expect me to do that? Why would you want to do that?"

"I need to train the telescope towards Delta Cassiopeia," said Max. "There's something I want to check out."

"I have no idea how to do that," said Jen.

"I know that the downlink frequency is 2255.5, I looked it up. Does that help?"

"Well, I might - no promises - be able to tap into the downlink and get some data, but turning that into anything meaningful is another story. Besides, there is no way that we could point the Hubble Telescope in a specific direction. Max, why do you want to do this?"

Just then, Doug walked in.

"Ah, I was told you might be here. Abi just told me what's troubling you, Max. If there is even the faintest chance that it is not all a bad dream, I think that we'd better have a talk about this."

"I was hoping that Jen could help me get some proof,"

said Max.

"Except you won't tell me what you are trying to achieve," snapped Jen. Her Australian accent became much more pronounced when she was riled.

Max took a long breath.

"I have reason to believe that a large alien vessel is headed this way... and they are not the friendly type."

"How do you know this?" asked Jen.

Max pointed upwards. "The dolphins told me."

"So, they are ringing you up now, is that it?" asked Jen.

"Look, don't take this lightly,' said Max. "All that I can say is that they or it has communicated with me and told me that a race they call 'The Old Ones' is less than a month away from devastating Earth."

"Max wants to use the Hubble Telescope," said Jen, "but I don't think that's going to work. Even if we did manage to get an image of it, and that's a big if, it's only going to be a fuzzy point of light at that distance. It's not going to prove anything."

"She's right, Max," said Doug. "I think we should be looking at asteroid hunters. They can detect small objects at great distances by comparing photographs of a particular part of the sky over time. They look at points of light that are moving in a particular way. Much more telling. I think I'll speak to my friend Rahul Singh - he's more up on that kind of thing than I am."

* * *

A large black helicopter flew low over the Grand Canyon. Inside, two men were deep in discussion.

"You are an idiot, Landers," said David Faulkner, head of Faulkner Avionics - one of the world's major helicopter manufacturers. "Why do you want to destroy this research facility? I agree that the technology you are telling me about would put an end to the helicopter business for good, but I would much rather have it than destroy it."

The thick-set man opposite looked out the window at the breath-taking view below.

"I just thought that you'd want the competition eliminated," said Landers. "If they start selling these things, you will be out of business in no time."

"Have you actually seen one of these…aircraft?" asked Faulkner.

"Yes, I have. From about fifty feet away, or less, right above my head," lied Landers.

"And where was this?"

"In a forest in Suffolk on the East coast of England. That's where their base is."

"Do you have any pictures?"

Landers produced a printout of a photo from a ufologist's blog.

"There. These guys got a photo of one in that forest."

Faulkner peered at the photo.

"Not much to go on. You said that you were in military intelligence? How did you find out about this outfit?"

"It all started off as UFO rumours," said Landers, "then we did some investigating. We were monitoring where the top people in avionics were moving and found this English avionics company called McGregor Aerospace. They have people from Russia, China, India – all the countries at the forefront of aerospace technology. They were actively headhunted and have been developing this anti-gravity technology for the last ten years. It's way ahead of anything we've got. I also know that McGregor Aerospace is just a small part of a much larger international consortium."

"Yes, I've heard of McGregor Aerospace but I thought they were just minnows," said Faulkner. "Very interesting, but I'm even more convinced that we should adopt this technology instead of destroying it. Hell, what do you think you are going to destroy, one factory? That won't eliminate the competition. They probably have branches around the world making the same things as we speak."

Landers listened and kept quiet.

"Now, if you were able to get me some specs or pictures of these things, we would make it worth your while. You must have the resources to do that?"

Landers nodded, but he had been all through this before – with disastrous results and humiliation.

"Yes, I have the contacts. Leave it with me. What is the best way to get in touch?" said Landers.

"My private email," said Faulkner, handing him a business card. "Send me a note when you've got something concrete."

The helicopter swung back in the direction of Las Vegas.

CHAPTER TWENTY-THREE

Thompson was now laying low in the backwoods of Florida and Walker had disappeared off the face of the Earth. Landers was going to have to do this himself. He needed a new identity – all the others had been compromised. He had contacts: time to call-in some favours.

He was holed-up in a place called Indian Springs, fifty miles North West of Las Vegas. There wasn't much there – a truck stop, a handful of houses and an air force base. He had old friends there.

Landers smiled as he opened the pack that had just been dropped-off by a UPS courier.

"Christ, these guys are good," he mumbled aloud.

His new identity papers said 'Major Michael Grant, US Army'. It wasn't surprising that the fakes were good: they were produced in the same print shop as the genuine articles. Not only that, but his back-story had been injected into the databases that mattered. He was now a major in a covert US Army division so secretive that it did not exist. Well, it didn't. That's how he had always worked. Now, all he had to do was to hitch a lift to England and a military transport plane carrying supplies to Suffolk would land him on McGregor's doorstep.

In England, as he left the C-17 cargo transporter, Landers handed over his fake sealed orders. He was assigned some quarters and went off to see the quartermaster. What he needed was a night vision headset and a sidearm. He had already packed his black-ops uniform and a video camera with low light capabilities. He also needed a civilian car, preferably black, a satnav and a set of heavy duty wire cutters. All were provided.

He was about fifty miles from Mewton Base and found it difficult to keep to the correct side of the roads. They were narrower than he was used to and it was dark. At first, he thought it didn't matter what happened to the car - there was no comeback. But then he realised that if he wanted a ride back home, he had better not annoy anyone.

He followed the satnav until he got within a few miles of Mewton, then he pulled over and studied some high-res aerial photos on his laptop. The forest showed up as dense and a perimeter fence encircled the base. All he had to do was find the best spot to make a hole.

He slung a backpack over his shoulder and donned the night vision goggles. It was hard going through the vegetation but he pressed-on.

When he eventually came to the fence, it was even stronger than he had imagined: thick chain links and razor wire on top. He took out the anti-tamper wires and bridged them across with jump-leads. It was necessary for him to stand on the wire-cutter handles to exert enough force to cut through the wire links. This precluded cutting any links more than a foot above the ground. Eventually, after re-adjusting the jump leads, he managed to bend the fencing back enough for him to squeeze through. It was difficult but after pausing several times for breath, he managed to get through the small gap. He left his backpack on the outside and just took his video camera.

The forest was still thick as he used his wrist compass to head North West to where he knew the clearing was. As he got near, he could hear the rattle of a roller door opening and a glow from inside. He hunkered down behind a tree and waited. The hive of activity inside told him that something was about to happen. His heart beat faster. Further rattling opened the hangar door fully and he could see the silhouette of something edging its way out into the clearing.

"Oh, boy!" he said, as Auntie Gertie cleared the door opening and came to a rest in the middle of the clearing. He flipped back his night vision goggles, pulled the small video camera from his pocket, and switched it on. In the viewfinder, he could see the Delta aircraft in all its glory. He pressed the 'record' button.

The aircraft started to hum and lifted slowly into the air. It hovered for a few minutes and then shot straight upwards into the darkness.

Stunned, Landers then zoomed-in on the still open hangar. He could see two more aircraft and some men scurrying about before the shutter door rolled down. Then he was in complete darkness again.

The footage was good, but he wanted more.

"It's probably a complete waste of time," said Max. "I don't think our optics are up to it, but we have to try everything."

Abi took Auntie Gertie a hundred and fifty miles up.

"The plan is to take high-res photos of Delta Cassiopeia from points on both side of the Earth as far apart as possible, and everything in-between. When the photos are stacked, any moving object will be at a slightly different position relative to the star and will show as an elongated shape."

"Do you think that will work?" asked Abi.

"Don't know," replied Max. "We might not have enough magnification."

It took three hours to move between the different vantage points. Max couldn't tell much from his helmet display. From this altitude, with no atmospheric distortion, he could see thousands of stars around Delta Cassiopeia of all sizes and colours. Any movement among them would not be obvious until the photos were processed. He took spacial co-ordinates of each of the shooting positions. If he took photos from the exact same positions on subsequent nights, any object that had moved should be fairly obvious on the stacked photos. In astrophotography, stacking photos involves overlaying multiple exposures in exact registration, difficult to do manually but easy for a computer.

"That's enough for tonight," said Max. "Time to go home."

Ali pressed the 'home' button and Gertie obliged.

As Gertie hovered over the landing dollies, Max looked round the clearing with his helmet display.

"I wonder how they are getting on with the work to mask the earth movement," he said to himself. "Yes, it's better, but still some way to go."

"Whoah!" he said. "Hold on Abi, there is something odd out there."

Max cycled through the wavelengths of his helmet display. There was a bright infra-red dot amongst the trees.

"I think we might have a visitor," smiled Max. "Look South East about a hundred yards out."

"Yes," said Abi, "I can see it. What shall we do?"

"It's a job for security," said Max, "I'll call it in. Just go ahead as normal."

Gertie settled on the landing dollies and glided into the hangar.

Max headed straight for Doug's office.

"Doug, can you ask Jen to download the photos from Gertie's computer and get them off to your Mr. Singh. I think we have a problem outside. An interloper. I've called security."

"Aha," said Doug. "We expected that might happen at some time or another. Security are well prepared for such a situation."

* * *

Landers couldn't believe his luck. He had footage of the Delta taking off and landing and a pretty good shot of the interior of the hangar showing the other aircraft and equipment. Faulkner should be pleased.

He put away his video camera and pulled the night vision goggles back down. He knew that the hole in the fence was due South East but with all the manoeuvring between trees, he couldn't pinpoint the exact spot. He decided to head for the fence and then skirt along it. When he reached the fence, he was not sure whether to go right or left. It all looked the same. He walked to the left for five minutes. No hole. He headed back the way he had come and walked to the right. The hole in the fence was small, but he did spot his jump-leads completing the circuit in the anti-tamper wires.

The hole looked even smaller than he had remembered but he had got in through it, so he must be able to get back out. He took off his goggle harness and pushed it through the hole. He was going to have to feel his way through. He stuck his arms through and then his head. When he tried to get his shoulders through he became stuck.

"Fuck!" he yelled.

Much as he wriggled, he couldn't move backwards or forwards. He decided to cool down and think this through. *It was the same hole, wasn't it?* Just then he was aware of footsteps.

The sole of a heavy boot met his head and pushed down hard.

"For fuck sake," he cried, "take your goddamned foot off me."

Landers saw the flame of a cutting torch come to life beside his head and could feel its heat as it cut through the links above him. Hot sparks burned his skin. Then it moved across to the other side and the chain fence was lifted and he was dragged through.

Four armed security guards looked at him lying on his face on the ground. Without a word, they hauled him to his feet and prodded him at gunpoint along the outside of the fence. One of the guards found his back-pack and took it, along with the night vision goggles.

It was several hundred yards before they came to a gate. A guard held his hand up to a pad at the side of the gate and it opened. Landers was pushed and shoved until they came to a camouflaged door in the side of a small hill. They went through.

* * *

Max looked at the sorry figure in the locked room on CCTV.

"Yes, he looks familiar," said Max, but the only time he had seen Landers was by a lake in Canada – in another realm.

"Here is his laptop," said Doug. "It is password protected and I would very much like to see what is on it. I'll see if Jen can get in. His video camera has some very good shots of Gertie taking off and landing and some very compromising shots of the hangar interior."

"I wonder who he is working for?" asked Doug. "The Americans?"

"I think that you will find out that he is working for himself," replied Max. He had liaised with the CIA in the other realm to track Landers down and catch him, but only he, Sergei and Jen knew that. It was too difficult to explain to Doug.

"Let me have a word with him," suggested Max.

"I think I'd better come with you," said Doug. "How are we going to handle this? Is it good cop, bad cop, or do we go for the full Gestapo routine?"

"I've never done an interrogation before," said Max. "Let's see how it goes."

An armed guard let Max and Doug into the small room where Landers was being held. They didn't have a cell as such, just an unused storeroom that had a security camera installed.

"Perhaps you would like to explain why you were snooping around our premises?" asked Max.

Landers, still dressed in his black uniform and with his face blacked, held a middle finger in the air and said nothing.

Although he wasn't from Glasgow, Doug managed to pull a strong Glaswegian 'hard man' accent out of the air.

"You," he said as he pointed at Landers provocatively, "you'd better start talking if you know what's good for you."

Max motioned at Doug to calm down.

"You do realise, Mr. What-ever-your-name-is, that now you've seen what we have here, we can't let you go," said Max.

Doug ran a finger across his throat to press the point home.

Landers squirmed.

"It would be better for you if you were to tell us what this is all about," said Max.

Landers stared at the ceiling and said nothing.

Doug reverted to his usual soft Scottish lilt. "Okay, be like that. You're not going anywhere."

They closed the door behind them and a key turned in the lock.

"I think that we'll have to hand him over to the MOD," said Doug. "I'm sure that they are better at this kind of stuff than we are. Now, let's see what we can get off his laptop."

"I've got the composites back from Rahul Singh," said Doug. "But as you suspected, you don't have high enough magnification. He is going to run the same tests through some Earth-based observatories. They have a network that searches for rogue asteroids. That sounds like a better bet."

"How long will it take?" asked Max. "Time is running short."

"Short for what, exactly? Even if we have confirmation that this thing is headed Earthwards, there's still not a lot we can do about it."

Max looked grim. "Yes, I know."

It was two days before the new composites arrived by email. The accompanying note confirmed that there was an object moving near Delta Cassiopeia's position in the sky.

"Better get this stuff over to HQ," said Doug. "I'll set up a meeting for first thing in the morning."

"What about our friend in the storeroom?" asked Max.

"We are taking him along," said Doug. "The MOD are going to pick him up at headquarters, we can bring them here."

Tony Davidson shook his head slowly. Max had just finished telling the assembly his story and the room had gone deadly quiet.

"If this is true, we can't keep it to ourselves," said Tony, "but I can't just ring up the Minister and tell him that somebody had a dream that we are about to be invaded by aliens. Is there any proof?"

"We have a composite photo taken over a few days that shows that there is definitely something moving from the direction we are expecting," said Max. "It's either an asteroid, too far away to be of any danger, or a bloody big spaceship. Meanwhile, back here on Earth, we have a space navy of two and a half Deltas armed with six railguns each and we have no idea what we are up against."

Tony tapped his pen on the table.

"I wasn't supposed to mention this but what you have just told me changes everything," he said sternly.

"You are well aware that McGregor Aerospace is part of an international consortium. We share a certain amount of technology, but each country is autonomous and responsible for their own R&D. There are other aircraft that use G-drive technology. Both China and Russia have them. I don't know very much of the details about the vehicles other than," he coughed, "China have a base on the Moon and have had for the past five years. Their G-drive craft are considerably larger than our Deltas. The Russians also have larger craft and have been experimenting with weapons too. Again, I am not privy to the details but I have heard that there is some sort of gravity energy weapon. I think that the time has come to pool our resources."

Max paused before continuing. "What about the Americans?"

"Yes, them too. This is too important for petty nationalism and commercial considerations. Our world is at risk."

Max tried to probe Tony for more details about what the Chinese and Russians were doing but he wasn't inclined, or able, to elaborate.

"Tony, something else we didn't mention," said Doug. "We caught an intruder in the grounds at Mewton Base. He's obviously American but not connected to any legitimate part of the military. I'm passing him over to the MOD to see what they can extract from him. I have his laptop and we are trying to hack it to see if there is any useful information. So far, we haven't had much luck."

"Mmm, I like to know how he found us," said Tony.

"Yes, we know that we have a signature in the infra-red due to the excavations. We are sorting that out at the minute," said Doug.

"But it means that he must have had access to satellite imaging," said Max. "Maybe he is more military than we think."

"The MOD will be able to sort that out," said Tony. "They have their ways."

"Now, how do we tell the world?" asked Doug.

"Ahem, we don't," said Tony. "If the world is going to end in a couple of weeks it is better to keep it quiet or all hell will break loose."

"Shouldn't we, at least, tell the governments?" asked Max.

"What?" asked Tony. "You want to get politicians involved? They will just end up arguing until it's too late to do anything."

"But what can we do?" Doug interjected.

"If we are going to solve this dilemma," replied Tony, "I'm not saying that we can, but I would like to keep it in-house. Who know about this at the minute?"

"Just the Delta crews, Doug and you," said Max.

"Right, let us keep it that way," said Tony, slapping the table. "Not a word to anyone!"

Katie was surprised to see Max home so early. She hadn't expected him and didn't have any food ready.

"Don't worry, love," he said, "we can pop out for something."

Katie was dressed for a night in so she had to find some suitable clothes.

"It won't be anything fancy," called Max, "how about the White Swan?"

"Is it all right?" asked Jen, "have you been there before?"

"No, but I'm told that it is quite good," answered Max, which wasn't strictly true. He had been there with Jen in the other realm but he didn't want to have to explain that to Katie.

Max recognised the same waitress that served him and Jen. He was worried for a minute that she might recognise him too but that idea was absurd. It was in a different universe.

"Max, what's wrong?" asked Katie, "you are just not yourself these days."

Max leaned across the table and stroked her hand. "There's nothing wrong, Katie. There really isn't."

Katie gave him a dirty look. She knew Max too well for him to let that pass.

"Is it something at work that you can't talk about?" she asked.

"Katie, I said that there is nothing wrong. Why will you not believe me?"

Luckily for Max, the food arrived at the table so the situation drifted. Katie was only drinking mineral water, so Max had a whole bottle of Chardonnay to himself. He should have known better.

"I'm not going to let you drive home," she said, insistently. You've had far too much wine. I'm going to have to drive."

"But, you've never driven my car," said Max, with a slur. "It's automatic."

"How hard could it be?" teased Katie. "You can drive it and I'm a better driver than you are."

If anybody else but Katie had said that to him, Max would have had a fit. It was bad enough having a female pilot that was better than him, now this.

"I'll mange just fine," said Max, "it's only round the corner."

"Well, if you're driving, I'm walking," said Katie angrily. The thought of Katie walking home late at night bothered him even more that the prospect of her driving his car. He pushed the keys across the table.

"If you go over a hedge, there'll be hell to pay," said Max.

"I'll be ever so careful," she said in her most angelic voice. "Just hang on there for a minute while I powder my nose."

Max was aware of Katie trying to press the non-existent clutch a few times but he had to admit, she did pretty well. He remembered his first attempt in an automatic car and the embarrassment it caused. He wasn't going to tell her that though. When they got home, Katie parked in the middle of the driveway - she wasn't taking any chances. The BMW was much wider than her Mini, so she left plenty of room. Max headed straight for the bedroom and passed out, fully clothed.

* * *

It was nearly morning when Mr. Burrage appeared in Max's dream. The bottle of wine had masked any earlier dream state.

"Can't you do something? Anything?" begged Max.

"You know that I can't," said Mr. Burrage. "I cannot interfere in your realm, it would cause ripples right across the multiverse."

"Can you tell me about their craft, their weapons. Please give me something."

"I can tell you but you won't be able to do anything about it," said the master. "I told you before, they are far more advanced than your race. Their craft is five of your kilometres long and two and a half kilometres across. It can travel at 0.2 light speed. They destroy planets using biological weapons but they also possess directed energy weapons. You have no defence against such power."

"Don't they have any weakness?" asked Max.

Mr. Burrage was amused at the question. "If they have a weakness, it would be their arrogance. No race has every stood up to their onslaught, never mind beaten them."

"So they expect to win with no opposition?" asked Max.

"Oh, they have been opposed many times, but it has never affected the inevitable outcome," said Burrage. "Much more powerful races than yours have tried, but it didn't make any difference. They will just sail straight in there and that will be it."

Max was just about to ask another question when the alarm clock went off. He cursed it. Katie was not beside him but he could hear the cistern flushing.

"Good morning," she said cheerily. "Have you got a hangover?"

"My head's all right but my mouth tastes like a vulture's armpit," he grimaced.

"I'll have to take your word for that," she said, whacking him with a pillow. "Get up!"

Max made a large mug of very strong filter coffee.

"You know, your blood alcohol level will still be above legal," said Katie. "Can't you call in sick for once?"

Max had never called in sick in his life.

"I'll be fine after another coffee," he said, wrestling with his jacket.

"Coffee won't make any difference to your blood alcohol," she snapped.

"Maybe not," said Max. "But it will sure as hell wake me up enough to avoid police patrols."

Max left with his shirt tail hanging below his jacket. Katie went after him and tucked it in. She kissed him goodbye. "Be careful!"

Max wondered if the pretence of swapping into a 4x4

was worth the trouble now. Did it really matter if someone saw his BMW drive into the front track up to Mewton Base? Did anything matter? The thought of taking his wonderful machine along a rough, dirty track potholed with muddy puddles took him to the procurement offices car park where the Land Rover was waiting.

As soon as he exited the Land Rover in the Mewton base car park, one of the maintenance workers told him that Doug was waiting for him and that he should hurry.

"You look a bit rough," said Doug. Sergei, Jen and Abi were already waiting in Doug's office.

Max flapped his hand and sat down.

"Tony has been on to his counterparts in China and Russia overnight," said Doug. He's just taking a short nap and wants to see us all here at twelve.

"What has he found out?" asked Max.

"He didn't say," said Doug, "but we will find out in a few hours."

CHAPTER TWENTY-FOUR

Tony Davidson addressed the team gathered at the small meeting room at Mewton Base.

"I've had a lengthy discussion with our Chinese and Russian colleagues during the night. As you know, we share certain technologies with these other companies – the G-drives, the fusion reactors and, as you will have found out Max, your helmet technology. Other than these basics, each arm of the conglomerate has played its cards pretty close to the chest. They have developed these technologies in their own way and in diverse directions, no doubt with some influence from their governments. Just as we have technologies that they don't - Sergei's radiation deflector and the, em, inertial damper - they have ideas that we don't have."

Sergei butted in, "The inertial damper is only available in Delta 3, we have no idea how it works and we certainly can't reproduce it."

"Yes, I understand that, Sergei. The Chinese have come up with a different method of deflecting radiation on their trips to their moon base, 'YuèGōng'. You might understand the technicalities, Sergei, I don't. YuèGōng means 'palace in the moon', a feature of ancient Chinese folk tales. It is in a deep crater at the Moon's south pole. Most of the facility is underground to keep it hidden, and to protect it from radiation. They have six craft that carry crews and supplies back and forth between their bases on Earth and on the Moon. From what I understand, each craft has five large G-drives, which gives them much superior lifting power to our Deltas."

"What about the Russians?" asked Max.

"I was coming to that, Max. The Russians invented

the micro fusion reactor and have made some significant advances on that since we got the initial designs from them. They have increased the power output fourfold without increasing the size. Unfortunately, there is no way to retrofit these into our Deltas, certainly not on the timescale we are looking at. In addition to increasing the power and speed of their craft, they have managed to create something else. Call it a tool, call it a weapon, it can be used either way but it is a method of directing a pulse of gravity waves. At low power, it acts much as your railgun does in providing a powerful kinetic kick. When it is used on full power, it can rip matter apart at a molecular level. This is your science fiction disintegrating ray. The trouble is that it only works at a very short range – a few kilometres at best."

Tony stood up and looked round. "That, ladies and gentlemen, is what we have. As I've said, I don't begin to understand these technologies or their implications; that is your job. I would like you have a meeting with the Chinese and Russian scientists ASAP, preferably today."

"And where will that meeting be?" asked Max.

"YuèGōng," said Tony, pointing upwards. "You can't get much more secure than that. Has Delta 2 been fitted with radiation deflection, Sergei?"

"Yes, just last week," he answered.

Tony continued, "Much as I would like to go myself, we are short of seats. I suggest that Max, Doug and Li Yan go in Delta 3 and Abi, Sergei and Jen go in Delta 2. You should also take Delta 1 along - it can't carry people but it can take supplies."

"Why Li Yan?" asked Max.

"The Chinese scientists do speak passible English," said Tony. "When it comes to technical stuff, they might struggle. From what I know of Ms. Li, she has a good command of technical English and Chinese. Has she been up in a Delta before?"

"Only once," said Doug. "She didn't like the disorientation of weightlessness and the G-force made her physically sick."

"That shouldn't be a problem in Delta 3?" asked Tony.

"No, she hasn't been up in Gertie recently. The weightlessness won't be a problem either as we won't be floating around, we will be travelling at full pelt."

"Good," said Tony. "Get on with it, and keep me updated. I'm just about to have a very awkward chat with certain Americans."

"Jen, have you had any luck with that laptop?" asked Max.

"Yes, easy peasy, " said Jen. "It wasn't a military computer, it was a personal one. It only took a few minutes to crack."

"Anything interesting on it?" asked Max.

"Depends what you mean by 'interesting'," she grinned. She showed Max some photographs.

"Apart from the smut?" asked Max.

"There are satellite photos of Mewton Base, quite hi-res. I don't know how he could have got those. There are also some interesting emails with someone called David Faulkner."

"David Faulkner?" asked Max in surprise. "THE David Faulkner?"

"Who's he?" she asked.

Max punched-in the number for Doug's internal phone.

"Doug, is Tony still here?"

"He left just literally a second ago," answered Doug. "I'll see if I can catch him."

A few minutes later Tony answered the phone.

"Yes, Max?"

"Tony, can you come down to Jen's lab. We have something here you should see."

Tony read the emails through several times.

"They have been very careful with their words," said Tony. "Nothing that would hold-up in court, but I can see what is going on here. This guy, John Landers, is an industrial spy and he is trying to sell information about our operations here to the head of one of America's biggest helicopter manufacturers. Here Max, have you seen this photograph of a Delta landing in the forest off some nutty UFO site?"

Max looked at the screen.

"Just a UFO, nothing to worry about," smiled Max.

Tony scowled.

"Jen, can you forward this stuff to me at HQ. It is all good ammunition when I speak to the Americans. I don't want to rush you, but don't you guys have a meeting somewhere?"

* * *

As the trio of Deltas swung in towards the south pole of the Moon, they saw two pentagonal craft rise up to meet them.

Max scrutinised them intently.

"Yes, they are big," he said to Sergei beside him. "I was half expecting to see a large yellow Chinese star on the top; they must have had another reason for building them that shape."

"Makes perfect sense to me," said Sergei.

A voice came over the radio.

"Hi, McGregor craft. Please follow us down."

As they dipped into the crater, Max could see other craft sitting on the surface connected up to a central tower with walkways.

"It's just like an airport down there," he said. "What are

those oval ones?"

"I think that you'll find that they are ours," said Sergei. "They must have beaten us here."

"We can only go as fast as the occupants of Delta 2 allow us," said Max. "Your comrades must have really felt the Gs."

"They are tough," said Sergei.

"I can see a major problem," said Max. "We don't have any airlocks. We can't hook up to one of those umbilicals."

Just as he spoke, he could see a large hole open on the surface.

"Ah, they think of everything, these Chinese," said Max.

Deltas 2 and 1 followed him through the opening in the ground. The roof over their heads gradually closed. Max was about to open the hatch when Sergei stopped him.

"Wait for the green lights on the wall," said Sergei. "It takes time to pressurise a hangar bay as large as this."

It took five minutes before the green lights lit up. Airlock doors at the side opened and figures in spacesuits came towards the Deltas.

"Welcome to YuèGōng," came an accented voice on the helmet speakers. Max could see one of the figures waving. Then he beckoned.

Max opened the hatch surreptitiously. There was no rush of air but a strange smell filled Gertie's cockpit.

"I didn't realise that the Moon had a smell," said Sergei.

"At least it doesn't smell of cheese," said Yan.

They cautiously jumped down from Gertie's hatch. The one third gravity made it happen in slow motion. Max could see the occupants of Delta 2 had the same experience. The welcoming committee shook their hands and lead them through an airlock. Once they were all inside they removed their helmets.

Immediately, Li Yan stepped forward and started gibbering in Chinese.

"English, please," said the taller Chinese man with barely a hint of an accent. "You must mind your manners," he scolded.

"I am Michael Zheng, Director of YuèGōng. I welcome you. This is Xu Wěi, our chief scientist. Please come this way and we shall have some tea."

Yan went over to Xu Wěi and said something. His eyes lit up in recognition. They obviously had some history.

After removing their suits, Michael Zheng led them into a large room. The architecture and furnishings were a strange mixture of ultra modern and traditional Mandarin. He beckoned for them to be seated round a long, low table.

"We have much to talk about," he said and then stood up. Four other people entered the room.

"Sergei," one of them called and came running over.

"Andrei!" said Sergei, standing and embracing his old friend.

"We were at high school together," said Sergei, presenting the man to the others.

"This is Viktor, Dmetry and Nina," said Andrei. Each of the Russians gave a small bow as their names were called.

"Please take a seat," said Michael Zheng. "Ah, here is the tea." For a few minutes, the group chatted informally, then Michael Zheng stood and spoke.

"And now, ladies and gentlemen, we have some serious issues to discuss. I will ask Mr. Sinclair to begin the briefing."

Doug stood up.

"I am Douglas Sinclair and I am Director of Research at McGregor Aerospace in England. You have probably been given a brief idea of why we are all here today in this rather splendid conference room, congratulations Michael to you and your people. It is indeed a 'Palace in the Moon'"

Michael Zheng nodded in appreciation.

Doug continued. "But I am going to hand you over to

Max Hayden who can give you much more detail about what we are up against than I can. Max?"

Max stood shakily to his feet.

"Sorry, can't get used to this gravity," he smiled.

"Yes, our problem…"

Max started from the very beginning. He wasn't surprised when both the Chinese and Russian contingents admitted that they too had encountered the playful dolphins two hundred and fifty miles above the Earth. They sat speechless as Max recounted how Gertie was dragged into a rift in spacetime and how he, Sergei and Jen had their first conversation with the intelligence. They asked lots of questions that Max couldn't answer. He went on to tell them about his more recent dreams where the intelligence was communicating with him through the proxy of Mr. Burrage.

"Dreams, how dreams?" asked Anna, the Russian female. She had the frame of an Olympic athlete.

"I believe that on our first visit, they implanted something in my brain," said Max. "Nothing physical, like a computer chip, it is more like reprogramming part of my brain to act as a conduit. It only works when I am asleep."

"Quite," said Anna.

"It was in one of these dreams that I was told that the race they refer to as 'The Old Ones' were on their way towards Earth and the most likely outcome is our annihilation," continued Max. A stunned silence enveloped the room. "Now is the time to stop our petty nationalistic feuding and join together to try to defend humanity against this external threat."

Everyone nodded.

"What can we do?" asked Xu Wěi. "If they are as powerful as you suggest and your friends are not prepared to side with use, how can we protect ourselves."

"That's what we are here to discuss," said Max. "I

think that the best plan is to have a look at each other's technology. I have to say from the outset that we can't share our inertial damper with you. We have no idea how it works. If you saw the circuit board the intelligence modified, you would be as much in the dark as we are. There have wiring that goes nowhere!"

"We Chinese can copy anything," insisted Xu Wěi. "Let me inspect this circuit board."

"You can look at it, certainly," said Max. "Be my guest. Why don't I show you Delta 3 first, we call her 'Auntie Gertie'". He didn't feel like explaining why.

The assembly moved to the hangar bay where the three Deltas were sitting on makeshift landing gear. They had none of their own.

"Delta 3 is our latest and most advanced craft," explained Max. "Sorry, but there's not much room inside."

The Chinese and Russians took turns to examine the Deltas. They ran their hands over the sleek exteriors and climbed into the cramped cockpits two at a time.

"Reminds me of one of your British sports cars," said Michael Zhang.

"A very good analogy," said Doug. "It is especially good on corners."

Sergei climbed into Gertie and removed an access panel.

"You wanted to see the special circuit board," he said to Xu Wěi. "Have a look at this."

The Chinese scientist's jaw dropped when he saw the wiring that went into a hole on one side but didn't emerge from the other. Sergei further confounded them when he stuck a pen into the hole as far as he could and showed that it didn't appear on the other side.

"No, too difficult," said Xu, shaking his head. Then he smiled.

"Let me show you our dàpéng," he said proudly. It is a large magical bird in Chinese legend."

The umbilicals to the Chinese craft were pressurised and had the correct atmosphere so they didn't need to don their spacesuits.

There was a definite maritime influence in the dàpéng interior. No attempt had been made to conceal conduits and the whole effect was one of utilitarian efficiency. There was loads of room, like a deck on a naval destroyer. Xu explained how a ramp could be lowered on the underside to allow moon buggies to enter and exit with soil and rock samples. No mention was made of any armaments so Max had to ask. "Do you have any weapons on board?"

"Why would we need weapons?" asked Xu. "There's nobody to shoot at us up here."

Max noticed the Russians smiling at one another.

"Let me show you a real spaceship," said Andrei. He led them all down to the central hub and back out to one of the Russian craft. Through a porthole in the umbilical, Max could see that the Russian vessel looked quite different from his first impression from above. There were no sweeping curves - the oval-shaped craft was faceted like a cut diamond. The individual facets seemed to be made of finely corrugated metal. Max pulled Doug over to see.

"That's an interesting construction technique, why did you do it that way?" asked Doug.

"Easy to make," said Andrei, "and in space, you don't need streamlining."

"What about your drives?" asked Max. "How many do you use?"

"Five," said the Russian. "One large one in the middle and four smaller ones for, how you say, orientation."

Doug nodded.

"And what is that large dish at one end, communications?" asked Max.

"Ah, no. That is our gravity projector. It focuses gravity waves at a distant point."

"This is the weapon we have heard about?" asked Doug.

"Weapon, what weapon," smiled the Russian. "It is for dismantling things."

"Things?" asked Max.

"Yes, anything that gets in its way," said Andrei. "Junk satellites, small asteroids. Stay away from in front."

The inside of the Russian vessel was grey, stark and even more battleship-like than the Chinese one. The Russians certainly believed in function before form.

Michael Xu came over and joined them at the control panel.

"Quite different solutions to the same problem," he said. "Now, all we have to do is to work out how we are going to use them."

"If only we had more of them," said Doug. "Oh, where did the girls go?"

"I asked if they wanted to see the Earth space navy or go for a buggy trip up to the edge of the crater. They chose the sightseeing. They can see around the craft when they get back. If you want to have a buggy trip, you're welcome. Later, we are going to have some food. We have a very good chef here at YuèGōng. I'm sorry that we can't offer any local produce."

After the meal, which turned out to be a full-blown banquet, Xu offered them a dormitory to stay the night. Max was keen to get back, so he declined, thanked Xu for his hospitality, and he and his crew headed back to the suiting room. He had a last long look as they lifted off. They had three Deltas, four Chinese freighters and three Russian gunboats to protect humanity from oblivion.

* * *

"How did you get on with our colleagues?" asked Tony Davidson. Doug and Max sat opposite him in his large office.

"Very interesting," said Doug. "We had a look at each other's craft. Everybody brought something new to the table. If there was time and we could combine all these technologies, we would have a very formidable war machine. Unfortunately, we don't have that luxury. We will have to work with what we have."

"You spoke to the Americans?" asked Max.

"Yes. I didn't want to get mixed-up in politics so I phoned an acquaintance at NASA. Needless to say, he was shellshocked. He agreed about not telling the politicians just yet – except for the President. They don't have any viable G-drive technology, as we suspected. He was flabbergasted to discover that other countries did. What they can bring to the table is their deep space telescopes and 'orbital defence initiatives', as he called them. He said that he would have to get on the 'red phone' to the Whitehouse so that his equipment requisitions didn't get held-up by committees and bean-counters. Anyway, I have passed-on the co-ordinates you gave me. They will report back as soon as they have something."

"That bloody great spaceship is not our greatest problem," said Max. "It's time. We simply don't have time to do anything. Two weeks, that's nothing."

Tony stared into the distance.

"I wish that I had a solution for you Max, well, for all of us. I just don't."

Max and his team gathered in the Mewton Base meeting room.

"So what's happening?" asked Doug.

"Tony has someone at NASA trying to spot the thing. They have more technology at their disposal than anybody.

They can point everything they've got in that direction and plot an accurate path and ETA. They have ground-based nukes that they can send up when it gets in range. Something tells me that 'The Old Ones' aren't going to let that happen."

"Do you know what I think," said Doug. "I think it might never get that far. Sometime in the next two weeks, somebody else is going to spot this thing and tell the media. They will fall over themselves to see who can scare the most shite out of people. There will be utter panic. I very much doubt if there will be anything left for the aliens to destroy, we will do that for them long before they get here."

"I think that there is some truth in that, Doug, but please don't underestimate man's instinct to survive. We have faced great threats before and came through."

"Survival always favours the fittest, Max. Charles Darwin and his Theory of Evolution brought this to our attention quite some time ago. In this instance, I don't think that we are the fittest – by a long way. I reckon we probably have a week before all hell breaks loose."

Abi had been sitting taking all this in without comment.

"Are we one hundred percent certain that they are hostile?" she asked. "You claim to have been contacted by this … intelligence … in your dreams, Max. You could be imaging it, or, maybe you are being strung along. This intelligence might just have its own agenda."

"Yes, I know," replied Max, "the thought had crossed my mind … although my instinct says not. In any event, I think that another visit might be in order. We might not get access to their inner sanctum but we sure as hell have to try."

Jen was a very talented programmer but Max had come to admire Abi's bottle. To get where she did in The Royal Navy, she had real strength of character. He decided to take her and Sergei on the expedition to high orbit. Jen didn't seem to mind - she preferred to be at her computer anyway. Abi took the pilot's couch; Max, the co-pilot's; and Sergei was left facing backwards in the navigator's couch that Jen usually took.

"How will we find them?" asked Abi.

"We won't," said Max. "If they are inclined, they will find us. No guarantees. Even if they do find us, they may not want to take us home with them."

"Max," said Sergei. "Would it help if you went to sleep?"

"I don't think that I can," said Max.

"What if I sang you a nice Russian lullaby," asked Sergei, and started into a song.

"That is sure to keep me wide awake, Sergei. Shut up."

Max turned-off his helmet display and settled back. It was pretty boring just floating in space watching for blips on the radar display. It took an hour, but he eventually drifted off. Max dreamed, but there was no sign of Mr. Burrage. In his dream, he dreamt that he was asleep. There was another presence in his dream environment. It seemed strangely malevolent and was advancing towards him. He couldn't see it because his eyes were closed - he was sleeping in his dream after all. He tried to escape from the oncoming menace but he found that he was paralysed. He couldn't move any part of his body. Max was becoming increasingly terrified. The more he tried to get out of the situation, the more obvious it was that he couldn't. He tried to open his eyes, but they remained tight shut.

"Sergei," shouted Abi. "Max seems to be in some sort of trouble." She could see him twitching in the couch next to her and heard moaning over her helmet speaker. "It looks like he is having a fit. What should I do?"

"Give him a very gentle push," suggested Sergei.

Abi pushed and said "Max, Max. Wake up."

Max moved and moaned.

"Max, it's Abi. You are having a bad dream."

Max opened his eyes and lifted his head.

"Whaa," he said.

"Max, are you all right?" asked Abi.

"Aaa, yes, I'm okay. Just give me a minute."

Max breathed heavily. "Ohh."

"Were you dreaming?" asked Sergei.

"Yes. I was trapped. Couldn't move."

"That's quite common in dreams," said Sergei. "Sleep paralysis. It's caused by an erratic sleep schedule. Nothing to worry about unless it happens often."

"Oh," said Max. He wanted to rub his eyes but couldn't with his helmet on. "Any sign of our friends?"

"There are two targets about a hundred miles away," said Abi. "Don't know what they are but they are not coming towards us."

Max switched his display back on and looked around.

"I see them," he said. "Could only be dolphins. It's strange that they are not doing their usual performance."

"I don't think that they want to come closer," said Sergei.

"Why would that be?" asked Abi.

"Could be a number of things," said Max. "Maybe they don't want to have any further contact with us. It might also be because we have fitted railguns. They don't like weapons." He wanted to say that it might be because they had a female pilot but stopped short. Abi didn't take kindly to sexist remarks, as he had already found out.

"Well, if they are not going to play ball, we might as well go home," said Max.

Abi grunted and pressed the button.

"NASA have confirmed sighting the alien spacecraft," said Tony Davidson. "According to them, it is decelerating towards Earth and your ETA is about right, Max. Two weeks. The American president has been informed and he is going to take it to a special meeting of The United Nations tomorrow. It has been agreed that the situation is not made public and that any amateur sightings are discredited as far as is practically possible. They have infiltrators in all the ufologist and conspiracy theory websites to muddy the waters – but that's nothing new."

Max leaned back in his chair. "How can we even start to plan a strategy when we haven't the foggiest what we are up against."

"What do we know so far?" asked Tony.

"That it's bloody big, has travelled from another star system - we know not where - and that the occupants are thousands upon thousands of years more advanced than us. They first explored this planet when it was all just water and a few volcanoes. Long before life started here."

"So, from what you tell me, we haven't a chance?" asked Tony.

"That's what I was told by the intelligence," said Max. "They don't think we have a chance and I think that they have given up on us already. Just another casualty in the great scheme of things."

* * *

"Max, you are drinking too much," said Katie. He was half way down a bottle of Highland Park that he had only opened a couple of hours earlier.

"Are you just sore because you can't drink," he mumbled. "I'm drinking for two." He flicked through the television channels for something remotely interesting to watch. Suddenly, he went back a channel.

"Independence Day," he said.

"You've already watched that at least twice before,"

complained Katie. "Isn't there anything else?" she said reaching over for the remote. Max pulled it away from her.

"Wait a minute."

He was watching wave after wave of American jets launching nuclear missiles at a huge spaceship, only for them to explode harmlessly on a force field.

"Have you ever wondered what would happen if we were really invaded by aliens?" he asked.

"It's not something I think much about, Max," said Katie, "and I don't go chasing after the ends of rainbows for crocks of gold. I don't know for certain that there is no gold there, but I do know that the chances are really small."

"Yes, I know," said Max belligerently, "but just suppose, just use your imagination for a minute, what would you do?"

Katie thought about it briefly. "I would just wait for a couple of heroes in a captured alien spaceship to go up and hack their computers. There, simple!"

Max groaned. Did he really expect Katie to have the answer?

"No, that's too far-fetched," he said.

"Maybe they would succumb to our airborne viruses like they did in 'War of the Worlds'?" she suggested. Max had made her suffer many sci-fi films since they first met, both in the cinema and at home on television.

"They would have to land for that to be possible." In practically every sci-fi film that he'd ever watched, the aliens always had an Achilles heel. Some vital weakness that could be used to defeat them.

"Max, do we really have to watch this rubbish again?" begged Katie. He handed her the remote.

"I'm going to bed," he said and slouched-off.

Max had been up a couple of times in the middle of the night and daylight was just breaking as he snuggled up close to Katie and dosed-off again. Mr. Burrage was there.

"I have been told not to contact you," said Mr. Burrage.

"Is that why the dolphins would not come near our craft?" asked Max.

"If you mean our scout ships, yes. They won't come near you again."

"And you are not going to help us?" asked Max.

"I have been told not to contact you again," repeated Mr. Burrage.

"Well, that's a paradox" said Max gleefully, "because you have contacted me to say that you are not going to contact me."

Mr. Burrage waved his hand in dismissal of Max's facetious comment.

"Mr. Burrage, I know that you would never have told me the answers to questions in my exams, but you did, on a couple of occasions, suggest some reading that might help."

Mr. Burrage looked embarrassed, well as embarrassed as an apparition of an old schoolmaster standing-in for a huge, multi-dimensional collective intelligence could.

"Mmm. The only thing I could suggest, in that respect, is the work of one of your Ancient Greek writers – 'Homer's Odyssey'."

"I won't find any technological answers in there," said Max.

"No, if you try to use your technology, you will fail miserably and fatally," mused the master. 'The Old Ones' are very advanced and powerful, but with power comes arrogance and a sense of invulnerability. Use that to your advantage, Hayden, that and what you have already been given. This will be our last communication. I must not contact you again."

Max woke up with a start. He had some reading to do.

CHAPTER TWENTY-FIVE

Max struggled to read Homer's Odyssey. He had never studied the classics in his youth - his schooling had been more of a practical nature. Katie was more familiar with classical literature than he was, but it was the more romantic, later variety.

Having read through it once, he couldn't find anything remotely relevant. Yes, they slew various monsters but they used swords, spears, bows and arrows. What was Mr. Burrage trying to tell him? And, what exactly did he mean by 'what you have already been given'. They had been given an inertial damper facility – one. That was supposedly taken away again but they only removed the software, which Jen was able to restore from a backup. Was that an oversight or intentional? What else had they been given? Max couldn't think of anything else.

Max kissed Katie at the door as he left. He didn't get a hangover from good Scotch but he still felt the effects of the alcohol as he drove towards the car park at the procurement office. Maybe it was the alcohol or maybe his general tiredness, but he hit the kerb of a roundabout when doing a right turn. It wasn't long after that that he saw the flashing blue lights in his rear mirror. The police car pulled along beside him and an officer motioned for him to pull over.

Max wound the window down as the policeman approached.

"Good morning, Sir. Would you please turn off the engine and step out of the car."

Max toyed with the idea of driving off but thought better of it.

"Do you realise that your driving is a bit erratic, Sir?

Can I ask if you have been drinking?"

"I did have a drink last night, not this morning," answered Max.

"I would like you to take a breath test."

Oh, no, though Max. *Why does this have to happen now.*

Max was made to blow into a breathalyser and, sure enough, the red light lit up.

"Sir, I have reason to believe that you have above the legal limit of alcohol in your blood. Therefore I am arresting you and taking you to a police station where you will be asked to provide further breath or blood samples."

Max protested.

The policeman moved in close and whispered, "You people in your fancy cars think you are above the law. Not this time."

Max was shocked, but he could do nothing apart from lock his car parked at the roadside. He was ushered into the back seat of the police car.

At the station, his test confirmed that he had forty--three micrograms of alcohol per 100 millilitres of blood. He was taken to a cell and locked in.

"Christ," he thought to himself, "the world is about to end and they pull me in for drink driving."

He was brought a coffee. Instant. He refused to drink it. He asked for tea but was told he would have to wait.

It was six hours before Max was allowed to leave the police station. He was told that he could expect a one-year disqualification and a three to four hundred pound fine. The fine didn't bother him. The disqualification did, but then, the world might have ended in thirteen days. A driving ban was the least of his troubles.

Max recounted the experience when he got into Mewton Base. Doug looked horrified. Sergei took his side. Abi shrugged. What was he going to tell Katie? Time enough to worry about that. He told the team about his dream. None of them could help with Homer's Odyssey. Not a scholar among them. In the later meeting, they all tossed-in ideas about how to deal with the aliens.

Abi suggested laying mines in the path of the oncoming spaceship. They could transport nuclear warheads into high orbit and leave them there for the aliens to run into. It took Sergei to point-out that unlike the ocean, space is a big place, and three dimensional: the chances of hitting the small number of nuclear warheads that could be deployed were very slim indeed.

Jen thought that they could sneak-up on the aliens from behind the Moon and fire nuclear missiles. Max asked her how they were going to get nuclear missiles into such a firing position. "The big Chinese spacecraft, they have plenty of room inside?" she suggested.

"It would take weeks to convert one of those ships to carry anything useful, besides," said Doug, "I suspect that they would be well able to deal with incoming missiles with a force field or point defence weapons."

"The answer was in my dream," said Max. "I'm sure of it. I just don't know what it was."

* * *

To keep her happy, Max had agreed to go to look at a house with Katie. He though it was pointless. There were only twelve days to Armageddon.

The house was just the type that Katie longed for. Victorian, two floors and a living space in the attic, along with a beautiful garden with rose bushes and hollyhocks.

"Oh, this is just so wonderful," she said, taking his arm and walking him round the garden. "Let's look inside."

The estate agent opened the door and allowed them to step in.

The house was empty. Everything had been removed that was removable. The stained-glass in the front door glowed in the morning sunlight and cast coloured pools of light over the hallway walls and floor. They turned left into the living room. The tall sash windows, and lack of curtains, made the room look light and airy, despite the dark wallpaper. On one wall, a cast iron fireplace with well cleaned-out grate promised long winter nights by a cosy log fire. Behind the living room was a dining room with French windows looking out onto a sloped back garden. Another handsome fireplace graced the wall. At the back, the kitchen was small and looking a bit tired.

"Looks like it will need a new kitchen," said Katie, "but that's not a problem."

They went upstairs and examined the three bedrooms and the guest room in the attic. The estate agent pointed out the 'period' features in the bathroom. Max cringed.

They went back downstairs and looked at the living room again.

"I really love it," said Katie. "Maxie, what do you think?"

"Promising," muttered Max. "Needs a lot of work though."

Katie ran round the rooms once more, like a child. She had already chosen the baby's room and pictured the antique crib against the wall opposite the window.

The estate agent looked on nonchalantly as Max and Katie whispered in the corner.

"Shouldn't we put in an offer?" asked Katie.

"Hold on, hold on," said Max. "Let's not rush into things. We need time to think about it. You don't buy a house on impulse."

"But somebody else might take it," said Katie. Max could see tears in her eyes. "And it's just perfect."

Max turned to the estate agent. "Yes, we like it very

much but we'd like to sleep on it. Is that all right?"

"Yes, of course," said the man in a suit. "But don't take too long, a house like this won't be on the market for long, especially at this price."

On the way home, Max saw the police car with the officer that nabbed him going in the opposite direction. The policeman held a finger up to him.

"Huh," said Katie, "did you see that? Why would he do that?"

"Beats me," replied Max. "Maybe I was driving too carefully and it annoyed him."

"Meetings," sighed Max. "Not another bloody meeting." He had been told to be at headquarters for nine the next morning.

Max was first to be shown into the board room.

"The boardroom," he thought to himself, noticing the pile of coffee cups and jugs already laid out on the table.

"Morning, Max," chimed Doug, "seen anything of Sergei yet?"

"No, just got here myself," replied Max.

Tony Davidson ushered two other men into the room. They nodded. Max recognised the Secretary of State, Michael Reece, and his Minister, Ethan Shaw. Another man followed in behind them. Someone he didn't know.

"Good morning," said Tony Davidson. "I think everyone knows each other, except, maybe for Oliver Beresford who is representing the MOD." Tony introduced the others for Beresford's benefit.

"Everybody has already been briefed on the situation," said Tony, grimly. "The reason for this meeting, and others that will take place on a regular basis, is to monitor the latest developments. I will start with the news from NASA. As you know, they have confirmed the existence of this object on its way toward us. At the moment, it is only a pinpoint, but they are aligning all their orbital telescopes towards it to try and get a clearer picture. They tell me that it will be another week before we see anything significant. The object is in deceleration mode at present. If their technology is anything like ours, they will be travelling backwards, using their engines in braking mode. Of course, we have no idea what technologies these creatures have, all we do know, from Max's contacts, is that they never developed gravity drive technology. Maybe they have something better, who knows. They are a very ancient race and have had millions of years of development time."

"Indeed, that is very hard to comprehend," said Ethan Shaw. "I can't begin to understand what they might have at their disposal."

"Whatever it is," said Doug, "I very much doubt if it will defy the laws of physics. I think it is fair to assume that they will be subjected to the same ones as we are."

"I think it is very dangerous to make assumptions about the enemy," said the man from the MOD. "History has proved that."

Tony continued. "NASA have their top people trying to anticipate what the aliens will do. We know that they want the planet intact so that they can colonise it, which rules-out any large scale devastation with nuclear weapons, or whatever they use. It is more likely that they will release some short-lived toxic pathogens into the lower atmosphere. The most efficient way to do that would be to inject them into the various trade winds that circle the Earth and let the winds do the job for them."

"Or they could poison all the water," said Beresford. "All life on Earth needs water, either saline or fresh."

"Yes, that is another possibility," said Tony. "Can you think of any other ways? Remember, it has to be something that will work at a planetary scale over a short period of time with limited resources."

"Why do you say, limited resources?" asked Sergei. "We haven't a clue what they have or how much of it."

"Their spaceship is large, admittedly," said Max, "but compared to the size of the Earth, it is miniscule. They just couldn't carry enough gas nor generate enough heat to suffocate or burn us. They might be able to do that over time but not in an initial strike. In any case, I was told that they use biological weapons. We know from the two world wars how devastating they can be. You don't even have to breath them in; skin contact is enough to kill."

"So," said Tony, "when they get here, they will need time to identify the best injection points. They will probably need to send scout craft or something physical down into the atmosphere to allow them to create a weather map. These could be piloted or remote controlled, we can't tell."

The discussion went on for two hours with various theories tossed-in but Tony called the day's meeting to a close and agreed to arrange further meetings in the following days as intelligence came in. He told the assembly that the Americans wanted to hold the meetings on their turf but it was agreed that it would take too much precious time flying delegates around the world.

"Just one last thing," said Beresford, "the character that you sent over to us for questioning, Landers is his name, although he didn't tell us that, the CIA did. Apparently he was originally in the US Army but got booted out and joined a private army belonging to a right wing political group. He managed to get thrown out of that too and has set himself up as a one man industrial espionage outfit. Thank you for the laptop you sent across. It told us much more about him, his cohorts, and clients than he did. He was a pretty tough cookie to start with but when he found out that we knew almost everything already, he decided to co-operate. We have shared our findings with the CIA and he will be extradited … if we are still alive."

* * *

"Max," said Tony on the phone. "NASA still wants a face-to-face meeting. As you know more about this situation than any of us, I suggest that you go over to Washington and talk to them. If you take Delta 3, you can be there in an hour. Abi and Doug can go with you. I don't expect that Sergei will want to get involved with Americans."

Max gulped. The thought of landing Gertie on the Whitehouse lawn had a certain appeal. but Gertie was not equipped to land just anywhere.

"Don't worry, Max. NASA will be able to supply suitable landing gear. Get Sergei to give me the specs and I will pass them on. Now, get over there as fast as you can and see what they come up with."

"Ironic," said Max, "The Americans have wanted a glimpse of Gertie for ages, now we are landing her in their back yard."

"NASA doesn't have a back yard in Washington," said Doug. "We will be landing in a vacant building site a block down. They have arranged a three-point landing dolly, suitably sprung, and a car to take you to the meeting."

"You mean we are just going to leave Gertie there and so they can pour over her. Can she even be locked from the outside?"

"Yes, I can lock Gertie remotely," said Doug. "In the short time we are going to be there, they are not going to learn very much. No doubt they will take lots of photographs and give her a good feel, but they won't discover anything useful – not that it matters much now."

Max spotted the landing facility: it had been marked with an infra-red triangle as Sergei had specified. He brought Gertie down very quickly and came to a hover just feet above the landing gear. The last few inches he took very slowly. Max could see that they were completely surrounded by the blank, plastic-wrapped walls of a building site. There were no people or site equipment in view.

"I suppose that we will have to go through immigration first," joked Doug as two large black vehicles surrounded them. Max opened the hatch and they clambered out into the bright sunlight. It was early morning in Washington and the city was relatively quiet.

"Mr. Hayden," said the suited man with dark glasses, "would you please come with us."

Doug took out his mobile phone and tapped a few keys. Gertie's hatch closed with a soft clunk.

The fast drive to the car park under NASA headquarters only took three minutes. It was an unremarkable long, eight story office block, with no obvious signage or features. They were led to a large lift in the car park and accompanied to the top floor. A man and woman showed them into a room where they could change out of their flight suits. After a few minutes, they were taken to a meeting room, where there were four people waiting.

"Ah, Mr. Hayden, Mr. Sinclair and Ms. Bristow. Welcome to NASA headquarters. I am Jack MacNamarra, Head of Space Research. My colleagues here are Leroy Farrell, one of our eminent space scientists, Tyler Balboa from our deep space observation group, and Angela Ford, who represents the President, who can't be with us – but I can't for the world of me imagine what could be more important."

Angela Ford leaned over and whispered something in his ear.

"Oh, okay," said MacNamarra.

"I was rather hoping that we could have landed on the Whitehouse lawn like I've seen happen in films," said Max.

MacNamarra scowled. "I wanted this to happen somewhere more remote but here is the only place we could get this group together quickly."

Max went quiet. Abi crossed her legs.

"Mr. Hayden, this has all happened very quickly and I must admit to being in a state of shock. I was horrified to hear that you, the Chinese and Russians have all been doing your own thing and that it has all been kept from us."

"Just the way you have kept your secrets from Roswell and the UFO sightings by your astronauts on the Moon," said Doug. "And what about your Aurora project, high altitude scram-jet technology. You won't even admit that it exists."

MacNamarra shuffled uneasily and changed the subject.

"Look, we have only ten days until this spacecraft gets within spitting distance of our planet. We don't know what they will do. Will they observe for a while or will they attack immediately?"

Leroy Farrell broke in. "We haven't involved the military at this stage. I don't think that our military are going to be a lot of use to us in this instance. I've been thinking about the aliens' potential tactics. They are coming-in towards our north pole. They are coming straight here, not through the solar system, so they must know something of conditions here. If they were just exploring, they would be looking at the other planets too, but they are headed straight here."

"Yes," said Max. "They have already done their exploring a long time ago. They have obviously ear-marked Earth, being in our system's Goldilocks Zone, as a potential colony. I don't think they will know exactly how far Earth has developed since they were last here. They know it is a Class M planet of a particular mass and distance from the primary. It will probably just be one of many planets on their agenda."

"To change the subject for a minute," said MacNamarra. "I hear that the Chinese have a base on the Moon?"

"Yes," said Max. "It's called YuèGōng, Palace in the Moon."

"What do you know about it?" asked Tyler Balboa.

"What do you want to know?" asked Max.

Balboa didn't quite know what to ask.

"We've been there," said Abi. "We were made very welcome."

MacNamarra looked exasperated. "That is not very relevant to the current situation unless they have a deep space telescope there."

"Yes, they have an observatory," said Abi, "we were told about it but we didn't actually see it. I don't know anything about its capabilities."

"The moon base might not be relevant in itself," said Max, "but the Chinese spacecraft certainly are. We saw four of them at the moon base, they probably have more back in the wilds of China. They are about ten times the size of ours and are made to carry substantial payloads."

"Are they armed?" asked Angela Ford.

"Not as far as we know," said Max, "although I imagine that they could be adapted to carry missiles easily enough. The Russian ones certainly are."

"With what?" asked the President's representative. "Don't tell me they have high powered lasers?"

Max laughed. "They are way ahead of you there. There isn't an official English translation for what they have. Science fiction writers would call it a disrupter beam, I suppose. It uses gravity technology to scatter molecules. We didn't get to see a demonstration but I'm told that it can vaporise space junk or a small asteroid from a couple of miles away."

The Americans were visibly stunned.

Leroy Farrell spoke again. "A huge spaceship is not

going to be able to negotiate Earth's atmosphere. Whatever they are going to do, they will have to do it from orbit. That means that they will be sending down smaller craft, which might be more vulnerable to what we have at our disposal. Remember, they know as little about us as we do about them."

"Yes, but blowing-up something carrying a load of toxic biological chemicals in the Earth's atmosphere is not a good idea. The stuff will come down eventually, somewhere."

"Yes, you are right," said Doug, "we will have to dispose of it at a safe distance from the atmosphere. Easier said than done."

"Well, it's all conjecture at the minute," said Jack MacNamarra. "We really are going to have to play this out as it goes. Now, I would offer to give you a guided tour of NASA headquarters but, to be frank, there is nothing of any interest here. It is just an administrative centre – wall-to-wall filing cabinets."

"I would like to offer, on behalf of our President," said Angela Ford, "his most sincere gratitude for your trip here today. How long did it take you to get here, by the way?"

"Just under the hour," smiled Max.

The woman took a deep intake of breath.

They all shook hands and exchanged pleasantries before Max and his crew picked-up their suits and were shuttled back to their waiting Delta. They were glad to see it was surrounded by armed guards in Humvees.

"All this way and they didn't even offer us a coffee," said Doug. He tapped a password into his phone and Gertie's hatch cracked open. They climbed-in and donned their helmets. Max was talking to someone on the radio.

"We are clear to take-off in five minutes," he told Abi. "There is a lot more air traffic around here than we are used to."

Five minutes later, Auntie Gertie accelerated upwards

out of the building site. A loud supersonic boom was heard across Washington DC.

"Whoops," grinned Abi. "We're not supposed to do that."

Unusually, Max was home for supper.

"Have a good day?" asked Katie.

"Oh, yes," replied Max, not wanting to get into details.

"The estate agent rang up to see if we had made a decision on the house," she said. "We haven't really had a chance to talk about it, you are always so busy."

Max felt anger, but he didn't want to show it. He was trying to deal with an alien invasion, a drink driving charge, and all Katie could think about was moving house. He decided that he needed to go outside to cool down.

"Where are you going?" asked Katie. He was about to snap at her but kept his temper.

"I'll be back in a minute, just need a breath of fresh air. Been in stuffy meeting rooms all day."

He put the latch on the door and went out into the lane at the front of the cottage. He peered up at the sky. A few of the brightest star were already visible. A crescent moon hung in the sky. He would have loved to take Katie on that moon buggy ride to the edge of the crater. Maybe visit some of the historical landing sites to see that first step for Man. He could hear the click of dishes from inside and wondered what the future held in store.

"About the house," said Max. "It's nice but it needs a lot of work. I would prefer to buy a house where we could just move in and live in it without being up to the eyes in builders and decorators."

"We could still live here until it was ready?" suggested Katie. "It would only be for a month or two."

"I know you love the house," said Max, "but it's really

not my kind of thing. Old stuff makes me squirm. I suppose it reminds me of dead people."

"Oh, Maxie," she cried. "I love old things. They have history. They have character."

"They have baggage," said Max. "Let's find something we both like."

Katie fell back in her chair and pouted.

"We'll be here for the rest of our lives," she said, "and it's not even ours."

"We will buy a house," insisted Max. "All in good time."

"Will you at least come to the car boot sale with me?" asked Katie.

Max was just about at the end of his tether. He hated car boot sales and all the junk in them.

"Yes, okay," he conceded. "As long as it's quick."

At least the field was dry. He didn't have to jump over puddles of mud. Katie went into her honey bee routine and hovered between tables of domestic ejecta, picking things up and asking prices. Max spotted the occasional vintage camera, but most of them were too new and utilitarian to be of interest. Hell, why was he even considering buying cameras at all? He went into a daze and watched Katie, now with a pronounced bump, haggle amongst the stalls.

She came over to where Max was waiting.

"I've been buying toys," she said with a big grin. "Look." She had found a couple of dolls, a teddy bear and a wooden farm tractor.

"You are buying toys and you don't even know if it's a boy or girl?" asked Max.

"Oh yes I do," she smiled.

"You do?" asked Max, "and you didn't think to tell me?"

"I was keeping it a surprise," she said.

"Well, what is it?" asked Max.

Katie rubbed her tummy.

"One of each," she grinned.

Max rubbed his forehead. The abstract concept of 'baby' was suddenly a lot more focussed in his mind.

"Oh Katie," he said, giving her a cuddle. "You should have told me."

"I have now," she said, and kissed his cheek. It was most unlike Max, but he helped her back to the car, taking her arm and carrying the teddy and tractor in his other hand.

* * *

Max hadn't seen Tony dressed down before. He always wore a smart suit everywhere he went. He had come to Mewton Base in slacks, a jumper and an open-necked shirt.

"He'll be rolling-up his sleeves next," thought Max.

"I hear that you had a little brush with the law?" asked Tony.

Max lowered his head in mock shame.

"Yes, it was a fair cop," he said, "except that the cop wasn't fair."

"What do you mean?" asked Tony, with his eyebrows raised.

"I think I was being victimised for driving a Six Series BMW. The guy had a chip on his shoulder."

"Really," said Tony. "The law is very strict about drink driving procedures. If that policeman did not do it by the book, it could be thrown out of court. Let me talk to our lawyer, I'm sure that he will be able to swing something."

"I did admit to drinking and the breath test was over the limit."

"Well, we won't worry about it now," said Tony, "there are bigger problems."

"Yes, there are," said Max.

In the meeting room, Tony was standing at the table.

"I've just had NASA on the phone. They still haven't got anything worthwhile visually but they have been able to run some spectrographic tests. The spaceship is indeed coming in backwards and seems to be spewing plasma of some kind. It isn't enough to tell us about their propulsion methodology but it is enough to demonstrate that whatever it isn't too exotic. It is using reaction mass ejection like a rocket motor would, except that it is not a chemical rocket. Might be some sort of ion drive or atomic motor."

"Atomic motor?" asked Sergei. "What is that?"

"If it was possible, somehow, to create a continuous atomic explosion behind a spaceship, it would push it forward, Newton's Third Law and all that," said Tony.

"I've heard of pulsed explosions but never a continuous one," said Sergei looking a bit puzzled.

"Again, we are speculating about something with insufficient evidence," said Tony. "All should become much clearer in the next few days."

"Yes, it will be here in a week and we can ask them all about it," spat Max.

"You have to look at this philosophically," said Tony. "When you see a film of a lion chasing down and killing an antelope on some African plain, you always think 'poor little antelope', you don't consider that the lion is just trying to feed its young."

"Yes," said Max, "but try explaining that to the children of the antelope. That's what we are, the children of the Earth."

Tony quickly changed the subject. "How are Sergei's people doing with the railguns?"

Max answered, "All three Deltas are now equipped with six rails. Gertie has a magazine on each rail holding ten slugs. The others only have single shot capabilities at present. I don't know if we can upgrade Delta 2 in time, it's not a simple job."

"Right," said Tony. "Well, if I can be of any help, you know where I am."

"He's rolling his sleeves up," chuckled Max to himself.

Later, Max saw Tony in the hangar talking to Sergei. Tony was pointing at something under Delta 2's hull. Max drew closer.

"Yes, an excellent idea," said Sergei. "Might work. I'll give it a try."

Tony saw Max coming and pre-empted his question.

"Yes, Max. I didn't get to be head of McGregor's Aerospace by pushing paperclips. I was an engineer most of my earlier life. Sergei is a good engineer but he does things strictly by rote. This takes some divergent thinking. I've just suggested a quicker way to implement his automatically fed railgun slugs and he thinks it will work."

"Good," said Max, "but somehow, I don't think that railguns are the answer here. I'm going to have to out-diverge you on that one."

Tony did a double-take, but eventually got the point.

"We have to make the best of what we've got," said Tony, in his defence. "If we can cripple some bio-bomber outside the Earth's atmosphere, it is a job well done. There is enough dangerous material up there already, a little more won't make much difference."

Max nodded.

CHAPTER TWENTY-SIX

There was an atmosphere of excitement when the photos came in from the Chinese observatory.

"The buggers," said Doug, "they do have a high powered space telescope up in YuèGōng and they didn't tell us. Look what they have sent us."

What had previously been just a dot had now become a definite shape. It was blurry and indistinct, but it was not a dot.

"Having another point of view should help a lot," said Max. "Hopefully, the aliens won't notice our lunar outpost. I will tell the Chinese to keep their profile as low as possible, only tight beam communications back to Earth. As the aliens are approaching from the celestial north and the moon base is at the south pole, perhaps they will remain undetected. They are unlikely to attack the Moon as there is no atmosphere to spread their bugs."

"What about the Russians?" asked Doug. "They were only visitors to YuèGōng, as we were. They don't have any lunar presence."

"The Russians are going to have to co-operate with the Chinese, as are the Americans and everybody else that wants to come to the party. Do the French know anything about this yet?" asked Max.

"No, the French have been kept out of it so far. You know what they are like with their red tape," replied Doug. "They will be told when the United Nations meet tomorrow. It might be difficult to keep a lid on it after that."

"They have to keep it quiet," said Max. "The media must not get hold of this until the very last minute."

"Yes, they understand that, but with so many delegates something might leak," said Doug.

"Then they have to restrict it to a few key players behind closed doors. They have done that before. Let them call it a steering committee or something, I don't care what, but they have to keep tight wraps on it for as long as possible," said Max. "If the word gets out, all hell is going to break loose."

Doug played with his pen.

"Maybe so," he said, "but in the end, it's not going to make a great deal of difference. Whether it is a wailing or a whimper, the day of judgement will come whether you are a believer of not. Faith will not affect the outcome one way or the other. A neurotoxin in the atmosphere is a great leveller. In the end, we are all just a load of chemicals and subject to chemical reactions."

Tony Davidson was back in his suit and tie for the meeting at headquarters.

"I've been trying to tie-down what resources we have from our various partners. It's not easy. The Chinese were quite open. Apart from the four spacecraft you saw at YuèGōng, they have two others on the ground that are operational and another two in the process of being built. They are a few months away from completion so we have to discount those."

Tony drew six pentagons on the whiteboard.

"Can they be armed?" asked Max.

"I don't think we will get anything useful in the time available. They have cargo bays that can open to vacuum and could accommodate some missile launchers but their missiles are not designed for space - they need atmosphere for their guidance fins to work. They wouldn't be much better than a galleon's cannons."

"And the Russians?" asked Max.

"Not so forthcoming. I had to press them hard. They have five operational spacecraft of the type you saw at the

Chinese moon base. The have some earlier experimental models but they are only flying test beds. Their five 'flying saucers', I won't attempt to try to pronounce their words, have been fitted with their gravity beam projectors but they are only effective at a short range of about two or three kilometres."

Tony added five ovals to the whiteboard.

"What about the Americans?" asked Doug. "Do they have anything useful?"

"Ah, now, there's the surprise." Said Tony, "They have been keeping things up their sleeves. As we suspected, they have some frightening stuff in low Earth orbit – not so much planetary defence as planetary offence. Needless to say, it all points downwards and getting it to point outwards is not so easy. They have some serious stuff in bunkers that is designed to intercept asteroids a long way out. That could be useful. More interestingly, they do have something akin to our G-drives which they have reverse engineered from alien technology. Of course, they don't have the Russian fusion power plants that we and the rest of our partners have. Instead, they have some not-so-efficient fission powered reactors, but they do work. The bad news is that they only have one of these craft and it's not armed. On the other hand, we have been offered their entire arsenal of fighter aircraft which might be useful in the atmosphere." He did some more squiggles on the whiteboard representing missiles and a cloud-shaped blob with a question mark in the middle.

"But we have already discussed the folly of attacking anything carrying toxic material in the atmosphere," said Max. "We don't know if even a nuclear explosion would destroy the payload. We can't afford to take that chance. Detonating nuclear missiles in the atmosphere isn't a good idea either, so I think that we will have to discount fighter planes, from any nation, unless the situation changes drastically. This war has to be fought in space."

"And we don't have much expertise in that area," said Tony. "Then, there is our contribution." Three triangles were added with the other shapes. He drew a big circle round them all.

"There, that's it. All we have between life and death."

* * *

Doug answered the phone as he opened the door of his car.

"Hello, Rahul. What can I do for you?"

Rahul Singh sounded somewhat agitated.

"Doug, you asked me a few days ago to do a sweep in the direction of Delta Cassiopeia for any anomalies and I sent you the stacks. You didn't tell me what we were looking at. It was just something headed in this direction. I assumed that it was a comet. We have been keeping tabs on this object and, I don't know how to tell you this, but something very strange has happened."

"What?" asked Doug."

"It has altered course."

"Oh," said Doug, noncommittally.

"Comets don't change course," said Rahul. "What are you not telling me? The speculation is growing rife around here."

"I can't tell you that, Rahul. I really can't. For a start, I don't know, and secondly, I am not allowed to discuss it. Official Secrets Act and all that stuff."

"Are we having visitors?" asked Rahul. "People have to be told."

"Rahul, it is imperative that people are not told. Not yet anyway. You have to trust me on this one, believe me."

"Does anyone else know?"

"Yes," said Doug, "The leaders of the biggest nations

are abreast of the situation and we are taking appropriate measures."

"Appropriate measures?" screamed Rahul, "what measures?"

Doug realised that he had already said too much.

"I am sorry, Rahul. I really can't discuss this," said Doug. "A public announcement will be made shortly. Goodbye. Take care."

Doug slipped his phone back into his inside pocket. Max was listening to the conversation from the passenger seat.

"Do we have a problem, Doug?" he asked.

Doug exhaled. "These guys aren't stupid. They have spotted a course correction and are putting two and two together. I don't know if we can contain this much longer."

"I had better warn Tony," said Max, taking his phone out. "We have to have contingencies in place for when the shit hits the fan."

Doug and Max headed back to Mewton Base via the procurement office car park.

Max could feel the buzz as soon as he got out of the lift. People were talking.

"What is it, Jen?" he asked, taking her by the arm into his office.

"It's hit the net," she replied. "Only conspiracy theorists at the minute." Jen sat down at Max's computer and typed-in a web address.

"Look at this," she said. "Giant alien mothership headed towards Earth." The headline was accompanied by some very imaginative illustrations. One was an obviously computer-generated image of a huge alien battle destroyer armed to the teeth and firing green death rays in every direction. Another picture showed a really terrifying bug-eyed monster that would have done any horror film poster credit.

"Christ," said Max, "I knew something like this would happen."

"Look at the comments," said Jen, scrolling down the page of the blog. There were very few believers. Most of the comments were ridiculing the idea as preposterous. One even published the address of the illustrator's web site that the picture had been lifted from.

"I can see that our anti-conspiracy agents have been busy," smiled Max.

"Here's another one," said Jen, bringing up another web page. This time, the stacked images from the asteroid hunters showed the dotted path of the approaching object – complete with course correction.

"That more worrying," said Max. "It won't be so easy to rubbish that one."

"Oh, they have," said Jen. "Somebody has questioned the use of open-source software to produce meaningful results. What dingo-doo. Oh, excuse my Australian."

Max grimaced. "It's not so much the validity of the posts here, it's the fact that they are discussing it at all. That's just going to have more people going out and trying to find more material. There are a lot of amateur astronomers out there with very expensive kit. Now they will all be putting-in their tuppence worths."

"Max, have you seen the front page of The Post today?" asked Tony.

"No, I don't pay any attention to that rag," said Max, holding his phone to his ear with his shoulder as he typed-in the paper's web address.

He looked at the blurry photograph and scrolled down the page to read the report.

"Yes, they have lifted this off some guy's blog almost verbatim," said Max. "I wouldn't worry too much about anything that The Post prints, only complete idiots would believe that paper."

"They are getting worryingly close to the truth," said Tony. "Today, The Post, tomorrow, every national daily in the world."

"Do you know anything about the meeting of the United Nations Council?" asked Max.

"Not much," said Tony. "It was discussed yesterday by the inner sanctum, but a complete blackout has been put on it. It's not going to filter down to us mortals."

Max found Jen in her lab scouring the web for the latest conspiracy theories.

"Yes, it's really hotting-up out there in blogland," she said and pointed to some choice articles. Her phone rang.

"Max, it's for you - Tony."

"Max," said Tony Davison, "I've had some info in from NASA. Have a look at the email I've just sent you."

"Okay, I'll do it now," replied Max and headed off to his own office. The email was encrypted so he had to process it to see what was in it. His jaw dropped. The photograph wasn't pin-sharp but it did show something like he had never seen or imagined before. It was obviously foreshortened; he could only see, what he assumed, was the back of the spaceship. It had a bluish glow but the rest was quite indistinguishable. The text said that it was about the same distance from Earth as the Asteroid Belt between Mars and Jupiter but at right angles to the orbits of the Solar System, so it wasn't going to pass any planets on the way in. It was decelerating hard and had made several course adjustments. It would arrive in Earth orbit in five days or less.

Doug walked-in.

"You've seen this too?" asked Max.

"Yes," said Doug. "From the direction it's coming, it will

most likely go for a high polar orbit. That means that they can cover the entire planet with a few orbits."

"Do you think that they will attack right away?" asked Max.

"My guess is that they will take their time," said Doug. "They will want to plan their drops to hit the wind and ocean currents. It's not as if we are going anywhere."

"I want to get a closer look at that thing," said Max.

"That could be fatally dangerous," said Doug.

"Of all the resources we have at hand, Auntie Gertie is best placed to go out there and have a look. Gertie is well hidden from radar and anyway, they might not be worried about something so small and insignificant."

"I'd be more inclined to send Delta 1," said Doug. "Jen has shown very good remote control skills."

"Yes, it's all those computer games she plays," said Max. "I don't know. I think that Abi and I could get in close enough for a recce and Gertie can dodge anything thrown at her better than anything else we have. I'm not thinking of attacking it, just having a look at what we are up against."

"For when our massive space fleet come out from their hiding place behind the Moon and obliterates it with plasma cannons and photon torpedoes?" said Doug sarcastically.

Max didn't answer. The spaceship was still out of range but he was already planning his play.

* * *

Late in the afternoon, Abe Thompson drove up to the small store not far from his hideout in South West Florida. He had been talking to Ellie, John Lander's woman on the phone an hour before. She wanted to know if Thompson had heard from him. Of course, he hadn't. Lander's was locked up in a cell deep below London. He had told Ellie that he was going away for a couple of days. She assumed that it was overseas, but didn't know where.

"I bet he's gone to England," Thompson had told Ellie. "He has a bee in his bonnet about some kind of experimental aircraft that they have over there." Ellie wasn't at all interested in the details, she wanted to ask him if an offer that they'd had for the ranch was acceptable. She thought not but maybe John would be happy just to get rid of it.

Thompson picked up a newspaper from the stand outside the store and tucked it under his arm. He went in and bought some groceries and a six-pack of beer, paid in cash and went back to his car. He threw the shopping into the back seat and drove back to the small house he was living in, a mile down the road.

When he went into his house, he put everything down on the kitchen worktop. He put the beer into the fridge except for one he held back. They were already cold from the chiller in the store. He twisted-off the cap and sat down on a chair with the newspaper in front of him. He turned immediately to the sports page and checked out the Miami Dolphins. They were still underperforming in the league and Thompson wondered why he even bothered with them. He folded the paper and put it back down on the table face up. He took another slug of his beer. A headline on the front page caught his attention

"Massive alien spacecraft headed for Earth."

He nearly choked on his beer and coughed as he put it down and unfolded the newspaper.

"Nah, can't be. Another hoax," he thought to himself. "They'll print any cock-and-bull story to sell a few newspapers." He read on. All the sources were unofficial and criticising the government for keeping it all hushed-up. There was no word from NASA or the government. The story continued overleaf and as he poured through it, the more he began to believe what he was reading.

"Bloody hell," he said to himself."He needed to talk to someone else about this. He didn't trust his own judgement. He took the paper and went next door to Frank's house. He just walked in.

"Hey, Frank. Have you seen this?" he said holding up the newspaper. Frank laughed.

"Abe, I remember when they did a radio program on Halloween when I was a kid. Scared the whole country shitless but it was just a play about the Martians invading Earth. Orson Wells was in it."

"War of the Worlds?" suggested Abe.

"Yes, that's it," nodded Frank. "Sure put the wind up a lot of folks."

"This story looks pretty convincing," said Abe.

Frank waved his hand.

"I'll believe it when I see it," he said. "Dolphins aren't doing so well this season. All that money and they are playing like a bunch of schoolgirls."

Abe knew he wasn't going to get much sense out of old Frank and went off to see if anybody else was interested.

* * *

Four days to go and the news hit all the media. The United Nations made a terse official statement to the press.

"An extraterrestrial spaceship is headed towards Earth. We do not know their intentions at this stage but it is unimaginable that such an advanced race would be belligerent. We will welcome them with open arms and hope that our two cultures can find common ground for trade and cultural exchange. The United Nations is in the process of setting-up a welcoming committee. We do not believe that there is any cause for concern and look forward eagerly to this truly momentous occasion."

Max raised his eyes to the ceiling.

"What a load of bollocks," he yelled.

"I think that they've said the right things," said Doug.

"No!" cried Max, "too woolly. Typical diplomatic bullshit. They should have been much more positive. There is too much 'unknown' about this statement."

"But, we don't know," said Doug.

"Maybe, but we shouldn't say so!" exclaimed Max. "Now, there will be panic, you'll see. Look, I'm going to have to pop home for an hour. Katie will be frightened to death."

"Okay," said Doug, "but we have Tony coming over at four. Better get back for then."

"I won't be that long," said Max.

As he had expected, Katie had seen the one o'clock news on television.

"Oh, Max. Is this true?" she cried as he came in the door.

"I'm afraid so," said Max.

"Have you known about this all along?" she asked. "Weren't you going to tell me?"

Max gave her a tight hug.

"You know that I'm not allowed to discuss my work," said Max, "but now it's official, I suppose that it doesn't matter anymore."

"What's going to happen?" she asked.

"I wish I knew, Katie. We do not know what to expect."

"What if they are hostile?"

"Ah, you've been watching too many sci-fi movies," smiled Max weakly. "There are no indications that they are hostile."

"But can you be sure?"

"No, unfortunately we cannot be sure of anything," he said.

"What if they overwhelm us and take over our planet?" asked Katie, with a shake in her voice. "How long have you known about this?"

"A couple of weeks," replied Max. "There is a group of asteroid hunters who have been plotting its path and now NASA have sent us some blurry pictures."

"So this is why you have been dithering about buying a house," she said accusingly.

"Yes," he confessed. "We need to see the outcome of this before we can make any decisions one way or the other."

Katie sat down on an armchair and cried.

"Max. Is this it?" she asked.

"No, of course not," he reassured. "Everything will be fine. Who knows what marvellous technologies they will be able to share with us?"

Katie sobbed into a wet tissue.

"Katie, I have to go back to work now. I'll see you later,"

He put his arms lightly around her neck and kissed the top of her head. He left without looking round. He didn't want her to see his tears.

CHAPTER TWENTY-SEVEN

The reaction to the news varied wildly. Many just refused to believe it. Some wept. Some prayed. Some looted. Some just sat and stared at the floor, waiting.

Religious communities couldn't agree. Some saw it optimistically as a second coming. Others expected Armageddon with fire, brimstone and a wailing and gnashing of teeth. The airwaves were hot with discussions and interviews, with every politician and minor celebrity asked for their views. Little of it made any sense and only compounded the sense of fear and dread.

Some cities saw rioting and looting. What exactly they thought they were going to do with all the plundered booty was anyone's guess. Police and armies tried to hold back angry throngs of marchers, protesters, stone-throwing youths and armed militia hell-bent on overthrowing unresponsive governments and petty dictators who had simply vanished.

Buildings were boarded-up, although it became nigh impossible to get timber or boarding-up screens at any price. Some just dropped everything but a few personal belongings and left. Roads across the world became jammed as families packed their cars and headed out of town. For some misguided reason, they thought they were safer in the open.

Television newsreels showed entire blocks of buildings on fire. What the looter couldn't carry, they set light to. Cars were overturned and torched. Even boats in marinas had fuel poured over them and set alight.

Max couldn't imagine such chaos in his little corner of England. Folk were too genteel. They would all be down the pub drinking G and Ts and counting down the minutes like it was New Year's Eve. He thought of Katie at home all alone and what she must be going through. He wanted to be with her at the end but he had work to do.

Tony had now set-up base at Mewton. He was wasting too much time driving to and fro from headquarters. He spent much of his time on the phone and communicating via email.

"The reception committee are about ready," he said.

"What, that bunch of United Nations technocrats and stuffed shirts?" asked Max.

"No, Max. The Chinese and Russians are ensconced at YuèGōng. The Chinese craft have been fitted with some kind of missile batteries that can fire through the open cargo bay ramps. Sounds all very Heath Robinson to me. The Russians have their gravity beam weapons and some bolted-on missile launchers of dubious usefulness. Sergei's team are almost ready with auto-fed railguns on all three Deltas. We are about as ready as we can be."

"Tony, can I ask you something personal?" asked Max.

"What is that?"

"I would like to bring Katie over here. It breaks my heart to know that she is all by herself at home."

"I'm sorry, Max. If I allowed that for you, I couldn't say no to other people in the same boat. The base would be overrun with families all demanding attention and interfering with the work we have to do. It can't be done."

"I understand," said Max, trying hard to hold back his tears.

New photographs of the approaching menace came in by the hour. NASA's deep space telescopes and the Chinese telescope on the Moon offered the best views but were still not showing any detail other than a blue glow. Artists impressions of the ship showed-up on the internet, each trying to outdo the other. Many of them looked like the space-going battleships that had adorned the front covers of science-fiction paperbacks for the previous fifty years. There were flying saucers and things that looked like the steelwork of skyscrapers. There was even a huge black triangular one with drives at each corner. People wanted news but all they got was opinion and speculation. There was no news and the speculation was that the world was about to end.

Crowds congregated in city squares around the world. The families had left: these were the adolescents and the old who had come to recognise, if not accept, that the end was near. They listened to self-appointed visionaries and religious leaders. They stood silently. The panic and looting of the previous days had all but subsided as the miscreants finally realised that there was no point. The Earth was going to be levelled by destruction rays from countless alien saucers any time now. Vast atomic explosions would tear the planet apart.

"The doom-mongers are having a field day," said Doug. "They think that they have been right all along."

"Idiots," snarled Max. "There will just be more people having heart attacks and committing suicide because of their drivelling."

"Max," said Tony, "I think the time has come to go out there and intercept this thing. The longer we wait, the less time we will have to do anything useful. What is it? How is it armed? If you can get some photographs or video from a safe distance, it will give our strategists something to work with."

"I couldn't agree more," said Max. "Gertie is all prepped and ready to go. Should we take Delta 1 along too? We can afford to take more risks with a drone."

"No," said Tony. "When it comes to the crunch, Delta 1

will be useful in a battle. It is just as manoeuvrable as Delta 3 because there are no passengers to worry about. Delta 2 is going to be the weak one as there are no inertial dampers. Jen can use Delta 2 as the remote control base for Delta 1."

"Right," said Max. "Abi, we will leave in an hour."

Abi gave a very slight nod of affirmation. She didn't seem all that enthusiastic.

"Oh, no," said Tony, as he turned-off his phone. "The United Nations want to requisition one of the Chinese spacecraft to take a welcoming committee out to rendezvous with the aliens."

"And who will be supplying the translation and security services?" asked Max.

"They don't think of things like that," said Tony. "Anyway, I have refused point blank, on behalf of our Chinese friends. The diplomats made all kinds of threats against me and our partners but I told them to sod off. Diplomats can't handle language like that."

Max considered ringing Katie. He might not ever see her again but he really didn't want to tell her that.

Abi and Max were strapped-in to Gertie. They were given the all-clear from control but Abi was hesitant.

"What are we letting ourselves in for, Max?" she asked.

Max didn't answer immediately.

"We all have our day," he said solemnly.

Abi lifted Gertie into the air gingerly and then gunned straight upwards just under the speed of sound until she got to an altitude of fifty miles, then opened up fully. Gertie shot silently out into empty space.

"Don't head straight at it," said Max. "That could be interpreted as an aggressive move. Best to head off at an angle towards the Sun and then curve back in, but stay well back. We're only having a look."

Max set his helmet display at maximum magnification

and could see the blue glow of the ship's engines, but the rest of it was still very indistinct.

"It's just one big hazy blue glow," said Max. "Can't distinguish any structure at the minute."

"We are still a long way off," said Abi. "It's still half a million miles away. Twice the distance to the Moon."

As the hours passed, the view didn't improve significantly.

"I'm still not seeing any kind of structure," he said. "I think I can see a smaller green glow behind the large blue one. If the ship is travelling in reverse in braking mode, the green glow would be at the front. It's still going at a hell of a speed."

As they arced round towards the oncoming ship, the foreshortening decreased. Max could see two hazy glowing spheres, a large blue one and a smaller green one. He swept through the light wavelengths in his helmet display and couldn't comprehend what he was looking at. It just didn't make any sense. The extreme magnification of his viewing camera pixelated the image so all he could make-out was two glowing spheres and something in-between. Whatever it was, it didn't look like any spaceship he had seen in fact or fiction. As they moved-in closer, he still couldn't make out any detail.

"Abi, we are going to have to go in closer. This thing doesn't make any sense to me at all. At the slightest hint of them opening fire on us, use Jen's random evasion program and hold on tight."

"We are about a hundred miles off it at the minute, how close do you want me to go in?" asked Abi.

"Slow down and move-in to fifty miles," said Max. When they reached that distance Max shook his head. He reduced the magnification on his helmet and the image sharpened.

"Good God," he said. "What do you make of it Abi?"

"I'm as baffled as you are, Max. If I had to describe it, I would say that it looked like a sea creature - part squid, part lobster. It's very complicated."

"Yes, they look like tentacles, or tendrils, or a lobster's antennae, but there are too many of them. They seem to be holding that blue sphere at the back. There is a bulbous body in the middle and, what I assume to be the front, has thicker limbs holding the green sphere. It does look more organic than machine. And what are all those bits that look detached? No, they are connected when I shift wavelength, they are just beyond the visible spectrum."

"Max, this is just incredible," said Abi. "Look at those six big paddle things surrounding the blue sphere. They must be something to do with steering."

"Just watch out for any reaction to us," said Max. "Try edging in just a little more, I want to get some video. I can't find any words to describe this thing."

Abi closed the distance. The vast scale of the object took Max's breath away. Tendrils that must have been at least a kilometre long trailed out from the rear and mid-ships. There was no concept of symmetry: each of the tentacle-like appendages was completely different in shape and had branches coming off them like the twigs of a tree. Structures that, on a tree, would have been leaves, looked more like pieces of torn flesh. The entire surface of the ship cycled colours from magenta, to red, to orangey yellow. It seemed to have an ever-changing web of electrical arcs, like lightning covering skin.

"Look out," screamed Abi, "it's tuning towards us."

They watched the huge craft turn slowly. As the bright green sphere turned to face them and the paddle-like appendages around the blue sphere twisted and curled behind, Max could make out a central part that didn't glow. It was like black glass.

"Looks like a big eye," said Jen. "I think we should get

out of here." Max continued watching the ship behind them as they moved away from it at top speed.

"No, it wasn't turning towards us," said Max. "It was just turning round. Now the green sphere is at the front and the blue one is diminishing in intensity at the rear. It's heading for Earth orbit."

"I can't see anything that remotely resembles a weapon," said Abi.

"Apart from the drive at the back, I can't identify any part of it or its purpose," said Max. "I still don't know if it's a machine or an organic creature. At least, it didn't attack us. Get us home, Abi. We have to inspect those videos to try and see what makes that thing tick."

"The Americans are all ready to lob some nukes at it," said Tony. "The Chinese and Russians don't have the range that the Americans have but will follow-up as soon as they are in range."

"But well out of the atmosphere?" asked Max with his eyebrows raised.

"Of course," said Tony. "Now, are you going to show me the videos you took?"

The large screen in the meeting room lit up. Max had already edited-out the early, blurry footage and went straight for the full-screen medium shot that showed the entire craft.

There was a communal gasp in the room, followed by silence.

"What kind of mind could conceive of such a thing?" asked Tony.

"We don't know if it was built or grown," said Max. "It looks like it's a living creature yet it is manipulating what must be an enormous source of energy in that blue sphere."

The video zoomed-in on the surface texture.

"Notice how the skin is alive with electricity," said Max.

"It's like millions of electrical storms all happening at once."

"St. Elmo's fire," said Doug. "It's a phenomenon that happened in the rigging of sailing ships when the air became highly charged in electrical storms at sea."

"So, there's obviously a huge amount of static energy built-up in that ship," said Tony. "Maybe that's what powers their drive."

"And you say that it didn't react to your presence?" asked Tony.

"No," said Max. "Either it didn't see us or it didn't care."

"Was there any sign of it being armed?" asked Doug.

"Nothing that I could recognise as being a weapon," said Max, "but I really don't know what to look for. It didn't have gun turrets or batteries of missile launchers. Considering its size, it could have had thousands of them, but I couldn't see any."

"What are all these long, wispy things?" asked Jen.

"They could be antennae for long-range communications," answered Max, "but your guess is as good as mine."

"It will be with us tomorrow," said Tony. "It has slowed-down considerably. NASA says it looks like it is going to insert into a polar orbit but at quite a far distance – a thousand miles up initially but it might close-in on that."

"How is it going to introduce its pathogens?" asked Doug. "From what I can see, there are no shuttles or any means of delivering them."

"It's just so alien," said Max. "We can't begin to anticipate its methods. There are sections that seem to be detached from the main body, although my helmet shows that they are connected by something beyond the electromagnetic spectrum."

Six missile silo doors opened somewhere in the midwest

of North American. After a brief pause, five of them spat out long, nuclear-tipped missiles. The sixth exploded underground and sent a billowing fireball high into the sky. It wasn't a nuclear explosion as the warhead was not yet armed but it did spread radioactive waste over a wide area.

"We have five, repeat five, birds in the air," called a technician at a console. "Bird six has gone critical and self-destructed in the silo."

Cleanup crews in white radiation suits hung onto utility vehicles as they headed for the contaminated area. Chunks of twisted metal covered the ground and lighter material floated down like snowflakes.

"Birds one to five are nominal," called the technician. The powerful rockets jettisoned their boosters and continued skywards. Military top-brass gathered round a group of large displays.

"Go show 'em," shouted one uniformed figure, as the five white plumes disappeared into the heavens. One display on the wall showed the five missiles as slowly moving dots and their intended target still some way off.

"How long to impact?" asked one general.

"ETA is three hours forty three minutes," came the reply.

The men watched as if they were jeering-on a filly at a horse race.

More people came into the hall and peered-up at the huge screen. What was usually a very noisy control room was hushed.

When the target was thirty minutes off, nose cameras on the missiles kicked-in and broadcast their views onto a split screen display showing six images. One image was blank, the other five showed the same dot in the distance. At fifteen minutes out, a countdown counter overlaid on all the screens. The five images grew increasingly larger.

"Christ, look at that thing," said the general. "I've never seen anything like that in my worst nightmares."

"Five minutes to target," called a technician. The alien ship was quite distinct on the screen and rushing towards the cameras at an accelerating pace. Jaws hung open. The room was still.

"One minute," came the call. The wispy antennae on the object were now clearly visible and whipping to and fro at a leisurely rate.

"Ten, nine, eight, seven, six, five, four, three, two…"

"What happened," asked a very puzzled general.

"Telemetry shows that the warheads did not ignite. The birds are still flying."

"What, we missed?" screamed the general.

"Not according to the camera feeds," said the technician. "It looks more like they passed straight through it. We are still getting telemetry, oh, it's stopped now."

Thirty seconds later, a bright new star appeared briefly in the north sky as the warheads self-destructed. The target remained on its steady course towards Earth orbit.

"They dodged the missiles somehow," said another blue uniformed figure. "We were dead on target but the missiles just passed clean through. What are we up against, ghosts?"

"Sir," said a technician, "the thing is just hitting orbital insertion about eight hundred miles out. Looks like it's here."

CHAPTER TWENTY-EIGHT

The alien craft had achieved Earth orbit and in the first six hours, it circled the Earth five times. It had dropped its initial eight hundred miles altitude to three hundred and fifty. NASA had photographed it from many of their reconnaissance satellites but they didn't release these shots to the media. Instead, the television stations, newspapers and internet blogs published amateur shots taken by enterprising individuals with their own expensive gear. They didn't show any great detail because of atmospheric distortion. NASA's clear shots were considered much too terrifying to show to the public.

At first, it was referred to simply as 'the aliens', but some new-age hippy philosopher came up with the name 'Aquarius' in his blog and it went viral. 'The Age of Aquarius', that it alluded to, had many interpretations in astrology but was popularly accepted to be a new dawn of enlightenment for the human race.

Max read the article aloud to the team around him.

"A time of peace and prosperity. A time of love and understanding."

He rubbed his eyes.

"If that's what they want to believe, who am I to argue?" he said. "Bloody fools!"

"It will probably take two or three days to map the world's weather," said Doug. "Twenty polar orbits a day. They should be able to deduce what is happening in the lower atmosphere just from cloud movements. They won't need to send down any scout ships or drones to work that out."

"We need to hit them hard with everything we've

got," said Tony. "We can't afford to let them complete their survey and release their payload."

"After the American fiasco, let's hope that the combined salvo of Russian and Chinese missiles can have more of an effect. I'm not feeling good about this," said Max. "They need to detonate those warheads in a good spread all round the thing and as closely as possible. I think that the best way to do that is to take Gertie up and stage manage the detonations visually. I can do that from a safe distance and our radiation deflectors should be able to handle whatever radiation gets through."

"That sounds very risky to me," said Tony. "The radiation deflectors have never been put under that kind of stress. If they fail, you'll be fried."

"No, I'll be back far enough," said Max. "From fifty miles away, I'll get a good image on my helmet display. The missiles just need to get close and when I give the word, they can be remote detonated. There's no point in trying proximity detectors. That's what the Americans were relying on and look where that got them."

"Won't there be a parallax problem with only a single viewpoint?" asked Doug. "It would be much better if you had two or three views from different angles."

"Yes, you're right," said Max. "We'll have to take all three Deltas up. If they beam their video over to Gertie, I can build a 3D image in my helmet display. Should be able to get a pretty accurate bearing that way."

"Right," said Tony. "I'll get onto the Chinese and Russians and suggest it to them. The ship has settled into a stable orbit now so plotting an intercept point should be simple. Can we be ready in three hours' time?"

The Russian team thought it was a terrible idea. They took it as an insult that they could not be relied upon to hit 'a sitting duck' with their phalanx of missiles. Tony reminded them that the American missiles had apparently passed right through the thing as if it was vapour. There was nothing for proximity detectors to detect.

Eventually they agreed on a compromise. If the Russian targeting didn't work for the leading missiles, as they knew it would, Max could feed back timing information and they would remote detonate the following ones on his instructions. Max didn't like that idea at all. By the time he'd seen the failed hit, radioed it back to Earth and the Russians issued the remote destruct command, the missiles could have overshot their target by miles. He just hoped that the Chinese were more co-operative. He wished that he had been able to issue the remote detonation commands by himself, but neither the Russians nor the Chinese were prepared to relinquish their ultimate control.

Sergei and Jen took Delta 2. Abi and Max were in Delta 3. Jen had the job of remote controlling Delta 1 from her co-pilot's couch. The trio took off together and spread out as they hit the upper atmosphere. The alien ship was around the other side of the planet and heading in their direction.

"Right, I'm getting the three feeds in my helmet display," called Max. "Just a backdrop of stars at the minute."

The Chinese and Russians had been able to muster a total of nineteen nuclear missiles between them. They were all based to the north and south of Mongolia and primed ready to launch in volleys of four or five. When the alien ship was high over a remote part of Northern Russia, they would start launching. Max and his team were waiting.

"Russian tracking stations have confirmed the ship passing over the North Pole, should be here in fifteen minutes," said Sergei. "The first set of missiles have been fired to intercept. I don't like sitting here waiting for nukes to come towards me."

"They won't come anywhere near you, Sergei. Don't worry about that. I'm getting tracking information of the aliens and missiles on my helmet display now. Stand by."

Max was getting a 3D image in his helmet display. The missiles and target were still some way off, but closing fast. He tweaked the zoom setting on the alien craft. It looked like it was heading straight for him with its green glowing sphere clearly visible.

"Wow," said Jen. "Look at that thing. You would think that it would detect the missiles and take evasive action. It seems totally unperturbed. Come on, come and see what's waiting for you."

Max could see the first five nuclear missiles streaking upwards and the inevitable rendezvous point. The alien craft continued in its orbit regardless.

"Ten seconds to impact," he called. "Hey, what's happening?"

As he spoke, the grid of lighting arcing over the surface of the vessel expanded. It formed a huge egg-shape some distance from the hull, if there even was such a thing. Max could see the five missiles, in close formation. They hit the egg, passed right through it, and emerged from the other side. They continued on their paths. The alien ship was totally unaffected and continued on.

"Just as I thought," said Max. "Proximity detection doesn't work. It's like a ghost."

"Second wave coming up", said Sergei. "Max, you need to anticipate how long it will take your command to be implemented."

"I know," said Max. "First go is a practice."

Max counted down his instructions to the ground-based operators.

"Five, four, three, two, one, FIRE!" he called.

Again, the missiles passed though the giant egg and on the other side, exploded in a blinding fireball.

"Missed," shouted Max. "The delay is longer than I thought. I'll try to compensate."

This time, he started his countdown further back. When he called "Fire," the response was much faster. The missiles exploded before they reached their target.

"Damn, damn, damn!" he yelled. "This is the last four missiles. We've got to time this just right."

He did time it right. The missiles entered the egg. There was a slight ripple of sparks across the surface of the egg as the warheads exploded.

"What?" he cried. "They have managed to absorb the energy of four nuclear warheads. Just soaked it up like a sponge. The thing is completely undamaged."

Max could only hear groans in his helmet speakers.

"Better get out of here," he said, "fast." The three Deltas dropped Earthwards.

"If they can withstand a direct hit from four nuclear warheads, and ten near misses, we don't have a hope in Hell," said Sergei.

"I can't see any point of the Chinese craft with their bolted-on conventional missiles going in there, unless they co-ordinate with the Russians and their gravity weapon," said Max. "Maybe if they both attacked at the same time they would have a better chance."

"I think that attacking from above, instead of coming up from the surface, might confuse them a little too," said Sergei. "They will be approaching from the Moon, which they won't expect."

"Okay, I'll set it up," said Max. "I just hope that they aren't ready to deliver their poison."

"It's strange that they haven't fought back or even tried to evade our missiles," said Abi. "It's as if they didn't care."

"I was told they were arrogant," said Max. "I was also told that our weapons would be useless against them. So far, both have been proved right."

"The Russian craft are going to have to get very close for their gravity weapon to have any effect," said Max. "It doesn't have much range."

"Yes, that is worrying," answered Sergei. "You saw what happened to that last bunch of nukes, just swallowed up."

"I think we should go up for a front-row seat," said Max. "We don't need to be there but I wouldn't want to miss it."

Max and Sergei agreed to meet-up with the Chinese and Russian craft from the Moon and lay an ambush in orbit. Each vessel had its instructions and it involved the Chinese causing a distraction attack to allow the Russians to get in as close as possible with their gravity weapon. At least the Earth craft had speed and agility on their side, whereas the aliens were just orbiting at a relatively leisurely pace.

As all the craft converged towards an agreed rendezvous point, Max checked that the alien ship hadn't done anything unusual. It had not. The bright green sphere on its prow was now in sight on his magnified helmet display and it was closing fast.

The six pentagonal Chinese craft had their cargo bays open to space. Inside, adapted road vehicles armed with multiple rocket launchers were strapped-in with the missiles pointing outwards. It really was a ridiculous arrangement but its purpose was to distract: the more confusion it caused, the better. As the aliens came into range, the Chinese released a swathe of missiles, each tipped with high explosive warheads that would have ripped any ordinary spacecraft to shreds. All they did was produce a pathetic showers of sparks on the alien's hull.

The five Russian craft came in from Sunward, spread-out in a loose formation. They closed-in to within a few miles of the enormous spacecraft and the Russian commander gave instructions to fire at will. The craft took turns at firing from close quarters and veered-off to circle round for another run. The stabs of concentrated gravity beams must have hurt.

The protective egg expanded and seemed to solidify. There was just a solid wall of blue electricity. Long fingers of lightning stretched out and touched each of the Russian craft - they sparkled and went still.

"Oh, no!" cried Sergei.

"That's the first time they hit back," said Max. "The gravity weapons must have had some affect."

The Russian craft came back to life, veered off and moved away.

As they watched, the egg contracted and became transparent again. Inside, the alien craft was untouched.

"You realise that was our best shot," said Max. "Nukes, gravity beams, we've thrown everything we've got at them. We don't have any more cards to play. I think we've had it."

* * *

Tony was in a pensive mood. The team were strewn around the meeting room and nobody was saying much.

"We seem to have run out of options, unless anyone has any other ideas?" asked Tony.

Abi lifted a finger and withdrew it again. Whatever she was going to say, evaporated.

"Some people have gone to ground, according to the news feeds," said Jen.

"Somehow, I don't think underground stations are going to be of much use against pathogens," said Doug. "Bombs, perhaps, not biological agents."

"Not underground stations," said Jen. "There are

some places on the planet that are prepared for the event of a nuclear holocaust. Governments have them in a lot of countries. Some companies and research institutes have them for seed banks and charged particle experiments. A few very rich individuals have built nuclear bomb shelters and stocked them up for years. They have filtered air conditioning and recyclable water supplies. They could hang-on for years."

"And the Chinese have their YuèGōng and somebody is probably selling tickets," said Max.

"Aren't there some undersea cities somewhere?" asked Abi. "I'm sure that I read about them somewhere."

"So, the human race won't be wiped-out all that easily," said Tony. "We could survive in the lower levels here for some time but we don't know what's going to happen in the long term. The alien pathogens are supposed to kill-off all life so that they have a clean slate and can then terraform the Earth. No, 'terraform' is the opposite of what I want to say. Anyway, they will change the atmosphere to whatever they breathe, but that's not going to happen quickly. Presumably, they will set-up some bases here to generate whatever gases they use while the population remain up on the ship in orbit until the planet is more amenable to them."

"And we come out of our hidey-holes and take care of them," said Sergei.

"We still don't know what we're up against," said Max. "All this speculation is driving me up the wall."

CHAPTER TWENTY-NINE

With the alien spaceship in orbit round the Earth and seemingly unstoppable, Max decided to go home to see how Katie was holding up. When he went in, she had newspapers strewn across the living room floor and was sandpapering a small bookcase.

"Oh Maxie," she cried, "I'm so glad you're home."

She jumped-up and gave him a huge hug.

"What's happening, Max? Where have you been? I've been so worried. You haven't even called me."

Max kissed her and held her tight.

"Things have been quite hectic at work," he said. "No doubt you've been hearing all about it on the news?"

"I just don't understand what's going on," said Katie. "There's some strange extra-terrestrial spaceship circling the Earth and nobody knows why it's there or what it's going to do."

"No," said Max. "We've had no communications from it."

"Max, they are saying all kinds of scary things on the television, I don't know what to believe."

"In situations like this, people's imagination run riot," said Max. "Everybody has an opinion, and they are entitled to it. Just take it from me, it's all utter rubbish. Nobody in the world actually knows anything. We can only wait and see."

Katie nodded and went back to sandpapering.

"What are you doing?" asked Max, pointing at the bookcase.

"I have to do something, Max," she replied. "I just need something to take my mind off all this. How long are you back for?"

"Just until this afternoon," he answered. "Sorry, but national security has to come first."

"National security," she cried, "what does that have to do with you? You design bits for aeroplanes."

"Yes, very important aeroplanes," he smiled grimly.

Max went into the kitchen.

"Would you like some coffee," he called.

"Tea please," she shouted.

"Oh, it's good to have some decent coffee for a change," said Max pouring the hot water over the ground coffee in the filter jug.

He brought the tea and coffee into the living room and set it down on the coffee table.

"Thanks" said Katie. "Max, I've been talking to Martin next door. His house is floor to ceiling with books."

"I haven't been into his house," said Max. "I've only spoken to him a few times in the garden."

"He's a very clever man," said Katie. "He has several degrees to his name, in literature and philosophy."

"Oh really?" said Max. "I didn't know that."

"He's not the same since he had that fall," said Katie, "says he can't remember anything anymore."

"You know, I think I'll go and have a word with old Martin. He just might be able to help me with something that has been running round inside my head."

Max finished his coffee and went next door.

"Hello, Martin," said Max. "I just wanted to ask you something."

"Come in, Max," said the old man and showed Max into his living room. It was, as Katie had told him, piled-high with books, many of them looking very old, with leather bindings.

"Have a seat," said Martin, "can I get you some tea?"

"Oh, no thanks," said Max, "I've just had some."

"Interesting business, this alien spaceship," said Martin. "It was bound to happen eventually. It would be wonderful to have a conversation with them, I would really like that. So many things to ask. They must be very advanced and could teach us all kinds of things."

"Yes," said Max hesitantly. "Martin, I wanted to ask you something, and I hope that your academic background might help. You are familiar with Homer's Odyssey?"

"Yes, of course," said Martin, "what about it?"

"I tried to read it but found it hard going," said Max.

"The Greek?" asked Martin.

"Oh, no, the English translation," said Max. "And I've looked up references online but they seem very confused."

"Yes, nobody is sure that he even existed. His dates vary wildly. All we can be sure is that someone in Ancient Greek produced some very important works and they were attributed to 'Homer'. That might be one person or several, scholars are divided."

"And, the Odyssey?" asked Max.

"The sequel to the Iliad, tells of Odysseus's epic voyage after the fall of Troy, back to his home at Ithaca where his wife, Penelope, and son ,Telemachus, had given him up for dead. Yes, I can understand how you might find it difficult, the plot does wander about a bit."

"What can you tell me about the monsters he encountered?" asked Max.

"Ah, monsters," smiled Martin. "The Greeks loved their gods and monsters. Odysseus - his name means 'trouble' in Greek - had to battle both monsters and lovers. There doesn't seem to be much difference. He encountered the Sirens, the Lotus-Eaters, the Laestrygonians, Scylla and of course, Polyphemus, the cyclops."

"Mmm," said Max. "Tell me more about the cyclops."

"Cyclopes are, supposedly, one-eyed giants. They are reputed to have had a single eye in the middle of their foreheads. Odysseus gets Polyphemus drunk on strong wine and when he is asleep, plunges a burning stake into his eye. He and his men, the ones that Polyphemus hadn't eaten, escape by hanging under his flock of sheep. A great yarn," grinned Martin. "Then plagiarised by the Romans, who changed his name to Ulysses."

"Very interesting," said Max. "I remember seeing that in a film once. Thank you very much Martin, you have been very helpful. I'm sorry, I could sit and talk about this all day, but I have to get back to work."

"Of course," said Martin. "Lovely to see you. Please drop-in any time."

* * *

"I have an idea," said Max. Tony and his crew were sitting round the meeting room at Mewton base. "It's something that Mr. Burrage told me in a dream."

"We are clutching at straws, here," said Tony.

"No, listen," said Max. "The intelligence won't help us with this situation as I've told you before, but they did give me a clue. Mr. Burrage told me to read Homer's Odyssey and now, I think I understand what he was getting at."

"Go on," said Tony.

"That ship up there has two glowing spheres. One, we know is some sort of drive at the rear but there is a smaller one on the prow. It is green but there is a shiny black part in the centre. It looks like a big eye. Maybe it *is* what they use to see, a sensor array. It makes me think of the cyclops, the mythical one-eyed monster. Odysseus blinded the cyclops by stabbing his eye with a sharp stick. I'm thinking: big eye, sharp railgun slugs."

"Oh, Max," said Doug, "if all the nukes on Earth can't stop this thing, what chance do you have with a few pointy bits of metal."

"Do you have any better ideas, Doug?" asked Max. "If you have, I'm sure that we would all love to hear them."

"Max, it would be suicide," said Doug.

"It might be," said Max, "but we are all going to die soon anyway, what difference does a day or two make one way or the other?"

Doug bit his lip.

"Abi," are you willing to join me on this one?" asked Max.

Abi thought about it for a few seconds.

"I'll go."

Max put his hand on her shoulder.

"Good girl," he said. "I knew you wouldn't refuse. Sergei, can you get your guys to load Gertie up with railgun slugs. What have you got?"

"They are mostly just plain steel," answered Sergei, "but I have a few titanium ones for testing purposes."

"Load them up," snapped Max. "I'll give them a good testing!"

"Do you want to take Delta 1 along for support?" asked Doug.

"I think we'll be busy enough without having to operate a drone," said Max. "No, we'll be fine."

Max and Abi lifted-off from Mewton Base knowing well that it might be for the last time. Gertie went three hundred miles up in the space of a few minutes, and stopped dead.

"We are right in its path," said Max. "Luckily, it still hasn't deviated from its predictable orbit." The alien spaceship showed on his helmet radar display, coming in fast.

"I'm a bit worried about heading towards that thing at this speed," said Abi.

"We won't head towards it," said Max. "How are you at flying backwards?"

"Backwards?" yelled Abi, "you want to fly backwards in front of it?"

"Yes, it's easy," said Max, "Just go to the direction menu on the helmet display and turn it to 'reverse'. Your helmet will adjust so that you think you are chasing the aliens instead of them chasing you. You can turn round just before I fire."

"Er, right," said Abi, "here goes."

Her helmet display showed the giant spaceship going backwards and them closing-in on it.

"Get me in as close as you can," said Max, "but keep your finger on that 'random evasion' button."

Abi manoeuvred Gertie to align perfectly with the centre of the black part of the glowing green eye. She edged-in slowly. The alien ship seemed completely unconcerned.

"Rotate, now," ordered Max.

Max released salvo after salvo of railgun rounds into the black circle. They fizzled out in a shower of sparks as they got close.

"Nothing," yelled Max, "might as well be shooting peas from a pea-shooter. Get us away from here before they shoot back."

Abi operated the controls for a fast downward escape.

"Max, it's not working," she screamed, "Gertie is not responding to the controls."

A series of electrical fingers arced out towards Gertie and a web of sparks encased her hull.

"They've got us," yelled Abi, "I can't move."

Max didn't answer.

"Max, Max. Are you alright?"

Still no answer. Max was slumped in his couch and unconscious.

Max dreamed. He had seen this white misty environment before, when he first encountered the intelligence and when he first met Mr. Burrage in his dreams.

"Surely not," he dreamed to himself.

A figure stepped out of the mist towards him. A female.

"Maxwell, Maxwell Hayden?" asked the woman.

Max couldn't believe it. It was Miss Oakley, Miss Amanda Oakley, his other science teacher from school. Max had had a schoolboy crush on Miss Oakley, she was a stunner. Then, most of the other boys did too. They used to tell fanciful stories about secret liaisons with her, all lies of course. There was even a rumour that she had been seen coming out of a store cupboard in the physics lab with Mr. Burrage, straightening their clothes. It found its way into the annals of school mythology and was passed down from year to year. What was Miss Oakley doing here?

"Maxwell, you seem to be hell-bent in getting-up to mischief. What is wrong with you? Why are you doing this?"

Max gulped.

"Doing what, Miss?"

"You and your friends have been throwing stones and clods of earth at my car. Why?"

Max couldn't remember ever doing that. Some boy had once stuck a potato up into the exhaust pipe of her Morris Minor and she couldn't get the thing started. She had to call for a mechanic from the local garage, then was very cross with everybody for days afterwards.

"Miss, it wasn't me," said Max.

"Don't tell lies, Hayden. You were caught red-handed."

"But, Miss. You were going to choke us all."

"What?" she cried, "what a load of nonsense. Where did you get that idea?"

"Em, Mr. Burrage told me you had come to poison us all," whimpered Max.

"Mr. Burrage?" she cried, "ah, now I understand."

"Understand?" asked Max.

"Mr. Burrage tried it on with me in the store room once. I slapped his face. He didn't like it. Him a married man too."

"Oh," said Max.

The image of Miss Oakley flickered. When the flickering stopped, she looked much older. Fifty years older.

"Hayden, I have something to explain to you which you may have difficulty understanding."

Max waited.

"A very long time ago, millions of your years, Mr. Burrage and I were the same people - well, a group of people. Over the years, Mr. Burrage's people became enamoured with the idea of synthetic implants. They augmented their organic bodies with mechanical and electronic devices and eventually, there was nothing organic left. They became a machine, a massive thinking machine. My people had little use for machines and technology. We were a more spiritual race. For us, it was the souls that intertwined, not the brains. We became as one also. We had no animosity towards our cousins and we just went our own way. They saw themselves as guardians of life in the multiverse, but with a cold determination that everything should just happen in its own realm and that they should simply watch. We, on the other hand, travelled the universe taking with us the seeds of life. We took the basic building blocks required for organic life and spread it across the cosmos, where there wasn't any. We were responsible for the life that eventually evolved on your planet and many others. Of course, our cousins refer to us as 'The Old Ones', and we call them the same. We are two branches of the same tree."

"So, you are not here to wipe us out with some horrible pathogens?" asked Max.

"I think Mr. Burrage must be becoming senile in his

old age," said the elderly lady. "That's the trouble, too many things can go wrong with mechanical and electronic devices. Unlike organic entities that can heal themselves, if an electronic brain develops a fault, it simply ignores it and arranges a workaround. Mr. Burrage is in his dotage, I'm afraid."

In his dream state, Max was stunned at the revelation.

"We always return to the planets we have seeded to see how things have progressed," said Miss Oakley. "Some develop more quickly than others. I have been monitoring your planet since I arrived. I can see much progress and much discord. I can see the early beginnings of the splitting of mind and soul, as we did all that time ago. I can see history repeating itself."

"And what now?" asked Max.

"Like our cousins, we do not interfere with the progress of our prodigy. Now that my research is complete, I will be moving on. There are many other planets on my itinerary. I must say farewell for now. I won't be back for a very long time. I really hope that you don't make the same mistakes as we did."

Max woke up.

"Max, Max, are you okay?" asked Abi in a very concerned manner.

"Yes, I'm okay. You are okay. We are all okay," he grinned.

Abi felt the controls come back online.

"They've let us go, I have Gertie under control again."

"Yes, take us down, Abi," said Max.

As they dropped down through the atmosphere, Max could just see in his helmet display, the alien craft changing course and climbing out of orbit.

"What just happened?" asked Abi.

"I had a dream," said Max. "A wonderful dream. I can't

wait to tell everybody."

Tony Davidson shook his head slowly.

"Max, I don't understand. How were you able to communicate with this thing?"

"I didn't understand myself until I really thought about it," replied Max. "I remember Mr. Burrage telling me that our weapons would not work against the alien craft. He was dead right in that respect. He also told me that they were arrogant and that I had already been given the means to defeat them. He told me to read Homer's Odyssey. I did read Homer's Odyssey and I got someone who understands it better to explain it to me. I thought that I was being told to poke it in the eye with a sharp stick. That I did, and of course it didn't work. What it did do was to take me into close proximity with the alien ship, where they were able to communicate with me over my neural implant. The one that was put inside my head on our first visit with the intelligence."

"But Max, weren't you told that the alien ship was coming to destroy all life on this planet and that they were going to colonise it?" asked Tony.

"That's the thing," said Max. "It's partly true. They did come to this planet, but it was millions of years ago. They did alter the atmosphere and colonise it – that's why we are here today. On this occasion, they came to monitor the progress of their work."

"And, their arrogance, what was that all about?" asked Tony.

"I put that down to family differences," said Max. "Both branches of their tree - there may be more - believe that their way is the correct one and that the others are all wrong. They both call each other 'The Old Ones' by the way. One branch chose the disciplines of intellect, the other, the ways of the soul. Even in my relatively unsophisticated existence,

I can see that intellect and soul should live together. You can't have one without the other. It is arrogance on both their parts to think otherwise. For all their advancements, they are in fact, a failed society. The big worry is that we are going in that same direction."

"And they have showed themselves to us as the bad example?" asked Tony.

"Exactly," said Max. "They didn't have to reveal themselves at all. Their technology would have allowed them to stay hidden from our eyes. I think that they just wanted to make the point."

Tony sighed.

"They have certainly done that. We have to make sure that when this story is told, that the population of this planet take heed."

"That is the true battle," said Max. "Now, if you don't mind, I want to go home and see Katie?"

"Of course, off you go. Give her my regards," said Tony. "And, Max, that thing about your drunk driving, you don't need to worry about that, it's been taken care of. Just be careful in future, I might not be able to help next time."

Max threw the door of the cottage open.

"Katie," he shouted.

She came running out of the living room.

"I'm home," he smiled. "Have you seen the news?"

"No," said Katie. "It's too depressing. I don't even switch it on now."

"Katie, they're gone!" yelled Max.

"They're gone?" she asked. "Who's gone?"

"The alien ship in orbit. It has left orbit. In fact, it has left our solar system."

"What did it want?"

"Oh, just visiting some old acquaintances," grinned Max.

"But, will it come back?" she asked.

"Oh yes, definitely," he replied, "but not for a very long time."

Max switched on the television. The news channels were abuzz with stories about the alien ship having left. Again, there was more speculation than fact. People spoke of 'the second coming'. Others claim to have been abducted and returned. More at a factual level, the first televised images of YuèGōng were shown, to the shock of the entire world. When it was explained that it was a scientific research establishment and would be open to scientists from all nations of the world, fears subsided, a little. There was also news of a new trade agreement between the United States of America and the English, Russian, Chinese consortium that had the G-drives and compact fusion reactors. The Americans got the best of the deal.

"And, Katie," said Max. "I've just made an offer on that house you loved so much – and it's been accepted."

"Oh, Maxie," she cried. "I've never been so happy. Can we go and look at it again. Now!"

"Perhaps later," said Max. "I'm feeling very tired. I need a little nap."

The End.

ABOUT THE AUTHOR

It all started with Dan Dare in the mid '50s. In the Eagle Comic and on Radio Luxembourg, a young Joe Gillespie learned of 'spaceships' and 'Saturn' – and was hooked.

Born in Belfast in 1945, he won a place at The Royal College of Art and graduated with a Master's Degree in Visual Communication.

He worked in the advertising industry in London before setting up his own company, Pixel Productions, developing interactive multimedia for Apple, Microsoft and other leading technological companies.

An ardent classic sci-fi reader, he used his writing skills developed from advertising copy-writing and penned numerous short stories and longer projects that unfortunately ran out of steam due to pressure of work.

Now retired to sunny Dorset, he lives a less hectic life involving bird watching, astronomy and catching-up on ideas to change the universe for the better.